The Exigent Earth

Recently Placed on the Endangered Species List:
Humans

Beverly Knauer
and
Murray Rosenthal

Wise Words Press

Printed in the United States of America

Wise Words Press
1611-A S. Melrose Drive #265
Vista, CA 92081

First Printing, 2019

For information, address the publisher at: wisewordspress.com

Paperback ISBN-13: 978-0-9977303-5-7

ALSO BY BEVERLY KNAUER

The Line Between

The Soul's Hope

To the truth seekers. To those who think out of the box. To those who seek their highest purpose. To all the people who strive to make our world a better place by paving a more sustainable pathway to tomorrow.

Listen to the whispers and you won't
have to hear the screams.
—Native American Proverb

PROLOGUE
2039

DEEP BRAIN STIMULATION—WHERE they'd use increasingly stronger electrical impulses to probe his brain cells to extract information—was the least of his worries. There were more important concerns than the possibility they'd torture him.

Zac Sparkman knew he was in a large fortress-like building—most likely the U.S. government's highest-security facility, sitting threateningly, like an ancient gargoyle, on a hillside just outside New York City. Just moments ago, he'd been brought there by a V-45 vertical takeoff and landing aircraft. From the air, through the mesh covering his eyes, he caught a glimpse of the gray concrete facility—cold, silent, and foreboding—its rooftop capped with isotropic antennae radiating power in all directions.

The VTOL transport had hovered briefly before landing. No time had been wasted as they dragged him to a room where they uncovered his eyes just before shutting a thick steel door with a loud clanging noise that startled him. Zac was now in a prison pod so dark, he couldn't see his own hands in front of his eyes. The only thing visible was a small green light on the surveillance camera, scanning the area. They'd rough-handled him onto a chair, threatened him, and left.

All around him, the quiet reflected something ominous, something sinister. With his vision obscured, his sense of smell was heightened to the nauseating stench of rancid cheese and stale cigar smoke. Before the aircraft departed, they'd given him some kind of drug that even his special powers couldn't shake off. He could feel his pulse pounding in his temples as he clasped his hands in front of him, trying to hold back the trembling. An Aristotle quote kept repeating in his head. *"Fear is pain arising from the anticipation of evil."* The room felt cold and his teeth chattered, but it was probably due to his escalating anxiety.

He was in pain, not so much physically as spiritually and mentally. *What have I done? Why would they do this to me when my intentions are only for the good of humankind?* he thought. He wasn't certain how long he'd been in the room or what had even happened to him. All Zac knew, after they'd described various nefarious interrogation methods, was that they'd planned to extract information from him if he didn't cooperate. The drilling of holes in his skull to allow for two wired probes to be inserted deep into his brain tissue was something he definitely wanted to avoid.

The government was convinced that somehow Zac was the one creating the horrifying disasters happening around the world: earthquakes, cyclones, hurricanes, floods, even volcanic eruptions. With each prediction he gave, he created a greater separation of the two opposing camps of thought regarding his intentions. One side saw him as the hero, and the other one—the group now in charge—was convinced that Zac was the villain. While the two differing groups battled it out, world devastation was rising to cataclysmic proportion.

Why would they assume that I'm the cause?

Of course, he knew he'd never cause a disaster, but he understood how someone might misunderstand his intentions, knowing how often people's actions originate from a place of fear.

He chewed on the cuticle of his right index finger. His throat felt dry and parched, and as his eyes adjusted to the dark, he glanced around the area seeking something, anything, to quench his thirst. His mind was racing with thoughts. *I tried to explain and warn them about what was coming, but now I'm somehow considered the dangerous one—people always seem to need a scapegoat, so now I'm the one blamed for what they brought upon themselves.*

He rubbed his aching head, still groggy and unsteady, feeling sure that they'd injected him with a powerful sedative on his way to this fortress. He had a vague recollection of his captors, remembering snippets of their conversation. They'd referred to the doctor he was about to see as a specialist who knew how to deal with someone who resists authority. *What the heck does that even mean? Who specializes in such things?*

A sensation of doom washed over him, and a rush of panic set in. *There's no "us" and "them"—we're all in this together, and time is running out.* Despite all the challenges he'd overcome in his life, Zac began to fear this situation might be hopeless.

His anxiety heightened as he realized that even though his jailers thought they were in control, it would all mean very little, very soon if he couldn't escape and let the world know what was coming next. He couldn't shake his sense of dread.

At this point, what was the benefit of being a well-known scientist with all his accomplishments? He'd spent his whole life implementing ways to benefit the world. After all, he was the man who helped humankind weather the worst famine on record with crops treated using technology he'd developed. But now the man who had been compared to the greatest minds in history was locked away feeling useless and very alone.

His dark thoughts were making the room feel even more menacing and threatening. A shiver ran down his spine, yet beads of sweat dripped from his forehead and rolled down his cheeks. Nothing would matter if he couldn't escape.

A sliver of light expanded across the floor, and the stale smell of the room gave way to the fresher, ventilated air of the hallway just outside. The heavy door opened, and two men pulled him to stand and dragged him out the door by the arms. That's when he heard the words "The doctor will see you now."

This is it, he thought. Killing him, if that's what they intended, would be the end for everyone.

PART ONE
1988–1993

All truths are easy to understand once they are discovered; the point is to discover them.

—Galileo Galilei

CHAPTER ONE
VIRGINIA
1988

THERE'S A WONDER and awe in the universe that still hasn't been explained. Some scientists accept only proven data and empirical observations, while others acknowledge the existence of unsolved mysteries that cannot yet be measured or quantified. Virginia Sutter fell into the latter category, opting to approach her career with Einstein's belief that "the most beautiful thing we can experience is the mysterious."

Virginia, exhausted yet exhilarated, returned home to her condo in Los Angeles after receiving an award from the Society of Women Geoscientists for her contributions to advancing women leaders. After the ceremony, she'd been invited to speak to a group of female students on "How to Shatter the Glass Ceiling in the World of Science." She was a multilingual geologist and writer who specialized in the study of earthquakes. She was known as the plate tectonics expert who predicted the devastating 1985 earthquake in Mexico City. She was the volcanologist who was present in Antarctica at Mount Erebus in September 1984 when the volcanic activity increased and eruptions ejected bombs from the crater floor onto the rim. She was the speaker who always had intriguing stories to relay to her audience.

Relieved to finally be home after her hectic day, she couldn't get her key in the lock fast enough. She yanked off her suit jacket, kicked off her high heels, plopped down on the sofa in her living room, and massaged her sore feet.

As of late, she'd been more in demand as a speaker due to her writings about an emerging paradigm in the world of science that embraced a unifying holistic vision of consolidating ecological, social, and biological dimensions—a viewpoint she embraced to contend with the worldwide ecological crisis. She'd always been obsessed with new and creative concepts that lay just outside of man's comprehension—those ideas just waiting to be uncovered and explored—because then and only then were quantum leaps of change possible.

Barefoot, she padded down the hallway into the kitchen and, after digging in the back of the refrigerator, pulled the bottle of her favorite sparkling wine from the fridge, nicely chilled in anticipation of such an occasion. She popped the cork, filled her flute, and returned to her spot on the sofa, where she'd left a stack of mail to peruse. After setting her glass on the coffee table, she sorted it into four piles: bills to be paid, junk mail, invitations, and periodicals.

As she glanced at her *Journal of Geophysical Science,* her attention was drawn to one of the headings on the cover that mentioned the scientist Nikolai Sparsinsky. She flipped to page forty-six and learned that the normally reclusive Russian scientist would be speaking at an upcoming conference in Zurich. Virginia had read some of the generalities of Dr. Sparsinsky's work in the original Russian text, and there was a uniqueness to his thinking that piqued her interest.

This particular Swiss group of scientists to whom he'd be presenting his research was formed on the basis of the work coming out of the Santa Fe Research Institute. Their examination into artificial intelligence, economics, origins of life, and the dynamics of chaos and complexity theory was legendary. The institute attracted physicists, biologists, geologists, and mathematicians—any scientist asked to attend and join considered it one of the highest honors. Virginia knew she had little chance of meeting Dr. Sparsinsky one-on-one, but nevertheless, she wanted to attend his lectures.

After taking a few sips from her glass, Virginia impulsively picked up her phone to call her assistant, Jackie.

She answered on the first ring. "Hi, boss. Congratulations on your award."

"Thanks, Jackie. I do my best to be an advocate for the work I love, so receiving the acknowledgment is nice." Virginia took another sip and felt the bubbly elixir flow through her, lending to the feeling of relaxation she sought.

"So, what's next?"

"I'm just going to relax here on my couch with my wine that makes me feel like I'm drinking the stars. Anyway, I have something I want you to do for me, please and thank you."

"Sure, shoot."

"I'm going to send you a copy of an article I found about a conference I want to attend in Zurich. Would you please set everything up for me? And maybe research a few new restaurants you think I might like? I'll fax over the details to you."

"I'm on it! Springtime in Zurich will be wonderful. You know how it always seems to rain when you're there, so I'll be sure to pack an umbrella."

"Those are the details I count on you for."

"I'm green with envy. Bring me back some Toblerone?"

"Of course."

Three weeks later, Virginia arrived in Zurich tingling with excitement. She found the first day of the conference fascinating—so stimulating that her synapses were on fire with new information and possibilities. But she was more than surprised at her reaction to Dr. Sparsinsky. She couldn't quite place her finger on the provocative factor in the equation, but he intrigued her in ways no one else ever had. Not only was she attracted to the brilliance of his mind but to the essence of his character as well. His smile was disarming and playful, almost hinting at a rebellious side with a touch of mischief. She couldn't seem to disengage while he talked, and she stared at him as he paced the stage, microphone in hand, and shared his passion with the audience. *I certainly didn't expect this known recluse to be so engaging.*

Virginia had seen photos of him, but they didn't do him justice. He was handsome in an understated way, although she hadn't anticipated the salt-and-pepper hair, or the tanned skin that indicated he actually went outside to enjoy nature—not always buried in his books and studies as she'd imagined. And those mesmerizing eyes held a gaze that transitioned from penetrating to piercing.

She assumed he'd be a bit stoic and withdrawn, but surprisingly, he interacted with the audience more than she'd thought. He even told a joke or two. When he spoke, in his thick accent, he zeroed in on the audience, drawing them intimately into his world, nodding his head, gesticulating passion. He walked the stage like he owned it.

She read him as though he were an intriguing book. The chapters of his life were written on his face—each line, each furrow reflecting his strength of character, along with memories of lost love, tinged with hardship and sorrow.

After a delicious dinner held in the Grand Hall of the conference center, Virginia decided to take an evening stroll. It was a crisp spring night, and the moon was full. Her mind was awhirl with all the information she'd learned that day. A waft of a cold breeze blew, and she pulled her sweater tighter to her body as she scurried down the sidewalk. Out of nowhere, a man—well over six feet—literally bumped right into her. When she looked into his face, she was stunned. It was him. Nikolai Sparsinsky! *Out of all the people walking on this sidewalk, what are the odds of me running into him? Kismet perhaps?*

"Pardon me!" He looked flustered.

In her state of shock, Virginia failed to respond.

He tried a string of other languages. *"Mi perdono... Perdón?... Oprostite."*

Virginia understood all of his apologies but remained silent, simply staring at him. Now, face-to-face, she could see he had such depth in his eyes that it stopped her cold and rendered her speechless. They had such intensity, so blue they glowed—a look that disarmed her normal self-composure. His scent was heady, a mixture of damp earth and breath mints. Suddenly, his words came flooding into her awareness. Why the heck was he speaking several languages all strung together? Composure regained, she interrupted him, speaking in English.

"I think I owe *you* an apology for not responding. I'm just so surprised to bump into you. I'm here in Zurich for your lectures!"

"As they say, it is a small world. And joining me for a cup of tea would be a most acceptable apology." He reached out and touched her shoulder.

Hmm… not the antisocial man I thought he'd be.

With a slight tilt of her head, she gave him her most alluring look. "I just passed a small café on Beckenhofstrasse. I'm suddenly in the mood for a sweet. Care to share a Meitschibei as well as that tea? I've had a craving to try this particular pastry." She had never experienced such an instant rapport before. What was it about him that was so enthralling? A strong energy flowed between them, and apparently, the attraction was mutual.

As though it was meant to be, like they were picking up from another time and place, they took off arm in arm down the street. For Virginia, the rest of their story was written in the stars. At that precise moment, she knew: Nikolai Sparsinsky was going to be her husband.

CHAPTER TWO
NIKOLAI
1988

NIKOLAI SPARSINSKY HAD just given one of his presentations on cellular energy to a diverse group of scientists in Zurich, Switzerland. His first talk had gone well, yet he craved some time alone to figure out some changes he wanted to make for his next day's lecture. Despite all of the precautions the Russian security team that was monitoring him had in place, Nikolai snuck away for a meditative evening stroll, giving them a late-night slip.

Walking meditations offered Nikolai the quiet he needed to crystallize his ideas, allowing him to think clearly about the issues at hand—it was just how he functioned. On this night, he needed the time to sort out how much of his research he felt was safe to share in his talk the next day.

The secretive Russian government allowed Nikolai to give speeches about the general content of his work, but any written material on the details of specific research results could land him in a Russian prison. The government considered him its property and, at all costs, would do what was needed to protect the brilliant mind in which it had invested so much.

The early life of the Sparsinsky family had been a difficult one, and the hardships taught Nikolai self-reliance and that "Mother Russia" was not to be trusted. However, one opportunity the Russian system did offer to Nikolai was an educational advantage. Very bright students were identified, accelerated early, given a free education, and deemed a national asset. Nikolai was quickly identified as a prized possession. The greatest problem he presented his teachers with was which areas of study to accelerate him toward. His knowledge in chemistry, physics, and mathematics was extraordinary. While most pupils concentrated on one area, Nikolai mastered all three with ease. There was never a question—his was a genius to be revered.

What they didn't know was that Nikolai had uncovered secret, powerful fundamental principles of energy, and he'd decided to wait until he was truly free of the Russian regime to introduce his discovery to the world at large. Desperately, he wished he could live in a country where he'd be able to share ideas openly and without fear. Zurich would have to do for now.

After a full day of networking with fellow scientists at the conference, Nikolai was relishing the fresh air. It was a crisp spring night, and the moon was full—perfect for an evening stroll. He hadn't even bothered to change his clothes from the suit he'd worn for his presentation. *Overall, I'm pleased with how interested the audience seemed, how accepting of my work. If only I had the freedom to share the secrets of my discoveries. Together with other scientists in that audience, we could alter the world.*

He meandered down the sidewalk with his head down, arms swinging reciprocally at his sides, feeling the nippy evening breeze caress his face. As he drifted deeper into his thoughts, he lost awareness of the world around him. The next moment, he realized that he'd knocked smack-dab into something or someone. His right shoulder impacted the left shoulder of a woman walking toward him, slightly jarring her to the side. The bump quite literally snapped Nikolai out of his meditative trance. He couldn't help but notice her radiant beauty. Tall, fit, and elegant, she had the look of an exotic Mediterranean woman yet was dressed like an American. Her dark hair, olive complexion, and cognac-colored eyes were mesmerizing, and an energy radiated from her that rendered him weak in the knees—a sensation he'd long thought he'd never feel again. He simply found her haunting.

He was aware of her eyes scanning him from head to toe, but she said nothing. She didn't look angry or upset but locked eyes with him and didn't let go. *I need to speak*, he thought. *To apologize.* Nikolai suddenly, and without any defenses, found his heart racing. Transfixed, he thought about which language he should select to try to communicate with her.

"Pardon me!" he said, feeling flustered as he wondered what to say. He waited for her to respond, but she continued to stare at him. *Perhaps she doesn't speak English. I'll attempt something else.*

He tried a string of other languages. "*Mi perdono... Perdón?... Uprostite.*"

Still, she remained silent. What was this feeling coming over him? His eyes fell to her hand, looking for a ring. There wasn't one. How could he communicate with her?

He startled when she finally spoke, speaking in perfect English.

"I think I owe *you* an apology for not responding," the woman said.

He had no idea where his next words came from. "No, no... it was me not paying attention to where I was going. However, if you insist on apologizing, how about joining me for a cup of tea? That would be a most acceptable apology." He smiled and reached out and touched her shoulder.

What has come over me? Where's the shy man who has difficulty talking to women? What is this hold she has over me? Where is this boldness coming from?

She seemed a bit smitten in return and appeared to be giving him an alluring look. He sensed a slight hesitation in her movements and a sensual softness in her voice. He had an overwhelming desire to reach out and press his finger to her lips, but he restrained himself, lest he scare her off.

She spoke again, her voice almost lyrical. "I just passed a small café on Beckenhofstrasse. I'm suddenly in the mood for a sweet. Care to share a Meitschibei as well as that tea? I've had a craving to try this particular pastry."

The charming café was hidden, sandwiched between the tall city buildings—they almost walked right by it. The mingling scent of roasted coffee beans and spicy tea instantly permeated their noses as Nikolai opened the door. In contrast to the brisk night air, the interior felt warm and cozy when they stepped inside. Classical music played softly in the background. Despite the late hour, the room was filled with chattering people. Renoir prints decorated the light pink walls, and softly lit lamps, in lieu of overhead lighting, created an ambiance suitable for falling in love. Glass cases, filled with every delightful treat imaginable, lined the west side of the room. There was even a red velvet couch flanked by two striped, overstuffed chairs tucked in a corner area. A waitress greeted them and showed them to a small, round table with a glass top, in a corner away from the hustle and bustle. A small cream-colored vase with three yellow daffodils served as the centerpiece.

Nikolai placed his hand over his chest, wondering if this intoxicating woman could hear his heartbeat. He pulled out a chair for her to sit down. "Whenever I think of cafés such as this, I'm reminded of Hemingway," he said.

She sat and placed a rose-colored cloth napkin on her lap. "Ah yes, the literary Parisian cafés his generation made famous. This place is adorable."

After he sat across from her, he hardly noticed the décor of the room. All the sights and smells and tastes became invisible as he focused only on her. He watched as she subconsciously trailed her index finger over her lush lips.

"Dr. Sparsinsky, I guess you should know my name. I'm Virginia Sutter."

"I'm honored to meet you, Virginia. Please, you must call me Nikolai."

"Nikolai, I want you to know how much I enjoyed your talk today. I found it very stimulating. You're an intriguing person, and I'd really like to get to know you."

"Hmm… you are too kind. Intriguing? I'm not so sure that is how I would label myself."

"Then tell me how you'd label yourself. I'd like to know about you, your life… I want to know everything. I've heard you described as a true genius. So I'd say you are definitely intriguing."

His cheeks flushed red. "You flatter me. To condense my life story into a few minutes over a lovely pastry we share wouldn't be possible, do you think?" He touched her gently on her hand. *I'm not sure where my words are even coming from, but I'm so drawn to her.*

"Well, we may have to find a way to schedule ourselves some additional time to share all the vital pieces of our lives. But for now, tell me some personal things about yourself."

Do her eyes actually crinkle at the corners when she smiles? She seems so feminine and charming, yet strong and independent.

Virginia continued. "Do you come from a large family? Do you have siblings?"

"I am an only child. And you?"

"My parents have both passed, and I have one brother, Brian."

"My parents are no longer alive as well. In his day, my father was a pharmacist. It was difficult for them to have to flee the pogroms of rural Russia seeking the anonymity of a big city, so that I might flourish. They chose Moscow. They believed my arrival was a blessing from God and felt it was their responsibility to do whatever they could to help me realize my potential. They wanted me to have a better chance at a major university."

"Obviously, you made the most of that chance."

He bowed his head slightly, avoiding her eyes. "I did."

The young waitress who'd greeted them approached the table with pad and pencil in hand. "Coffee or tea?"

Virginia and Nikolai responded, "Tea, of course." Then they simultaneously laughed. They selected their choice of tea from a lengthy menu and ordered the pastry Virginia wanted to try.

Several minutes later, the waitress brought a pot of steeped tea and two teacups to the table. The perfume of the spiced tea floated through their nostrils. The waitress placed the pastry plate on the table with two forks. "Here you are. You sure you want to share it? It's so good, you'll want to eat the whole thing by yourself."

With her fork perched, ready to dive in, Virginia responded, "Oh, no, thank you. Sharing this will be perfect for us." At that moment, Beethoven's Fifth Symphony started playing over the speaker. The dramatic opening notes were a perfect prelude to her first taste of the pastry.

Nikolai watched Virginia take a bite. She literally swooned. "Oh my God. I've never had a pastry so delicious. This sweet hazelnut filling, the flaky crust..." She licked her lips and gazed at Nikolai. "It's just delightful!"

"I can tell. It will be our signature pastry in the future, and Beethoven's Fifth will have to become our song." He took a taste and nodded his approval. *I can't believe I actually just said that. How forward.*

"So, let's see… let me think of something to share with you to get to know me a bit better. Ahh… okay, I will tell you a story about how tea became an important part of my life. Back in the seventeenth century, tea became available in Russia. Did you know that our very precious tea was brought by traders on camels who came from China?"

"No, I didn't. However, that would have been an amazingly long journey."

"Yes, it took about a year to complete, so for that reason, tea was very expensive."

"Likely available to only the aristocratic class."

"That's correct. Then, when the Siberian Railroad opened in the late 1800s, it also opened up a new world. The length of the trip was shortened to about two months, and due to that change, tea became a treasure beloved by *all* classes."

"Oh—I have to tell you something. A year ago, I found a beautiful Russian samovar at an antique store, and I bought it. I make tea in it."

"You did? You do?" His eyes lit up. *Who is this woman? How is it we are so in sync?* "No matter what your social class, the samovar was always the centerpiece of a Russian home— a sign of Russian hospitality. We had a large, beautifully crafted urn made of copper that held a large quantity of water. Coal was used to heat the inside chamber to keep the water hot all day long. Each morning, I would see the small, decorative teapot sitting on top of the samovar, keeping it warm. It held a concentrate of very strong tea called—"

Virginia, in her excitement, interjected, "I know this. *Zavarka!*"

Nikolai shook his head, laughing at her outburst. "Are you sure you are not Russian? That is correct. Whenever I wanted a cup of tea, I just poured a small amount of *zavarka* into my cup and diluted it with the hot water from the samovar. It became a symbol of comfort for me."

"What type of tea?"

"We often used a blend that was smoked. Did you know that our traditional way is to sip the tea through a sugar cube held in the mouth? Watch, like this." He plucked one out of the bowl on the table and placed it in his mouth and took a sip of tea. "You try."

She placed the sugar cube in her mouth and sipped the tea, and they both burst into a fit of laughter. He knew at that moment in time that in spite of his logical mind, there are things that can't be explained with charts and equations. There are truths that go beyond verifiable evidence. His preconceived theory had been wrong, and he relented to the fact that, indeed, love at first sight really did exist.

"I hope you are not married? Engaged?" he asked a bit hesitantly, not knowing for sure if she was sharing the same feelings he was experiencing.

"No, I'm not. What about you?"

His shoulders slumped, his eyes downcast. "I was married once. To a lovely Jewish girl, named Miriam. She was a doctor, which made my mother very happy. Even if she weren't a doctor, my mother would have been thrilled, as I was very shy and did not have a way with the women. She worried that I would never marry."

"No matchmaker for you?"

"There were always matchmakers trying to make a *shiddach,* or marriage arrangement. None were right for me. My parents were very surprised when I showed up with Miriam, but of course delighted, as she was both pretty and a doctor."

"So, what happened? Did you divorce?"

"No. We had a very happy life while it lasted, both of us very committed to our careers, and we knew we both wanted to begin a family. Tragedy came upon us like a thief in the night and stole my life as I knew it. In the very hospital where Miriam practiced, where we decided to have her deliver our first child, she suffered a tear in her uterine wall that was undiscovered until it was too late. She and our child died hours later." His lips quivered, and he bowed his head. "I was beyond devastated. There are no words, no words."

Tears sprang to Virginia's eyes, and she placed her hand on top of his to comfort him. "I'm so sorry, Nikolai. Such a tragedy."

"I have to say I became bitter and forlorn. I just threw myself into my work and developed the reputation of being a dark and brooding recluse. I cared nothing for much, and certainly not politics. I just wanted the authorities to leave me alone so I could do my work. My fondest desire has always been to go to America, where I'd have the freedom I need and crave. I want to share my ideas openly, and between you and me, I have powerful fundamental principles of energy to share with the world that will have to wait until I am truly free."

Virginia sat back in her chair, put down her fork, and beamed.

"What is it you are so delighted about?"

"I have a brilliant idea, but a question first. How are you here now without being watched and scrutinized?"

He bent toward her and whispered over the table.

"Ah, I see," she said after he'd confided to her that he was likely being watched and scrutinized right this minute. "I do have an idea, but it's not for the ears in this room to hear. Shall we pay our bill and go for a walk? I know the hour is getting late and you have another talk tomorrow afternoon, but I'm feeling wide awake."

"As am I. I've never felt so awake in my life."

Nikolai's scientific mind hadn't allowed him to accept a belief in fate, but it was clear to him that the darkness of his days had finally shattered, and a glimmer of light had entered through the cracks. They paid the bill and left the café, naturally strolling arm-in-arm again, discussing their lives, their goals, their desires, and a plan... definitely a plan.

❈   ❈   ❈

Separating at a time when their love was just beginning to blossom was difficult but necessary. After the conference in Zurich ended, Virginia returned to California, and Nikolai to Russia, and they came up with a plan to be together that worked. Nikolai, in coordination with an American petroleum businessman—who just happened to be a Russian-born Jewish immigrant with ongoing close ties to Russia—was able to secure work in Russia for Virginia in the area of petroleum geology and production.

Once they were reunited in Russia a few months later, Nikolai felt complete and whole as they resumed their romance in his homeland. They registered their marriage at the local Citizen's Records and Licensing Bureau and began their life together as husband and wife, waiting for the right time to enact the second part of their plan: building their life in America.

Nikolai knew they'd encounter political hurdles to overcome. The

American government was still suspicious of anything Russian, and the Russians were not going to give up a brain as unique as his. As it often is with complex problems, Nikolai knew the simplest solutions are the most serendipitous; it seemed as if fate was paving the way for the newlyweds to find their way home to America under the shadow of the Iron Curtain falling.

Although Nikolai was not a practicing Jew, his heritage and the Jewish groups that politicked for his release opened a door that would get them out of Russia. Amid the confusion of an emerging society and falling Iron Curtain, he was suddenly out of Russia for good. With just two suitcases full of clothing, treasured journals and books, and his secret notebook that Virginia had carefully stowed in her oversized carry-on bag—information worth more than any dollar amount that could be placed on it —they headed for a land Nikolai had only dreamed of. For Nikolai, entrusting Virginia with the journal that contained the distillation of twenty-five years of his work, all bound in a handwritten leather book, was the most powerful gesture he could make. It reflected his profound love and trust in her, in their union.

The Russian government scientists were led to believe that Nikolai had left his life's work behind for other Russian scientists to study; however, Nikolai assured that that information would turn out to be a complexity of multiple doors leading to nowhere.

The Sparsinskys boarded a large jet in Moscow, and nineteen hours later, they arrived in L.A. as the Sparkmans. Nikolai wanted a fresh start, an American-sounding name, and a clean break from his painful past. The moment he stepped out of the international terminal and the California sunshine struck his face, the sorrow of his past began to melt away. A single tear rolled down his cheek. He stared up into the blue sky of a place he'd dreamed about his entire life. Looking around, taking in the scope and breadth of his new homeland, Nikolai grasped Virginia's hand. Pulling it tightly against him, he said, "My love, life is good. I'm finally free. I'm finally free."

CHAPTER THREE
OLIVIA
1990

THE WAY SHE met the Sparkmans was both a hardship and a blessing. Even at age fourteen, Olivia already knew there were two sides to a coin, a yin to the yang. But today, Olivia and her father, direct descendants of the great Medicine Crow—the most famous of the great Crow chiefs—were in trouble.

No cell phones at that time could have helped Olivia and John Medicine Crow that autumn evening in the foothills of the Pryor Mountains of Montana. As the sun set in the valley, John headed home in his old pickup truck with Olivia riding shotgun. The road had turned to muddy water in motion from a recent afternoon downpour. As they descended an incline on a narrow gravel road, a scrawny coyote suddenly darted across their path directly in front of them. Instinctively, John flung his arm out across Olivia's chest to protect her as he abruptly swerved the truck. He tried to maintain control, but he instead ran the truck into a shallow ditch, slamming his head into the steering wheel upon impact. Olivia saw her father slumped over, apparently unconscious. Unharmed herself, Olivia frantically attempted to assist her father, but she was unable to wake him, and a gash on his forehead was bleeding. She looked around for help but saw no signs of anyone in the vicinity. Scrounging through the glove compartment, she discovered some clean paper towels, and she gently dabbed, then pressed them against his wound.

Olivia opened the door of the truck, climbed out of the ditch, and stood by the side of the road, squinting as she observed an approaching vehicle a ways off. It began to rain again, and the road was pooling with water in the potholes. She hoped the car she saw in the distance wouldn't turn off, so she'd be able to flag it down to aid her and her father.

Fortunately for John and Olivia, Virginia and Nikolai were traveling through the foothills of Montana and Wyoming looking for the perfect spot for their new home and his laboratory. They were only a couple of miles from the house they were renting in the area when they saw Olivia jumping, waving, and shouting to them.

They stopped and rolled down the window to ask if she was okay. Olivia explained what had happened, and they rushed from their car to assist. John was coming to as they arrived, stating that he was fine except for a relatively minor cut on his forehead. After Virginia grabbed the first aid kit she'd stashed in the Jeep, she performed a cursory assessment, cleaned his gash, and bandaged it. Olivia watched with tears running down her cheeks.

"Is he going to be okay?" she asked.

"Aw, honey, don't worry. I think he'll be fine," Virginia said. She placed her hand on Olivia's shoulder. "No headache, nothing draining from his nose or ears, he's breathing fine, equal pupil size, normal speech… the cut on his forehead isn't deep and doesn't need stitches. But you won't be driving anywhere tonight, so you both are coming home with us. We're only a short distance from our rental house. We'll get the truck taken care of in the morning and take your dad to a clinic to be checked out."

Olivia released a breath she'd been holding, and the tightness in her chest dissipated. *Thank heaven for these wonderful people who are being so kind to us.* They carefully extracted John from the truck and out of the ditch and helped him slide onto the passenger seat next to Virginia, while Nikolai and Olivia climbed in the back. The sound of thunder bellowed. The wind was unleashed, and a downpour of rain followed.

Once they arrived at the rental house, they waited until the blast of rain subsided, and then Nikolai and Virginia assisted John inside and got him seated on the comfortable leather recliner in the living room. There were no clinics open in the area, and John seemed fine, but Virginia told Olivia she wanted to keep him engaged in conversation to observe him for any possible decrease in his level of alertness for the next few hours.

Then Virginia invited Olivia to help her make dinner, leaving Nikolai and John to chat.

She couldn't explain why, but Olivia felt an instant rapport with Virginia. There was something about her mannerisms that indicated her inherent warmth and sincerity. Her soft and comforting voice was soothing, like some kind of mind massage. She knew the feeling was mutual because they talked intimately, like long-lost souls reuniting. Olivia watched as Virginia tore the lettuce for the salad while she spoke. This simple act caused an aching, tender yearning in her heart for her mother, who had passed on when she was five years old.

She loved her father deeply, but she missed the influence of a mother in her life. She and Virginia chatted and laughed as they worked together as a team. For a brief moment, Olivia tuned out while getting in touch with the happiness she was feeling—like she was finally drinking from a full cup. After the brief inner reflection, she tuned in again, continuing to listen with interest to Virginia's self-revelations.

"So, we ended up looking for a permanent home here. I love this land, especially these sandstone, shale, and limestone mountains. I have dreams of starting a huge garden with lots of fresh organic produce and herbs this spring. I want to plant every herb imaginable."

Olivia raised one eyebrow and gave a slight curve at the corner of her mouth. "I can help you with that, Virginia. I'm kind of known as an herb expert around here. I make healing salves and tinctures. In fact, I'm making a nettle infusion next weekend."

"You are? You must show me. Would you like to come over and make it here? We could have lunch and then you can teach me."

Olivia beamed and nodded her head as they pared and sliced vegetables.

Virginia continued with her heart-to-heart. "Oh, and Nikolai and I have so many plans for our new home and our future, and you're the first to hear the next step in our plan. Do you want to hear it?"

"I do."

"I've really wanted to share this with someone because I'm so excited. We're working on getting pregnant. We've decided to start a family."

At that moment, when Olivia heard those words, a sensation floated through her. *I think I'm going to have some kind of role in this,* she thought.

Virginia lifted the cover of her slow cooker and sniffed the air. "Mmm... I love the smell of cumin. I have some chili cooking in this pot that I put on earlier this morning, and I made a pan of cornbread to go with it. This will be perfect for a chilly, rainy night. Would you like to help me make a dressing for the salad?"

Meeting the Sparkmans was more than Olivia could have hoped for. It wasn't typical for either her father or her to make friends with strangers so quickly. Normally a bit reticent, they both felt at ease with this new couple and broke bread together, laughing and enjoying the new companionship. She felt a developing bond—a knitting together of their past, present, and future. She understood and accepted that this would be a continuing relationship.

❋   ❋   ❋

At daybreak, the sky cleared and white cumulus clouds floated close to the horizon, with temperatures hovering in the sixties. After driving John to the closest clinic, Nikolai, Virginia, and Olivia waited while the doctor examined him. Once the doctor cleared him, they drove John back to the Crow Indian Reservation, where he had men who would help him retrieve his pickup. He expressed his gratitude to his new friends and gave permission for Olivia to go along with them to act as a guide in the area where Virginia and Nikolai were scouting for their new home.

Two eagles pirouetted through the sky as the three of them took off in the Jeep, passing through the sagebrush-dappled landscape with rolling pastures and the mountains off in the distance. It was the moment when they were descending a short pass through the hills onto a wide-open valley when Olivia leapt up in her seat and vigorously pointed.

"Look. Stop!" But Olivia wasn't looking at the foothills, the Pryor Mountains, or the ranch they'd just entered; she was transfixed by a beautiful white mustang that ran across a pasture toward their car.

Olivia whispered, "That mustang is known as White Cloud." As Virginia slowed the vehicle down, the horse stopped for a moment and stared directly at them. A stunned silence filled the car like a vacuum sucking up every sound from the environment. Olivia felt her breathing synchronize with the mustang's. As time suspended, the moment passed, and the great white steed seemed to vanish into the woods. Olivia noticed that when the horse left, sound once again returned.

This is the place, she thought. *I can feel it. I know it. They need to make their home here.*

"This is it," she said as she pulled the long strands of jet-black hair from blowing in her eyes. "This is definitely the place where you should live."

Nikolai laughed at her exuberance and turned to speak to her in the backseat. "We haven't even seen it yet, and there is something special I need if this is to be our home."

A typical teen, Olivia folded her arms across her chest and pouted. "Okay," she said a bit smugly, "but I already feel it. I'm telling you this will be the place."

Olivia marveled at how she already felt so strongly bonded with these people. It was such an instant connection. She knew in her heart they were special, and she had gifts meant to be shared with them. There was a purpose for all of this.

From the ranch's gates, she could see magnificent trees and the mountain foothills bordering the south end of the area that made the rear of the 5,000-acre property look like giant ocean waves. Driving over the crest of the road gave a commanding view of the property and beautiful farmhouse with manicured lawn, stables, pens, and barn. It was exciting for her to be with them when they first saw their future home.

Nikolai turned to Virginia and Olivia, eyes bright with excitement and awe.

"I must use an American term here," he said. "Wow! Virginia, my love, could this be the place?"

"We've found it. This is home!" Virginia said.

"Told you so," whispered a petulant Olivia.

An offer was made that very day, accepted by the end of the week, and soon the ranch was in escrow. The main house was a rambling four-bedroom home with a large kitchen that opened onto the garden and greenhouse. The large plate glass windows that framed the pastures and mountains in the distance brought bright light and an open, airy feeling to the house. And, of course, with two scientists in residence, there was a massive library to house their vast collection of books.

*   *   *

The weekend following the accident, Virginia picked Olivia up at the reservation to spend the day at their rental property so Olivia could teach her the art of herbal tinctures as promised. Her father had noticed her strong desire and excitement to spend more time with Nikolai and Virginia. Olivia was pleased that he not only allowed her to spend time with them, but found he enjoyed the company of Nikolai as well. Sometimes John would even accompany him on one of his meditative walks.

One morning before Olivia left to meet up with Virginia, the man of few words spoke his mind to his daughter. They took a morning walk down a dirt road behind their house, John keeping his eyes focused on the path ahead.

"Olivia, there is one thing I ask you to remember. Keep my ancestors' wisdom alive, and pass my story on when I die. The white man may never understand our ways. If you live in their world, you will have to protect the knowledge I've passed on to you. Our people tried to tell them important things generations ago and died for it. I trust these two more than any white people I have ever met, but, my daughter, even they may not comprehend our ways. It is to you I give the light that must live on."

Olivia grasped her father's hand and squeezed it and promised him the light would never go out. "I will, Father, I will."

*   *   *

Tight green buds of growth popped up everywhere, signaling that spring had arrived and that it was planting time at the ranch. Olivia and Virginia planned a large vegetable and herb garden and started out the annual and biennial seedlings in the greenhouse.

Early one morning when they were tending to the seedlings, Virginia noticed Olivia whispering as she placed each plant in the ground. "What's that you're saying?" Virginia asked.

"It's a little blessing I give to each of the plants. The beliefs of our Crow tribe are based on animism, that the universe and all things possess a distinct spiritual essence: animals, the trees, these mountains, and these plants."

"I like that. You know… I've wanted to mention something to you. You seem to have a knack for and desire to heal. Have you ever considered something in the field of medicine? Maybe studying to be a physician or nurse?"

Olivia stopped planting to glance at Virginia. "I haven't, but it's something to consider. Healing is in my blood. The shaman of the tribe is known as an Akbaalia, or healer. I'm from a long line of Native American medicine men, and being without a son, my father is passing his knowledge in this area on to me."

"Then I'm going to help you pursue further studies in this area. I think you have a gift. There's definitely a reason we were brought together.

There is, Olivia thought. *I have a very important purpose in your life that will reveal itself when the time is right. I just feel it.*

CHAPTER FOUR
NIKOLAI
1992

THE SEPTEMBER WILDFLOWERS—NATURE'S jewels— dotted the land like a magic carpet of blossoms. Nikolai was fascinated by the biological diversity with endemic species known only to that region. He was out for his walk before the sun was even up since sleep was almost impossible whenever his mind was running like a racehorse.

Walking the perimeter of their ranch property, Nikolai realized how truly happy and at peace he was. The past couple of years had come to pass exactly as he'd hoped. He relished the remote, quiet setting, where no matter which direction he looked, the scenery was breathtaking. This was the kind of home he'd only dared to dream about—the rolling, native grasslands and canyons with the backdrop of the majestic Pryor Mountains inspired his creativity. *Life is good*—that's the way he described it often.

Virginia filled her days with her writing and speaking engagements, but always seemed most fulfilled when she was outdoors working in her beloved gardens with Olivia. Nikolai cherished his time carrying out his research, planning and overseeing the construction of his lab, and working on special projects the United States government had requested from him in return for a handsome open-ended stipend without the drain of university duties. It was the freedom he'd so hungrily sought. The Pryor Mountains were the perfect place to continue his meditative walks and his research without interruption.

Now, he stood staring out onto the mountain range as the sun began to rise, reflecting on the past two years as he remembered how perfectly the whole laboratory concept had come together.

He'd felt an urgency to finish it quickly, keeping every step as surreptitious as possible, and he was surprised that it all had fallen together like clockwork.

There was one main condition Nikolai needed for his new laboratory: it had to be built into a mountainside. Only two top scientists, one from NASA and one from the National Institutes of Health, had the slightest of idea of the work Nikolai had brought with him from Russia, yet no one knew the full extent of its application. Not yet, he thought. Not yet. At the highest levels, the Israeli and U.S. governments had struck an agreement to fund the laboratory and subsequent research. Many key pieces of equipment had been developed in Israel by several of the physicists who had, like Nikolai, also fled Russia with the fall of the Iron Curtain.

Nikolai remembered a couple of years back when he'd first walked the grounds of the compound speccing out the area with Avram Epstein, his fellow scientist and closest friend. Avram had attended the Moscow Institute of Physics and Technology in the 1960s, specializing in mathematics, applied physics, and archeology. Having been falsely imprisoned for treason after being accused of passing on Soviet Union secrets to the West, he'd been part of a prisoner exchange, in which he'd ultimately been freed from Russian incarceration and immigrated to Israel, where he remained working with the Israeli government.

It had been a joy for Nikolai to see his old friend again and receive the benefit of his knowledge, wisdom, and, most of all, his confidentiality. Putting their two brilliant minds together, they'd given great thought to studying the land and determining the perfect location for the lab, looking at it this way and that, in the deliberative fashion that Nikolai had always applied to his work.

On that day, Avram and Nikolai walked the entire expanse of the area, stopping to examine the possibilities of one of the larger caves.

"This is a great location for your laboratory, Niko," Avram said. "These caves are not unusual for this part of the country; however, the size and scope of this one is unique. You found a prime spot, as there are some very unusual geological properties here."

Nikolai nodded his head slowly several times, subconsciously rubbing his jaw between his thumb and his forefinger as if deep in thought. "Virginia said the same thing and blessed it as geologically sound. I've been thinking. My suggestion is to construct the laboratory in three sections. For the first part, we'll build a sturdy shed with the back abutting this foothill. From the outside, it won't look any different than any other well-constructed farm shed, but the lab has to be constructed in such a way that it's both undetectable and shielded from micro, radio, and gamma rays.

"We'll create a faux wall along here." He pointed to the area with a beam of light from his flashlight. "I know the right guy to hire to install the best security system possible to control the locking mechanism of the door leading into the lab."

Avram followed Nikolai to the back. "Agreed. It's vital that the several-tons rock wall we discussed rests on pins so strong and balanced that, once unlocked, it will be able to be moved aside by a quiet electric five-horsepower motor."

Avram progressed a few feet farther into the dark cave. "Yes, this is impressive. You can use Virginia's vegetable garden as the cover story for having a gardening shed."

Nikolai used the high beam on his flashlight to light various sections of the interior and headed toward the back of the cave. "Avram, look over here. It's this expansive space here where we can create the second chamber. For this to be a success, it is important that each and every step of the construction be guarded for secrecy. This is of paramount importance."

A muscle twitched involuntarily at the corner of Avram's right eye, his mouth forming a rigid grimace. "But of course. I suggest that a wide variety of construction companies be used, and it'll be necessary for us to tell each one a different story for the various phases of the project. They must only see the blueprints relevant to the specific section of the lab that they are working on."

"And as with any secret, the less that's known, the better, so I will involve as few people as is necessary."

Avram waved his hand toward the expansiveness of the cave. "I agree with you, and after looking all this over, I'm convinced this location is perfect as it actually houses two caves, with the cave farther from the shed having a waterfall at the entrance. The waterfall will be perfect to form the back partition of the first chamber created by diverting the underground stream running through the adjoining cave. Behind the cascade of water, we'll create another wall. Embedded in that wall, we'll install a series of holes that, when stimulated in a specific sequence, will open the door."

"Thus making the rear chamber even more covert than the front."

"We'll also build hidden compartments into the walls for storage."

Satisfied they'd found the perfect spot to begin the construction, Nikolai wiped the sweat from his brow with the back of his hand. "I need a break. It's really hot out here. You know, hot summers and shorter, warmer winters have now become the norm in Montana thanks to climate change."

"I heard one of your ranch hands talking about how the intense heat is baking the nearby trout rivers, decreasing the fish population."

"Same with the moose population. Sad but true, my friend."

✻   ✻   ✻

Avram and Nikolai strolled back to the house, chatting about old times. After Nikolai unlocked the front door, they proceeded to his study and stood at his large, wooden desk that held the intricate construction blueprints for the lab that were still spread out where they'd left them.

Nikolai wet his lips. "First, let's nourish ourselves." He headed directly to the refrigerator in the kitchen. "Come join me. You'll find this a bit amusing. I make my own beet kvass. Nowadays, it's almost impossible to find real kvass in America." He pulled out the bottle, poured two glasses, and handed one to Avram.

Avram took a taste of the fermented beverage. "Ahh. So good! I haven't had this in a long time. Delicious, my friend. You could have a second career if this one doesn't work out for you."

They laughed, slapping each other on the back.

Returning to the task at hand, they walked back to the study and stood at the desk staring at the drawings. With pencil in hand, Avram pointed to an area on the blueprint. "Here's where we will direct the waterfall. It will be perfect for hydroelectric power." He traced the area with his pencil. "From here, it'll drain the aquifer from the mountain directly into a small pool that is the source of this stream that will run year-round through the ranch—"

"—creating a pond that will easily water the fields and pastures," Nikolai said, completing his sentence.

They nodded to each other, pleased with the plans. At last, they were ready to proceed.

❉ ❉ ❉

Avram stayed on with the Sparkmans in their guest room to help oversee the unfolding of the first part of the lab for a couple of weeks before returning home. Nikolai, although a loner at heart, appreciated the time shared with his good friend, especially one he knew he could trust implicitly and with whom he had a shared history. They worked diligently arranging and overseeing each detail. American contractors were utilized to complete the shed and first chamber of the laboratory, and Avram organized a small team of specialists who had constructed Israel's nuclear facility in the Negev desert, near Dimona, to complete the internal systems.

Nikolai had design ideas he'd never been able to test in Russia. Energized when challenged, he loved problem solving. The information he and Avram had swapped with the Israelis was worth the time, cost, and manpower they'd lent to Nikolai.

As Nikolai hoped, the mountain and rock walls shielded the laboratory. To retain the required level of secrecy, even the equipment that Avram obtained from Israel came from a variety of sources. Nikolai had assembled what he needed himself. No one could have guessed what the various pieces of equipment were for because he'd cannibalized what he needed from them. Anyone who ordered the same pieces would never have known which parts were for what use. For the rest of his needs, he'd requisitioned parts from so many sources, no one could trace their purpose as well. The deal that was struck between the U.S. and Israeli governments was to let Nikolai work in private until he completed his experiments, taking them from the theoretical to practical applications. They agreed to give him five years before he was asked for access to his work.

After the shed and first part of the lab was completed, Avram once again returned to the ranch for the second part of the challenge: the hidden lab. Their shared inherent mistrust of governments had led them to develop a clever scheme. The outer lab was well known to the U.S. government, but shielded from everyone else was the area that housed Nikolai's top secret work. Once the American government had inspected and sanctioned the outer cave, Avram sent word to his team, and the Israelis completed the plant in the deeper inner cave where Nikolai would conduct the clandestine part of his real work. Avram, a semi-retired Mossad asset, assembled the crew that completed the hidden cave. They knew how to keep a secret.

Upon returning home, Avram called Nikolai from Israel. "Niko, my team is perfectly capable of carrying out the remainder of the task, but if you need me to come for any reason, just send for me. Let me know when they've completed it, and I'll return to inspect the final product with you."

"Thank you for everything, my friend. I'll keep in touch," Nikolai said.

During the construction period, Nikolai kept busy working on the system to power his lab and creating the equipment he'd need for his projects. He was excited at the thought of finally being able to devise the experiments that had to be carried out in the confines of his secret lab. As soon as the hidden chamber was completed, Nikolai notified Avram, and once again, he returned, as promised, to inspect the completed second cave.

Nikolai demonstrated the covert system to enter the secret chamber, and he could tell from Avram's expression that he was impressed with how perfectly the moving wall functioned. The lab area was massive and subdivided into specific workstations, including a machine shop area.

Grinning with hands folded across his chest, Nikolai followed Avram with his eyes as he walked the room, taking it all in: the electrical transformers, microscopes, projection equipment, accelerators, electronic supplies and devices, tubes, electromechanical and X-ray devices, induction coil magnetometers, oscillators, large spools of wire, and other various unusual apparatuses—even glassblowing equipment.

Avram visually studied the space as he sketched a diagram of the area on his pad of paper, noting a projector and Nikolai's thick leather-bound journal in the corner on his desk. Avram pointed to the overhead projector. "Niko, is this your—" He stopped speaking mid-sentence when, in his peripheral vision, he caught sight of something intriguing he hadn't initially seen.

"So, my good man, explain to me what this unique piece of equipment is. Is this… is this your power source?"

Nikolai's eyes widened, his eyebrows lifted, and he beamed. "This is what I wanted to show you. I was waiting for you to notice. You're looking at my adaptation of the Tesla radiant energy system. What do you think? So here it is. I'm patting myself on the back because I succeeded in capturing energy from the air with a machine to convert that free energy into usable electricity. I did it!"

"I'm in awe. Let me take this all in." With curiosity, Avram touched and explored the components of the system.

Nikolai shook his head. "Life could be so much better today for everyone, for the Earth itself, if Tesla's concept of generating electricity hadn't been suppressed and he hadn't been stripped of his funding. Other scientists, like Moray, have also worked in this area, and he had his very life threatened because of it. So today we persist in using fossil fuels to generate electricity. We could do so much better for people and for our planet… so much better."

"Ahh, Niko—and please note my sarcasm here—why develop free energy systems that do not destroy the environment and have no ongoing cost to the user? Where is the money to be made in that? There is no economic incentive!"

"Such a sad statement, indeed. Well, I've made several prototypes of radiant energy machines. This is my most current, and I'll continue to modify it. My machine taps the highly energetic cosmic rays from the omnipresent ether and converts them to usable electricity. This whole lab is run on free energy.

Nikolai pointed to a piece of equipment the size of a small box. "In this device I created, I have a very special chemical vacuum tube. That tube is top secret. The antenna, the energy-receiving device, harnesses the power. And of course it must be grounded. The electrical current flows deep into the ground, which is negatively electrically charged and serves as the capacitor."

"Niko, I'm utterly fascinated. Even the light itself is different. It's more radiant. More brilliant. Your accomplishment will change the world."

"Problem is," Nikolai said, "I don't think the world is ready for it. If it can't be monetized in some way, no one will fund it, and it won't be developed further. And the other side of this is, I'm not sure mankind is ready to embrace it. Instead of thinking of the possibilities free energy could offer the world, I fear the initial response will be, 'How can I weaponize this?' "

"Sadly, this is true."

Avram put his stamp of approval on the laboratory and Nikolai's accomplishment. "Niko, old man... I'm filled with pride and admiration for you, my dear friend. This is better than what we even originally imagined. I'm grateful to have been a part of this project, and I can't wait to see the places you take it."

Nikolai jokingly punched him in the arm. "Who are you calling an old man? You're older than me! But thanks. I could not have done this without your assistance and your team. I am eternally grateful to you for helping make my dream come true."

"It was a brilliant move to use parts from so many places. No one will ever suspect that construction continued beyond the first cave," Avram said.

"I thought this was the best way to keep things concealed. I used technicians and workers from Canada, Mexico, and directly from Europe. Only the officially sanctioned Israeli scientists you found for the project arrived through the usual channels."

And only Yitzhak Shamir and the head of the Mossad know the whole story, on the Israeli side of it at least. Your laboratory will be one of the world's best-kept secrets. If you looked at the individual pieces of this lab project and tried to put them together, they would lead to a blind alley."

They vigorously clasped hands and declared it complete. *This is only the beginning*, Nikolai thought. "Now sit here with me and let's talk about zero-point vacuum energy, alpha fission, energy conversion technologies, and all the possibilities this could bring... oh, the possibilities!"

After a few hours of intense discussion, Nikolai's grumbling stomach indicated it was time to eat. As they closed up the lab, the sensation of the chill of the evening air and the darkening sky ended their discussion. Nikolai scanned his friend up and down. "Avi, you're too skinny, my friend. Do you ever eat? So now it's time to feed you. Virginia is probably wondering what happened to us. Let's head back to the house for some festivity. She insisted on making us an authentic Russian dinner. And, of course, I think some vodka is in order to celebrate."

❋   ❋   ❋

Now, over a year later, as Nikolai stood admiring his laboratory, he fully realized the plans had worked even better than he'd expected. The applications of the theories outlined in his journal were coming to fruition, and Nikolai was totally absorbed in his work, his dreams. Meanwhile, the American scientific community was well aware of Nikolai's departure from Russia and subsequent placement in the Pryor Mountains. Invitations to attend the Santa Fe Institute and major universities poured in with the hope of learning more of Nikolai's work.

Nikolai knew he was one of only a few major scientists in the world who had a deep understanding across the artificial boundaries university-based science had created. That's why he chose to work alone—within that sphere of isolation, he was able to unleash his unrestricted curiosity to pursue whatever he needed to get results. In time, he decided he'd join his colleagues and share what the funding government agencies would allow. But his lack of trust was always present, so even they would get only pieces at a time.

If he was correct, no one government should control this knowledge. It could be dangerous—very dangerous.

CHAPTER FIVE
VIRGINIA
1992

TO SAY THE least, Virginia was proud of her husband. She marveled at what he'd been able to create in the short span of two years. She supported him in his every endeavor and was fine with the time he needed alone to do his work. She kept busy with her own projects, tending to her garden and an orchard they'd planted, along with tutoring Olivia as she prepared to study for her nursing degree. But she experienced a certain stirring that often comes upon women when their biological clock signals time is running out to have a baby. She'd heard about it from friends, but now it was happening to her. They'd been trying to conceive since they'd first moved to the ranch, and frustration was overtaking her thoughts. *Maybe I'm too old. I'm pushing forty now. I hope I haven't waited until it's too late.*

With Nikolai having finished the lab and now working more specifically on his research and experiments, she thought she'd sit down and talk baby strategy with him. She knew how much he'd wanted to start a family, and she didn't want to let him down. Virginia planned to talk to him that evening over dinner, but as she looked out the dining room window, she saw Nikolai sprinting from his lab to the house.

He was breathless and appeared to be bursting at the seams. "Sit down, my love. I need to speak to you."

Hesitating before she perched on the chair in the family room, her chest tightened and her stomach churned—probably because he seemed nervous and unsure of himself.

"What is it? What happened? Please tell me."

He spoke so rapidly, it was hard to keep up. "It is important that I tell you this. Someone other than me has to know this information, and you are the one I trust to receive it."

Unable to contain his enthusiasm, he couldn't remain seated. He paced across the floor striking his closed palm into his hand. He raised his hands upward and looked toward the ceiling. "I've had a breakthrough, my love. I've cracked a key component to the problem of turning on higher energy states at the cellular level. I did it!"

Virginia inhaled a sharp breath, clasped her hand over her mouth, and said, "My God, Nikolai, this is profound!"

He bent toward her, placing both of his hands on her shoulders. "I have something I need to show you, and I need to do it now. I don't know how you're going to respond to this."

"Of course, you must. I'll be fine. Tell me more."

"It's a miracle. I've unlocked a fundamental secret of all cellular function that applies advanced physics to cellular energy. As you know, our cells can generate energy with and without oxygen. The key lies in the mitochondria. The mitochondria have their own DNA that's separate from the DNA in the nucleus of the cell, and the DNA in the mitochondria is handed down through the mother to her child. And, of course, each cell possesses a plethora of mitochondria that generate their energy supply."

"Okay… keep going. I'm fascinated."

He resumed pacing the floor. "So, at the atomic level mitochondria are very effective at capturing and using electrons and converting them into useful energy sources. You're not going to believe this, but—Virginia, I've found a way to amplify that energy without harming the host!"

Virginia slapped her hand to her chest. "I'm flabbergasted. This is earth-shattering. The potential is…" She shook her head.

"I know. Usually such an increase in energy produces heat, but my cells emitted waveforms that could transform the cells around them."

"Transform them in what way?"

"The mitochondria grew somewhat larger with an increased complexity of their inner wall. By my calculations, the energy produced could ramp up to the point that the waveforms admitted by the cell actually enhance the activity of the cells around it."

Virginia pondered the concept. "You've mentioned this possibility previously. So, say for plants, what would this mean?"

Nikolai sat briefly. However, unable to contain his own high energy, he jumped up from his seat and began pacing again. "In theory, plants would grow larger with the capability to protect themselves from pests more efficiently. All the while, the core DNA would change the protein it produced."

"So, all things considered, the negative effects of genetically modified foods could possibly become a thing of the past? My God, Nikolai, this is huge. This is life-altering!"

"At this point, I'm not exactly sure how the whole plant system would respond or if seeds could even be programmed. I'm slowly working my way up the chain of simple cells in order to advance to lower plant life, then animal life."

"I'm dumbfounded, and the possibilities of this are overwhelming my brain."

"I know, and I have so much to do, but I can't share this with others. I learned that from experiences in Russia. The *only* one I can trust with this information is you, my love."

Virginia knew of the basics of Nikolai's work, but she also understood that he needed to shield her for safety and security purposes, not for lack of trust.

"I will show you more and more of what I'm doing over time, but for now, know that I love and trust you. If my work is successful, there will be many who would do anything to own it. In the wrong hands, this would prove to be very dangerous. People have been killed for their new technology."

"I understand this, Nikolai. I know you'll give it to the world when you're ready and have determined *the world* is ready. I do understand that this technology in the wrong hands, and developed too early, would be like giving the secrets of atomic weaponry to every undeveloped country in the world before we knew the power of the atom."

"Exactly. For now, you have to have deniability. There's just no telling the results… and heaven forbid if such information is weaponized. Now, under the cover of night, you must come with me to the lab." He grabbed for a handkerchief he carried in his back pocket and dabbed at his face.

Virginia reached out with concern, gently touching his cheek. "Nikolai, are you feeling okay? You're sweating profusely."

"I'm feeling a bit off, but I'm probably dehydrated. I haven't had much water all day in my excitement. I feel I need to show you everything, and it may seem confusing at first. But you are brilliant, my love, and in time you will understand the whole picture. I need for you to understand."

She wasn't sure, but she thought she saw a momentary flicker of the old sadness in him, and then it was gone. She knew he hadn't been up to par lately, and it concerned her. She hoped he wasn't feeling this urgency to show her something because he had some kind of premonition.

No, I'm just feeling paranoid. I need to let go of these worries. I can always deny I've ever been to the lab later, if it ever comes to that. For now, I need to know everything.

"Nikolai, please drink some water before we head out," she said.

They walked hand in hand to the lab. There was nothing more reassuring to Virginia than to feel the strength of his calloused, strong hands: leathery, with visible veins, scarred and weathered from hard work—these were the hands that comforted and reassured her; the tender hands that brushed a tear from her eyes when she was sad; the hands that gently pushed her hair back from her face when the wind blew; the hands that caressed her and held her at night. Now the sensation of his hand in hers, the comforting squeeze he gave her, released her anxiety, effectively unknitting her brow.

Virginia felt so proud of her husband. Not a day went by when he didn't impress her, stimulate her, or dazzle her. She loved everything about him, especially his independent, audacious spirit. This was his dream, and she was enjoying every second of the magic carpet ride she was on with him. *I wonder what he's going to show me.*

"Now, as I've told you, I haven't showed you how to access the hidden portion of the laboratory for security purposes. But now I feel I must show you how to safely access it."

He unlocked the door, and they entered the shed. It looked like it always did when Olivia and Virginia stored their gardening tools and other equipment there.

"Now you go ahead and put in your code to enter the lab as you always do."

She punched in her code, a green light flashed, and the faux wall quietly opened. They entered the lab.

"Okay, now come over here to the entrance of chamber two—the hidden portion of the lab."

Nikolai explained how the waterfall at the rear of the first cave became the entrance to the second and how, behind the cascade of water, he and Avram had created another wall. Embedded in that wall, they'd installed a series of holes that, when stimulated in a specific sequence, opened the door.

"Watch carefully," Nikolai said. He bore into her with his penetrating eyes. "This is what I want you to memorize. Here lies the secret. Each hole actually represents the first notes of our song, our symphony."

"Beethoven's Fifth, of course."

"Two four-note motifs. Get it right, and the wall becomes a door that opens to my hidden lab. It will close automatically." Carefully, he punched in the sequence.

"Okay… ," she said. Her breathing accelerated. *What am I going to learn?*

The opening door created a bit of noise—this partition was evidently far heavier than the first. They stepped into the room. No lights came on until the door closed imperceptibly behind them. Virginia inspected the environment, taking in the vast array of computers, hoods, tanks growing cells, analyzers, and projectors. In the corner was a study area with a large desk, oversized whiteboard filled with equations, and wall shelves covered with books. Next to one of the bookshelves was an easy chair.

Virginia sighed out loud, taking it all in. "Nikolai, it's… it's… huge and such a special place. I had no idea it was going to look like this."

"Also, there are hidden areas we built into the walls where I keep many of my notes and papers. I always store my leather notebook in here." He stepped over to a specific location and pressed inward on a rock. It opened a door to a cubicle in which Virginia saw a stack of documents.

Nikolai spoke rapidly. "Now come here, my love. I must show you this fascinating discovery."

He switched on the projection scope, and on a high-definition screen, Virginia actually saw history unfold before her eyes. She was in both shock and awe. There, in front of her, was a synchronized dance of the cell Nikolai had created. No matter what kind of damaged cell he placed near it, they seemed to join, and then like some silent symphony, they danced together.

"Nikolai, there are no words! It's magical how they appear to move together."

"Well, actually, the activated cell causes the damaged cell to increase its vibrational state until they vibrate at the same frequency. Watch how the damaged cell moves away from my activated cell, how now it's glowing in a similar way as the master cell. Amazing."

"What, what is this, what does this mean?" For the first time in her life, Virginia was seeing something inexplicable. "Did that cell just heal the other? How did... What?... Nikolai, what's going on?"

"Watch for now and I'll explain. The array of equipment I've programmed to unlock the 'big bang gene' is the microscopic answer Einstein looked for with his unified field theory. It—"

Virginia interrupted. "Wait... wait... let me digest this a second. This is the theory Einstein spent his remaining years of life trying to solve by attempting to tie together all known phenomena with the intent to explain the behavior and nature of all the energy and matter in existence. In other words, essentially unlocking the secrets of the universe. Yes?"

He grinned at her enthusiasm. "Yes, the key to the primal forces in cellular energy. My first experiments were on unicellular organisms, and then I found that..."

"Okay, go on..." she encouraged.

"Anything my activated cell came into contact with became energized. So just imagine food sources, for example. Imagine them being energized and growing hardily even in the most compromised environments, imagine food that would impart better health for all who consumed it."

Virginia could hardly contain her excitement. "The possibilities for feeding the world would be staggering."

"Absolutely. But I'm also very aware of the implications and what could happen if this information got into the wrong hands."

"Of course, there is always the yin to the yang. So, what is going on here?" Virginia pointed to the far end of a wooden table.

"That, my dear, is my next planned experiment. Plant cells respond to the energy shifts by increasing the energy states around them. So the question is: how would a mammalian cell react? That is a mammalian cell in a special solution under my dissecting microscope."

"So what's this camera hanging above the scope for? And this odd-looking device off to the side?" She paused briefly and stared at him with a stern expression. "Nikolai, you're sweating again, and I see you rubbing your jaw. Stop talking for a moment and look at me. I want to know that you are okay."

"I'm fine. I'm fine. I've just been working hard and not sleeping well. Maybe I have a bit of a toothache, I think, and I'm feeling a bit nauseous. But never mind that. Right now, I have all of these questions to answer, like, what's the potential for unlocking these energy states in an animal? Could tissues regenerate? Could we possibly even reverse disease? I can only imagine the results at this point, but the mathematical theories and calculations are essentially complete." Nikolai gestured toward the whiteboard, filled with mathematical computations. "I'm ready to program the system, and you, my love, will bear witness.

"I believe in the next few days, I'm going to change the world of medicine. Who knows what lies on the other side of this one singular experiment? Virginia, it's extremely important that you remember the sequence I've shown you on how to enter the lab. Do you have it imprinted in your brain?"

"Of course. No worries. For once in my life, I'm rendered speechless. I'm finding all of this excitement very stimulating. Now let's go home and celebrate this phenomenal discovery." She slipped her arm around his waist, slightly cocked her head to the side, wet her lips, and gave him her best sultry look.

His face softened, and with a confident slight raise of his left eyebrow above a smoldering blue eye, he let her know he understood her message.

"Yes, let's."

CHAPTER SIX
NIKOLAI
1992

EARLY THE NEXT morning, still brimming with the excitement of the previous day, Nikolai needed to calm himself and decided to take one of his meditative walks and check out their property. He felt a sense of relief that he'd finally shown Virginia how to access the secret portion of the cave and shared his discoveries with her. While living in Russia, he couldn't even conceive of the life he ended up living here, in all this natural splendor. Not just finding the love of his life, but having the freedom to do the work he was passionate about—well, it was almost beyond the scope of his comprehension. Yet it was real. He'd found the happiness he'd sought, more than he could have asked for. To Nikolai Sparkman, life was complete exactly as it was. Always one to take each day as it came, he put every ounce of what he had into each moment. His motto had always been carpe diem, seize the day. Not one to look a gift horse in the mouth, he was grateful, but he wouldn't at all mind if he and Virginia would be blessed with a child. He had so much he wanted to share and a legacy he wanted to leave to a daughter or son.

Everything felt perfectly in sync—within his very being, he felt a rhythm and beat he was in tune with. Deep in thought, he wandered outside of the perimeter of their compound as he mentally reviewed all of the calculations one last time before the final step of his experiment. He clicked off the checklist in his brain; timers were already set, and then there would be the birth of a mammalian cell that was the first of its kind. It was an emotional experience for him.

Virginia and Nikolai felt blessed to share their ranch in Montana with the grand wild mustangs, and he recalled the one, called White Cloud, that appeared the first time they visited the ranch. Nikolai had seen him several times over the years; however, the horse always stayed a safe distance away. But now, outside of the compound, that same magnificent white mustang Olivia had first seen on the property temporarily distracted him. He'd never seen him so close up.

The horse stopped and stared at Nikolai. Frozen in the moment, he noticed for the first time that the horse had blue eyes, and he found himself mesmerized by their color and soulfulness. He didn't take flight. His ears were forward, as though he were totally interested in Nikolai. He approached Nikolai with his head held high, tail flagged, then relaxed. His flowing mane whipped as the wind blew through it. Puffs of moisture escaped from his nostrils. The horse snorted and nodded his head in Nikolai's direction as if trying to make some kind of nonverbal contact.

Nikolai didn't move a muscle. He just stood still, eye to eye with the horse, sharing a Zen moment. The great steed again snorted and pawed at the ground.

At that moment, Nikolai recognized what was happening. He felt the squeezing sensation and fullness in his chest as visions of the future floated through his head.

His breath shortened and became increasingly shallower… and he saw an image of Virginia.

This is it. My final moments on this beautiful Earth. I am grateful to die a happy and blessed man.

He broke out in a cold sweat… and he saw Virginia giving birth.

He strained to inflate his lungs… and he saw he had a son.

He fell to the ground, supine, and stared up into the sky. The clouds seemed to be circling overhead in some kind of mystical dance, inviting him to join in, then parting to expose the most brilliant sunlight he'd ever seen. The clouds looked so white against the blueness of the sky.

He clenched both of his hands into fists until his knuckles were white… and he saw an image of Virginia clasping hands, walking on the ranch with their child.

He wasn't afraid… he could feel his body shutting down… he knew everything was going to be okay.

He gasped a final breath as the sensation of a dark curtain fell over him… and he saw a vision of himself running free with the wild mustangs. He'd felt that glorious sense of freedom once before when he'd first arrived in California with his beloved wife. Now he felt it one more time. And once again, Nikolai was free.

CHAPTER SEVEN
VIRGINIA
1992

U NFATHOMABLE. SHOCKING. INCONCEIVABLE. Overwhelming. There weren't enough adjectives to describe what Virginia felt. Last night they had one of the most exciting, intimate moments of their lives; now her world had crashed.

Virginia had been busy in the kitchen making a breakfast of *syrniki* for Nikolai, waiting for his return from his morning walk. The tea was steeping, and she'd set a small bowl of homemade jam on the kitchen table when she checked her watch, wondering where he was. Typically a precise person, it was odd he wasn't back when she expected. After another twenty minutes passed, she set out to follow the usual path he walked to find him.

After searching for a while, she saw something unusual, slightly outside the boundaries of the compound. It was the great stallion, White Cloud. He appeared to be watching her. When she approached within a few feet, she noticed something near his hooves. There he was. Her Nikolai. Her love. Her life. She ran to him but already saw his spirit had left him. She sank to her knees, holding his face in her hands, feeling a desperation unfamiliar to her. His body was lifeless, but she sensed him around her.

Oh, my Nikolai, my love. Why did you leave me alone? How can I go on without you?

In a panic, she jerked her head to the left, then the right, searching for someone, anyone, to help her. There was no one. *I need help! I don't want to leave him alone.* She felt some solace that the white mustang continued to stand watch. *It's almost as if he's protecting my Nikolai.*

Virginia had no other choice but to run back to the house and call 911. After making the necessary call, she raced back to be with him while she waited for help to arrive. The mighty steed was still standing guard. But what was this odd thing that was happening? What was the stallion doing? It was a wild horse. No one had ever trained him. But what she was seeing was real… or at least she thought it was. The horse actually bowed down! To her knowledge, only horses trained to do tricks would do something like that. *What does this mean?* Then, as if he understood his duty was completed, the horse rose and galloped away. Soon, she heard the disquieting sound of sirens approaching as she lay next to Nikolai, clutching his lifeless body.

I often say that time is short, she thought. *I guess we don't believe it until it's in our face—until we are forced to endure the unthinkable. No one wants to believe that time has literally run out.*

Prior to the attendants taking Nikolai away, Virginia tenderly gave her husband one last kiss. *I'll never again see the stars in his eyes.* Tears wet her cheeks, her eyes clouded over like a heavy fog in the meadow, and she whispered her final good-bye.

❋   ❋   ❋

Stunned, Virginia staggered back to the house. She rested in the living room, staring out the window, feeling numb and paralyzed. She had no energy, feeling drained of her life force. She couldn't even manage to call Olivia. *I don't know what to do next.*

Even though Nikolai was quite a bit older than her, Virginia had imagined he would always be there by her side. After all, they were a team.

For one who studied earthquakes, how could she be so unprepared when the Earth metaphorically shifted, creating a huge quake that caused her world to come crashing down around her? All that remained of her emotions was the rubble. It was as though the ground had opened up and swallowed her whole.

Why did this happen? She wondered if Nikolai had risen early to work in the lab before his walk. Had he left any signs there? Any note for her?

Suddenly, reality hit her. She needed to immediately get to the lab and be sure his notes, papers, and journals were securely hidden. She was now responsible for protecting his work.

Rushing to the shed and standing before it, Virginia fell to her knees and cried. Wiping her tears with the back of her hand, she stood up, steadying herself. *I have to go in.* She unlocked the door of the shed and rushed to the code pad for the main lab. In her stressed state of mind, Virginia fumbled to punch in her code and waited for the wall to open, then entered.

First things first—she needed to check around the room for anything that needed to be hidden. It appeared that all the papers and equipment that had been left out were things Nikolai would have deemed safe for others to see. *I need to get into the secret part of the lab. I need to be sure he hid his journal and notes on the mammalian cell experiment.*

Virginia remained in a heightened state of emotion. Her hands shook, and her chest rose and fell with rapid breaths.

Next step—open the wall behind the waterfall and get in. *Do I remember exactly what Nikolai told me to do? Beethoven's Fifth. Yes… the first notes. I can do this.* She'd imprinted on her brain what Nikolai had shown her. Taking two deep breaths, she recalled their favorite symphony and began. *This better work.* Carefully, she punched in the sequence and heard the sound of the wall moving. Success!

Almost imperceptibly, the wall to her left moved inward. She stepped into the black void as the wall closed behind her.

Lights automatically illuminated the area. Wiping tears from her eyes, Virginia moved slowly through the space that had been his, gently gliding her hand over the surface of his desk as if she were still touching him.

Drawn to the far end of the lab, she focused on the elaborate projection scope that was pointed toward the petri dish shielded by a translucent box containing the mammalian cell. To get a closer look, she wedged herself between the strange-looking projector and the table. The projector was at a forty-five-degree angle to the dish with the recording device hung above the system, ready to document the experiment. Virginia peered through the microscope and saw one cell in the middle of the field, immediately recognizing a HeLa cell, which scientists had used for decades to study diseases. Curiosity drew her more closely to the cell as she tried to get a better view by wedging herself even more tightly between the tip of a piece of equipment labeled ACCELERATOR, the table, and the microscope.

What's happening! I think I hit something I shouldn't have, she thought. The timers Nikolai had set suddenly, and without warning, started the mammalian experiment. A subtle glow developed around the apparatus that grew into an unusual colored light. In a fraction of a second, the entire room lit up and then plunged into darkness. Virginia scanned the room but remained in place, frozen with fear. Had she done something wrong? She heard a clicking sound followed by a sharp pain that pierced her abdomen, causing her to faint onto the table, pushing the projection scope to one side and the accelerator to the other. The experiment was over.

Virginia woke to silence. *What time is it? How long have I been out? What did I do?* Other than opening the secret lab, which automatically turned on the lights, and wedging herself in front of the projection scope, she hadn't touched a thing.

She didn't know what had happened, but she knew she still hadn't completed her task of hiding Nikolai's work. Glancing around, she saw that his leather journal and two fat notebooks were stacked on the desk. She grabbed the whole pile, and after recalling the storage area in the faux stone wall that Nikolai had shown her, she pressed on the rock. The door sprang open, and she shoved the journal and notebooks on top of other papers and tapes already housed in the hidden nook.

In her haste, the bracelet she wore caught in the locking mechanism. *If I yank on this, I'm going to break it.* Because of its sentimental value, she hesitated—it was a gift from her brother, Brian—a black pearl bracelet he'd brought her from Fiji. She knew she had no choice. She pulled her wrist upward to release the bracelet, and the moment it broke, black pearls scattered all over the floor. *I need to hurry.* She scurried to gather the errant pearls and pocketed them to restring them later. She knew she didn't get them all, but she'd come back later.

Before she closed the storage compartment, she decided she should also hide the petri dish and various items on the table used in the experiment. Once those were concealed, she double-checked the room one more time as she headed toward the exit. Still feeling somewhat disoriented, she stumbled out of the hidden lab and heard the door close behind her, accompanied by the clang of multiple locks.

Virginia exited the main lab into the shed. Through the window, she could see that the sky had clouded over outside. And just as she was retrieving her keys to lock the door, she saw them approach. *Oh no! Not now!* There was no mistaking who they were. They all looked the same. Two government agents were climbing up the path from the house to the herb garden toward the shed. They'd come and gone for years; they could change clothes but not their persona. She recognized one who had occasionally met with Nikolai in his study. Virginia knew she had to pull herself together quickly.

The taller one, with sparse white hair, spoke. "Dr. Sparsinsky, we just heard the sad news, and we're very sorry for your loss."

"It's Dr. Sparkman. We're the Sparkmans now," Virginia said curtly in reply, "and you know that."

"Yes, sorry, I know you don't want any ties to the past."

Virginia nodded.

He continued. "So were you looking for something specific in the laboratory?"

It took her a moment to answer—she was astounded at how fast the news had spread after just one emergency phone call, and even more astounded at how quickly the agents had shown up. *Boy, they're not losing any time trying to get their hands on his work!* "Actually, no. I've spent many hours with my husband in his beloved lab, and I wanted to be somewhere private where I could feel close to him. I was playing some records we loved."

The second agent, short and rotund, responded. "We're sorry to interrupt you in your time of grieving, but surely you're aware of the gravity of your husband's work that we've been funding. We're here to collect his papers and equipment."

Virginia stood tall and wiped tears from her cheeks that she hadn't even known she'd cried. She felt Nikolai standing beside her, supporting her, as she stepped forward toward the agents—they were not going to intimidate her. Nikolai's work was now hers to protect. She briefly closed her eyes and brushed the hair from her face. "Gentlemen, I'm not all that familiar with Nikolai's research projects. Feel free to go into the lab and take what you need. You're also welcome to come to the house and look at the documents in his study. I'll wait outside while you do your work."

Her openness disarmed them. "Great, we appreciate that. If you wouldn't mind opening the lab, then?" The shorter agent looked at the taller one. "You start—I'll go get the boxes from the car."

As Virginia entered her code to access the main lab, she gave a silent prayer of thanks that she'd had time to secure Nikolai's work. Then she went outside, to the side of the shed, and let the men do what they would.

They were in there over an hour, hastily packing up everything they thought might be valuable—papers, folders, ledgers, slides, small equipment and larger equipment. At one point, Virginia overheard the overweight agent call from Nikolai's desk, "Boss, over here! There's a secret compartment under his desk drawer. And there are some crystal-like particles and pieces of black stone on the desk. Do you want those?"

"No, but take everything else," the taller agent called back.

The afternoon was dull and gray. Inside, Virginia felt the same, glad of only one thing: *Thank God my wise and skeptical Nikolai had the foresight to carefully place his Trojan horses that will eventually lead the agents to a dead end.*

Finally, boxes packed in a tall pile, the men paraded them back to the car one at a time and left with a brusque good-bye.

❈   ❈   ❈

Shaken and emotionally wrought, Virginia trudged back to the house. There, waiting on a rattan chair on the front porch, was Olivia. Next to her were two battered suitcases, a duct-taped cardboard box, and a golden retriever puppy.

Olivia stood as Virginia approached, then ran down the stairs and enveloped Virginia in a loving hug, holding on to her rigid and weary body. Reluctantly, after their silent exchange of grief, Virginia released her embrace.

"I heard," is all Olivia said, turning to follow Virginia through the front door. "I'm moving in."

CHAPTER EIGHT
OLIVIA
1992–1993

FASTER THAN A subatomic particle can travel, the news of Nikolai's death reached Olivia. Horrified and dismayed, she knew it was time to fulfill her calling. This was it. She informed her father, who agreed with her decision, then she packed her bags. Her father dropped her off at the ranch, and with a sense of knowing and sadness, he bid her good-bye. She waited impatiently on the front porch with her golden retriever, Delta, for Virginia to come home. *Where is she?*

When she finally saw Virginia walking up the path from the lab, Olivia raced to embrace her. After sharing mutual hugs and tears, she settled her bags in the room she'd always stayed in when visiting and showed Delta around her new home. Olivia hugged Virginia again and scanned her from head to toe. *She's running on very low energy at the moment.* Olivia didn't say much other than, "I'm here for you. You're not alone." Then she headed to the kitchen to put on the tea. In a tribute to Nikolai, she poured the boiling water into the samovar Nikolai cherished and made a pot of zavarka the way he'd taught her.

Together, they sat at the table pouring out their hearts and sipping tea as they typically did, but the situation was no longer a typical one. Virginia, through her trembling and bouts of tears, relayed her painful story of finding Nikolai, the horse, the agents… and how they'd cleaned out the laboratory. No tea would console the grief they held in their hearts that day.

✳   ✳   ✳

That's how they spent the next couple of weeks. Virginia talked. Olivia listened and comforted. Sometimes Olivia chanted. Sometimes they took turns crying—one minute it was Olivia, most times Virginia.

Over dinner one evening, Virginia confessed to Olivia her need to open up and share a secret. They'd just come from the garden after picking some fresh herbs and were busying themselves in the kitchen making basil pesto. Olivia thought the comfort and nurturing warmth of a kitchen was always a good place for women to release their emotions and for personal confessions.

Virginia vigorously picked the stems from the basil leaves as she spoke. "I wanted to talk to you about something. I know you don't judge, and this is a bit awkward for me; however, I feel compelled to share it with you."

"Of course, anything you say is safe with me."

"Well, I've been having dreams. I know this is nothing strange to you, but it is to me. I'm a scientist, but I do accept there are unexplainable things in this universe of ours. But... I believe... I think that my Nikolai comes to me in my dreams. I've actually felt his presence at my bedside. That familiar sensation of him stroking my hair like he used to when he was alive. His tall figure, his deep-set eyes. He's come several times, but when I wake up, there's no one there of course."

Olivia didn't look up as she crushed pine nuts in the mortar with the pestle. "I don't find that unusual at all. Just because you haven't found an explanation for something doesn't mean it didn't happen. Actually, I find it very comforting."

"Well, last night he came to me in a different way."

"How so?"

"He stood before me with that disarmingly sheepish grin of his, and he repeatedly pointed to my lower abdomen. And then poof, he disappeared. What do you make of that?"

Olivia didn't miss a beat—still not looking up from her task—and responded matter-of-factly: "You're pregnant."

Virginia opened her eyes wide and raised her eyebrows. "Why—why do you think so?"

"I don't think so. I know so."

✳   ✳   ✳

Olivia knew she was right—she had long been having her own dreams. Virginia took the pregnancy test, and sure enough, Olivia was correct. She acted nonchalant but intrigued as a new side of Virginia developed. Some curious things began to occur. When anything unusual happened around her, Virginia believed it was Nikolai guiding or communicating with her. Although this was unconventional for her—the metaphysical world was not front and center in her line of thinking—it was commonplace for Olivia.

It was true that odd things were happening in the household, and Olivia was acutely aware of the phenomena. She noticed how Delta, her dog, was drawn to the baby growing in Virginia's belly, often nuzzling her head against Virginia's abdomen. The corner of the sunroom had a grand view of the mountains, and it was Virginia's favorite place to read. It was apparent that the plants that surrounded her favorite chair had long since passed their blooming phase. One day, she looked up from her book with a shocked expression, glancing over at Olivia, who was studying at the nearby table.

"Olivia," she said, "have you noticed how all the plants in this area have started to bloom again? So many strange things have been happening. I think it must be Nikolai."

Olivia agreed, but she knew Virginia was only partially correct.

The weeks passed quickly. At first, Virginia told Olivia that she wanted to hold off on knowing the sex of the baby. But when Virginia couldn't wait any longer, Olivia attended Virginia's ultrasound appointment with her at the twenty-week mark. As the technician ran the transducer over the gel on her belly, the obstetrician stood to the side and pointed to the monitor.

"I'll bet money on this one," the obstetrician said. "It's a boy."

At that moment, the ultrasound machine made a strange clanking noise and shut down.

Not only did flowers bloom around her, but also electrical equipment seemed to go haywire whenever Virginia was around. The TV would flicker. Lights would dim. Watches would stop working while wearing them.

Olivia and Virginia spent hours planning for the arrival of the baby, and they derived great pleasure from searching through books, picking out the perfect name. Virginia decided to give her son a Z name, in honor of Nikolai's father, Zev."

"Which name do you like better, Olivia? Zeke or Zachary?" Virginia asked.

"He's a Zachary," Olivia responded.

"Then Zachary, Zac, it is!"

Olivia observed Virginia—a researcher by nature—spending time reading articles on various kinds of birthing methods. Olivia was familiar with the Leboyer method of childbirth, using low lights and soft music, and she told Virginia about it. With this method, baby Zac would immediately be placed on Virginia's abdomen, and shortly after, he'd be immersed in a small tub of warm water to replicate the floating weightless sensation of the womb. Virginia wanted the least amount of trauma for Zac, so she decided on a home birth. Together, Olivia and Virginia met with a number of midwives, and after many interviews, they found one, named Martha, that both women instantly liked. She was in her fifties, experienced, and skilled at delivering all forms of life, both human and animal.

❋   ❋   ❋

They still had preparations to make with only a few weeks left before the birth. Virginia and Olivia painted the walls of Zac's room in a shade of pale blue, then they added atop that background white-crested ocean waves that undulated beneath colorful airbrushed sailboats. Olivia, being the only one who could still climb a ladder, decorated the ceiling with dark indigo paint and pasted glow-in-the-dark stars in the formation of constellations.

Olivia circled the day on the calendar that she *knew* Zac would be born. Sure enough, Virginia began contractions that evening. Martha was stunned. No sooner had the delivery begun than it was over. Delta let out a howl, and lightning cracked in the sky. One hour was all it took for the fastest, most pain-free delivery Martha had ever attended. She meandered around the bedroom, running her fingers through her curly red hair. "I've never seen anything like this in my life," Martha muttered. "It's like the boy delivered himself."

Virginia didn't have the perspective that Olivia and Martha had when Zac came into the world. After Zac bonded on Virginia's abdomen, Martha picked him up, cradled him in her arms, and gently immersed his tiny, naked body into a tub of warm water she'd prepared. As Olivia watched, she was mesmerized at how he appeared to be looking directly at Martha and smiling. Olivia began to chant to the divine Mother Earth to give thanks for the gift she'd given to the world.

Later, while Virginia slept, Olivia first held the swaddled baby. *This is the most amazing thing I've ever experienced.* From there and ever after, she referred to Zac as "the Child of Light." At the moment of his birth, Olivia had found her purpose: she was meant to be Zac's spiritual guardian for life. Olivia gazed into his eyes and stroked his face between her thumb and index finger.

"You, my Child of Light, are a very special boy. You'll be of great service to humanity during these major times of change. You must remember this saying, and I'm here to remind you: darkness cannot exist where there is light."

PART TWO
1997–1999

The greatest threat to our planet is the
belief that someone else will save it.

—Robert Swan

CHAPTER NINE
VIRGINIA
1997

ZAC SPENT THE first years of his life surrounded by horses, eagles, a variety of men who came to work on the ranch, and two women who loved him: Virginia and Olivia.

For Virginia, keeping a gratitude diary became an everyday activity. After the passing of her husband, it helped her to concentrate on the good things she had in life. The greatest of her blessings was the gift of her son, of course, and next on her list was her friendship with Olivia—not only for the bond the two women shared, but also for the great love she saw Olivia bestow upon Zac. The affinity they had for each other was special and unique. Currently, Olivia was the only one, other than herself, who had any awareness of Zac's unusual qualities and abilities, and she was fiercely protective of him, assuming the role of both his angel and his warrior.

The two women worked out a system of caring for Zac so that one of them was always with him. While Olivia completed the clinical and classroom requirements for her nursing degree, Virginia continued her work as a geologist, with some limited speaking engagements and geological site visits. A major shift in her priorities happened once her boy was born—she no longer had the desire, the drive, to pursue her professional goals with the same fervor she had earlier in her career, preferring now to research and write in the quiet of her home and spend time with Zac.

After Nikolai's death, Virginia had lost her equilibrium, and as she floundered to regain it, she'd buried herself in too much work. It was a good distraction, but after an intense four months, she realized fatigue comes in two forms, both mental and physical, and if not monitored and kept in check, it spirals into exhaustion and depression.

Virginia was a woman who knew she needed balance in her life, and she understood how to achieve it. It was so easy for her to immerse herself in the world of science, but she also knew when it was time to connect with nature, to stay in touch with her inner essence. After being in such high demand from others in her field of work, she felt her stress bucket begin to overflow—she knew she needed to get away for some rest and relaxation and to create some wonderful childhood memories for Zac.

Growing up in Vermont with her brother, Brian, she had a New England type of practicality and self-reliance. She'd always been fiercely independent and competitive. Brian had been the dreamer while Virginia was the hard-driving, pragmatic one. Their world had been teeming with books, music, and summers filled with hiking and sailing off the coast of Cape Cod.

As she fondly remembered her childhood summers, she knew where she wanted to take Zac now. Desperate for a respite, there was only one place for her retreat: Cape Cod. A rendezvous with her brother would have been the icing on the cake, but she found herself disappointed when he had to decline her invitation. She hadn't seen him since he'd come out for Zac's second birthday. It seemed their schedules were never in sync, and sadly, this time was no different. So, while Brian headed off to Europe, Olivia, Zac, and Virginia headed off to the East Coast for some quiet, quality family time.

※　　　※　　　※

It was mid-autumn on Nantucket—Virginia's favorite time of year, when the tourists had finally gone home and a serene ambiance settled over the island.

On their first day there, Virginia, Olivia, and Zac spent the afternoon combing the perfectly windswept beach for seashells. The quaint, weathered fishing cottages, sailboats, and old lighthouses seemed more welcoming in the fall. Enjoying the fresh seafood, the oysters and lobsters, was always a treat. The undulating ebb and flow of the ocean, the salty, briny smell of seaweed, the steady roar of crashing waves, and the winding dirt bike paths felt like home to her: calming and comforting.

Virginia watched as four-year-old Zac, barefoot with his pant legs rolled up to his knees, bent down to pick up a lady crab shell with leopard-like spots. Always inquisitive, he rubbed the shell between his thumb and index finger, turning it over and back, apparently wondering about the life that it had once held inside.

He held the shell out for Virginia to examine. "Mommy, can I take this shell with me? I like it."

She accepted it from him and held it between both hands, feeling the energy within. She turned to him and placed the shell back in his palm. "Lady crabs molt during the summer, and they leave their beautiful shells behind on the beaches. You can enjoy it best by just looking at it. People shouldn't remove shells from beaches."

"Why? There's nothing in it anymore." He gazed at her with his curious, steely blue eyes.

Virginia's long hair blew in the breeze and feathered across her cheeks as she brushed it out of her eyes, gently finger-combing through the strands. "We must always do our best to protect nature. If you take that shell, Mother Earth wouldn't like that because it might hurt the little creatures that use the shells as their homes. Did you know that lots of shells on the beach disappear during summer vacation when so many people are here? They take them because they don't know any better. But now you do!"

"What good are they just resting here on the beach?" Zac asked.

"The empty seashells are important. Sometimes they're used for making birds' nests, and sometimes crabs or other little animals use them for protection."

He squatted down, patted an indent, and gently returned the shell to the sand.

Olivia, who'd been wading in the waves, barefoot with leather sandals in hand, approached and listened. "I have another way of looking at it," she said. "My ancestors thought of shells and other things in nature as being magical. Each one of these shells is filled with spiritual energy. It's like the special energy, the light, that's inside you." She reached over and tousled Zac's hair. "In fact, the abalone shell has been used by my Native American people in our spiritual ceremonies for many centuries. They think of the abalone as a gift from the sea."

"Olivia, is it okay if I pick them up and hold them? I like how they feel in my hand... And what's an abalone?"

Olivia gave him a tender smile. "Yes, it's okay to pick them up and hold them. Just be sure to return them to the beach after you feel the power of their energy. We must honor Gaia, the spirit of the living Earth. And an abalone is kind of like a big snail that lives inside a shell."

A loving sensation of warmth rushed through Virginia's body as she watched Olivia standing next to Zac with her long black hair, her strikingly high cheekbones, and her erect, almost royal posture. *I feel so happy when I'm with the two of them.* Virginia noticed how Zac gazed at both Olivia and her with wonder and amazement, presumably drinking in their knowledge and experience. She observed him as he discovered a clam shell, picked it up, held it between his two hands and whispered something to it, then returned it to the beach where he'd found it.

The intensity of her feelings for Zac still caught her off guard sometimes. She couldn't imagine loving him any more, yet each day her love deepened. She reached for his hand and tenderly held it in hers. "That's the power of science and spirituality, my son."

Virginia hoped their walks would inspire Zac to love nature as much as she did. She considered her own early interest in geology, wondering if it came from the hikes she'd taken with her father in the Adirondack Mountains when they'd tow the family sailboat up to the lakes in upstate New York. Always the outdoors type, she'd spend her days tramping around collecting samples of this or that for her and her father to examine together.

Now, she watched as Olivia walked hand in hand with Zac, marveling at their connection. *What would I do without her?* Olivia brought out another side of Virginia—the side that balanced her infatuation with science. Olivia gently reminded her to adjust and even herself out when she obsessed on all things scientific. She couldn't help herself—she loved all aspects of it, especially the esoteric thinking of people on the fringes of science. Virginia had discovered early in her life that original thinking is always out of the mainstream, and for that simple reason alone, she sought it out.

At that moment, a seagull flew overhead, breaking her out of her reverie. The comforting autumn sun warmed Virginia's shoulders and neck, and the scent of nearby chimney smoke and wet leaves filled the air. The seagull's screech brought her back to the present moment, where nature took over the healing of her spirit, soothing, energizing, and nurturing her soul.

While she wandered into the foaming waves along the shore, Zac and Olivia built a sandcastle. She plunged her feet into cool sand, feeling the grains escaping through her toes, and breathed in the salty aroma of the gentle breeze. As restored and renewed as she felt, she had to admit to herself that she was feeling a bit melancholy too—strolling on the beach always reminded her of the many times she'd walked arm in arm with her husband along a shoreline. As if on cue, she heard Zac's laugh carried by the wind.

If only Nikolai could hear that treasured sound, just once. I miss him so much. He should be here with us today.

❉   ❉   ❉

That evening back in their rental cottage, Virginia set a pile of tinder ablaze in the fireplace and headed to the kitchen to make chowder. While she was preparing the scallops and quahog, she heard the unmistakable sound of Zac crying. She dashed to the living room to see what was going on. Olivia was with him, soothing him after he'd tripped going up the wooden steps to the loft, skinning his knee.

After examining his wound, Olivia glanced up at Virginia. "I've got this. It's an opportunity to put my nursing skills to practice. I'm going to give him his bath early tonight and wash off his knee and all the sand from our day at the beach."

"Great. I'm making us chowder for dinner, and it'll be ready soon."

Upstairs, Olivia filled the tub with warm water and "magic bubbles" as Zac undressed. He stepped into the tub and sank down into the white foam, then he started his endless chatter and splashing the bathwater with his toy boat.

"You having fun?" Olivia asked. As she soaped up the washcloth to clean Zac's wound, she noticed that the skin had already completely healed and there was no longer any sign of an injury. She wasn't surprised.

"Yep."

She folded up the washcloth and placed it on the rim of the tub. "There. Your knee is all better and you don't have to cry anymore now."

"Why do I cry sometimes, Olivia?"

"Because it's your emotions that make you human, my Child of Light."

"Why do you call me your Child of Light? My name is Zac."

"Because that's what you are, and you'll understand someday when you recognize who you are deep within. Long ago, ancient civilizations told about a prophecy—that's something they believe is coming in the future—about some important changes that will happen to our planet Earth. Those changes are happening now. So you are here to help people. It's your purpose."

"Okay, Olivia." He shrugged his shoulders. "Why you are here?"

"I'm here to help you keep your light shining."

He looked down at his belly button and then his feet. "I don't see a light in me."

"I do. There is something called the Divine Source of Light. And I see it in you. It's perfect and it radiates and shines."

"Like the sun?"

"Yes. You'll understand this someday when you're ready. Right now, it's hard to appreciate, but when I say it to you, part of you will hear my message. When something is 'in the light,' there can be no fear, no darkness. We have the power to help heal the Earth to lessen the difficult changes it's going through. You're here to help guide people by shining your light. Your role is to help heal the planet and to awaken and motivate human beings who are living in the dark to keep them from self-destruction. You can help others to see their light."

He shook his head. "I don't know what that all means, but it sounds like a big job, Olivia."

"It is, my Child of Light." She toweled him off and dressed him in his pajamas.

By now, Virginia had been standing outside the door, listening to them interact for some minutes. Tears were in her eyes as she remembered one of Nikolai's favorite sayings: "Love is where the wise man builds his home." *I'm always home with these two.*

She wiped her cheeks, put on a smile, stepped into the bathroom, and clapped her hands. "So… who's hungry? Soup's on!"

CHAPTER TEN
VIRGINIA
1999

I T HAD TO be kept a secret. But how? What they knew, what they had knowledge of, could prove to be dangerous to all of them. Virginia wanted Olivia to understand her perspective—her thoughts about Zac and his birth.

Both she and Olivia knew that the government agents who used to meet with Nikolai at the ranch were still suspicious that she had more of her husband's important research papers. Every so often, but less frequently now, a ranch hand would report someone coming to the property feigning they were lost and asking directions, looking like the government agents from years before. They'd steer the conversation to Virginia or ask about interesting things that might be going on at the ranch. They always left empty-handed.

Determined to keep Zac's life and childhood as normal as possible, the two women found it difficult to prevent others from seeing his unusual talents. One thing they couldn't control was how Zac was as drawn to animals, both wild and domestic, as they were to him. Virginia observed how Zac and the animals seemed to connect on some otherworldly level.

First, there were the farm animals. Virginia would never forget the day when Zac wandered into an open cattle pen. The men were in the process of moving a couple of hundred head of cattle out of one pasture and into another, temporarily placing them in a holding pen near the main barn. The cattle bellowed out honking noises, rising in choirs of discontent as they were forced into a confined space.

One moment Zac was at her side, and then—after the slightest distraction that drew her sight elsewhere—he was darting under the lower rung of the wooden fence. Suddenly, he was inside the pen with dozens of cattle wandering in a disorganized manner, all looking for a way out.

The usual commotion of frightened animals in a herd halted momentarily. In the midst of the herd, with the animals all facing him in what seemed like a silent tribute, stood Zac, his cherubic smile not the least bit faded from his face. The ranch hands all looked around at one another, stunned, as the cattle arranged themselves in a circle with their heads all facing Zac. And then... there was silence.

Zac positioned himself next to a calf, looked directly at Virginia, and pointed. "He's hurt. Help him." That's all he said.

In the eerie silence, Virginia didn't hesitate. Quickly and cautiously, she grabbed Zac by the arm, pulled him to safety, and rushed him back to the house. He gazed at her with woeful eyes. "But, Mommy, the baby calf is hurt."

Later, Gus, the ranch foreman, told Virginia that he was amazed at what he'd witnessed. After moving the larger cows out of the pen, he'd examined the calf Zac had identified and found that it did indeed have a broken leg.

These are the incidents I worry about, Virginia thought. She'd always been fond of Gus and trusted him, but not enough to tell him Zac's secrets. She knew he was one of the "good guys," but she wasn't ready to share what she knew of Zac's abilities with anyone.

One morning, not long after the incident at the corral, Virginia invited Gus up to the house to sample her freshly baked coffee cake. As they broke bread together, the quiet and reserved man opened up and told her a bit about his life story. Gus was Comanche and proud of it. He'd grown up on a reservation and decided early to honor the Comanche traditions, yet he was aware that the best job opportunities were on the big ranches of the white man. In Nikolai and Virginia, he'd found compassionate bosses who treated him and the other ranch hands with respect. They even participated in a profit-sharing plan—unheard of on the other ranches. As a foreman, Gus did well enough that he was saving his money for a ranch of his own, and it was now a viable dream.

Virginia was especially fond of Gus for his special affection for her son—she could see they were the best of buddies. All of the ranch hands looked out for Zac and enjoyed his company, but Virginia could tell he liked Gus the best. Like Olivia, he knew the old ways, and he was passing on to Zac the same family stories that had been passed down to him. He often spoke to Olivia about Zac, probing a bit here and there, and Olivia would share those conversations with Virginia. Apparently, Gus couldn't quite put his finger on it, but he was clear that Zac had a gift, and to Gus, gifts were from the Great Spirit. The episode in the cattle pen had sealed his belief—he agreed with Olivia: Zac was a spirit on Earth.

Although Gus wasn't directly connected to his former tribe any longer, his wife was active in their community, and she told him of the gossip on the reservation. An old woman, the last descendent of the tribe's shamans, told of a coming child who would have the spirit of the land within him, and the animals would know him before any humans did. Gus had initially dismissed her story as an old woman's rants meant to keep the old beliefs alive, but after he saw the cattle in the pen with Zac, he accepted her words as prophecy.

Participating in the ranch activities was something Zac loved to do, so Virginia often took him to hang out with Gus. With Zac, Gus was patient and loving, and he never talked down to him. Despite his young age, Zac would ask probing questions that required intelligent answers: "Why do we plant this way?" "What is that for?" "How does it work?" The questions never stopped, and Gus fielded them all with the seriousness with which they were posed.

Of all the things Zac and Gus did together, Zac talked to Virginia the most about how much fun it was riding in the big, air-conditioned, bright green John Deere tractor. He enjoyed sitting up high where he could see everything around him. Everywhere Zac rode on the tractor with Gus, field after field they traversed would turn up green the next day. This was the type of thing Virginia had no way to hide or conceal.

How can I keep that a secret? she thought. *How can I ever explain something I can't explain to myself?*

The more of his special talents Zac exhibited, the more protective the women in his life became.

*   *   *

It was an autumn day, and the pumpkins and squash were ready to be harvested. Needing a rest from their gardening, Virginia and Olivia leaned against the wooden fence rail watching Zac ride the John Deere with Gus while Delta barked and chased rabbits.

Virginia noticed the familiar scowl on Olivia's face. "What's wrong?" she asked.

Olivia shook her head. "Nothing's wrong, but I just don't know how we can protect him."

Virginia nodded in agreement. "I'm also getting more concerned about how many people are witnessing Zac's unusual talents. I worry for him. I worry someone will take him. Steal him from us. Perform experiments on him. I don't know a good cover story for this."

"I'm aware of that too. It's hard for me to trust anyone."

"Well, at least I trust everyone on this ranch. They all love and adore him. But I worry that the stories will get to outsiders."

"It's our job to protect him. We need to think of something."

"Protecting Zac consumes my thoughts, and there's something more that makes me smile yet at the same time makes me afraid… I wonder if Zac might be more than just a combination of Nikolai's and my genetics."

"What do you mean?"

"I got this odd feeling one night when I remembered how I'd passed out in Nikolai's lab the day he died. Something happened. Something extraordinary. He had a timer set for an experiment. He'd told me that. I think I triggered the experiment or was a part of it in some way. I don't know what to do. How can we guide a child living in uncharted territory? I mean, what's the extent of his powers?"

Olivia folded her arms across her chest and deepened her scowl. "No. He's not the result of a science experiment, Virginia. I refuse to believe that. Spirits like Zac are written about in our ancient text. They walked the world in times gone by. They were the children of the light and connected to Mother Earth. That is who Zac is."

Virginia shrugged her shoulders. "Maybe. I don't suppose we'll ever know for sure."

"I already know for sure," Olivia firmly stated.

They made a plan, and both she and Olivia met with the key ranch hands and pleaded their case and convinced them that Zac had to be protected and the stories were not to leave the ranch. They all agreed, but Virginia was clear that Olivia still didn't find peace in that solution.

✳   ✳   ✳

Buz Stephenson owned the ranch right next to the Sparkman ranch. He hardly looked the part of a ranch owner—short and stocky, he lacked the swagger, replacing it instead with a modified waddle. But he was tough, and had been a bit of a showboat during the prime of his life. Buz ran his ranch efficiently with little of the respect Virginia and Nikolai showed their ranch hands, but the men needed the work and tolerated his abrasive style. There was no love lost between Buz and his ranch hands, and he easily mistook their fear of his anger for loyalty. When he needed to, Buz could also turn on the charm, but Olivia often told Virginia he was a fake, someone trying too hard to impress.

He'd lost his own wife many years earlier, and Virginia was aware of his flirtatious behavior with her after Nikolai's death. He'd often seek out reasons to visit her ranch. He was always on his best behavior, and she believed Olivia was pleased that she tolerated his neighborly attention but with little personal interest. She knew Olivia watched and observed him with disdain; she was as protective of Virginia as she was of Zac. But Virginia trusted that Zac's gut instincts would let him know if Buz was a problem, and she didn't see signs of that. He enjoyed his time with Uncle Buz.

Gus shared Olivia's dislike for the man. Stories about Buz circulated among the ranch hands, and Gus had heard them all. He tried to explain and justify the changes he'd seen in the man over the years to Virginia. As Gus saw it, hard living had taken its toll on Buz. He'd had a lot of losses in his life and a residual overall sense of failure. He was different than the "old" Buz they used to know—the guy who'd been fast with a joke and a smile.

But now, Gus was no longer a fan. He relayed stories to Virginia and Olivia about the lack of compassion Buz showed his ranch hands and his tendency to make a fast buck at the expense of others. He told them how Buz often obsessed about the mustang, White Cloud, and his desire to capture the magnificent creature. That only furthered Olivia's distrust of him, but Virginia felt more sympathetic toward him.

Over time, Virginia noticed that Olivia relented a bit in her disapproval because she, too, noticed that Zac seemed to enjoy his time with Uncle Buz. Buz liked to teach him things, like tying knots and rope throwing, and Buz did show a sensitivity to staying clear of topics that could potentially upset the little boy, like branding or hunting.

And Buz was a great storyteller. He regaled Zac with tales of the places he'd visited in the merchant marines as a young man, with stories of far-off lands and people. Faraway places called to Zac, and he dreamed of the adventures he'd have when he was older.

Although Olivia never wanted Zac to be out of her sight unless Virginia was with him, she did her best to convince Olivia to loosen up the reins a bit to give Zac more of a sense of freedom, and she even agreed to allow Buz to take Zac fishing. The worries were always centered on the unusual things others might observe; Olivia argued that she didn't want Buz to see how the fish seemed to be drawn to Zac and swarm toward him, but Virginia appreciated how Buz explained to Zac that the fish they caught were for food, not a trophy. Before Zac's first visit to Buz's ranch, the staff was ordered to carefully remove all of the wall-mounted trophies. *That's a good sign,* Virginia thought. *He's being sensitive to Zac.*

✳   ✳   ✳

After dinner one evening, Virginia snuggled next to Zac on the oversized chair in the living room while he was deeply engrossed in a book. Not wanting to disturb their bonding time, she avoided answering the phone when it rang. But when it sounded for the third time, she decided to answer. A few minutes later, she called out to Olivia to join them. Olivia sat on the couch waiting for Virginia to deliver her message.

"Well, you two, this is interesting." Virginia slid back into her spot on the chair with Zac. "I just got a job offer, and I think I'm going to take it if you can take care of Zac while I'm gone, Olivia."

"I'll make it work. What is it?"

"As you know, I've followed the 1994 Northridge earthquake and its aftermath with great interest and have done some writing about it. I was just asked if I'd examine and report on some unusual seismic activity in the Mojave Desert. Sounds intriguing to me."

"So, would you go there?"

"Yes, my former editor asked if I could make a quick trip. Fly to Barstow and take the train south to the region."

"I'll be here. Don't worry."

"It'll only be a couple of days. I'll be working again with the U.S. Geological Survey guys I knew as a grad student."

Zac sat in the chair listening to the conversation.

"Zac, I'm going to go on a business trip for a few days."

"Can I go too?" he pleaded.

"Not this time. I have to work, and you'll stay with Olivia."

"No. Then you can't go." He crossed his hands over his chest and pouted, and then, out of character, he began to cry."

Virginia leaned over and gave him a hug and ran her hand through his hair. "Honey, it's only for a couple of days, and I promise I'll bring you back something interesting from the desert. It'll be a surprise. You'll have fun with Olivia. You always do."

"I want an adventure too." He stuck out his lower lip.

"We'll find something else for you to do. This trip wouldn't be fun for you because I have to work."

✳   ✳   ✳

The next day, Buz dropped by the ranch. Olivia and Virginia were outside having coffee, keeping Zac company as he studied.

Buz moseyed up to them, looking proud of himself. "Mornin', ladies. Hi there, Zac," he said, reaching down to pat his head.

They all nodded and greeted him.

"Mind if I join you for a minute?" He removed his hat and set it on the porch railing.

Virginia pointed to a vacant chair. "Have a seat, Buz, and I'll pour you a cup of coffee. What brings you here today?" She noticed the scowl Olivia got on her face whenever Buz was around and gave her leg a nudge.

"I was just returning some stuff I borrowed from Gus and thought I'd swing by the house to—"

Just then, a mountain bluebird perched on the porch rail behind Zac, circled over his head three times, and flew off.

Virginia saw Olivia close her eyes, probably hoping Buz didn't see what just happened. But he did.

Virginia didn't miss the look on Buz's face either. He stared at Zac, then looked up in search of the bird. "Well, if that don't take the rag off the bush. What the…"

As he turned his head back to face the ladies, he noticed the advanced mathematical equations that Zac was working on in his notebook. His eyes widened, his eyebrows lifted, and he formed a close-lipped smile.

"I came to extend an invite to this one here," he said, pointing to Zac. "Me and a couple of the guys are gonna fix up the old wooden bridge at the far end of my property. Thought Zac might find it fun to go on an overnight camping trip with me and several of the crew. There'll be plenty of ranch hands, male and female, to watch over Zac, so no worries."

Zac immediately jumped up. "Can I, Mom? You said I could have my own adventure. This is it!

Virginia saw Olivia trying to communicate with her eyes, telling Virginia to say no, but Virginia thought Buz was harmless, and when she saw the joy in her son's eyes, it relieved a bit of the guilt she felt for leaving him behind. *He deserves this.*

"I think that sounds like a fine idea. It'll be his first overnight camp-out."

Zac jumped up and down. "Thanks, Mommy." He threw his arms around her neck.

Buz gave Olivia a side-glance, slightly curling the right side of his lip, then patted Zac on the back. "Pack your plunder, Zac, we're headin' for an adventure."

No sooner had Virginia made her decision than she regretted it. When she saw how visibly distraught Olivia was over her decision, she thought about backpedaling. *Maybe I should just take him with me. He can see what I do for a living, and he'll still get his adventure.* But then she thought, *No, he has his homeschooling, and I'll get more done without having to monitor him the whole time.* She went back and forth in her mind while she went to her room to start her own packing. By the time she came back out, Zac had his gear already packed and was sitting by the front door, clearly excited.

At the sound of Buz's horn, he gave his mom a hug and kiss goodbye, then looked deeply into Olivia's eyes. "Don't worry Olivia. I'm a big kid now. I'm going to be okay." Olivia forced her lips into a fake smile and waved as Zac ran out to Buz's truck.

As they were driving off, the car arrived to take Virginia to the airport. She hugged Olivia tightly. "I'm sorry. It all happened so fast, and I felt so torn. He wanted to go so badly. And it's only for one night."

"I know. I'm just a bit overprotective, and I was looking forward to some time alone with him. But like you said, it's only for an overnight. Don't you worry—I'll take great care of him while you're wearing your geologist hat."

"Of course you will. I wouldn't be able to go anywhere if it weren't for you. I'll always be eternally in your debt. I love and adore you, Miss Olivia Medicine Crow. You're like a daughter to me."

"And you're the mom I've always wanted. I love you too. Safe travels."

Olivia waved and stared off down the dirt road long after the car was out of sight and then returned to the empty house.

CHAPTER ELEVEN
OLIVIA
1999

OLIVIA HAD A terrible, restless night, and she couldn't wait for Zac to return later that day. *I don't know why I have these feelings about Buz. Virginia likes him. Zac likes him. But I don't.* Olivia checked her watch. Again. They were late, so she ventured outside and glanced down the road. Chugging up the hill in the distance, she saw Buz's old truck and released the breath she'd been holding. He stopped in front of the main house, and Buz hopped out of the driver's side, making a loud thump as his feet hit the dirt ground. He waddled over to open the door on Zac's side, helped him down, and grabbed Zac's overnight bag from the back and handed it to Olivia.

"Mornin', Olivia. Sorry we're late. Got a late start on breakfast." He glanced over at Zac as he walked toward the house. "Bye, Zac. I hope you enjoyed your adventure."

Olivia immediately cringed. *What's wrong with Zac?* He didn't respond to Buz, showed no excitement, and didn't speak a word. His shoulders were slumped, he held his head down, and if she didn't know better, it seemed as though a part of his light had gone out. No greeting for her. No hug. No kiss. He just grabbed his bag from her hand and dragged it up the porch steps without looking back.

Oh my God, what happened?

As Buz climbed up into the driver's seat in his truck, Olivia tore over to him and grabbed him by the back of his shirt, yanking him down.

"What the hell happened?" She drew her lips back as though she were a snarling dog. "Why's he like this? Answer me!"

Buz backed away from her, holding his hands out in front of his face. "Hey, little lady. Calm yourself down. Everything's fine. One of the ranch hands shot his pistol at a rabbit, killing it, and Zac got all balled up. He'll get over it. It's part of life. He's fine."

Her fury turned into a full-force hurricane. "Clearly, he's not fine! I swear to God, if you've done anything to hurt that kid in any way, you'll have me to contend with! Do you hear me?"

"Don't even try bulldozing me, Olivia. I said he's fine. He'll get over the damn rabbit!" He stormed off, got back in his truck, and sped down the road.

After racing back inside the house, Olivia found Zac lying facedown on his bed.

She sat on the side of the bed, stroking his back. "What's wrong? Talk to me. What happened?"

"I don't want to talk, Olivia."

"You need to talk to me. It's important. What happened?"

"Nothing."

"Yes, something did. Are you upset about the rabbit?"

He turned his face to the side and glanced up at her. "What rabbit?"

"The rabbit that was shot. Who shot it?"

He closed his eyes and blew air through his quivering lips. "I don't know about any rabbit."

"No one shot a rabbit?"

"No. I don't want to talk, Olivia."

"I know you don't, but I'm not going to let you lie here on this bed hurting because something is wrong. I'm here for you. I'm always here for you."

Delta hopped up on the bed next to him and licked his ear, then lay on the bed, whimpering.

Zac refused to engage any further, and Olivia sat on the bed next to him, stroking his back until he fell asleep. Olivia crept away to call Virginia. *She needs to know about this.* She couldn't reach her, so she called Gus and briefly spoke to him. About thirty minutes later, he arrived at the house. Olivia put a pot of coffee on, and they sat at the kitchen table.

Olivia's hands were shaking as she held her cup. "I'm in a bad way here, Gus. Did you get any information from Buz's ranch hands?"

He slowly wagged his head. "One of the guys who went on this so-called camping trip told me what happened."

Oh no, whatever happened, it's all my fault. "So tell me." Olivia tried to remain calm.

"It's bad."

Gus relayed the story he'd pried out of Cameron Birch, one of Buz's ranch hands, after he cornered him in the cattle pen on his way to the Sparkman ranch. While Cameron chewed on his dirty cuticles, he spilled what he knew: "So Buz told us his whole plan. I'm not sure how he could think the story would never come out, but it seems Buz had been working on this crazy plan for quite a while. He'd figured out the kid could communicate with animals, see. I've never seen it myself, but I've heard some stories."

"Go on," Gus prodded him.

"He was determined to get the kid—"

Gus interrupted at that point. "His name is Zac. Call him Zac."

"Yeah, right. Zac. Okay, so he was determined to get Zac to help him get his big prize. The one he's chased for years—that wild mustang everyone calls White Cloud.

"So, every few years, the Bureau of Land Management allows a few of the animals to be captured to keep the herd level below one fifty—"

"Come on, Cam. I know that. Get to what I don't know."

"Well, obviously, Buz was never able to catch him. The horse almost seemed to taunt him, and it's always ticked him off. He became obsessed. The horse would prance around the perimeter of his land but was always smart enough to avoid his traps. No truck, no rented helicopter, nothing could track him down. He seemed to just disappear."

"So, he used Zac…"

"At first he thought the kid, I mean Zac, would help him. Then he realized he'd never voluntarily do it."

"He needed a ruse and the right opportunity."

"Yep. The question was how to get Zac to attract the horse without causing him to be suspicious. And Gus couldn't say the horse was hurt, because Zac would know it was a lie." Cam took a breath here, then continued. "So he told Zac he wanted photos of the horse, and Zac just needed to get him to the right spot. Of course, Buz had his trap all set up beforehand."

Gus closed his eyes and shook his head.

"Buz only needed to mention the horse and the photos, and Zac took the bait and offered to help," Cam said.

"Sure, he wanted to please his Uncle Buz." Gus pounded his fist into his open hand.

"Yep. So Zac said, 'He's my friend, Uncle Buz. Do you want to meet him?' The kid was actually joyful! And then Buz says, 'I do, li'l man, I sure would.' "

"So how'd he do it?"

"I could see Zac from my vantage point, but he couldn't see us. It's kind of hard to describe. Buz had us all ready with the trap. Then Zac stood really tall, and he kind of scrunched up his nose and turned toward the forest. Then he raised his hands to the sky. He stood really still for what seemed like an eternity while Buz tried to hide himself so the horse didn't see him. Then all of a sudden, the horse appeared, and he came right up to Zac from out of nowhere. Right into the canyon. He actually nuzzled Zac's neck. This wild horse actually nuzzled him! But then the horse must have spotted Buz."

"What did he do?"

"The horse spooked. He curled his upper lip, then reared up on his hind legs with his forelegs off the ground. He let out something that sounded like a high-pitched, ear-piercing scream."

"How did Zac react?"

"God. Man. He freaked out. Seemed totally scared and confused. The horse spun around, still on its hind legs, and then he tried to bolt. But Buz sent the signal, and one of the ranch hands fired the tranquilizer dart at the same time two of the guys threw lassos around the stallion's neck. The sedation subdued him so they could transport him back to Buz's ranch."

"Oh, Zac... oh, Zac... ," Gus muttered.

"The kid froze. Mute. Then he let out the most bloodcurdling wail

I've ever heard in my life. I keep hearing it in my head. Buz totally betrayed Zac, and he'd set all of us up too—we had no idea he was using him. We wouldn't have done it if we'd known."

After Gus finished relaying the story, Olivia jumped from her chair and started for the door.

"Where are you going?" Gus asked.

"Where do you think?" At that moment, it seemed as though Olivia broke. Her whole body began to shake, starting at her feet, working up to her head, and the veins on her forehead threatened to explode. Her face contorted, and her nostrils flared while her hands closed into fists.

"You're forgetting something very important. Zac. You have to be here for him now. He needs you. Go to him. I'll take care of Buz. I have my ways. Let that anger go now and do what you're meant to do."

Gus's words acted like a valve on a tire, unscrewed to release the air. Olivia allowed herself to deflate. He was right. Anger would resolve nothing. She had a young boy she loved with all of her heart to attend to. Her shoulders relaxed, her face softened. "I've got this, Gus. Thanks." She turned on her heel to check on Zac.

While he slept, Olivia tried to call Virginia again but still was unable to reach her. From the itinerary Virginia had left on the hall table, Olivia knew she'd be out in the field right now, about to go live on TV. She woke Zac up and asked him to join her to watch his mom giving her report. He wandered into the living room in a trance-like state. Olivia sat on the overstuffed easy chair with the remote and tuned into the right channel.

"Come sit here next to me, Zac." She patted the spot next to her on the chair. "Mom's going to be on TV soon. It's almost two forty-five. Let's watch, then we'll call her later."

When Virginia's image appeared on the television a few minutes later, Zac perked up. There she was, microphone in hand.

"... Dr. Virginia Sutter-Sparkman, speaking live from the Hector Mine near the Mojave Desert. We've been experiencing a sequence of twelve foreshocks of up to magnitude—"

Zac's eyes widened and his eyebrows lifted. "Olivia, what's wrong with the TV? Why's Mom shaking?"

Olivia stood up, also thinking something was wrong with the

television, but then she heard the rumbling, saw the shaking, and watched as Virginia suddenly disappeared from view.

"It appears we have lost our connection with Dr. Sutter-Sparkman," the announcer said. "Now back to our studio."

Olivia clicked off the television set, then didn't move a muscle.

※　　　※　　　※

The Hector Mine earthquake was a magnitude of 7.1, rupturing in both directions from the epicenter. Olivia received the dreaded call early that evening. The TV crew that accompanied Virginia had warned her about standing too close to the edge of the cliff where she wanted to film, but strong-willed Virginia was back in the geological limelight and she wanted dramatic footage. After Olivia hung up, she leaned against the wall to brace herself. She could hardly see, she could barely breathe. Even in her shocked state, she was focused on only one thought: *Oh my God. Now they're both gone. How is my Child of Light going to withstand this pain? What can I do to help him with an unfathomable loss like this?*

The fault rupture lasted roughly ten seconds, but that brief moment in time was about to change the lives of Olivia and Zac forever.

※　　　※　　　※

As Olivia and Zac staggered through the days and nights that followed, they shifted from a state of numbness to one of pure agony. Olivia faced the fact that this was her time to be there for Zac; this was her purpose. She just never knew she'd be responsible for keeping Zac's light burning as she delved into a world of darkness of her own. She wanted to reside there, in the numbness, in the void, forever. It was too much loss: her own mother, Nikolai, and then the woman she loved so dearly, Virginia. And now she was responsible for this innocent little boy. Brian, Virginia's brother, was on his way back from a sailing trip on the other side of the world. As Zac's legal guardian, he'd arrive for Zac soon.

Olivia spent her days trying to get through to Zac, helping him cope. With the same energy he'd used to light the world around him, he reached deep inside and extinguished it. No more hurt. His light went out. Dealing with loss is a part of the human experience, and this was something Olivia clearly understood. The wound had to be dealt with. She knew what she had to do.

✳   ✳   ✳

Symbolically, the light was dimming outside as well, as the shorter days of November heralded the dark winter days ahead. Olivia needed to help Zac find his way again while they still had this time alone together.

She built a crackling blaze in the fireplace and sat cross-legged on the floor with a big burlap bag beside her. She called out to Zac. "Come here, my Child of Light. I have something for you."

He obediently plunked down on the floor next to her. "Olivia, I don't think I'm a Child of Light anymore."

She rested her hand on his knee. "Oh, but you are and you always will be. Okay, so this is what happened to your light. Imagine this for a minute. When you're outside and look up into the sky, sometimes the sun is blocked by endless gray clouds. But they eventually move, and the sun shines again. That's what has happened to you. The clouds of sadness have blocked your light temporarily, and they'll float away, and you'll brightly shine again."

"I don't know, Olivia."

Olivia pulled him close to her. "Zac, this is hard for you to understand because you think everyone is like you. But they're not. You have a very special gift that I've never seen before."

"What is it?"

"You know how all the animals come to you, and it's like they want to be friends with you? Do you know how the dry, brown earth becomes green when you're around, and plants that are dying bloom again when you are near? Do you know how when you rub my temples, you make my headache go away? Or how when Delta was limping, you healed her paw by touching it with the light from your hands? That's a very special gift you have that other people don't. In your life, you'll have to learn how to use that light to help others. It's a very good thing, and you'll learn how to use it wisely as well as when not to share it with certain people. This will come to you. Trust me."

Zac didn't respond verbally. He leaned into her and rested his head on her arm.

After a moment of shared silence, Olivia sat up straight, clapped her hands, grabbed the bag, and placed it in her lap. "So, I brought us each something."

Zac sat up too. "Can I see?"

"Of course. But first, in the shamanic way, we know that things leave us when they no longer serve us. As we allow ourselves to feel sad and grieve, our eyes open to the wisdom. If we do not heal the grief, just like the clouds, it can block our light. My father has gifted us with a very sacred tool—healing drums. Drumming is very powerful, and it awakens the memories of the soul. As we beat the drum, it'll calm us and put us into a trance. Through that, you will find your way and find peace. You must take care with your drum because it's a special gift."

Zac's eyes were wide. "Can I see it?"

Olivia withdrew a fourteen-inch drum from the bag and held it in her hand. "We use these for healing. This is yours. It's the horse drum. See, it's a wooden hoop with stretched rawhide and lacing." She turned it over. "The back is laced to form the symbol of a medicine wheel with the four cardinal directions, and that's where you hold it in your hand. My father smudged them while they were drying with sacred herbs like sage and sweetgrass."

She placed the drum in his hands. "My dad made it for you, and he left the face of the drum blank, so you can paint whatever you want on it. Yours is darker in color and lower in tone than mine, and yours is made of red cedar."

He examined the drum as though in awe. "This is for me?"

"Yes, it's a very special gift for you."

She withdrew a second drum from the bag. "This is mine. Mine is a red stag deer drum. See, it's lighter in color and has a different tone.

"As we beat our drums, we'll connect with the heartbeat of the drum. It will connect you to your own heartbeat and the heartbeat of Mother Earth."

She handed him his drumbeater. "This is what you use to beat the drum. It has a pouched-shaped head on a stick that my dad decorated with feathers."

At that moment, a splinter of Zac's inner light broke through the darkness he'd been residing in: he smiled.

Olivia turned on some haunting flute music, and they sat on the floor in front of the light of the crackling fire, drumming to the music as they connected to their heartbeats and the wisdom of their souls. Their beats began to sync together, and they drifted off on an inner voyage, losing track of time.

✳   ✳   ✳

After they'd gone to bed for the night, Olivia fell into a deep sleep. She woke in the early-morning hours to a familiar sound. As she padded out to the living room in her bare feet, there sat Zac, with Delta at his side. He was clutching his gift, eyes closed, steadily beating the drum in time to the soft flute music wafting through the air—hoping to once again find his light.

PART THREE
1999–2000

*You cannot teach a man anything, you can
only help him find it within himself.*
—Galileo Galilei

CHAPTER TWELVE
BRIAN
1999

B RIAN, VIRGINIA'S YOUNGER brother and only living rela-
tive, stood in the living room of the Sparkman home, somewhat
helplessly, in front of a silently grieving six-year-old child and a
young Native American woman who seemed equally in pain. He didn't
really know what to say. He'd met Zac only once before when he'd
attended his second birthday party but hadn't previously met Olivia.
On top of this unusual situation, he was also in mourning, in shock,
about his sister's sudden, tragic death. When Zac was born, he'd agreed
to become his legal guardian should circumstances demand it, but he'd
never once even imagined that this role would come to pass—that he'd
actually be the one to raise him. Brian Sutter had just inherited a family.

First things first. He had to concentrate on taking care of the legal
issues involving the ranch; his grieving would have to wait. Like his
older sister, Brian had a brilliant mind and had received his doctorate
in physics and math by the age of twenty-four. Early in his life, he was
nicknamed "Brian the Brain." He had formidable credentials, but after
being pushed too hard academically, he'd burned out early and dropped
out of his applied physics program. By age twenty-six, all he wanted was
a quiet life with the freedom to develop his ideas in private, avoiding
politics and unwanted public attention. He was, in many ways, similar to
the brother-in-law he'd barely known.

Brian had found a simpler life teaching mathematics at a small college in Bennington, Vermont. He was perfectly satisfied with his peaceful
existence as a single man who was a bit of a loner, so adding a boy he

hardly knew, a young adult woman, and a dog to the mix was quite the change in lifestyle. But he was trying his best to view this as a new adventure, as a gift bestowed upon him by the loss of his sister.

Brian, Zac, and Olivia formed a most unusual model of a family. At Olivia's urging, Brian consulted with the tribal leaders. It was decided that the Sparkman ranch would be held in trust for Zac. The tribe agreed to manage the ranch and cattle for a percentage of the profits, and Brian would invest the rest of the income for both Zac's future and maintenance of the property.

Brian lived frugally, but over the years he'd invested wisely. When his parents died in a car accident, they'd bequeathed a substantial estate to Brian and Virginia. At that time, Brian, the mathematical whiz, had become the family investor, a role he continued even after Virginia married. Neither Nikolai nor Virginia had ever shown any talent in investing. Brian had immersed himself in understanding the stock market. Be it luck or skill, he was successful—he had almost an uncanny, intuitive sense. He didn't really know what convinced him to invest in a tiny online bookstore called Amazon back in 1997. Upon Virginia's death, she'd left her money to Zac and Olivia, naming Brian as the executor of her estate.

After the legal issues were settled, Brian called his first family meeting around the fireplace in the living room. He was nervous about how Zac would respond to what he was going to say, and he subconsciously dragged his thumb and forefinger up and down the scraggly beard on his strong jawline, then used his index finger to push his round, wire-rimmed glasses from the tip of his nose to the bridge. He just stood there for a minute with his lithe and trim runner's body, with his sister's coloring, his now salt-and-pepper hair, and his cognac-colored eyes with circles under them, indicating a man who stayed up late solving complex equations.

He rubbed his hands together and cleared his throat, a small smile on his face revealing the lines there that were etched with a gentle kindness. "I'm not sure where to begin. We've all been through a lot. I know you're still in shock and, of course, I am too. But the reality is, my work is back in Vermont and I need to return. I already had someone covering for me while I was on my sailing trip, and then the university was very understanding about the bereavement leave I've taken here. But I'll lose my job if I take any more time off. I'm really sorry to make another big change in your life, Zac, but you're going to have to come live with me. Trust me, you'll love it in Vermont. I promise you. I'll take great care of you and love you like you're my own son. Heck, I already do!"

Zac jumped up and yelled, "No!" He threw himself on Olivia. "No… no… no! I'm not going to leave Olivia!"

Olivia peeled him off of her, coaxing him to sit on her lap. She looked directly into his eyes. "Do you for one second think I would leave you? Oh no, not me. Brian asked me to come too. I'm coming with you, of course. In fact, I've been filling out paperwork to apply for my Vermont nursing license. No more worrying about that."

He looked up into her eyes, finding the comfort he'd always found there. "But what about Delta?"

Brian grinned. "We're driving across country and bringing back all your prized possessions. Delta too. Road trip!"

Zac's shoulders relaxed. "Well, okay, as long as we all go. Bad things happen at this house. Bad things."

He lifted his head from Olivia's chest. "What about Gus? What about your dad?"

"They're going to be fine. Gus is staying on here as foreman, with help from the tribe—including my dad. It's all going to be fine, sweetheart."

❄   ❄   ❄

It wasn't until close to the end of November when they had all the loose ends sufficiently tied up and could begin the long cross-country trip. Brian figured it would take about five or six days with Olivia sharing the driving. In spite of the extended hours in the car, the trip was fun-filled with games, riddles, jokes, and stories to pass the time. Brian lit up with joy seeing how much Zac loved the adventure. As their journey drew to a close and they merged onto VT-9E, they experienced an unusual drop in temperature down to a chilly twenty-four degrees. Zac pressed his nose to the cold car window, apparently mesmerized by the sudden onslaught of white falling from the sky.

Brian talked to Zac in his rearview mirror as he drove. "Like the snow, big guy? We'll be doing lots of sledding and tobogganing this winter."

"I loved sledding on the ranch. Can Delta go with us too?"

"Wouldn't go without her!"

❉   ❉   ❉

The casualness of Brian's mannerisms and style of dress was reflected in his rambling colonial-style house—like him, it was a bit disheveled and in need of some fresh paint. As they pulled into the driveway of the canary yellow house with blue shutters, which sat on an acre of wooded land, Zac's eyes widened. Small in comparison to the ranch, the cozy house was nonetheless nestled among tall oaks that seemed to sing as the breeze blew through them.

Zac bolted from the car and broke into a run to the porch, laughing and giggling as Brian unlocked the front door.

"You and Delta go take a look around," he said, "and then you and Olivia can pick whichever bedroom you each want, except for the one that's obviously mine." Zac tore through the house with Delta barking behind him.

The main floor had a spacious living room with a wood-burning fireplace, a formal dining room with built-in cabinets, and a cheery, bright kitchen with a breakfast nook. Brian's study was covered with papers and books on the floor, the desk, and the shelves, but Zac didn't notice any of it as he headed upstairs, focused more on which bedroom would be his. There were other perks besides the three bedrooms on the second floor: a finished basement with a carpeted rec room, a fruit cellar, a darkroom, and a woodworking shop. In the back of the house, there was an inviting covered porch, a stone patio, and mature landscaping with a forest of oak trees. As a bonus, there was a tree house for Zac.

Brian could tell Zac felt right at home as he ran from room to room upstairs trying to figure out which one to claim. Brian breathed a sigh of relief, as Zac seemed to be adjusting much better than he'd anticipated.

On the west side of the house, Zac stood in the doorway of one of the bedrooms. "Uncle Brian, can I have this one?"

Brian turned to Olivia and raised his eyebrows. She nodded yes.

"Sure, and we can decorate it any way you want."

"In my room on the ranch, I had glow stars on the ceiling. Could we paint the universe on the walls, with planets and solar systems and stuff like that?"

"Anything you want. Olivia and I'll help you."

Zac ran outside to bring his things into the house. He pulled Delta's dog bed from the rear of the car and placed it next to the twin bed that was now his. Methodically, he unpacked his suitcases and cardboard boxes, setting his prized possessions on the empty bookshelves. He carefully stacked his favorite books and puzzles on the bottom shelf. On the middle shelf, he placed his stuffed animals—his golden retriever and white horse—along with his sacred drum and beater. On the top shelf, the most important one, he placed a framed photo of his mom and dad, a picture of his mom and him as a baby, a photo of Olivia and her dad, and one of Gus and White Cloud.

This is good, Brian thought. *He's already making this home.*

Brian didn't mind that Olivia immediately set about making the somewhat disorganized house an organized home. Only his study remained off-limits due to what Brian referred to as his "mess." It didn't bother Olivia; she was used to seeing books and papers lying around Nikolai and Virginia's library at the ranch.

❆   ❆   ❆

Things were going better than Brian had expected; however, he did feel concerned about getting Zac the proper schooling he'd need. Having been homeschooled up until now and having arrived several months after the school year had begun, Olivia and Brian wondered about Zac's ability to adjust to so many changes at once. As a teacher, Brian knew Zac would have to be tested and worried that his homeschooling would leave him ill prepared on many levels. He and Olivia could not teach him at home as Virginia had, and although Olivia was aware that Virginia had begun Zac's comprehensive curriculum at a very young age, she wasn't sure how much he actually knew or how far along he was. For days, prior to his first school interview, Brian drew Zac out and then began his own assessment. Aware that his entire life had been spent solely around adults, he feared Zac might not have the social skills of a normal first grader.

By his own students, Brian was well respected but also known to be a bit eccentric and whimsical. For entertainment purposes, he'd sometimes put on disguises or perform comedy routines during some of his lectures. He believed students learned best through humor, and he enjoyed a classroom filled with enthusiasm and laughter. When the spotlight was on him, the normally reserved scientist let loose with the zany side of his personality. In a spontaneous moment one afternoon, he decided to reenact one of the skits he'd used with his students for Zac.

He greased his hair, parted it down the middle, and glued a black mustache onto his upper lip. He dressed meticulously in a cutaway coat along with white gloves and a derby hat. Tiptoeing down the stairs, he peeked around the corner to see what Zac was doing. Zac was sitting at the dining room table putting together an intricate jigsaw puzzle when he looked up to see his uncle pacing back and forth in front of him with his hands clasped behind his back, stepping with a light bounce. Brian stopped, stood before Zac, and spoke using a different voice:

"I was born around midnight, somewhere between July ninth and tenth in 1856 during a violent lightning storm. Midway through my birth, the midwife wrung her hands and announced that the lightning was a bad sign. 'This child will be a child of darkness,' she said, to which my mother replied, 'No, he will be a child of light.' "

With that, Zac's eyes rounded in wonder and he laughed. "That's what Olivia calls me!"

Brian waggled his finger in Zac's face. "If you want to find the secrets of the universe, young man, think in terms of energy, frequency, and vibration."

Zac bit his lip to hide a smile. "Mom said your character—the one you're dressed up as—had an earthquake machine in his laboratory that shook when he did his experiments."

Frozen in a momentary paralysis, Brian splayed his hand to his chest. "Wait... who had an earthquake machine?"

"The man you're dressed up as. Nikola Tesla. He had some kind of earthquake machine. It wasn't really one, but Mom said it was a high-frequency oscillator."

It took a minute or two for what Brian heard to sink in. His eyebrows lifted, and his lips spread into a grin. "Your mom taught you about Nikola Tesla? Holy cow, Zac. What else did she teach you?"

The discussion that ensued revealed Zac's understanding of physical principles, and Brian was stunned. "Zac, do you understand how smart you are? I need your help here."

This is going to be a real challenge. Zac's not your typical kid, and I don't want him to be ostracized, like I was, once he goes to school. He needs peers he can relate to. Brian knew painfully well how an exceptional child can quickly go from marginalized to socially isolated to burnt out. *This isn't going to be easy, but if I can't help him, who can?*

Brian called to Olivia in the kitchen. When she saw him, she didn't even flinch at his unusual get-up—she was already getting used to his sense of humor.

"Okay, everyone, sit. We've got a dilemma here," Brian announced. "Zac, you're a darn smart kid. Probably more than smart, probably a budding genius. The problem is, Olivia and I can't homeschool you. You have to go to regular school, and, to be honest, that may be hard for you. You've only been around adults your whole life, so you haven't really practiced being a kid. I'm afraid in a short period of time, you're going to know way more than your teachers. I think if you were formally tested, you'd probably be at high school level. But that's only in the smarts department. Socially and emotionally, you're still a young kid and you need to do things other kids do. I was a smart kid myself, and I know this can be a hard combination."

"Why? Did the other kids tease you?"

"Mercilessly. I'll teach you some additional things here at home to advance your knowledge, but you also have to go to school and learn to be a kid and get along with others your age. I want you to learn to be a six-year-old. This won't be easy. If you trust your uncle Brian, we'll play this by ear and see how it goes. Okay?"

Zac pouted and crossed his arms over his chest. "I don't know. Why can't I just stay here with Olivia?"

"Let me explain why," Brian continued. "I learned from my own experience, and I don't want you to have to go through what I did. I kept more to myself as a kid, and I was pretty quiet and shy. I loved to spend hours playing music and building a ham radio or piece of electrical equipment. I was a math whiz, and my parents accelerated me pretty early. In hindsight, that was a detriment to me socially, and it made my shyness all the more painful for me.

Zac unenthusiastically nodded. "I wish I could just stay here."

With the instincts of a shaman, Olivia came from behind Zac, putting her arms around him, and her gentle hug removed the tension from his body. "I can't teach you all the things you're going to need to learn, though. You're way too smart for me. And once you make a connection with other kids, you'll be glad you did. It's less lonely. Playing and hanging with the others will be so good for you. I know this won't be easy, but all three of us will work on this together, okay?"

Zac broke eye contact and lowered his chin to his chest. "Okay, if you say so."

✳   ✳   ✳

Brian was right that his work was cut out for him. He recognized that Zac didn't have even the street smarts of a small-town boy. Zac did exceptionally well on his entry test despite allowing himself a few staged mistakes, but even with that, it still put him in the most advanced curriculum the college-town school would allow.

In the coming weeks, when Brian talked to Zac's teacher, he reported that Zac spent most of his days by himself, and he didn't seem to make a connection with any of the other kids. Zac sat in the back of the room and ate lunch alone. He participated in classroom discussions when called upon, but mostly he kept to himself. Brian felt it was his mission, his purpose, to help Zac thrive. He was concerned.

That is, until Sarah Brooks moved to town.

Chapter Thirteen
Zac
1999

LESS THAN A month after Zac started school, he was suddenly no longer the newest member of the class. Sarah Brooks had arrived.

Zac liked her immediately—maybe it was her air of nonchalance, or her deep-from-her-belly laugh, or the carefree way she tapped her feet as she listened to a tune playing in her head. After introducing her as the new girl from California, Mr. Kirkman, the classroom teacher, asked her to say a few words about herself to the class.

She looked like a girl who favored sunshine and sports: medium height with an athletic build and a tanned face, suggesting she'd spent time on the beach. Her light brown hair, with a halo of sunlit streaks, curled around her face and tumbled over her shoulders and down her back. She stood in front of the class with complete confidence, her pale green eyes sparkling with curiosity. She wore a woolly navy sweater with a large white snowflake on the front, a black skirt, dark leggings, and black booties. Animated and energetic, she gestured with her arms as she talked, telling the class about her life before Bennington. But what Zac liked the best was that laugh of hers. How could he not smile when he heard it? This was the first kid his age with whom he'd felt an instant connection.

❋   ❋   ❋

That day at lunchtime, Zac sat alone at the table where he usually ate, unwrapping the sandwich Olivia had made him, when Sarah slid next to him on the bench.

"Want to share sandwiches?" she asked, capturing him with her smile.

Taken by surprise, Zac grinned and responded, "Sure, what do you have?"

"Today, it's peanut butter and jelly. What's yours?"

"Meatloaf. Want half."

They exchanged half a sandwich, and Sarah bit into Zac's and chewed. "This is really good," she said between bites. "Thanks for sharing it."

"You're welcome." He licked jelly off his fingers. "I'm Zac. I'm new here too. Actually, I just started a couple of weeks ago. I used to live in Montana. How come you came here from California?"

"It's a sad story. Can you handle it?"

Zac nodded and wiped his lips. "Yep, I think I can."

Sarah wore a pained look on her face and focused her eyes downward on the table. "My dad died a month ago. He was the head of a project with the Scripps Institution of Oceanography. In San Diego."

"Oh no! What happened?" Zac felt sick to his stomach. She was going through the same thing he was!

Her voice wavered. "He died several hundred feet underwater. Something cut the tether to his research vessel."

Zac didn't even know how to respond. She lifted her eyes to look at him, and he reflected back his anguish.

Sarah continued. "My aunt lives here, so my mom moved us back here to stay with her. Maybe for a couple of months. It's all so sad. I miss my dad a lot."

Zac cleared his throat to find his voice "That's really awful, Sarah, but do you know what's weird? The same kind of thing just happened to me. My mom is a—was a—geologist, and two months ago, she went to the Mojave Desert to report about it on TV. She was standing right there talking when the earthquake hit and killed her." He stopped speaking for a moment as he felt his eyes well up. *I don't want to cry now. I don't want kids to tease me.* He bit down hard on his lower lip, then continued. "I'm living here now with my mom's brother, Uncle Brian, and Aunt Olivia."

They met eyes and read each other at a soul level, forming a deep bond and connection. Sarah reached over and squeezed Zac's hand, and they resumed eating their sandwiches.

A few minutes later, Sarah asked, "You want to share one of the chocolate chip cookies Aunt Myra made? They're really good."

"Sure." Zac reached out to take the cookie she handed him.

"Mr. Kirkman put me in the advanced reading group," Sarah said, wiping chocolate from her lips.

Zac nodded and beamed. "Oh good! I'm in that one too."

"It's funny that I got here just in time for winter break to start, but that's kind of cool because we can get together and play. You'll have to come over to my house and meet my aunt and our dog."

"And your mom?"

She shook her head. "No, my mom went back to England to get better. An old friend of hers invited her. She used to go to college there. I overheard my aunt tell my mom to go. It made me mad because she told my mom not to mourn too long—that she should catch herself a rich man while she was still young and beautiful. I mean, really." She rolled her eyes. "My mom gets obsessed with things like that. Anyway, my aunt is taking care of me until she gets back."

"Do you miss her?"

Sarah shrugged her shoulders. "Sometimes, but Aunt Myra is really cool. Oh, and our dog just got pregnant—I can't wait for her puppies to come."

"We have a dog too. She's a golden retriever. What kind of dog do you have?"

"Have you ever heard of a puli?"

Zac shook his head.

"Her name is Dorje. It's a Tibetan name that means 'the indestructible one.' This kind of dog has been in our family for a long time, and my daddy just loved Dorje."

"I like that name. My dog's name is Delta."

"Nice name. Dorje is from one of the very best puli bloodlines. There's lots of champions in the family. My dad was kind of obsessed with protecting Dorje's family line. It's up to me to keep it going."

"I don't know that kind of dog. What does she look like?"

Sarah released one of her belly laughs. "She looks like a big mop! Like she wears dreadlocks!"

Simultaneously, they doubled over. They were in sync—two peas in a pod. Connected. Kindred spirits.

Olivia is right. It's great to have a friend.

Sarah wrote on a scrap of paper and handed it to Zac. "Here's my phone number. Call me over winter break and come over and meet Dorje."

❋   ❋   ❋

Full-fledged fun was on the horizon. Zac was on break from school, Brian was on break from teaching, and Zac had a new friend to spend time with. Life was good.

When they lived on the ranch, Virginia and Olivia never really made a big deal out of the holidays, so Zac didn't know what to expect from Brian. Olivia didn't like the idea of cutting trees down simply to allow them to die inside the house, and Virginia didn't like the idea of spoiling kids with gifts. But Brian loved every second of it all—the planning, décor, holiday foods, festivities, gifts, and merriment.

Olivia and Brian introduced themselves to Sarah's aunt, and after that, Zac and Sarah were free to play with each other.

❋   ❋   ❋

On December 21, Zac awakened to a large figure looming over him in bed. It was Brian, standing over Zac looking like a lumberjack in a plaid shirt, wool cap, suspenders, jeans, and boots. He was holding an axe in his hands. Another child might be terrorized, but Zac pulled the pillow over his face to stifle his laughter.

"Hurry up, big guy. Get dressed. We're going to Pleasant Valley Tree Farm. It's this great eighty-acre lot, and we're going to do the 'choose and cut method,' where we pick out the best Christmas tree we've ever seen and we cut it down ourselves."

Zac sat upright in bed. "So I get to use the axe?"

"Umm… that would be a no. It was only for effect. They have saws there, and we'll use those. I already checked with Myra, and she said Sarah could come along. So hurry up, shower, and get dressed. We're picking her up at ten. And you two can go on a hayride while I load the tree in the car."

✳   ✳   ✳

On their way to the farm, Brian pulled the car into the driveway at Myra's house to pick up Sarah. She was already waiting on the porch, wearing bright red mittens and a matching stocking cap. Zac opened the door for her while she waved good-bye to her aunt and ran to the car, but she didn't look happy.

"Uh-oh, Uncle Brian. Sarah looks sad," Zac said.

Brian's grin slipped for a minute. "How do we turn that frown upside down, Sarah?" Brian asked, looking into the backseat and focusing on her forlorn face.

"Oh, I'll be okay. I'm just a bit disappointed." Her voice was soft and a bit strained. "My mom just called and said she isn't coming for Christmas. I guess she's having a hard time without my dad around anymore. I overheard her and my aunt talking about how her friends are helping her feel better. I thought maybe we could make each other feel better, but…" Sarah stopped for a moment and stared at her mittens. "Maybe she'll come after New Year's."

"Aww, Sarah, I'm sorry to hear that," Brian said. "But we want to make you feel better, and you and your aunt can share Christmas with us. Now put your holiday spirit on, and let's go have some fun!

✳   ✳   ✳

The day left an indelible impression on Zac because it was the day he learned to let loose with complete abandon and have fun with a friend. One moment he was sawing down a tree, and the next he was on a bumpy horse-drawn hayride with his new pal.

At day's end, through snow that was deep and powdery, they dragged the freshly cut, eight-foot pine tree into the house, and even with Olivia's help, Brian struggled to set it upright in the tree stand. Although it ended up crooked, Brian said it gave the tree character, and he set out to perform the tedious task of stringing the lights, all the while singing every Christmas carol he could think of at the top of his lungs. Tattered boxes full of ornaments sat on the living room floor waiting for Zac and Sarah to open them. Unwrapping each ornament, one by one, and hearing

Brian talk about the history behind them was interesting for Zac. Some of them had been his mom's when she was a little girl. *I wish she were here decorating the tree with us.*

Zac never realized before that the Christmas season had so many smells. Everywhere he went, delicious scents flavored the air: the comforting aroma of vanilla, the top notes of cinnamon and cloves, the spicy scent of mulled wine, the aromatic blend of toasted marshmallow and charred firewood, the essence of cranberry and oranges, and, best of all, the permeating perfume of freshly cut pine wafting through the house; it was as powerful a scent to him as the smell of hay or freshly mown grass on the ranch. All the scents combined into a symphony Zac called "Christmas music for the nose."

When the tree-decorating task was complete, Brian told Zac he'd been given the privilege of turning on the lights. Olivia, Brian, and Sarah stepped back from the tree for a better view in anticipation of the lighting.

Zac flipped on the switch, and the room lit up with twinkling colored lights. "Wow, that's beautiful," he said.

❄   ❄   ❄

As Brian promised, the school break was filled with winter recreation: sledding, ice-skating, building snowmen, and, of course, snowball fights. Myra took Zac and Sarah to a holiday arts and crafts show and shopping on Main Street to purchase gifts, which they secreted away once they were home.

On Christmas Eve morning, Sarah arrived at Zac's house carrying a big bag of gifts to wrap. Zac grabbed his own bag, and they headed to Zac's tree house in the backyard. There they created their own version of a wrapping station, with rolls of wrapping paper, scissors, tape, and ribbon. After an hour of production, Zac held up one of his haphazardly taped and wrinkled packages—complete with crooked ribbons and bows—for Sarah's inspection.

"I don't think this is the career I'm going to pick. I'm not too good at this," Zac said.

Sarah cracked a smile and said, "I think that's why they say 'it's the thought that counts.' " And with that, she fell backward on the floor, holding her stomach as she laughed boisterously. Zac's lips curved upward until he, too, broke down in hysterics.

He'd never known before just how good it felt to laugh so hard with someone.

For Christmas Day, Myra invited them over for her version of a New England feast. Olivia had helped with all the food preparations over the past few days. It was Zac's first time experiencing a traditional Christmas, and his beaming face and wide eyes drank in all the magic in the rooms Myra had decorated. The house was ablaze with lights and colors with a crackling fire burning in the living room and twinkling lights flickering everywhere: on the tree, the fireplace mantle, wreaths in each room, as well as spiraling around the stair banisters. Tall candelabras graced both ends of the dining room table with their glowing gold and silver tapers.

They all took their seats at the table, with napkins in lap, waiting for the festivities to begin.

Myra welcomed everyone. "I'm so pleased to have you all here. Olivia and I cooked a lot of love and joy into the foods we made for our feast today. We hope you enjoy it. Before we dive in, Olivia told me something interesting about all the lights you are admiring in the house. Olivia, would you mind sharing that with the others before we begin?"

"I'd love to. In many ancient cultures, the winter solstice was celebrated, and it still is by many today. It's a tradition I like to continue. The winter solstice, in the Northern Hemisphere, marks the day with the shortest period of daylight and the longest night of the year. What I love about it is how it represents the beginning of our return to the light—the turning point. We celebrated this at our house three days ago, didn't we, Zac?"

Zac jumped into the discussion, nodding his head. "Yeah, Brian, Olivia, and I made luminaries. Olivia bought these cool paper bags that had holes punched in them, and we filled them with sand and stuck votive candles in glass holders inside. Then we lined them up along the driveway and lit them at night and they glowed! They were really awesome. After that, we beat on drums to welcome the light."

"Yes, it's a celebration to welcome the light," Olivia continued. "It reminds us that there's a place for the darkness in our lives, which we often think of as sadness. We need to yield or surrender to that darkness when it comes into our lives and allow it to be transformed by the light.

"We've all been through some difficult times this year, so Myra and I put a small votive candle by each of your plates as a reminder. Please light your candle and think about yielding to those dark moments you've been going through and appreciating your light."

Zac reached for his lighter, lit his candle, and watched it glow. He looked around at each face at the table and recognized that maybe, just maybe, he could work with his gift. Perhaps he could let his light come out after all.

CHAPTER FOURTEEN
OLIVIA
2000

I T ALL STARTED with a phone call. Olivia had a knowing sensation that it was going to be an opportunity for Zac to deal with his inner struggles, and she was prepared to play her supporting role. But that didn't mean it was going to be easy. *Is it harder to go through something painful yourself or watch someone you love go through it?*

Maybe the odd Vermont weather they were having was some kind of sign. Olivia stood at the kitchen sink, washing vegetables, as she stared out the window that overlooked the backyard. The sun had just set, and snow pellets began to tap on the windowpane while a growl of thunder roared nearby. Out of the corner of her eye, Olivia saw a flash of lightning. She'd heard of thundersnow before but knew it was very rare. *How unusual,* she thought.

Watching the snowfall had a hypnotic effect on Olivia, stirring up her deep thoughts—thoughts that often centered on Zac. During the previous month of January, she'd noticed his happiness quotient exponentially increasing. It was the little things that gave her clues: a warmth in his voice, a constant upward turning of the corners of his mouth, a lighter step in his gait. These little nuances indicated to Olivia that tiny tendrils of joy had started to wrap themselves around his heart due to his friendship with Sarah. They were like-minded and brought out the best in each other. Although this provided Olivia with a sense of peace, she also held it in the forefront of her mind that Sarah's time in Bennington was temporary, and she understood Zac would endure another loss when the time came for her to leave.

It was a comfort to Olivia knowing that Zac was no longer feeling alone and isolated, the way Brian had described his own school years. Sarah and Zac shared their lunches every day, walked home from school together, played with each other on the weekends, and frequently phoned each other when they were home. Brian called them Tweedledum and Tweedledee.

How different Zac was from just a few months ago! He now seemed to be thriving, burgeoning forth with a newly discovered sense of confidence, and Sarah's presence in his life seemed to soothe the internal woes and sorrows he struggled with.

Olivia knew Zac still had issues coping with the paralyzing anxiety of his gift. It was a sensation no one else would understand. He'd blocked that gift—shut it down. But that didn't mean he'd erased it. It still hid dormant within, waiting for the right time to be released while the pain and sense of loss of his mother's death would be woven into the fabric of his life.

Zac seemed to be finding pleasure in the common everyday activities that kids his age enjoy. When Valentine's Day approached, he asked Brian to take him to the Bennington Village Chocolate Shoppe for a heart-shaped box of chocolate-dipped strawberries for Sarah, and he signed the card, *To my best friend, from Zac*. It didn't take any special powers to know that Sarah's departure would hit him hard.

As Olivia stood at the stove finishing up her dinner preparations, she heard Zac hanging up the phone after talking to Sarah. He sauntered into the kitchen and plunked himself down on a chair, leaned back, and crossed his legs with his feet on the table.

Olivia swatted his shoes with the back of her hand. "Zac, feet off the table where we eat!"

He snapped his legs down. "Oops, sorry, Olivia." His voice was rushed and breathy. "I have some exciting news. Sarah just called and said Dorje's puppies will be born any day now. The vet thinks she's going to have three. She asked me to invite you to the delivery because she knows you like Dorje and thought it might be a good idea to have a nurse there too."

"That's so nice of her to invite me. I'd be honored to be there for the whelping process and to watch the miracle of life. You know, I've attended many animal births over the years, and each one is always exciting."

"The vet said everything looks like it's going to go okay, and Sarah and Myra made her a nesting box. They had to find a box big enough for Dorje to have room to stretch out. And they lined a laundry basket with blankets and towels for the puppies. I want to help while they're being born."

"There isn't much we'll need to do unless something goes wrong. Usually the momma dog wants to go off by herself and have privacy. She'll want space, so we won't want to hover over her too much. I'll tell you what to expect to prepare you for the experience."

"Why, what'll happen?"

"First, would you go tell Brian to get ready for dinner?"

"Sure." Zac yelled into the other room. "Uncle Brian, get ready for dinner."

Olivia pressed her lips together and glanced out of the corner of her eye at Zac. "Well, I meant to go get him. I could have yelled to him myself."

He snickered. "Yeah, but not as loud as I can."

"Would you please set the table while I finish plating the chicken?"

"Sure." Zac set the table with three plates, glasses, and silverware.

Brian bounded into the kitchen with twinkling eyes, rubbing his hands together. "Something smells delicious. What's for dinner? What can I do to help out?"

Olivia glanced at his smiling face. "Well, you look like you had a good day today. We're all set, and all you need to do is sit, relax, and enjoy your meal. We're having tahini roasted chicken with a vegetable medley and mashed potatoes."

With the steaming aromatic dishes on the table, they sat down, passing around the platters of food, helping themselves.

Brian took a forkful of the chicken. "Olivia, this is just delicious. So what were you talking about before I walked in? Catch me up."

"I was getting ready to prepare Zac for his participation in whelping Dorje's puppies. He said they're due any moment now."

"That's a really good idea," Brian said. "I remember being really surprised when I watched our terrier having her pups." He turned to Zac. "I thought they came out looking just like furry, cute little puppies, but they don't."

Zac scooped up a mouthful of mashed potatoes. "So what do they look like?"

At that moment, Delta, smelling something worthy of a trip to the kitchen, meandered over to Zac's chair and plopped down at his feet, waiting for a bite or two of chicken to come her way.

"The process is really fascinating," Olivia began. "First, Dorje will start out in labor. She might lie down or walk around a bit. She'll look swollen, and she might pant."

Zac's eyebrows furrowed and then released. "Does it hurt?"

"I really don't know the answer to that, but getting the first puppy out is usually more work than the rest, and she may moan or whimper a bit. She has to push the puppy down her birth canal. First, you'll probably see a shiny, gray sac hanging between her legs, kind of like a water balloon."

Zac didn't say anything, but his eyes grew wide.

Olivia continued. "When the sac opens and fluid comes out, it means the puppy's on his way. He'll come out wrapped in a membrane that makes it seem like he's covered in plastic wrap. It might look to you like Dorje is pooping the puppy out, but she's not. When it's finally out, Dorje will lick the membrane off so the puppy can breathe. He won't be able to see or hear for a while, and he won't be able to lift up his head. He'll kind of squirm and wiggle around because he'll want to nurse. Dorje will chew off something that looks a bit like rope—that's the umbilical cord. Then she'll start the process of birthing her second puppy."

Brian reached for the bowl of vegetables. "It's good to know ahead of time what's going to happen."

"You saw births happen on the ranch while you were growing up, Zac," Olivia reminded him. "You've just forgotten."

"I did? I don't remember. I just know Sarah's really excited, and I am too."

※　　　※　　　※

That night, at 11:00 p.m., the phone rang, and Brian roused himself from a deep sleep to answer it. He knocked on Olivia's bedroom door, then Zac's, and announced it was time: the puppies were on their way.

Zac was prepared with his sweatpants and hoodie by the side of his bed, ready to throw them on at a moment's notice. Olivia quickly dressed and grabbed a bag of some medical items to bring with her, and they drove to Myra's house in the dark of night.

Myra greeted them at the front door and invited them in, leading them back to the family room. Dorje was in her whelping bed, reclining on her side, looking very swollen.

Sarah clapped her hands when she saw them. "I'm so glad you're here. Dorje's in labor!"

Zac stood a fair distance away. "Does it hurt her?"

"She isn't crying or anything."

Olivia kept her eye on Zac to see how he was taking it. He seemed fine—wide-eyed and curious. Sarah and Myra sat to the side to let nature take its course as the vet had instructed. Zac continued to stand back, appearing increasingly agitated.

After the first puppy was born, Dorje licked off the membrane as Olivia had described. Olivia heard Zac taking huge, deep breaths and noticed he looked pale. Then, several times, he blew out his cheeks and released the air. The muscles in his face quivered, and his excessive gulping was audible.

"You okay, Zac?" Olivia whispered.

Zac stepped farther away from Dorje, and Olivia thought he might take off. "Olivia, take me home now. I have to leave. I'm feeling sick, and I'm going to throw up." He bolted out of the room.

Olivia opened her hands in a palm-up gesture and shrugged her shoulders. "I'm sorry, Sarah. You help with the puppies. I'm going to take Zac home. Call me if you need my help."

Zac sat in the passenger seat of the car with his head turned toward the window. As Olivia drove home, she asked him, "Zac, did I not prepare you well? What's wrong? What's going on?"

He began to cry—quietly at first, then deeper sobs with heaving shudders. As soon as the car stopped, he opened the door and rocketed to the house, leaving the door open behind him. He dashed up the stairs and threw himself onto his bed with Olivia following close behind him.

Brian woke from the commotion and stood in Zac's doorway in his pajamas. "What's up, buddy? What happened?"

Zac didn't respond. Olivia spoke to Brian with her eyes—she raised her shoulders and shook her head, indicating she didn't know what was going on. Brian looked on, helpless in the face of his nephew's tears. As soon as Olivia went to the side of the bed, Zac sat up and threw his arms around her neck.

His voice shook with fear. "Olivia, help. Help! I don't know what to do! Dorje's pups are sick and no one knows it. Only I know it. How can I tell them without... you know... without explaining? How do I tell them what's going to happen? They're all going to die, and I'm scared. I'm scared for Sarah and Dorje and her puppies."

Olivia glanced at Brian's confused face. "Brian, is it okay if I speak to Zac alone for a few minutes? I'll fill you in later. I promise."

"Okay," he said hesitantly, looking upset and perplexed as he headed back to his room.

Olivia lay down on the bed next to Zac and slowly and gently pulled his face toward hers with her open palms covering each of his cheeks. Their eyes met, activating the bond they'd held from the day he was born.

She spoke in a soothing tone. "We both knew this day would come, and I'm only your guide. I can't live this for you, or I would. You must learn about these decisions and how and when to use your gift."

She felt him squirm and try to wiggle from her face-hold. She knew she needed to toss him a rope to draw him out of the well he'd fallen into. Who else was going to understand what he was going through?

"Dorje's very sick, Olivia. She has a virus, and it's going to kill her and her puppies and hurt my best friend in the whole world. I don't know what to do! I don't want any more hurt for anyone." He continued to struggle and squirm away from her.

"Zac, hold yourself still now and listen to me. Let what I have to say sink deep into you. Let your 'inner you' hear my message. You can select where and how to open your light. This is your choice. You were never meant to live your life in darkness. You're wise beyond your years, and yet you're still a boy. This will not be the last time you struggle with this decision, my Child of Light. Use every experience that comes to you as an opportunity to learn—learn about yourself and what you have been given. Learn to use your gift wisely and for good. You were given the gift of being able to heal with a special energy that comes through you. Remember the time you held a sick butterfly in your hands and all of a sudden it got well and flew away? You have the choice to determine when you will use that energy. Whatever you decide, I'll be here. I'll support you. This is my best advice. The darkness that surrounds and stops you from using your light is fear, and fear deceives you. It makes you weak. Do not live where darkness hides.

"You're being tested. All people get tested. Now you need to turn up your light. Let it shine brighter. Again I'll repeat this because it is so important: do not live where darkness hides."

Zac's face, pillow, and shirt were wet, and Olivia tenderly wiped his eyes with a tissue.

Zac turned over on his stomach and buried his face in the bedding. Olivia continued to lay next to him while he mulled over her words. About an hour later, there was an incessant ringing of the doorbell, and she heard Brian go downstairs to answer it. Then she heard his footsteps coming back up the stairs to the doorway of Zac's bedroom.

"Zac, Sarah is here to see you. I didn't know if you were up to seeing her or not. What should I tell her?"

"It's okay, Uncle Brian. Let her come up."

"Okay, I'll go get her."

Olivia could hear Sarah's light footsteps running up the stairs.

"Can I come in? Zac?"

Zac sat up next to Olivia on the bed. "Sure, come on in."

Sarah sat down on the edge of the bed and scanned his distraught face with a baffled expression. "What happened to you? I've been so worried! As soon as the last puppy was born, I snuck out of the house and rode my bike in the dark over here. Aunt Myra doesn't know I'm gone. Are you sick? The puppies are here—all three of them, and they're fine. Dorje's doing okay. Do you want to name one?"

Before answering, Zac paused. "I'm glad to hear they're all okay. I'm really sorry I ran away like that. We're best friends, but there's something you still don't know about me. I'm nervous, but I'm ready to tell you."

He glanced at Olivia and she nodded. "Do you want me to go?" she asked.

"No, stay here while I tell Sarah, please."

Zac slowly began to tell her bits and pieces from his childhood—his experiences with animals, with other living things like plants, what happened with White Cloud on the camping trip with Buz. "I used to know when certain things were going to happen or when something or someone was sick and needed healing. But I didn't want to know, and so I turned it off. I stopped my gift. I don't want it to be used to hurt anyone or anything."

Sarah furrowed her brow and tilted her head to the side. "I'm so sorry about what happened to that horse, Zac. It's really awful. But what does this have to do with Dorje?"

He pressed his hand against his forehead and shook his head. "Sarah, something's terribly wrong. Dorje and the puppies are very, very sick."

"But, Zac, the vet, Dr. Arnold, saw Dorje before she started labor, and he said she was in good health and the litter would be small but fine. They all seem to be doing okay."

Olivia knew that what Zac had left out was his own healing powers; he hadn't wanted anyone to know about that—not yet.

"Sarah, sometimes I just know things. I can't explain it. I know Dorje is sick and the puppies are too. I think you need to get them to the vet right now."

Olivia saw the seeds of doubt and worry about Dorje's well-being in Sarah's eyes.

"Olivia, would you drive me home?" she asked. "I need to tell Aunt Myra that we need to go to the vet. I know how late it is, but I'm really worried now."

Olivia agreed, and she and Zac took Sarah home and waited to be sure she got safely inside. Then they drove home without speaking, but Olivia could feel Zac's despair.

✳   ✳   ✳

About 6:00 a.m., the frantic call came.

"Zac, please. I need your help. Aunt Myra wants to wait until the vet's office opens, but… but… this is what you were trying to tell me. I want to go now. I can't seem to make Aunt Myra understand. Please, please can you and Olivia help? They're sick. All of them! I stayed up with them after I got home, watching them to be sure they were really okay. Dorje and the puppies started vomiting a little while ago and then shaking."

"Hold on a minute," Zac said. He explained to Olivia what was happening, and she grabbed the phone from Zac.

"Sarah, this is Olivia. Listen to me. We're on our way to your house with the van. Tell your aunt to call Dr. Arnold immediately, and tell him it's an emergency and to get to his clinic as soon as possible. You two need to be ready when we get there. Have Dorje in her box and carry the puppies in the laundry basket you prepared. The one with the handles. We'll be out front in a few minutes."

Olivia was already up and dressed, having anticipated the urgent call. Within minutes, they were in Olivia's van heading to Sarah's house. Olivia raced to the front door, and Myra handed her the box with Dorje in it. Olivia carried the box to the middle seat of the van and set it down next to Sarah. Then Myra carried out the basket of puppies and placed it in the rear seat with Zac. Myra climbed into the passenger seat, barely getting her door closed before Olivia took off driving down the street.

As she drove, Olivia watched Zac in the rearview mirror. Their eyes met, and she gave Zac an almost imperceptible nod. Zac nodded back and selected the one puppy he knew had a chance of surviving, knowing it was already too late for the others. Pulling the wiggling little guy close to him, then under his coat, his hands worked as if they had never forgotten how to heal. Olivia alone saw the aura as Zac's hands engulfed the puppy with his light and energy. Zac closed his eyes and went on his inner healing voyage.

As Olivia pulled up to the vet's building, Dr. Arnold met them at the car, took the box with Dorje inside from Sarah, and headed to his office. "It can't be too serious," he said. "Dorje checked out fine the other day." Sarah followed him, carrying the basket with the two puppies.

"I'll bring this puppy in," Zac told her as he got out of the van. "I'm trying to keep him warm. He's really shivering, and I'm using my body heat."

Once everyone was in the back room, Dr. Arnold placed Dorje on the cold exam table and went to work on her. The IV fluids he gave her didn't stop whatever was happening, and he told them he needed more sophisticated diagnostic tests to determine what was going on. But before he could try anything else, Dorje went into convulsions. Moments later, she was dead.

Sarah clutched Dorje's still body, gently petting her beloved dog. Myra stood to the side, stunned and silently crying, distraught that her niece was having to endure yet another tragic loss. Olivia reached over to touch Sarah's shoulder in comfort, but she quickly withdrew her hand as she felt the sharp sting of Sarah's sorrow ripping through her heart.

By the time the vet turned his attention to the two puppies in the basket, they were also gone. When Dr. Arnold gently pulled Sarah away from Dorje's body, she turned into Olivia's stomach and let Olivia's arms envelop her. "Daddy!" she screamed through her sobs. "I'm so sorry! Daddy! Daddy." Her weakened body melted to the floor.

Again, Zac exchanged subtle nods with Olivia. Silently, he stepped forward, kneeled down, and opened up his hands. "Sarah" was all he said.

She glanced at him with a pained expression before the movement caught her eye. There in his arms was a bouncing male puppy, whimpering but otherwise healthy. Sarah's eyes stared right into Zac's. No words needed to be spoken. He had given her a gift of immeasurable worth, one that moved her very soul. The Dorje bloodline would live on and the memory of her father with it.

"Damnedest thing I've ever seen," Dr. Arnold muttered. "Why did this one pup survive? All of them were clearly infected with something… It'll take a few weeks to get the reports back, to figure this out…" His voice trailed off. Then, recovering himself: "Take this one home. No contact with other dogs. He's not out of the woods yet and will need a lot of care. I'll give you a list of instructions on how and when to feed him, how to keep him warm. He doesn't have a mother now, so taking care of his needs is up to you. Give me a call if you have any questions or concerns."

✳   ✳   ✳

The four of them rode home in silence, each lost in their own world of thoughts. Sarah and Zac sat in the back seat focusing on the puppy. Olivia knew it would take Sarah some time to process another loss in her life.

Olivia blew out the stagnant, suffocating air from her lungs. Zac had faced his challenge, his fear, and he'd heard the message that he no longer needed to live where his darkness had been hiding. *This is a life-altering moment for him*, she thought.

Now that Zac had opened himself to his gift again, Olivia's intense work with him would begin—nothing a shaman couldn't handle. She knew she needed to teach him how to manage his special energy: how to control it, hide it when necessary, and bring it out upon command. It would take training and meditation. She'd immediately begin to teach him to lower his state of vibration, how to channel and release his energy, and how to use his body to ground it.

Sarah gently stroked the surviving puppy as she rewrapped the blanket around him and cuddled him to keep him warm. Olivia listened to her conversation with Zac.

"Sarah, I know how sad you're feeling about Dorje and the puppies. Do you want to come stay with us for a while so we can help you out with this little guy?" Zac asked.

She shook her head. "No, thanks so much for offering, but I think I should stay with my aunt to take care of my poor puppy. We're both so sad." Her voice cracked and wavered again. She turned to Zac and took a deep breath. "I don't know what you did or how you did it, but this is something I'll never forget. Not ever. I have no idea how to thank you. I owe you everything. This little guy is all I have left of my dad. Whenever I look at this little guy from now on, in my mind, I'll hear and see my dad walking Dorje or sneaking treats to her. Each time I hug this puppy, a part of me will feel like I'm hugging my daddy."

"I'm really glad I could help you with that, Sarah," Zac said.

※　　※　　※

Olivia knew the next learning opportunity for Zac would follow soon, and she was right. A few weeks later, she heard Zac talking on the phone and could tell from the conversation that Sarah's mother had returned and that Sarah would be leaving Bennington shortly. Her mom, Lesley, had found a good job outside of London, she'd even been in contact with an old flame she was thinking about reconnecting with. No amount of persuasion by Myra and Sarah had been able to change her mind—she was set on starting a new life a continent away.

Oh no… does this have to happen right now? I guess there really is no "right" time.

Once again, Olivia held her tear-ridden Child of Light in her arms hoping the comfort and love she so deeply felt for him would soothe some of the pain he once again had to endure. She could feel his small hands clenching at her, pulling at her to share her strength with him.

I'd do anything to protect him from the pain, but I know only he can walk this. I'll always be there to walk beside him.

"Zac, I have an idea," she whispered in his ear. She told him what it was, and he nodded.

Zac invited Sarah over to his house to say his farewells on her final day in Bennington. Her mom's driver dropped her off at the house and would return to pick her up in two hours. After that, Sarah and her mom would be on their way to a new life in England.

Brian, Zac, and Olivia answered the door. Sarah's tear-streaked face and bloodshot eyes showed Olivia she was experiencing the same pain of separation Zac was going through.

Together, they walked into the family room. "Sit a minute, Sarah," Zac said. "We have something for you."

Olivia took her cue and went upstairs to retrieve the mystery gift.

While Olivia was on her mission, Brian asked Sarah, "So how's the puppy doing?"

"He's doing really well. Zac's helped out so much by stepping in as a substitute mama dog. Dr. Arnold said we needed to bottle-feed him every two hours for the first seventy-two hours. After that, it was every three hours with a four-hour stretch at night. There's so much to learn, and we want to do everything right.

"Did you know puppies can't even poop and pee on their own 'cause their mom usually helps them? So with Dorje gone, Aunt Myra has done that part. And you have to keep them at the perfect temperature, so we had to get an incubator and watch that he doesn't get too hot or too cold. I never knew how important the momma dog's role was in this. But now I have to leave my aunt, Zac, *and* the puppy, so I feel really sad. He just isn't strong enough to travel yet, so he'll be staying with Aunt Myra until he's older and can handle flying."

"I was wondering about that," Brian said. "So what's his name?"

She turned to Zac with raised eyebrows and an open mouth. "You didn't tell him, Zac?"

"I forgot! She named him after me—Sparkman. His name is Sparky! Isn't that cool?"

"That's great, Zac. Perfect name."

"My aunt said Zac can come over as much as he wants to bond with Sparky and to help him get strong."

Brian nodded at Sarah and smiled, and they all turned and watched as Olivia came down the stairs holding a cardboard box. She handed it to Zac.

"I have something for you, Sarah," Zac said. "It's my good-bye gift to you, and it'll help you heal the sadness you feel. Brian, Olivia, and Sarah, please sit on the floor, cross-legged, and we'll make a circle."

As they got into formation, Zac reached into the box and retrieved two new sacred drums made by John Medicine Crow. He handed one to Brian and one to Sarah. "These are for each of you, and I'll explain what they're for in a minute. This one's Olivia's, and this one's mine." Zac glanced down at the face of his drum where he'd lovingly painted a picture of White Cloud. He handed Olivia her drum and held on to his.

Zac told the same story Olivia had originally shared with him. "We use these for healing," he began. His voice was confident and strong. "They're much more than the drums you see." He held his up to demonstrate. "See, it's a wooden hoop with stretched rawhide and lacing. When you turn it over, you see the back is laced like a medicine wheel, and this is where you hold it in your hand. Olivia's dad made these and smudged them with sacred herbs while they were drying."

Brian and Sarah examined their drums as Zac spoke. Olivia beamed with pride. *He remembers everything perfectly.*

"This is incredible," Brian said, his voice cracking with emotion. "I've seen you and Olivia use yours many times. I feel honored, really deeply honored, to now have one of my own. Thank you, Zac. Thanks, Olivia."

Sarah slowly and lovingly drew her fingers over the taunt, stretched leather face of the drum. "This is really for me?" she asked.

Zac nodded. "Yes, it's a very special gift for you. The face was left blank so you can paint whatever you want on it that's important to you.

"As we beat our instruments, we'll connect with the heartbeat of the drum. It'll connect you to your own heartbeat and the heartbeat of Mother Earth."

He handed a beater to each of them. "This is what you use to make the sound. And, Sarah, whenever you need to feel me near you, sit in the quiet and beat your drum. I'll beat mine too, and we'll connect wherever we are in the world. Olivia and I'll show you how, and you both can try it with us. It'll help you heal from losing Dorje and the puppies. And... us not being with each other."

Sarah placed her hand over her heart and nodded as tears slowly rolled down her cheeks.

Olivia turned on the familiar haunting flute music, and they sat in a circle on the floor, playing in harmony with the music as they connected to their heartbeats and the wisdom of their collective soul. Their beats began to sync together as they drifted off on an inner voyage, losing track of time.

Olivia stood and quietly tapped Brian on the shoulder, signaling him to slip out of the room with her to let Zac and Sarah sync their eternal friendship.

❋   ❋   ❋

The phone rang in the kitchen, and Olivia quickly answered it. The two hours had already passed—it was Myra calling to inform them the driver was on his way back to pick up Sarah. After that, Sarah and Lesley would be winging their way to England.

The black limo pulled up in front of the house, and the uniformed driver held the door open for Sarah. All four of them walked down the sidewalk toward the car, with Zac and Sarah holding hands.

When she reached the car, Sarah gazed into Zac's eyes. "I always knew I wouldn't be here forever, but now that it's happening, I feel so sad. But you helped me, Zac, and gave me the greatest gift I'll ever get."

"You too, Sarah. You helped me bring out my light again. You're my first real friend."

"I guess we both helped each other, huh? You're the most special person I've ever met. I won't forget you. We'll write and stay in touch and get together when we can. We're forever friends. You know how I love Winnie the Pooh? Well, when Pooh says to Christopher, 'Forever you and me,' that's us."

She placed her drum and beater on the car seat and turned to face Zac.

"Forever you and me," Zac whispered. "There are no good-byes, only see you laters."

Sarah grabbed Zac and pulled him in for a prolonged hug, then turned away. She climbed into the backseat of the car, and the driver closed the door. They waved at each other as the car drove off.

Zac stood still, not moving a muscle, as tears flowed down his cheeks. Olivia walked to the end of the sidewalk. She saw the anguish in his eyes. They didn't speak—the words to express their feelings hadn't been created yet. She put her arm around his shoulder and walked back into the house with him. They met each other's eyes in the unspoken way they had.

Olivia flipped on the music, and Brian, Olivia, and Zac sat on the floor in their circle of three, picked up their drums, closed their eyes, and returned to their journey of healing.

PART FOUR
2006–2011

The day science begins to study non-physical phe-
nomena, it will make more progress in one decade
than in all the previous centuries of its existence.
                                           —Nikola Tesla

CHAPTER FIFTEEN
OLIVIA
2006

I T WAS MID-JANUARY, and the Pryor Mountains were blanketed with a light dusting of snow. Olivia pulled the collar of her red winter coat up around her neck to ward off the chill, then, after throwing her suitcase in the back, she slid into the driver's seat of her rental car. Driving often put her in a pensive mood, and she had much to think about. It was a funeral that brought Olivia back to the ranch. She'd been aware that Gus's wife, Nadi, had been gravely ill, so Olivia wasn't surprised when she received the news that Nadi had died after suffering complications from pneumonia. To a shaman, death is a doorway to a new beginning, and it was an opportunity and responsibility for Olivia to call upon her ancestors and the Great Spirit to help heal those left behind who were suffering and in pain.

Gus had asked her to lead the ceremony that would assist Nadi's spirit in her transition as well as help those in mourning. When she gave Gus a long hug in greeting, she could feel the anguish he was holding inside, and so she gave him a shamanic healing session to release his toxic energies, to help him shift back into balance, before the two proceeded to Nadi's ceremony.

Afterward, Olivia returned to the Sparkman ranch to have some alone time and regroup. In the past, every time she stayed at the house, she'd planned to do a deep cleaning as well as an energy clearing to remove the lingering negative energies from Virginia's death and Buz's betrayal. Now was the time.

She began with a thorough cleaning of all the rooms. *It's amazing how thick the dust collects from visit to visit,* she thought. Running her dust cloth over the bricks of the fireplace, she felt a rough edge poking into her hand. She paused and took a closer look—the mortar between the brick on the top and bottom appeared loose, a bit crumbled.

After grabbing a table knife from the kitchen, Olivia pried at the crumbled mortar to clean it out. The brick almost fell into her hand. In its place was an open space with something in it. As she reached back into the hollow area, she felt two notebooks that had been stuffed into the small opening.

Inhaling deeply, then blowing her breath out slowly, she pulled them out, one at a time, and examined them. The first was cloth-covered, with Virginia's handwriting on the cover, and the second was a small drawing pad of sketches and notations in Nikolai's handwriting. *Why would they hide these here instead of in the locked lab?* She held Virginia's locked journal and determined it was her diary. She had a vague memory of Virginia writing in it every night before bed, so maybe keeping it in the main house was easier for frequent use. She decided to take both of them back home with her, as they might be something Zac would treasure as keepsakes.

After thoroughly cleaning the house, and in spite of the cold temperature outdoors, she opened the doors and windows prior to performing a smudging to eliminate the low-level vibrations and unhelpful energies that were never previously cleared.

Olivia placed her herbs—sage, tobacco, and sweetgrass—in her abalone shell and lit the mixture with a wooden match. As the orange embers glowed and smoke rose from the herbs, she walked from room to room fanning the smoke with her feather while chanting. When finished with her smudging, she felt the shift in the energies of the house—it felt purged and more balanced again. *Now the house will be ready for Zac when he decides to visit.*

※　　　※　　　※

A week later, after Olivia had returned to Vermont, Zac teared up when she handed him the notebooks. Zac didn't usually ask Olivia much about his parents, but she knew he would when he felt ready. He was eager to go to his room and read through them to see what he might learn; however, he noticed his mom's journal was locked. He remembered how Sarah had received her first diary—complete with a key—for Christmas, and she'd told Zac that a diary was the place to write down secret "girlie stuff."

Three days after she'd given him the booklets, Olivia drove to the school to pick up Zac. He was standing on the sidewalk, patiently waiting, wearing his heavy jacket and tundra boots with a backpack thrown over his shoulder.

After she pulled to the curb, he slid into the passenger seat and pulled the door shut.

"Hi, Olivia. Can you take me to RadioShack? I want to get some supplies."

She grinned at his cherry-red nose and pink cheeks. "Hi yourself. Sure, we can go now on the way home." She looked quizzically at him. "Supplies for what?"

As Olivia drove slowly on the icy road, Zac dug into his pocket and pulled out a piece of paper. "I was looking through dad's drawing pad that you brought back. There's a picture he'd sketched of something I want to try to re-create on a smaller scale."

She turned her head to glance at the sheet he held. "What kind of things do you need?"

He started reading a long list: "PVC pipe, magnetic wire, insulated hard wire, a 2N2222A transistor, a 29k resistor, an on/off switch, a nine-volt battery and connector, a Ping-Pong ball, aluminum foil, a CFL bulb…"

"Oh my. Okay, we might also have to stop at Home Depot for some of those things. Whatever are you making?" Olivia asked.

Zac scribbled something on his sheet of paper with a pencil from his backpack. "I'm re-creating genius," he said without looking up.

Olivia shook her head and chuckled. "Of course you are. Just don't blow the house up or electrocute yourself, okay?"

His lips spread wide showing a set of straight, white teeth. "I'll try not to do that. Uncle Brian said I could use his workroom. I'll need his mini drill, the hot glue gun, and his solder iron. He gave me his empty CD spindle case to use for the base."

"That's a very weird assortment of equipment."

Zac nodded his head. "It is. If I can make it work, you'll see how it comes together. I'm making a wireless power transmission system."

"From looking at a sketch?"

"Yep."

"Just please be sure to follow all the safety precautions your uncle went over with you for whenever you're in his workroom. Proper ventilation, make sure you have the fire extinguisher present—"

"I remember them all."

✳   ✳   ✳

As soon as they arrived home, Zac changed into his sweats, grabbed his bags of supplies, and disappeared downstairs into the workshop. Olivia was emptying the dishwasher when she heard the sound of the drill, but otherwise it was fairly quiet. *I think I'll see what he's doing.* She bounded down the steps to check on his progress.

Olivia stood next to Zac at the workbench, peering over his shoulder. "How's it going? I'm glad to see you have safety glasses on."

He glanced up from his task. "So far so good, I think. What time is Uncle Brian going to be back tonight?"

"Around six. He's going to stop on the way home and get some take-out for dinner… So I'm curious what all of this stuff is going to add up to. Where's the PVC pipe?"

"Right here." He pointed to a wire-wrapped tube. "I sawed the pipe to the right length. Then I wound this magnetized copper wire around it about two hundred and fifty times. That was pretty tedious."

"What's that for?" Olivia pointed to a gold-painted box.

"That's the spindle case Uncle Brian gave me. I drilled three holes in it, cut out an opening for the on/off switch, and spray-painted the exterior. Then I glued the switch in. It's my base."

He pointed to various items as he spoke. "I inserted the wire extending from the bottom of the tube through this hole and glued it. After that, I glued the tube to the base. I coiled the primary wire three times around the bottom of my tower, then fastened a bottle cap to the base and soldered the transistor to it. The primary coil and resistor were soldered to the on/off switch, and the resistor and secondary coil to the transistor base. I connected the primary coil to the transistor collector. Next, I—"

Olivia stuck her index fingers in her ears. "Ugh... no more! Good heavens. Sorry I asked. This is total Greek to me, and I don't understand any of it."

"Look, I'll show you. You can learn. Now I'm inserting this battery into the terminal and gluing it down."

Zac handed her the Ping-Pong ball. "Here, Olivia, you can help. Cover this ball with a piece of aluminum foil and then trim the end off."

She accepted the ball, set it down, and tore off a piece of foil. "Does it matter how?"

"No, just cover the whole thing and trim the excess."

She wrapped the ball and trimmed it with the scissors as directed.

He continued his demonstration. "See, I'm gluing this end of the secondary wire from the top of the tower to the bottom of the wrapped ball you made and hot gluing it to the top of the tower. And voila, it's done."

Zac pushed the safety goggles up on his head before continuing. "Now I'm going to let you do the honors. Hold this CFL bulb in your hand near the tower. What do you see?"

She looked confused. "Nothing. Am I supposed to see something?"

"No, you're not. Let me turn off the lights first."

As Zac skipped over to the basement light switch, Olivia asked, "I'm not going to get a shock, am I?"

"You shouldn't." He let out a laugh. "Okay, flip the on/off switch to on."

She did as she was told, and the lightbulb she held in her hand lit up and glowed. "Wow, it's like a magic trick. The bulb isn't connected to anything! That's amazing, Zac. How does that work? Never mind. I don't really want to hear the answer."

At that moment, they heard Brian's footsteps upstairs, and he called out to them. "I'm home! Where are you guys? I have hot Chinese food."

"In the workshop. Come on down," Zac yelled back. "Olivia, flip the switch to off before he gets here."

Brian thumped down the steps and scanned the setup. "Why are you working in the dark? What are you guys making? What is that?"

"Watch," Zac said. "Olivia, do it again."

She flipped the switch back to on, and the lightbulb lit up again.

Brian raised his eyebrows and opened his eyes wide. "Holy cow, Zac! Is this what you said you were going to try to create from studying your dad's sketches?"

"Yeah, Olivia took me to get the parts."

"What did you use for that ball on top of the tower?"

"A Ping-Pong ball."

"What's the purpose of all of this?" Olivia asked.

"Like I told you in the car—it's a wireless energy transmission experiment."

"Brian, do you understand this?" Olivia asked.

He nodded. "I do."

"Then I'm leaving you guys to it. I'll set up for dinner."

Brian headed toward the stairs with her. "I'm starving, so I'll come back down and look at everything in detail after we eat. Zac, be sure to turn everything off before you wash up for dinner, please."

Zac just nodded absently and mumbled that he'd be up in five.

Upstairs in the kitchen, Olivia unpacked the containers of food while Brian dug out chopsticks from the drawer. "He's moving forward very quickly, Olivia. He's like a sponge that drinks up everything there is to learn. We need to get him some more advanced tutoring. He already blew by all the tutors we've gotten him so far, and pretty soon, he's going to surpass my level of knowledge too—at least in the areas he's interested in studying. I worry that I won't have enough to offer him."

"Well, this is all certainly outside my area of expertise. It's in your hands, Brian. I leave the details of his education up to you. Whatever you decide, I'll support."

"Thanks. I want to do my best for him, but I'm torn. He obviously doesn't belong in the public school system intellectually, but I'm still reluctant to accelerate his education so quickly that it outpaces his social and emotional development. And we have no way of knowing if the government is still after more of Nikolai's secret work." Long ago, Olivia and Brian had agreed to try to keep Zac's intelligence under the radar—not draw any unwanted attention to how exceptional he was. "I know the plan has been to slow him down as much as he can tolerate—at least in school—but I can't justify not doing whatever else we can do here at home to nurture that incredible brain of his. I'm going to check out some graduate-level tutors at the college right away. I really think this brilliant kid can make the world a better place."

"His possibilities are limitless," Olivia said.

CHAPTER SIXTEEN
BRIAN
2009

WHERE DID THE time go? It was Zac's sixteenth birthday, and Brian wanted to create a special day for him. As he sat in his study, barefoot, in jeans and a blue T-shirt, with a huge box of loose photos on his desk, he reminisced about his life with Zac and Olivia. One of his birthday gifts was a photo album reflecting the past decade with Zac—Brian's way of memorializing the special moments he'd loved sharing with him. Both he and Olivia spent hours sorting through the images, recalling their fondest memories. Even though Brian started preparing the gift weeks in advance of Zac's birthday, he made very slow progress—each photo distracted him as he mused over the past. *This has been the best ten years of my life,* he thought. *I love this kid as if he were my own.*

The ticking clock on his desk returned Brian to his task. Zac would be home soon, so he had to stay focused and finish his gift. He opened the album to fill the final blank pages.

Although dwelling in reflection wasn't typical for Brian, it seemed almost impossible for him to avoid drifting into the pleasant reverie each photograph elicited. His life hadn't turned out as he'd imagined it would when Olivia and Zac first came to live with him—it was much better than he'd envisioned. He loved his unique family.

Almost instantly, Olivia and Brian had developed a natural fondness and special caring for each other. Although Olivia encouraged Brian to date, which he did, he hadn't found that special someone he wanted to settle down with long-term. His fulfillment came from teaching, spending time with Zac and Olivia, and sailing.

Olivia's fulfillment came from combining the healing practices of nursing with the healing aspects of shamanism. Both Olivia and Brian had a deep comfort and respect for each other and their roles in the life of a very special boy. It was enough—more than enough—for both of them. It didn't bother them in the least that other people found their arrangement odd.

Brian had divided his album into sections. He dug into the box and pulled out a photo of Zac and Sarah posing with Dorje. It reminded him of how, prior to Sarah's move to Bennington, he'd been concerned about Zac's inability to connect with other kids his age. His own childhood memories of isolation still haunted him. But Sarah had brought the best out in Zac. After she moved to London, Brian had worried that Zac wouldn't seek out new friends, but once he'd opened his light to heal Sparky, he found a new level of confidence that helped him socially.

For the first month after Sarah moved, the two of them talked on the phone frequently—too frequently. When Brian opened his phone bill, he'd been shocked. With the five-hour time difference, Zac had snuck in some phone time with Sarah during the early-morning hours before she went to school. Brian had no idea why Zac always seemed so tired then. But once the secret phone conversations were discovered, Brian limited the overseas calls. Zac didn't know it at the time, but Sarah's mother did her best to control Sarah's activities and curtail her communications with Zac. According to Myra, Lesley was insistent that Sarah cut ties with her American past and move on with her new British life.

Brian fastened that photo into the album.

*   *   *

Next, Brian studied a great shot of his sister and Nikolai posing on the porch of their ranch house. *She was so beautiful, inside and out, and one of the best people I'll ever know.* His heart ached, and he wiped his eyes, thinking about the times they'd shared when she'd been alive.

She'd been his best friend growing up. Even though, as adults, they hadn't seen as much of each other as they'd have liked due to their different schedules, they'd always stayed in contact. Virginia's death had been such a tragedy, and Brian missed her every day.

He looked closely at the image of Nikolai and was surprised at how much Zac now looked like his father. Tall and lean, with the same intense expression on their faces, the same piercing blue eyes. *It's sad they never got to meet each other.* A product of Virginia and Nikolai's mixed genes, how could Zac be anything but a genius? Fortunately, he was able to handle his smarts in ways Brian hadn't been able to, and Zac had learned to blend in with his peers.

The last time Brian talked to Zac's school counselor, he could tell Zac was still following the plan they'd laid out in middle school. He was pacing himself academically, staying near the top of his class but never allowing himself to dash to the very top, where he knew he belonged. He was aware of the possible scrutiny by the government that Olivia and Brian feared, so he reserved displays of his true intellect for outside of school—at home and with the tutors Brian hired for him. But Zac had learned just about all he could learn from them, and as Brian suspected—in all of the hard sciences outside of his own fields of mathematics and physics—he himself had taken Zac as far as he could by age fourteen. Brian was truly in awe of his nephew.

He attached the photo of Nikolai and Virginia to the inside cover of the album.

✳   ✳   ✳

On the left side of his desk, Brian had a stack of pictures of Delta taken before she'd passed. *I miss her too. She was such a sweet dog.* He selected two for the album—one of Delta leaping up into the air catching a Frisbee mid-flight, and one of Zac and Delta cuddled up on the living room couch in front of the fireplace.

✳   ✳   ✳

Brian wasn't sure which of the sports photos to include—there were so many. Zac's sports activities provided him with a sense of camaraderie and team spirit with the other kids his age, and for that, Brian was grateful. For the most part, Zac's peers had different interests than he did, but sports was their common denominator. Through the years, his body had grown long and lanky, and he'd become an accomplished athlete in both track and field and swimming. There were so many pictures from his competitions; it was hard to choose.

Brian randomly picked two and placed them in the album.

✳   ✳   ✳

Unique to Brian, Olivia, and Zac was their passion for ancient and primitive instruments. Brian focused his attention on a picture taken last year when the three of them had been invited to play as a musical ensemble for the Bennington High School Christmas show. He grinned as he remembered how each of them had worn a Santa hat while performing "Carol of the Bells." It was the highlight of their holiday season.

Olivia had introduced both of them to drumming years ago, but as Zac was digging through the attic looking for treasures one day, he came across Brian's didgeridoo leaning against the wall behind a stack of boxes. Brian had told him it was a remnant of his trip to Australia and he should feel free to try it out. A few weeks later, strange, rhythmic sounds pervaded the house accompanying a cassette of Aboriginal songs. Brian explained to Zac that the chief who had given him the instrument told him it was said to embody the voice of Earth itself.

Zac had always been musically inclined, and his drumming with Olivia had prompted him to engage in some intensive research on primitive music. Finding himself totally mesmerized by the sound of an instrument he discovered on the Internet, he was compelled to own a hammered dulcimer—a multi-stringed trapezoidal instrument that's struck with hammers. Apparently, it was an invention of the ancient Persians and brought into western Europe in the fifteenth century.

Zac's enthusiasm intrigued Brian, so they decided to send for a do-it-yourself kit and had spent hours building one in their workshop. After their great success with the hammered dulcimer, they found plans online to build a tongue drum set—one of the world's oldest instruments and a favorite of Brian's.

Once Olivia heard them playing, Brian instinctively knew what would happen. He heard her footsteps galloping down the stairs soon after their magical notes started sounding. He laughed when he saw her bouncing on the balls of her feet to keep rhythm, anxious to join in. "Music is the heart-beat of the human spirit," she'd said. "I need to play too." Her idea was to form their own musical group. As a longtime owner of an ancient, closed-voooool instrument called an ocarina, she joined their ensemble.

Brian believed the flute-like instrument that had been known through-out many cultures over time and was used in many rituals—often by shamans to connect to the world of spirit—was the perfect instrument for Olivia. Brian and Zac were in awe of the sounds it produced—haunting and mysterious, buoyant and otherworldly. Both Zac and Brian loved to compose, and they spent hours at a time creating original pieces for the three of them to play.

Brian placed their Santa hat ensemble photo on the final page of the album.

❉   ❉   ❉

Rushing to finish before Zac charged through the door, Brian still had open-ings for a few more photos in the back of the album. These were reserved for their sailing adventures—Brian's other great passion he shared with Zac. They both loved spending time on the *Quark,* his thirty-six-foot Catalina sailboat. Sailing was their duo adventure just for the guys—Olivia, prone to seasickness, had no desire to participate; however, she was emphatic that Brian teach Zac, as she knew it would be important to him someday. Brian never questioned Olivia on those things. He understood she had "knowings."

Zac and Brian sailed the *Quark* together every chance they got over the springs and summers, and Brian enjoyed teaching Zac everything he knew of the sea. Although they never left the coast, Brian knew his nephew had dreams of sailing the world someday.

Ever since he was a little boy, Zac loved adventure stories, and he fre-quently begged Brian to share his tales of sailing. The one that Zac asked him to retell over and over was about his trip on the *Don Quixote.*

Brian remembered back to when he was telling Zac the story for the fifth time as he sat at the helm of the *Quark* with Zac standing next to him. "So I sailed around the world on the *Don Quixote* with Oscar Sanchez," he said. "My friend Oscar—he's one of the good guys. Such a special charm and charisma about him, you know? You'll really like him when you get a chance to meet him. But I was the one who had the heart and soul for adventure. Just like you! We were known as the 'adventure brothers.' Now you and I are adventure buddies."

"Tell me again about where you sailed," Zac said, encouraging him to share more.

Brian yelled over the sound of the waves breaking against the hull. "We sailed the salty seas to the Caribbean, through the Panama Canal to the Galápagos Islands, then across the Pacific to French Polynesia. On one of the Marquesas Islands, Oscar fell in love with a lovely Polynesian woman named Lea. He'd learned enough French to convince her to marry him two years later. What do you think of that? We both loved that area and the people. You and I'll have to go there sometime. You'll never see a land so filled with wild fruits, lush vegetation, and loving, giving people."

"When can we go?"

"When you're older. You've still got more to learn before we take that kind of a trip."

"Where else did you go?"

"From there we sailed the Cook Islands, Fiji, New Zealand, and Australia. There's this great story—we'd been lucky enough to help an Aboriginal man whose boat had capsized. He appeared to be a common worker who turned out to be a local chief. We were rewarded with entry to ceremonies few white men have seen and our very own didgeridoo. The one you like to play."

"So what happened to Oscar?"

"After a year of sailing, Oscar went off to get his PhD in virology, and I went for my degree in physics. Oscar rose through the ranks of academia, while I chose a quieter life at a small college, away from the limelight. He lives in Atlanta, Georgia, now and works for the Centers for Disease Control and Prevention. He has two kids."

Zac patted him on the shoulder. "And you have one."

Brian glanced at him with a tender look. "I do." *What a sweet thing to say*, he thought.

They had many enjoyable sailing trips along the coast, where Zac learned everything Brian could teach him. One of his favorite pictures was of Zac holding a sextant as he sat on the transom of the *Quark*. In his mind, he could hear the tone of Zac's voice, taste the salty air, and feel the rocking momentum of the boat.

It took him back to the day when they were sailing off the rocky Maine coast near Portland, where Brian kept his beloved sailboat. They had just passed Monhegan Island. Brian, holding the box with the sextant in it, paused near the main sail roller furling and looked at Zac sitting at the helm with a smile on his face that anyone who loves to sail would've recognized. He clearly remembered their conversation.

"We should drop anchor, Zac. We'll need to tack so we can get closer to shore."

Once they dropped anchor, they sat side by side on the boat's bow and set to work.

"Well, big guy, you're a fast learner and you know more than many about sailing, but I'm going to teach you something not a lot of others know, and you have the math skills to handle this. The next thing I'm going to teach you is celestial navigation, also known as astronavigation. You're going to learn how to use a sextant. Before all the fancy gadgets and devices we now have, sailors used them to plot their location at sea."

Zac gave him a broad grin. "Awesome. So, you line up stars to find your own place on Earth?"

"Actually, you can use the sun, the planets, the moon, Polaris, the stars… For hundreds of years, sailors used them to plot their location on the sea. You like ancient things—it's an ancient art."

"Sounds interesting to me."

Brian placed the box on his lap and unsnapped the fasteners on both sides. "Sad thing is the Naval Academy dropped the program for this in 2006. I think it's a big mistake."

"Why?"

"Dumb move if you ask me. We should never let ourselves be vulnerable."

"Why not just take advantage of the advanced geolocation technology?" Zac pushed his sunglasses up on the bridge of his nose and pulled down his visor to block some of the intense sunrays.

"Well, think about that, Zac. I'm not saying don't use technology.

I'm saying be prepared with a backup if it fails. Current-day technology is great, but it's vulnerable. You always have to be prepared for emergencies: electronics go out, batteries die, lightning strikes, and there's human error. We're subject to cyberattacks. Even our own systems can be pulled if national security feels the need. Satellites aren't fail-safe. They get outdated. They need updates. The best technology can fail. I don't want to rely on something with a single point of failure, do you?"

"Good point." Zac cocked his head and paused as he thought about what Brian had said. "Well, here's what I think, based on what you said. They may have to shut down GPS to keep enemies from using it or to protect it if under attack... or the signal could be jammed by a local military base... or there might be spoofers. During war or when it goes dark, satellites could be down, radar not working... and you don't want your electronics to be monitored. All sorts of things can take out a GPS system or disrupt it."

Brian slapped Zac on the back. "There you go. Now you're thinking. Okay, you get the point. Besides, Olivia has strongly encouraged me, if that's even the right word, to teach you how to use this, and I never second-guess what she says."

Zac guffawed with delight. "That's for sure."

Brian opened the box, removed the sextant, and held it in the air. "Okay, here it is." He handed the instrument to Zac.

Zac held it and examined the different parts. "It's cool. Feels heavier than I thought." He held it up to his eye and peered through the sighting scope.

Brian pointed out the various components. "This baby will measure the angle between the horizon and a celestial object. See, there's a telescope, shades, mirrors, index arm, eyepiece... I'll go over all this with you in detail, and we'll use the tables to do our calculations. You game?"

"Of course. Let's start now."

Brian shook his head to bring himself back to real time and stretched out in his chair. *Those times spent on the boat with Zac were some of the best of my life.*

Brian added the final four photos to the album.

✳   ✳   ✳

All the memories the photos brought to mind made Brian feel gratitude for the opportunity of having Olivia and Zac in his life. He checked his watch. Zac would be back from practice soon. The dinner reservation was for 6:30. With haste, he wrapped the album, along with another smaller box, with brown paper and leftover ribbon. *I hope he likes his presents.*

✳   ✳   ✳

Olivia, wearing teal-colored scrubs with a stethoscope around her neck, breezed through the front door, breathless and rushed, carrying a pink bakery box. Brian rushed to relieve her, setting it on the kitchen counter.

"Hey, Brian," Olivia said. "If you can believe it, after work, I almost forgot to pick up his favorite cake from the bakery. But I got it, and I also have the candles. Do you have his gifts ready? Please tell me you finished the photo album."

"I just finished it. By the way, Zac said we could skip the candles."

She didn't look up. She didn't miss a beat. "We're doing the candles."

Brian laughed under his breath. He found her stern ways endearing. "He wants steak, so I made a reservation at the Publyk House."

"Sounds great. Did you invite Kelly to go along?"

"Wait. Who's Kelly?"

"Oh, good grief, Brian," she said, rolling her eyes. "The girl he's dated a few times now?"

"Oh, sorry. It slipped my mind. Should I call her now?"

"No. We're leaving in a few minutes." Olivia smirked and shook her head. "I'm going to go change my clothes before he gets here."

"Okay, me too. He'll be here any minute."

✳   ✳   ✳

The Publyk House, rated one of the most beautiful restaurants in Vermont, bustled with energy. Their seats were in a prime location at a table with a magnificent *view of Mt. Anthony. After indulging in their delectable steak dinners, they headed back to the house for dessert.*

While Zac changed into his sweatpants, Olivia prepared the cake, punching sixteen blue and white birthday candles into the thick, white icing, then carried it to the dining room table. Brian stood with lighter in hand, waiting for Zac to return. As he walked into the room, Zac laughed at all the lit candles. *Yeah, he acts like he's too old,* Brian thought, *but he'd be disappointed if we didn't do the candles.*

"Make a wish and blow them all out," he said.

After stuffing themselves with chocolate cake, Brian announced, "Time for your gifts. Oh, and here are some cards that came in the mail for you."

Zac opened one with a yellow envelope. "Hey, it's from Gus, and he gave me a gift card. Awesome! That's so nice of him."

Brian reached across the table and handed him the first box.

As Zac untied the ribbon, he chuckled. "Obviously, you wrapped this, Uncle Brian. I think I take after you in wrapping abilities."

"Yeah, yeah… my talents lie in other areas."

"I'm actually surprised you aren't sitting here dressed as a clown or some other character as you have for many of my birthdays."

Brian leaned forward with his elbows on the table supporting his head in his hands and grinned. "I thought the cutoff for that should be age sixteen."

"I'll love it even when I'm fifty, Uncle Brian."

Zac pulled the photo album from its wrapping. Suddenly quiet, he turned the first few pages.

"A ten-year summary of our lives together." Brian's voice cracked a bit. "Both Olivia and I worked on it."

"This is so awesome. I can't thank you guys enough for doing this for me." He thumbed through the pages. "Okay, I think I'll do this later in the privacy of my bedroom since I can tell I'm going to tear up, and I don't want you staring at me when I do."

"It's okay, I teared up a few times myself putting it together. So did Olivia. But looking at it later is fine. Here's one more gift from Olivia and me." Brian shoved the second package across the table in Zac's direction.

Zac unwrapped it, opened the box, and let out a yelp. He closed his eyes and threw his head back. "You guys… this is incredible. This is too much! Who waited in line for it? Thank you." He jumped up from his chair and ran to stand behind Olivia. He pulled her jet-black ponytail to the side and hugged her around her neck, then plunked a kiss on her cheek. Then he repeated the hug for Brian.

"I can't believe it. My first iPhone. And this is even the new release! A 3GS. Unreal."

Brian handed him the contract. "I waited in line, but you're worth it. And we bought you the 32-gigabyte version, along with a service provider contract. I had them set it up for you at the store, so it's ready to go."

Zac tapped the camera icon and did a little dance around the room holding up the phone and aiming it at various items to see how they looked on the screen. "I love it. Thank you! But hey, guys, what my new album is missing is a picture of today with the two of you. Lean in together so I can take a shot of my two favorite people in the world with my new phone camera."

They posed and he snapped the picture. Another memory of a special day for his album.

Olivia picked up the discarded wrapping paper and ribbon and wadded them into one ball of trash. "Zac, you don't have to sit with us while we drink our coffee if you don't want to. You can go play around with your new phone."

"Not yet. I can do that later. You know what I want to do?"

"What?" they both answered in unison.

"I want to jam. The three of us. Let's go down in the rec room and make some music."

As they stood to go downstairs, Brian turned to Olivia and said, "Hey, you do know how to play 'Happy Birthday' on the ocarina, right?"

She gave him a thumbs-up. "Of course I do." she said.

Brian stood in the doorway of the rec room watching Zac and Olivia take their usual spots. As he took his place to join them, he thought, *I don't think I could be happier with how this story's turning out.*

CHAPTER SEVENTEEN
ZAC
2009–2010

FOR EVERYTHING, THERE is a season, and Zac wondered if it was time to return to his childhood home. For months after his sixteenth birthday in June, he'd been drawn to the photo album Olivia and Brian had given him. Even though it caused a lump in his throat, he kept turning to the photo of his mom and dad. Thoughts of the father he'd never met kept popping into his head—he had a yearning to learn more about him.

Early on, Olivia and Brian had told him it was up to him when and if he wanted to take a trip back. Zac was aware that on a twice-yearly basis, each of them flew to Montana—Brian to monitor the ranch and review finances with the family accountant, and Olivia to visit her father and friends on the reservation.

I wonder what's held me back from going? Zac thought. He finally admitted the reason to himself after Olivia returned home from her most recent trip back.

She stood in the doorway to his bedroom and said, "My Child of Light, I'd like to talk to you for a minute. May I come in?"

Zac was studying at his desk. He turned around and grinned at Olivia. "Of course! Come in and sit down. What's up?"

Olivia plopped down on the comforter on his bed. "I have something important you need to hear. As you know—because I've said this before— things happen for a reason. Years ago, something very painful happened to you when you were a little boy. You learned about betrayal, that humans can be cruel and that not all people have your loving heart. The terrible situation with White Cloud compounded by the loss of your mother shut you down, and you still carry the heavy pain of that day with you."

Zac lost the grin he wore, looked down at his hands, and didn't respond.

Olivia continued. "At the ranch, I was talking to Gus. I think you should know what happened. It's news about Buz."

Zac cringed at his name and felt a churning in his stomach.

"I'll just say it. Buz was found dead in his barn under somewhat mysterious circumstances. The coroner couldn't find anything but an insignificant bruise on his chest, about the size and shape of a horseshoe. His death was subsequently ruled a cardiac arrhythmia."

Zac began to shudder from head to toe. Something dark, like a black fog, released from his body as he exhaled. He instantly felt lighter and more at peace. He gazed deep into Olivia's eyes and nodded his head for her to continue.

"The fence he used to corral White Cloud appeared to have been broken down from the outside, and White Cloud disappeared without a trace."

Zac stifled his tears and closed his eyes. He sat motionless. What once threatened to devour him, to internally eat him up, was finally gone. It had departed. Nothing had ever felt as good as this sweet release of buried anger.

Olivia let him process the information and sat in silence with him.

At last, Zac stood from his chair, walked over to Olivia, and bent down to kiss her on the cheek. "I love you, Olivia. Thank you," he said. And he left the room.

✳   ✳   ✳

As with all teenagers, Zac was going through internal shifts as he matured. By the middle of his junior year, school had become beyond boring for him. He found himself less patient with his teachers, and his open corrections of their mistakes didn't win him any favors. For years, he'd only been attending public school for the social aspect—to have friends and fit in with his peers—doing most of his real learning on his own, down in Brian's workroom.

But now Brian, Olivia, and Zac all agreed he was ready. He'd held back to avoid suspicion long enough, and he was tired of hiding his intelligence, tired of faking wrong answers on tests just to avoid outshining all the other students. Now, he no longer cared who knew how smart he was, how brightly he shined. He had a mission and a dream, and he didn't want to wait another day going after it. So that spring, Zac took every test he needed to take to graduate early, then he earned a perfect score on his SATs. He was done with Bennington High School months before the semester ended. Then he set to work in earnest applying to his colleges of choice.

Further schooling required money, so Brian decided it was time to fill Zac in on his financial status. The monies that were held in trust for him would be released at the various milestones that Virginia had had the presence of mind to lay out. Profits from the ranch since his parents' deaths—the funds accrued from the cattle and the crops—had accumulated nicely over the years and had also been set aside for Zac's future. Then there was Virginia's own inheritance that she'd passed on to Zac, which Brian had invested with substantial success. Basically, Brian summed up, Zac would be more than financially comfortable for the rest of his life. Noting his uncle's talent for investing, Zac asked Brian to teach him how to do it himself, and Brian was more than happy to oblige.

As he was getting ready for bed one night, Zac once again found himself leafing through his photo album. The picture of his parents kept calling to him, setting off a quiet longing. He had no memories of his father, and now his memories of the ranch were beginning to fade along with those of his mother. He knew it was time to finally return for a visit, and because Buz was now gone, he could do so with a sense of freedom and excitement. First thing in the morning, he'd ask Brian and Olivia to go along with him for moral support.

The arrangements were made quickly—as soon as Brian was done teaching for the year in May, they'd all set out together. Before Zac knew it, he was back on the land of his childhood home. As Brian drove the Jeep down the main road of the ranch, Zac was transfixed by every tiny detail around him. Some of it looked familiar, but most of it didn't.

As they drove up the bumpy incline to the house, Gus was the first to race to the car to greet Zac, shaking his hand vigorously. Zac was happy to see him again, and he surprised the normally reserved man by pulling him close and giving him an old-fashioned bear hug. While Olivia and Brian settled in, Gus eagerly took Zac for a walk to show him all the changes around the ranch. The first rush of melancholy enveloped Zac when Gus talked about the grieving process he'd gone through when his wife died. So many things had changed over the years. Many of the same ranch hands were there, with several new additions as well. Gus reminded Zac of how they used to ride together on the old John Deere—now replaced by a newer model—and pointed out Delta's favorite spots to chase rabbits. Vivid images of his mom and Olivia working in the garden formulated in Zac's mind.

After the tour, Gus left Zac on his own, wanting to give him some space to reminisce about his childhood in private. Zac had no idea what to expect as he began his exploration of his past. His pulse pounded in his temples, his hands shook, and he nibbled at his cuticles.

He walked through the house, down the halls, filling in the mental holes in his mind as he peered in each room, recalling them one by one. When he came to the family room, he had a clear memory of seeing his mother disappear in the middle of her televised news report. He touched the top of the old TV that was still in its place. *I miss you so much, Mom.*

He wondered if Olivia had set out all the photos that speckled each room. He didn't remember there being that many—photos of his mother, his father in Russia, both of his parents together, Olivia with his mother, his baby photos, Gus, even one of him with Buz. Zac picked that one up from the fireplace mantle, opened the frame from the back, took out the photo, and tore it to pieces. On the way to his bedroom, he emptied his hand into an open trash can.

Once in his room, he sat on the edge of the bed. Memories flooded his brain as suspended moments in time. He could hear the gentle voice of his mother soothing him, singing to him, loving him. He felt the warmth of Delta curled up next to him, gently snoring in his ear.

As he made his way to the kitchen, he clearly recalled the smells and tastes of food on the stove. He could see his mother making her special vegetable soup, with its comforting scent rising up through the air. Looking out the window, he noticed that the garden had been kept up and that a plentiful supply of vegetables and herbs was growing. *That would make Mom happy.*

Olivia wandered into the kitchen breaking Zac's reverie.

"How's it going? Memories coming back?" She stood next to him with her hand on his shoulder, peering deep into his eyes.

Zac nodded his head. "Yeah, I'm okay. It just all feels weird to me."

"Zac, now that we have some time alone where others can't hear us, I need to talk to you—it's about your father. Have a seat and I'll get you some iced tea while we talk."

Oh no, now what kind of bombshell is coming? He plopped down on one of the kitchen chairs. "Okay, lay it on me."

Olivia filled a glass with ice and tea and placed it on the table in front of him. She sat next to him wearing a serious look on her face. "I didn't want to discuss this with you until you were ready to return to the ranch, and that decision had to come from you. Of course you've been given information about your father's background and his areas of research. You know he was a brilliant scientist and that he did confidential work for the government. What you don't know is that he had a special lab built for him here on the grounds. It was supposed to be a place he could privately carry out his work and experiments. The government helped fund it, and agents came here often to check on any developments. I'm thinking you'll probably want to go look around it and spend some time in what used to be his private sanctuary."

Zac's eyebrows shot up immediately. "Definitely. I definitely want to see it."

Olivia proceeded to tell him about the shed, the lab, the day his father died, how Virginia had fainted in the lab that day and thought it had played some part in his birth, and how the agents showed up only hours after his father's death to clear out his desk and workspace.

"Wow," Zac said, hardly able to take it all in. "Can we go see it now?"

Olivia grabbed the keys hanging on a hook inside one of the kitchen cabinets and headed out the back door. As they made a quarter turn from the vegetable garden and continued down a pathway, they came face-to-face with the shed.

It looked like an ordinary garden shed to Zac, and yet he was drawn to it. He was curious as to why it was built into the side of the hill, not a more practical place for a toolshed, closer to the fields.

Olivia showed him the key to unlock the shed and opened the door. Zac looked around. From first appearances, it didn't seem like anyone used it any longer. Nothing appeared to have been disturbed for years. He noticed a workbench, a Peg-Board with tools, old bags of soil, fertilizer, and pots.

"Now, this is how to enter the laboratory. I'm the only living person who knows this code," Olivia said. She showed him how to enter the code, and a green light flashed.

To Zac's amazement, the door slowly opened. It was so cleverly concealed that its movement startled him. *Amazing how it still moves so quietly after all these years.* The lights flickered on as Zac walked into a room that apparently had been cleared out of equipment and papers. *Unbelievable! This was my father's laboratory—or what's left of it anyway.* He felt tears spring to his eyes.

"I know this is overwhelming to you, Zac. Would you like some time alone in here?"

He nodded, unable to speak.

"Okay, I'm going to visit with Gus. See you in a bit." She gave him a hug. "When you want to talk, I'm here for you." She left the lab.

Zac examined everything, touching furniture, tabletops, stray paper clips and staples, even the walls, while imagining his dad working in his sacred space. He removed the books that hadn't been confiscated from the shelves and thumbed through the pages, but his eyes kept diverting to the waterfall at the back of the room. It intrigued him. Why was it there? He grew more and more curious. What was powering the lights? Whatever it was, it appeared to be self-contained, but he couldn't tell from where. Zac continued to go through his father's books for something he didn't know he was looking for.

As he sat at his father's desk, he found a small black notebook stuck between two physics books. It was filled with mathematical equations, but on one of the pages there was a diagram of a staff of notes. Reading the notes, he could hear the song in his head. It was the beginning of Beethoven's Fifth Symphony. *What's this doing here with all these scientific drawings?*

The waterfall repeatedly nagged at him—it was consuming his thoughts. He walked toward it to observe it more closely. With his keen sense of hearing, he noticed a different sound where the water splashed against one side of the wall. Apparent to Zac, the wall was not as solid as it appeared.

Something else is back there. Zac used his musical ear to listen as he tapped on the rear wall. He wasn't sure, but he thought he'd heard a change in tone. He felt compelled to inspect it further. After tapping on various spots on the wall with the edge of his hand, he heard the hollow sound again. He pressed on the specific area, and in the semi-darkness, eight red laser lights appeared to emanate from the wall.

Some kind of code is needed to enter another area. I just know it. Eight lights. The number eight flashed in his mind. The drawing in the book—it had the eight notes of the symphony. *Could that be the code?... Oh my God, I think that's the code! Starting with G-G-G-E-flat... Here goes...*

His mind drew a musical score around the dots of light, and he tapped out the motif. The lights in the lab went out and he heard a creaking sound. This time, the opening door created some noise, as this partition seemed to be far heavier than the first. Zac was unprepared for what unfolded before him.

What am I seeing? What the heck is this? It looks like some kind of secret room!

The second, much larger cave was alive with electronics and some other kind of power-generating equipment the likes of which Zac had never seen. The waterfall on the rear of the first cave had become the entrance to the second. He didn't have a full understanding of physics yet, but with what he knew, Zac could tell this had a special purpose, and he recognized this chamber was top secret and had apparently only been known to his father—and maybe his mother. Even Olivia didn't know about it—she would have told him, he felt sure. He stood for a moment in silent tribute to the man he'd never met.

In the corner was a study area with a large desk, a desk chair, a whiteboard covered with equations, a box filled with his father's notebooks, papers, and tapes, and wall shelves jammed with books. Some kind of experiment had been set up on a worktable, adjacent to the desk. There was a projection scope that was pointed at a forty-five degree angle toward something that was presumably missing, with a recording device hung above the system. He opened it but didn't see any tape inside. There was also a microscope and a piece of equipment labeled *accelerator*. *I have no idea what that is.*

He stared at the chair his dad had sat in to do his clandestine work. *I'm not ready to sit there quite yet. Not yet...*

He didn't think he could decipher all the math equations on the board, but maybe with Brian's help? He examined everything. Next to one of the bookshelves was a large easy chair—Zac elected to sit in that one instead, to observe his father's private world from that vantage point. As soon as he settled in, he heard a clicking sound. The lights dimmed, and three beams of light converged over the desk, projecting a 3-D image of Nikolai. A second later, a recorded message started to play. Zac started crying the moment he heard his father's voice.

"Whoever is listening to this message, a few things are clear: I am dead and you are here. For you to have gotten this far, I can only hope your intentions are noble, for what you are about to see and hear can dramatically impact the human race. Your presence here places in your hands the burden of the responsibility for my work. Please use what you are about to learn wisely. Whatever fate brought you here, I hope it will give you the guidance you'll need. My name is Nikolai Sparkman, and this is my life's work..."

Even as Zac listened to every single word his father uttered, he was bombarded by his own thoughts: *I don't know what to think or feel. What responsibility is being handed to me? Am I up for the task? I don't know what to do right now, where to turn. Who was this man? Why is all of this hidden?*

❈   ❈   ❈

Zac lost track of time. It was all so overwhelming. What was he meant to do with all of this information? Who knew about this besides him? He felt an invisible thread connecting him to the father he never knew. Now he had the opportunity to get to know him through his work. Finally, reality woke him from his trance.

Surely by now, everyone would be wondering where he was. He decided to return to the house as quickly as he could, making sure both labs were securely locked before he exited the shed. Then he headed back the way he'd come, toward the garden.

When Zac entered the kitchen, Olivia and Brian were seated at the table drinking iced tea. He didn't even know where to begin. "We—we need to talk," he stammered. "Privately." He pulled out a chair and sat down next to them. He shook his head, as though to clear it of distractions.

Seeing his agitation, Olivia put a hand over his. "You don't have to tell us exactly what you've discovered if you don't want to, but we just need to know how important it is and if there's anything you need us to do about it."

Zac stared out the kitchen window. "You two are my only family, and my home will always be wherever the three of us are. But I believe I need to be here for a while—that I'll need to come back on a regular basis now. The demons that kept me away no longer exist. I'm not sure how much I can or should tell you… and I'm far from being able to understand everything I just saw in that lab myself… but I have a feeling it's something we absolutely cannot share with anyone else. Honestly, guys, this is more than I can handle on my own. I'll have to count on both of you for some guidance on this."

"Of course," they both agreed.

"You need to see it for yourself. There are no words."

Olivia faltered. "I don't think I'm meant to see whatever you discovered, Zac. Take Brian and show him, okay? Then you two can tell me anything I need to know."

"Okay. You ready, Uncle Brian?"

"Couldn't be any more ready. Let's go."

※   ※   ※

What was supposed to have been a week's trip turned into a month-long exploration of the ranch and the secrets it held. Throughout it all, Zac and Brian engaged in intense conversations about the possible implications of Nikolai's work. First Zac needed to understand it fully before he could know what to do about it. And that meant diving into his higher education headfirst.

He'd already been accepted to start at Princeton in the fall. But now that he knew exactly what course of study he wanted to pursue, Brian got some referrals to scholars on campus who would hopefully be able to help Zac work through the intricacies of his father's research. After making a few calls, they settled on a mentor they hoped they could trust. In the meantime, Zac planned to master all of the physics and mathematics Princeton could offer him. Inherently, he just knew: he was meant to continue his father's work.

✳   ✳   ✳

As the end of their stay approached, Zac had one more thing he had to do before they returned to Bennington. *I need this to satisfy my soul.*

After waking up in the morning, he heard Gus in the kitchen with Olivia and Brian, having breakfast.

"Hey, sleepyhead," Olivia said when he walked in, "do you want some banana pancakes?"

"No thanks. I'm not really hungry. Olivia, you told me my dad used to take meditative walks and that there was one specific path he liked to walk daily. Do you know which one?"

"I do, because my dad used to join him sometimes. Do you want to walk it?"

"Yes. But I'd kind of like to do it on my own."

"Sure, let me sketch it on a piece of paper for you." She stood to grab paper and pencil off the counter and made him a quick drawing. She handed him the paper, and he set off.

The path was quiet and peaceful, and Zac understood why his dad liked this particular route. He absorbed the beautiful scenery that his dad had witnessed every morning: the expansive view of the Pryor Mountains, the sage, the wildflowers, the trees. It was as though he could feel his presence walking next to him. Although he never got to meet his father, he felt especially close to both his parents when he was on the land they loved and spending time in his dad's private lab. There was so much to contemplate regarding what he needed to do next. Clearly, he was meant to figure out the legacy his father had left behind.

Zac stepped outside the perimeter of the compound and stretched. It was time for him to turn on his inner light once again. After his experience with Sparky, Olivia had regularly worked with him over the years to teach him how to control his light, his energy. He stood erect, closed his eyes, and carried out his deep-breathing routine. Then he uttered a chant Olivia had taught him to ground and center himself. He scrunched up his nose like he did as a child and turned toward the forest. Then he raised his hands to the sky, brought forth his light, and mentally called out his message. He stood still and waited and waited.

A cloud of dust rose in the distance, and he heard the sound of galloping hooves beating on the ground, coming closer. He held his breath. *Is it… him?* He exhaled slowly. It was. It was White Cloud. Zac's emotions overpowered him. He fell to his knees as he covered his face with his hands and sobbed, draining out all the guilt, the pain, the sadness he'd held in his heart for the past eleven years. His beloved friend was not only alive, he was free.

White Cloud stopped several feet away. Zac stood up, ready to let him make the moves. The magnificent steed approached with his ears forward, his tail curled. He snorted and tossed his head to the side as though acknowledging their past connection. He approached, slowly moving closer until both of them were nose to nose, sharing a common breath. White Cloud softly blew a breath in Zac's face, and Zac returned the same. Then he nuzzled his head up against Zac. White Cloud stepped backward, and they stared into each other's blue eyes. Then Zac's special friend turned and galloped off back toward the forest.

At that moment, Zac knew: if an animal could indeed forgive, then he'd been forgiven.

CHAPTER EIGHTEEN
BRIAN
2010

TIME WAS PASSING all too quickly for Brian, and Zac would be heading off to college in a few more months. Brian remembered the quote "Life is a series of natural and spontaneous changes," and he was aware of many changes that would be happening soon in his own life. Like retirement.

Fortunately, he'd maintained his track record of picking winners on the stock market—not just Microsoft and Amazon, but also Google, Netflix, and Priceline in the past decade—and once Zac realized how much they were worth after his crash course in investing, he'd insisted that Brian stop living quite so thriftily. Day after day, Zac had nagged Brian to buy a bigger, newer boat, since the *Quark* had seen better days, and to move somewhere closer to the water.

After putting a great deal of thought into it, Brian agreed. He was ready for a change of scenery, and the house in Vermont would seem so empty without Zac. Portland, Maine, seemed like it would be ideal, as there was nothing as delicious to him as the smell of salty shores and the squawking of seagulls, and there was always one more rocky harbor, one more fishing village, and one more island or passage to explore.

So, while Zac was still home with them to take part in the decision making, they all went house hunting in Portland. In spite of many hours spent online looking at available properties, the right house was harder to find than anticipated, as Zac took a stand that Brian had to purchase an energy-efficient home. They weren't too plentiful, and Brian had no desire to get involved with renovations.

Finally, at the end of July, the real estate agent found a new type of house—three bedrooms, three baths, set on a beautiful wooded lot—that was so efficient that it actually produced more energy than it consumed. Brian quickly bought it, put his own house on the market, and the three of them were all packed up and on their way to their new home in less than a month's time. Once again, as in Bennington, Brian turned the setup and decorating of the house over to Olivia, who was both delighted to do it and good at it. It worked out well for both of them, as Brian wanted to focus all of his attention on his new fifty-two-foot catamaran with all the bells and whistles, appropriately named *Quark II*. *This is my dream,* he thought.

✳   ✳   ✳

As summer memories began to fade, the trees gave a hint of the multicolored explosion that was soon to come. Zac was off to college. Olivia and Brian drove him to Princeton and got him settled in, but on the six-hour drive home, they both started feeling the effects of empty-nest syndrome. They hardly spoke, and now and then, Brian saw Olivia turn her head toward the car window as she tried to muffle her sniffles. Although they knew Zac would be coming home during school vacations, they antici pated missing his daily company. Grateful for modern-day technology, at least they could make video calls while he was away.

Brian planned to spend as much time sailing as he could, and he was hopeful for another circumnavigation around the globe with Zac, and maybe even Oscar, in the future. After he'd resigned from his job at Bennington College, Brian felt the freedom of more time to have the adventures he craved. He also noticed that with less need to concentrate on Zac's life, Olivia was allowing more time for herself as well. After the passing of Gus's wife, she spent more time back at the reservation utilizing her shamanic abilities with the tribe. The budding romantic relationship with Gus was something Brian sanctioned. Gus was a good man—kind and compassionate. Olivia was often a bit stern and stoic, and Gus had a knack of bringing out Olivia's witty, fun-loving side.

The next surprise in Brian's life came quite quickly. Almost immediately, he discovered that he wasn't ready to retire after all, that he missed being in the classroom, particularly his interaction with the students. So when he saw an opening posted for a part-time teaching position at Bowdoin College, a liberal arts and sciences college on the coast of Maine, about a thirty-minute drive northeast of his house, he applied and happily accepted when offered the opportunity to fill in indefinitely for a professor who had gone out on extended medical leave. Utilizing his tried-and-true comedic lectures to engage the students, Brian quickly became well loved, and the college had to create a wait list to enroll in his classes. He was convinced that the humor he injected into his lectures helped his students retain more of the information.

✳   ✳   ✳

Opportunities come when a person is open to them. At least that was Brian's philosophy. He had seen her on campus several times—the last time was in the Hawthorne-Longfellow Library and once when he was on his way to the Searles Science Center. In November, he attended a show on campus at the Pickard Theater in Memorial Hall, and as if it were fate, he was seated next to her. They finally introduced themselves. Her name was Hannah Mae, and she was an assistant professor of anthropology with a focus on Native American and other indigenous communities, doing her research on indigeneity, sovereignty, and politics. She was of Hawaiian background and had grown up on the island of Maui.

Brian instantly liked her and had an inspiration to introduce her to Olivia, who would be a wealth of information for her research work. After the show, they decided to have a drink together at a nearby pub.

The sky was a black canvas painted with twinkling stars as they meandered down the sidewalk crossing the campus. Hannah wore a red satin blazer, a black leather pencil skirt, and three-inch high heels that caused her to walk slowly and wobble on the bumpy surface of the sidewalk. She laughed at herself, telling Brian she was not used to wearing heels. They stopped to sit on a wooden bench, where she slipped them off, exchanging them for a pair of flats she carried in her large purse. At that moment, Brian found himself a bit smitten with her. He liked that she seemed a bit shy, perhaps coy, with him, but she talked with passion and exuberance about her work.

Once they were seated at the bar having a glass of wine, he wondered if other people made things up when they looked at someone—like make-believe stories about who they are and what they do simply by the way they look and speak and move. He decided Hannah was someone who'd stick her tongue out to catch a snowflake or scream with her arms up in the air when riding on a roller coaster, or someone who'd catch a spider—one that had found its way into the house—in a jar and release it outside instead of smashing it with her shoe.

He guessed from the career and accomplishments she outlined for him that she was about forty-eight, but she looked no more than forty. The lights in the pub cast a shine on her chin-length dark hair, which looked like a metallic finish on a new car. *What does she do to make it so glossy?* Her smoky, cinnamon-colored eyes were twinkly and bright— a sign that she was probably not an insomniac like him. She was trim and lithe, so he decided she enjoyed juicing kale and carrots and went to Pilates. Her elongated, elegant neck reminded him of a lovely swan, and once she'd discarded her heels for flats, she moved as gracefully as a cygnet gliding on a lake.

The evening turned out to be a pleasant surprise for Brian. *This is the perfect time for a new friendship,* he thought.

❋   ❋   ❋

Brian carved out a portion of each day to study. Following the discovery of the covert portion of the laboratory back at the ranch, he was more intrigued by Nikolai's work than ever. He'd returned to Montana once since then for his regular check-in with the accountant, and while he was there, he spent time going through a box of journals and books he and Zac had gathered off Nikolai's shelves. He selected a few that looked interesting and stuffed them into his already-bulging briefcase. When he returned home, he was ready to dig in to his reading.

After a late-night dinner, Brian reclined in his leather easy chair by the fireplace. The living room drapes were open, and a full moon shined its pale yellow light through the window while the fire blazed and crackled. Brian opened *The Character of Physical Law,* published in the 1960s.

Some time later, Olivia entered, precariously balancing a tray holding two overly full cups of hot cocoa. She placed one on the side table next to Brian.

Brian idly fingered a stone while he read—a black stone he'd found in a little pile in the back of Nikolai's desk drawer. He looked up from his book. "Oh, that smells delicious. Thank you. Perfect evening, isn't it? A full moon, a blazing fire, an interesting book, and homemade hot chocolate. With marshmallows."

She settled herself into the chair next to him, cradling her ceramic cup with two hands. "I was thinking the same thing. What are you reading?"

He held the book up for her to see. "I brought a couple of books back from Nikolai's lab to see if I can help decipher any of his work. I thought I'd start with what he was reading. The papers and notebooks he left out are interesting, but I have a feeling there is much more. I assume the government believes that too. I doubt the agents think they got everything."

"But you and Zac did a thorough search of the hidden lab and Nikolai's study, didn't you?"

"We did, but we came up short. We were looking for something that would explain how his energy system worked."

"You know, he was doing some experiment right before he died. Virginia told me it was going to change the world as we knew it."

"Really?… That information must still be somewhere. I doubt he left it where the agents could have confiscated it." Brian opened the book and showed Olivia the writing on the inside front cover. "When I looked at this, I realized I'd grabbed a book that wasn't even his. There's a name and contact information from a person called Avram Epstein inscribed here."

Olivia opened her eyes wide. "Avram… Avram. Oh, I remember him! Back in my teenage years. He was a close friend of Nikolai's and helped him plan and build his lab. He lived in Israel. Tel Aviv, I think. They kept their friendship off the grid. He didn't want the connection made between him and Nikolai's lab or his work. He was like a chameleon in the shadow of the night." She chuckled. "He arrived in the night and departed in the night."

"So he was there during the construction?"

"Yes, even before that, with the planning."

"Then he'd know about the secret part of the lab."

Olivia shrugged her shoulders. "I never really thought about it before since I didn't know about it myself, but yes, I believe so. He probably helped devise it. Everything with the two of them was very hush-hush."

Brian was quiet for a minute. *He could be a very valuable link for us if I can locate him.*

"Olivia, I wonder what he knows. He may be the missing link to understanding some of Nikolai's work. Does he know about Zac?"

"No, I'm pretty sure he doesn't. Virginia did try to notify him, but he took part in covert operations in Europe and the Middle East as an agent for Israel's intelligence agency, the Mossad, so he was hard to track down, and Virginia felt so sad about that. She said Avram even had to avoid coming to Nikolai's memorial service in order to continue their denial of working together. He held his own memorial service in Israel."

"That's fascinating. A spy in our midst… I'm inspired to try to track him down."

"He has to be going on seventy by now, so I'm sure he's retired. If anyone can locate him, it's you."

"I'm going to look for him and make contact if I can."

❋   ❋   ❋

It was much easier than Brian thought to find Avram Epstein. If the contact information he'd found online was still valid, he currently lived in Tel Aviv. Brian carefully crafted a letter explaining who he was, his relationship to Nikolai and Virginia, and that the two of them had had a son, Zac. He wrote that he'd love an opportunity to talk with him.

It was weeks until Brian heard back. When he excitedly opened the envelope and read Avram's letter, it was short and to the point. Avram explained he didn't want to communicate anything of a sensitive nature over email. He told Brian he had checked him out—Brian was fascinated with how he'd done so—as it was always best to be careful. He proposed a specific date and time to speak on the phone, and—adding intrigue to the mix—Avram instructed Brian to purchase a burner phone for the call, saying he'd explain why when they spoke.

Brian eagerly waited for the day of the call. It turned out to be everything he'd hoped and more. After hanging up the phone, Brian yelled downstairs for Olivia to come talk to him in the kitchen. She joined him at the table.

"I'm having a glass of wine. Want some?" He stood with a bottle in hand, poised and ready to pour a glass for her.

"Sure. So what did he have to say?" She accepted the glass he handed to her.

Trying to contain his enthusiasm, Brian sat and began to relay the conversation. "Olivia, this man is so interesting. We had a really intriguing talk. First, you were right. He didn't know about Zac and got a bit emotional when I told him. Said he was protecting Nikolai and his work by keeping his distance from the family but sad he missed out on knowing Zac. He probed me with lots of questions about him. I asked him if he knew about the hidden lab, and he was a bit hesitant to speak about it. He wondered how we figured out how to get in and if it still stood. After he heard of Nikolai's death, he figured the agents came and took everything, and he didn't want them to associate it with him or to contact him. I told him what you told me—that the agents took the 'Trojan horse' journals, equipment, and notebooks."

"Wow, this really is intriguing. What else did he say?"

"Sorry I'm talking so loud and fast, but this is exciting." He rapidly tapped his fingers against the table and said, "Well, here's the bombshell. There are concealed compartments in the walls of the hidden lab. What the heck! He said we'd find an extremely valuable journal and notes within the walls. In the walls! I want to go there right this minute. But of course we'll wait for Zac's winter break. We can all go back then to find that journal.

"And that's not all! Avram invited us to Israel this summer. He'll arrange a dive trip to Eilat, along the Red Sea, as our cover. You're invited too."

Olivia reached out to place her hand on top of Brian's. "Brian, you're the kindest man I've ever met, and you've been exceptionally good to me in the same way your sister was. She'd be so proud of you and how you've taken care of her son and treated him as your own. But this part of the journey is for the two of you. I would only hold you back. I don't dive, and I don't understand even half of what you and Zac talk about. I'll stay here and take care of the house for the summer and spend some time with Hannah. And I'll go back to the ranch for a couple of weeks to visit my dad and Gus. I'll be fine. Make your plans. Zac will be thrilled. This is a terrific adventure for the two of you."

Brian stood up, reached for her hands, and pulled her up from the chair to hug her. "I love you, you know that, don't you? With all my heart and soul."

"I love you too. You're somewhere between a father and an older brother figure to me. I couldn't have asked for a better life than the one I've been spending with you and Zac."

"I'm going to have to figure out a way to get this news to Zac securely. I think I'll take a train down to school this weekend to tell him in person."

❋   ❋   ❋

When Brian met up with Zac in Princeton, he found his nephew on an adrenaline rush. He let Zac give him his school updates before getting to the purpose of his visit, and he wasn't surprised to hear that Zac was doing extremely well and surpassing his targets in his studies.

At a nearby diner over lunch, Brian broke the news about Avram, about the invitation to Israel over the summer, about the hidden storage compartment in the lab. Zac almost jumped out of his skin. He leaned across the table, grabbing Brian's forearm, his eyes a little crazed, and he let out a string of exclamations. It was all Brian could do to keep Zac from leaving school right then and there to start their quest. Brian understood Zac's zeal and his eagerness to meet his father's trusted friend. What excited Zac the most was the journal: *What will we find in the journal?*

❋   ❋   ❋

Semester's end arrived quickly. On the plane ride to Montana, Brian and Zac made plans for their trip to Israel. They'd read that the best time to scuba dive in the Gulf of Aqaba was September and October, but of course they had to stick with their plan to go earlier, according to their school schedules. They'd just have to deal with the crowds and the higher temperatures in June. In preparation, Zac told Brian he'd signed up for a course in Hebrew. He planned to devote all of his free time over spring break to studying the language.

"Avram said he can get you into places," Brian said. "You know… hook you up with people who can help you understand all the tapes your dad left and any information we find. I have this feeling, Zac. I have this feeling…"

※   ※   ※

Once they landed at the airport in Billings, they sped to the ranch in their rental car. This time, only Gus knew they were arriving.

After pulling into the driveway and parking the car, they immediately grabbed the keys to the shed from the kitchen cabinet, hurried down the hill, and made their way inside. After they entered the code to the first chamber, they looked around the room from the doorway—everything looked as they'd left it. Zac hurried to open the second door, revealing the hidden chamber, and scanned the room from top to bottom with his eyes. "Okay, now we need to find these mystery storage areas. Brian, you visually inspect, and I'll auditorily listen. I was originally able to find this hidden chamber by the variations in sound. Different materials vibrate differently. It's all about the vibration." He knocked along the walls with his knuckles, listening.

Brian scanned the walls in a sequential manner—top to bottom, right to left. Next, he moved to the far section in the rear of the cave. "Zac, over here." He'd found something on the floor and picked them up. He held out his hand for Zac to see the four small objects he held.

Zac took one from his palm and inspected it. "Round, almost perfect sphere. Iridescent black-green, about twelve millimeters in—" He stopped short to look up at Brian, who was breathing heavy. "Why does your face look so weird?"

"I recognize these," Brian said.

"What?"

"Yes, they're black pearls. From Fiji."

"How do you know that?"

"Because I bought them. A beautiful black pearl bracelet I gave your mother for her birthday after my sailing trip with Oscar... So the way I see it, something happened right here that made the bracelet break."

Zac tapped and listened on the wall directly behind Brian. "I hear a different vibration here. Yes, definitely a change. I wonder how we open it?" He pressed inward with one hand and felt a push back. He pressed harder using two hands, and that portion of the wall popped inward, then out. A door opened, revealing something that looked like the insides of a wall safe. It was filled with papers, notebooks, and documents, and on top of all that was the pièce de résistance—Nikolai's thick leather-bound journal.

"Finally!" Zac exclaimed. "I can't believe we found all this. It's odd that there's no code needed to open this."

"I'm betting that was to gain rapid entry," Brian said. "Push in, it opens, stash the documents, and push it closed." He paused, staring at Zac.

"What? What are you staring at?" Zac asked.

"Sorry, I was thinking. I had a flash. I think your mom was in here and maybe was shoving stuff in here quickly before the agents could find her... Look, a piece of silk thread is hanging off the catch here. That must have been where her bracelet caught and snagged. If she was in a rush, she wouldn't have had time to pick them all up."

"Why wouldn't she have come back to get them?"

"I don't know, but Olivia said after that day, she never returned to the lab again."

"Wow. Well, we found the mother lode. There's also a bunch of crystals and pieces of a silver-black stone. I wonder what they're used for?"

"Pack it all in this satchel, and we'll look them up online later. We can come back and look for more storage areas too. For now, we have enough. Let's go back to the house and start sorting through everything."

※   ※   ※

They sat up all night going through Nikolai's notes, sketches, and papers. Brian rubbed his temples and cupped his hands over his eyes. "I guess I'm too old to pull an all-nighter anymore. This headache feels like someone's jackhammering my brain. I want to keep going with you, but I'm not seeing straight."

"Uncle Brian, you're forgetting my many talents. I think I can help Loosen your clothing, go lie down on the dining room table, and relax. I'll release your energy blockages."

Brian did as he was told. Zac stood behind his head and activated his energy by rubbing his hands together several times. After his hands filled with warm pulsations, he laid them lightly over Brian's eyes, then temples, then behind his neck. An unusual glow emitted from his hands. As he slowly moved them over various parts of Brian's body, he felt a soothing sensation, a deep relaxation, then a tingling, vibrating feeling. When Zac finished, Brian stayed still for a few minutes realizing his headache had melted away.

Brian slowly sat up after the treatment. "Thanks, Zac, that was incredible. I should take more advantage of living with two healers." He rubbed his hands together with renewed energy. "Now back to business. I think the time difference between here and Israel is nine hours. Hand me my burner phone, please. I want to let Avram know we found the journal and lots of other information."

Brian placed the call. The message was short and sweet: "We've got it. Mission accomplished."

❋   ❋   ❋

Zac and Brian continued sorting through the treasure trove all day, alternating long stretches of silence as they studied this or that with spurts of animated discussion to go over what they were finding.

"I'm glad I started to take Hebrew lessons because a lot of my dad's notes are written in Hebrew. More covert, perhaps? And I know my dad was a genius, but honestly, some of what I'm seeing here are things beyond what mankind has imagined," Zac said, shaking his head in disbelief.

"I know what you mean," Brian agreed. "I feel like someone must have felt over four hundred years ago when they first uncovered da Vinci's drawings. There are so many entries on different topics here—energy principles, philosophy, botany, chemicals, math equations, geology, musical scores, physics, astronomy, and pages and pages of sketches of inventions. There's about—what?— fifty notebooks here... but it's the leather one that's most intriguing."

Zac slowly nodded, glancing up at Brian. "These sketches seem way ahead of his time. But at least we don't have to view them with a mirror like people had to do with da Vinci's work. This is what someone looking at da Vinci's helicopter or submarine would have felt like. Some of it looks... well, otherworldly."

They both stared down at Nikolai's work for a minute.

Then Zac lifted the open journal to show Brian a specific page. "Look at this. This sketch is exactly like the box that's the energy source in the lab."

"That's like hitting gold, Zac," Brian said. "Now we just need someone to help us understand all this." He stood up to stretch his legs and head into the kitchen for more coffee, calling back, "Maybe Avram can do that."

Zac continued to slowly thumb through the drawings in the leather journal, then suddenly stopped. After contemplating what he was looking at for a few seconds, he yelled out, "Brian... Brian, come here. Come look at this."

Brian hurried back into the room and slid down next to Zac. Peering over his shoulder, he said, "What is it?"

"Honestly? I have no idea."

They slowly took their eyes off the page to instead stare into each other's eyes.

Brian's jaw dropped. "What the hell is that, and where did it come from?"

CHAPTER NINETEEN
ZAC
2011

ZAC WOKE TO the sound of rain pattering on the roof. He forgot for a moment that he was home from school and in his bedroom in Maine. There was so much to look forward to—school was out for the summer, and today he was flying to Israel. He'd packed his suitcase the night before, so he only needed to throw in his toiletries. *I've been looking forward to this trip for half a year.* He'd often thought about meeting Avram and getting to know someone other than Olivia who'd known his dad. He felt closer to his father after having listened to hours and hours of the tapes that documented his experiments and reading through his many journals and notebooks.

Both Brian and Zac were concerned about internationally transporting Nikolai's documents for Avram's review. Zac talked with Brian about the best way to carry some of the top secret papers—there was no way they were taking the leather notebook anywhere—so he spent time scanning the most relevant items to a USB flash drive. Zac was aware that Brian was equally concerned about the government getting its hands on the documents. They'd thought the agents might have forgotten about Nikolai's research, until one day in April at Princeton, when Zac had had an unexpected interaction.

As he was leisurely strolling across campus, a short, stocky man had approached him. "Hi, Zachary Sparkman, right? I'm Robert Parker."

Zac stopped to greet the man and sized him up. *He's dressed like a Fed,* he thought.

"Yes, I'm Zac Sparkman. What can I do for you?" He reached out and shook the man's hand.

"I heard you went to school here, and I was on campus meeting someone and thought I'd introduce myself. I knew your parents and used to visit your ranch in Montana years ago."

"Nice to meet you." Zac was hesitant to say any more than he had to, as the man was obviously on a fishing expedition. *How did he even know what I looked like to track me down? Clearly, I'm still being monitored.*

"You ever find more of your dad's journals or work on any of his experiments?" Mr. Parker asked.

There it is. He's just going to shoot straight and ask me directly. Okay then, I'll just play it cool and smooth. Zac did his best to act convincing when he replied, "You know, I really did try to find more of his work, but I guess you guys took everything worth taking." Then, wearing a look of genuine innocence, he added for good measure, "If you guys would give me access to what you found in his lab, maybe I could figure some things out for you?"

"Not sure anyone could get access to that now, kid. It was top secret and never declassified. I just wanted to meet you for myself. I'm out of that game and retired over ten years. All the best with that brain of yours. You come by it honestly."

Guess he doesn't think I'm all that smart if I'm not suspicious of what he's doing here.

The agent stared at Zac for what seemed like an eternity. "I hear you have some highly unusual talents for science and math. Word has it you're a super-genius."

"Well, you know what they say, Mr. Parker." Zac never averted his gaze. "You shouldn't believe your own PR."

They both chuckled.

"So, if I may ask… what are your plans for your future?"

Zac slightly turned his lips up at the corners. "Still undetermined for now. Time will tell."

"Well, my best wishes to you. See you around."

They shook hands again, and Zac watched the man stroll down the pathway. He stopped, turned back to look at Zac, and waved.

That confirms it. I'm still on their radar.

✳   ✳   ✳

He pulled himself out of his daydream to finish his trip preparations. Zac decided he should look presentable when he got off the plane, but comfort was also key for a long flight, so he decided to wear his loose khakis and a long-sleeved Henley shirt. Then he double-checked that he had everything, including a gift for Avram. He was ready to go. He'd been working unusually hard at his studies and was looking forward to having fun with Brian.

Olivia and Hannah drove them to the airport. Zac was pleased to see that Brian was pursuing a friendship with Hannah—he didn't want him to be lonely when he was at school and Olivia was spending time in Montana. Typically a forthright man, Brian had yet to open up and confess if this relationship was anything more than a friendship, but Zac knew he'd get it out of him while they were on vacation.

✳   ✳   ✳

Luggage, passport, phone, security check-in… and they were off. The fifteen-hour flight to Ben Gurion Airport in Tel Aviv was uneventful, and Zac was able to catch up on some sleep for over half the trip. He was aware that Israel was tight on security, so once they were through immigration and passport control, they breathed a sigh of relief and looked for their driver. They found him, in uniform, holding a placard for Dr. Brian Sutter and Zac Sparkman. The driver loaded their baggage into the black limo, and they set off on the nineteen-kilometer drive to Avram's place. He'd insisted they stay with him—there was no talking him out of it.

It was June, and the temperature was a humid eighty-four degrees at noon. As Zac stared out the car window, he thought there was something heart-pumping about waking up in a new country and actually seeing the things he'd read about coming to life. Not surprisingly, the city looked very modern, and he'd heard about the wonderful beaches, great restaurants, and enjoyable nightlife spots.

Finally, they arrived in front of an attractive apartment building.

After the security guard gave them entrance, they dragged their luggage into the elevator and headed up to the tenth floor.

As the elevator door opened, Zac could see an older man standing in the open doorway of his apartment. Avram looked like he'd imagined him: medium height, lean, late sixties, sparse white hair, very tan. Zac noticed a scar beneath his right eye. Just looking at his face, Zac observed the reflections of the harsher side of his life, his secret spy life that others weren't aware of. His eyes told a story—eyes full of grace and knowing, a wisdom from his years of experience. As he smiled and walked toward them, he exuded charisma and an enthusiastic energy.

Zac felt Avram's gaze glide over him from head to toe, and he watched his face soften—his eyes were like a faucet with a leak, releasing one drip at a time. He placed both his hands on Zac's shoulders and looked him directly in the eye.

"I am Avram Epstein, and you are the spitting image of my dear friend Niko. We must embrace." He gave Zac a bear hug. "We are family. It brings me great joy to meet you, Zac. To think I could have gone to my grave without knowing of your existence! Ahh… your father would be so proud of you. He was a good man, a great man. No one else like him in the world. He had a mind the likes of which I'd never seen before. He died way too soon. I miss him terribly."

Avram reached out for Brian and gave him a hug as well. "And you are the man, Brian Sutter, who has stepped into the role of father and raised this wonderful boy. You are an incredible human being. Now quit standing out in the hallway and come in to my humble home."

Avram walked with a definitive limp into the well-appointed living room, waving them to follow with their bags. "I will show you to your room. In my day, I was an avid hiker and rock climber, but as you can see, I have some trouble making it into the kitchen these days.

"Sorry for the cramped quarters, but this is the way it can be in Tel Aviv. This is a very expensive city and three-bedroom apartments are hard to come by, so I get by with two. The guest room has two beds and should be comfortable for you. Please settle in after your long journey. You must be hungry, and my lady friend, Yaffa, has made us something to eat when you are ready. Yaffa will be leaving tomorrow for a period of time to care for her ailing mother who recently had surgery, but you will meet her before she leaves. I am overjoyed that you are here with me today."

❋   ❋   ❋

Over the next week, the three men spent hours talking as Avram enlightened them with great tales about young Nikolai as well as his own fascinating life stories. They went over pages and pages of Nikolai's work, with Avram filling in many of the holes Zac and Brian had wondered about. Between the work of reviewing the documents and journals, Avram took them to impressive places to explore.

"Today you must visit the city market with me to get a true sense of Israeli life," Avram said. "Such a world of plenty filled with spices, cheeses, fruits and vegetables, and many specialties."

At the market, Zac and Brian found some exquisite pieces of jewelry that they bought for Olivia and Hannah. Zac's curiosity was resolved—Brian did admit there was something a bit more than friendship going on as he selected a special necklace for Hannah. They enjoyed the city nightlife and spent an evening with Avram sharing wild stories while they smoked hookah at a local café.

Their days were very busy—between tourist visits to places such as Old Jaffa, Jerusalem, the White City, and museums, there were visits to the Israel Institute of Technology, Hebrew University, Tel Aviv University, and various homes of some well-known scientists Avram lined up to speak to Brian and Zac.

One morning at the start of their second week there, prior to leaving the apartment to visit a fellow physics specialist, Avram prepared a quick breakfast to serve out on his balcony, overlooking the water.

"This is where I'd be sitting every day," Brian said as he relaxed on a white, wooden chair. "What a great view of the beach."

Avram plopped down in the chair between Zac and Brian. "Yes, it is very pleasant to sit here. We will leave shortly to visit my friend after we eat. I have many connections in the international scientific community, and we will go and personally meet the key players. The face-to-face contact is important, and these are people that I have literally trusted with my life. They will help you. You do not need to be here to consult with them, but you are welcome to stay with me whenever you like. We can set up conference calls with any one of my contacts while you are in the States if you like. There is an Israeli-based company that understands security, and we will establish a secure conferencing system for you. When you have a question, you will have instant access to the brightest and the best."

Zac sipped from a glass of freshly squeezed juice. "I'm so appreciative for all your help. Just since being here, I feel I've made huge leaps in understanding my dad's focus and intention. We've met so many inspiring people."

Avram gestured, throwing his hands up in the air. "This is good. Good for you, and good for mankind as well. Ah… here I sit without the food I prepared. I will go get it."

Zac saw Avram wince in pain as he started to rise, and he jumped up from his chair. "No, you sit. I'll get it." He returned from the kitchen with a platter of sliced fresh tomatoes, feta cheese, olives, flatbread, and hummus. "This looks delicious." Zac set the plate in the center of the round table and returned to his chair.

"Help yourself!" Avram said.

Zac took a plate and scooped out some hummus with his flatbread.

Avram continued. "Are there other areas you wish help with that we haven't touched upon yet?"

Brian nodded. "Yes… actually, yes. There's an arrangement set up on a table in Nikolai's hidden laboratory. He must have been in the middle of an experiment. We think this is all critical information, as it seems to be the last thing he was working on before he died. On that table, is a projection scope and an accelerator with a recording device hung above the area as if to record an experiment. We were excited to see it but found no tape anywhere. And it appears the experiment was actually carried out, as it had been set on timers. But where would the tape be?"

Zac wiped his mouth with his napkin before adding, "We checked all the faux storage areas, and there were no documents, no notes, no tapes relating to this."

"Let me think for a minute," Avram said slowly. "I have a feeling this is something important to pursue. Zac, your father began experiments on enhancing cellular energy years ago. He knew that if he could crack the fundamentals of cellular energy and synthesize the information into practical applications, he could create great advances for mankind. It was his passion to find a means to end hunger and feed the world. Perhaps you should expand your studies in yet more areas, to delve deeper into his work—cell biology and developmental biology, I'd say. And oh… I have a person to connect you with who is a microbiologist. He is completely trustworthy and could most definitely be helpful. You could send him photos of the setup and equipment. At the least, even if he can't pinpoint what Nikolai was doing, he can shed light on the experiment."

"Excellent suggestion," Brian said.

Avram layered some tomato slices and cheese on his plate. "When I was there years ago, Nikolai was looking to cellular energy as a way of creating micro energy circuits that could be harnessed to power nanoparticles, but he discovered something that he kept to himself. He was looking at the mitochondria of a cell, the powerhouse, as an untapped energy potential. It has its own DNA, and many believe it evolved separately before being integrated into cells as the power generator.

"As Nikolai explained it, he felt the potential was universal and the key to the door of a new understanding of life from the cellular to the planetary. He was determined to unlock a fundamental secret of all cellular function that applied advanced physics to cellular energy. I imagine he was working on this at the time of his death. There must be a tape on this."

Zac shook his head. "I know. I keep thinking that too. There's a ton of them, and they aren't well labeled, so I've been getting through them slowly. Much of what I've heard I haven't understood, so that's been frustrating to me, and I'll have to go back and listen again as my knowledge base increases. But all your suggestions are really helping. Thanks."

Avram patted Zac's knee. "We will get this figured out. And we will stay in touch. I can't believe our time together has already flown by and you must ready yourselves to leave. My place will feel empty without the two of you. But you still have a great adventure in store—diving in the Red Sea. This trip will do you a world of good. I wish I could join you."

"Avram, we'd love to have you join us," Brian said.

"There was a day when I was so active. I loved sailing like you, diving, all sorts of things. Then this accident… and poof, my leg doesn't work well and is always causing me such pain. I would like to come to your town and join you on your boat sometime, but the pain becomes too much."

Zac looked up and stared at Brian, silently asking him a question. Brian received the message, closed his eyes and nodded.

Zac leaned forward in his chair, his elbows resting on his thighs. "Avram, Brian and I talked about this. I can help you with your pain."

Avram's eyebrows rose a notch. "How? What do you mean?"

"Let's just say I have the magic touch. Let's go into the living room and have you recline prone on the couch. I'll show you."

They all headed to the living room, and Avram stretched out on the couch as instructed.

"Now just relax and close your eyes and let me do the work."

Zac vigorously rubbed his hands together until he felt the familiar warm pulsations and an unusual color emitted from his fingertips. As his hands began to vibrate, he lightly touched the base of Avram's neck and slid his hands down his spine to the base. He repeated the motions, only this time, holding both hands a few inches above his spine, moving and gliding both hands up and down. Then he placed his left hand above Avram's painful hip, and with his right hand, he made a scooping motion, pushing the energy away from Avram's body. Zac redirected the energy several times.

"What are you feeling?" Zac asked.

"Like I'm vibrating," Avram said in a muffled voice.

"Okay, good. Let's get you standing now."

Avram slowly rose from the couch, and once he was solidly on his feet, Zac continued working the energies in Avram's body, clearing and releasing. He looked like a conductor moving his hands over an invisible outline of Avram's frame, rhythmically and methodically.

When he was finished, Zac said, "Now sit down and stay relaxed for a few minutes."

While Avram did as he was told, Zac and Brian went about clearing the breakfast things from the patio and doing the dishes in the kitchen. About ten minutes later, Zac heard quiet sobbing coming from the living room. Following the sound, he found Avram sitting on the couch, resting his head his hands, mumbling to himself "It's gone. The pain is gone! The agony has disappeared."

Zac held out his hands to him and gestured for him to rise. At first, Avram was wobbly. Zac placed a hand on Avram's shoulder for support. "Take your first steps slowly. Walking is going to feel different to you now."

Avram almost stumbled with his first step, but Zac held on to steady him. "Slowly. Let yourself bear equal weight through both legs now."

Hesitantly, Avram started walking across the room, increasing his speed little by little. There was no trace of his limp. Returning to Zac, he threw his arms around him in an embrace. "What have you done? What is this gift you have? I've not seen anything like his ever! The pain is gone. This is some kind of miracle. How can this be? Does this last or will it return?"

Zac teared up himself. "It will last."

Avram shuddered and put his hands to his face again, letting his tears release his emotions. "What is this gift? What is this gift of yours?"

Zac looked upward and then into Avram's eyes. "I wish I could answer that for you. I don't know, and it's something I want to, *need to*, know. I don't know where it came from. Do you know if my father had such a gift? Brian said my mother did not."

"No, Niko did not have such a gift. This I would have known."

They both sat on the couch. "I'm preaching here to the king of covert," Zac said, "but of course no one can know about this. I try to keep my gift controlled so as not to draw attention. Only a couple of people know about it. The fact is, I can heal things. I don't want people to know, as my life would no longer be my own. There would be lines to get to me, people following me everywhere, needing to be healed. I want to do good with my gift, but not in that way, and I'm not sure how that will play out yet. I trust in you completely that this will remain between us."

"Of course." Tears continued to roll down Avram's face. "The relief is incredible. I do not know how to thank you."

"You already have. The feeling is mutual."

Bidding farewell to Avram was more difficult than Zac had anticipated. *Now that he's pain-free, maybe he'll come visit us in the States.* Certainly Zac would return to visit him again. He felt a strong connection, an unbreakable bond—an invisible thread that connected him to his father. *There are no good-byes, only see you laters.*

❈   ❈   ❈

The diving trip to the Red Sea was better than Zac could have imagined. Anywhere he went with Brian was always a good time. Brian lived in the moment and appreciated life with a sense of lightness and good humor.

The location was beautiful, and the diving was beyond their wildest dreams. Brian had done his research and knew the requirements ahead of time, so they came prepared with their diving certificates, their professional logbooks showing they'd been on a dive within the past six months, and proof of their insurance. They rented their equipment and were assigned a master diver to provide them with an experience like no other. It was an interesting change from their typical dives, as the dive spots were reachable right off the shore. The coral reefs, of all different varieties, were like nothing they'd ever seen before—almost like alien life-forms. The colors were saturated, brilliant, and vivid, but Zac knew that the fluorescent colors meant the coral was suffering from heat stress.

It pleased Zac to see there were some protections in place for the marvelous reefs, as he was well aware that global warming was causing their destruction as the ocean waters heated up, along with ocean acidification and, of course, pollution. It caused him great sadness to think of the coral no longer thriving, but it was only a matter of time if action wasn't taken. The number of snorkelers and divers was regulated by park staff in an attempt to ensure that the ecosystem continued to thrive.

As usual, the sea creatures around Zac swam close to him, attracted to his energy. Brian and Zac snapped some great shots that would rival photos in *National Geographic*—the best one capturing Zac face-to-face with a Hawksbill sea turtle. They vowed to return to dive there again someday—maybe Avram could even join them.

❋   ❋   ❋

The long plane ride home gave Zac the space he needed for thinking through everything that had happened on their trip—sorting through the information he'd received, the emotions he'd experienced—and contemplating where to focus next. Helping to relieve Avram's pain was a highlight, and he realized how much his healing gift could help others. But he needed to understand where it came from. *I'm really becoming obsessed with these thoughts.* Since Avram confirmed it didn't come from his father's genes, and it wasn't from his mother, where did it come from? Was there any other person in the world like him? It made him wonder: *Just who am I?* That question was going to be one of his priorities. He was on a mission to find out the answer.

He had to.

PART FIVE
2025–2027

Though free to think and act, we are held together,
like the stars in the firmament, with ties inseparable.
These ties cannot be seen, but we can feel them.

—Nikola Tesla

Chapter Twenty
Brian
2025

WITH HANDS ON hips, feeling slightly overwhelmed, Brian stood in the center of his backyard storage shed, staring at the wooden shelves lined with row after row of old, dilapidated cardboard boxes. He shook his head. *Why didn't I take the time to label any of these? I don't even know where to begin to look.* Hannah often teased him about his tendency toward disorganization, and Olivia loved to accuse him of being a hoarder. He took their teasing in stride, characterizing those traits more as attributes than character flaws. In his mind, he simply thought it was prudent to be well prepared for emergencies. His easy-going, nonchalant nature had come in handy during the past fifteen years or so that he'd shared this home with his two favorite women. He always wondered what the neighbors thought of their unusual arrangement, but it didn't really matter—it worked for them.

Shortly after returning from his trip to Israel with Zac in 2011, Brian and Hannah finally professed their mutual love and commitment to become life partners. There was a bit of hesitation on Hannah's part to move in with Brian; she didn't want to place her best friend in an awkward situation, worried that Olivia might feel like she was intruding and move out. But after a family meeting, they'd all agreed that the three of them living together was what worked best. Both women made frequent trips to the Crow Reservation: Hannah, to work on her research and writing, and Olivia, to assume her role as the tribal shaman, to help care for her diabetic father, and to provide seasonal nursing services at the reservation clinic. And, of course, she wanted to spend time with Gus.

This arrangement also worked well for Brian, alleviating him from his guilt whenever he decided a sailing adventure was in order. They were three people who loved one another but also enjoyed maintaining their independence and pursuit of their individual interests.

Over the years, as the original *Quark* had begun to deteriorate, Brian stockpiled spare parts that he'd stashed in the storage shed at the back of their property. He called it his "just in case" project, assuming that any piece of equipment that can go wrong will. Fortunately, many of those older spare parts could still be used on *Quark II*. Not knowing exactly where to find what he was seeking, Brian reached up and pulled down the box closest to him from the top shelf. In this circumstance, he reluctantly acknowledged that Hannah was correct, wishing he'd been better organized and had clearly marked each and every box. While rummaging through the shed, he felt that familiar sense of excitement—next on the agenda was another sailing trip with Zac and Avram, and Brian needed to finish readying and provisioning *Quark II*. And he'd never leave without the boxes of spare parts.

Brian was so pleased that Avram agreed to join them on this particular cruise. It was hard to believe that well over a decade had passed since Zac healed Avram's leg pain. Was it a coincidence that Avram's general health had miraculously improved since then? Brian didn't think so. As impossible as it seemed, at age eighty-four, Avram possessed the vitality and spirit of a man twenty years younger. No one was more enthusiastic about this trip than Avram, calling it his "last hurrah."

Feeling the pressure to quickly grab what he needed and get to the marina, Brian rapidly yanked down one box after the other, placing them on the floor. Zac and Avram were already there preparing the boat, completing a safety and equipment check and stocking it with the nonperishables. Zac was in charge of assuring that all of the paperwork was in order and organized—original ownership documents, registration, all permits and licenses, clearance papers, insurance certificates, logbook, passports and visas, and other necessary records—while Avram was tasked with checking the communication system and inspecting the sails, lines, and rigging.

Noticing that one of the boxes had something illegible scribbled on the side in Zac's penmanship, Brian pulled open the flaps to see what was inside. To his surprise, it was filled with mementos, each one reflecting a special moment in Zac's life. *I feel so old looking at all of this stuff.* It was hard to believe he was already seventy and Zac, thirty-two.

Even in his rush, Brian couldn't help but become a bit distracted and caught up in sentimentality as he time-traveled with the items he retrieved from the box. As he picked through some of them, he welled up with emotion. He was so impressed with the man Zac had become, and he could feel his sister smiling at him with gratitude. During college, Zac had come home whenever he could—the two of them had a strong connection. Even when Zac worked on his experiments at the ranch, he always asked Brian to join him, and their mutual love of adventure and the sea would always be a shared bond.

Over the years, Avram—true to his word—had set Zac up to study abroad and work with various scientists during his vacations, and Brian was always included.

From the bottom of the box, Brian picked up Zac's cap and gown and his black and orange tiger sweatshirt—reminders of his university days at Princeton. Wanting to do something grand to celebrate his degrees in physics and mathematics, Brian had gifted Zac with the sailing trip of a lifetime.

Of course, Olivia and Hannah had also been invited on the trip, but Olivia still had no love of the sea and had been content to stay home on dry land in Maine along with her frequent trips to the ranch and the reservation. Hannah always supported Brian's love of sailing and went on short trips with him where she wouldn't lose sight of the coastline. She was perfectly satisfied busying herself with teaching, writing, and researching.

Brian and Zac were thrilled when Oscar agreed to take some much-needed leave from work to join in on the action for several months, and after picking up Avram at the marina in Sibenik, he also accompanied them for a few weeks. Digging down deeper into the box, Brian discovered a bag of dried figs and a Šestine umbrella in a paper bag. He grinned as he remembered the places where they'd found those souvenirs.

They'd been gone for the better part of a year. Brian had made a commitment early on to help Zac maintain a balance between his intense studies and relaxation. The day before they'd left on their trip, two government agents showed up at the house to talk to Zac—something that seemed to happen more frequently since Avram entered their lives—so the guys were even more eager to get away from the scrutiny of the government. It had been a magnificent trip—one Brian would never forget. The best part had been when all four were cruising Croatia's Dalmatian Coast together.

For six years following their sailing trip, Zac had buried himself in his studies, and during breaks, he'd confined himself in the lab poring over his father's work. Based on Nikolai's notes, Zac felt compelled to pursue additional areas of study, so he'd attended graduate school at Harvard, earning a master's degree in astrophysics followed by a doctorate in biological sciences. Never one to be impressed with certificates and awards, Zac had unceremoniously rolled, tied, and tossed his diplomas into the box. Brian decided that later, he'd frame them and hang them in their rightful spot on Zac's bedroom wall. He knew this gesture wouldn't matter to Zac, but Brian was incredibly proud of his nephew's achievements.

Brian glanced out the window, pondering Zac's life track. To fully understand the drawings of this father's that he'd always described as 'otherworldly,' Zac next decided to attend the Krieger School of Arts and Sciences, Center for Astrophysical Studies, at Johns Hopkins. The program even allowed him some online studies. To other people, the vast array of subjects Zac pursued made no sense, but Zac was honed in on a specific goal, and he and Brian both knew what he had to do to get there.

A final look in the box revealed some papers from Zac's teaching days. It had been Brian's suggestion, actually—to ease some of the weariness that had developed in Zac after all those years of being a student and to lift some of the heavy weight of responsibility he carried on his shoulders. Having sat in on many of Brian's lectures in the past, Zac had learned the art of making teaching fun, and now it was his turn to try his hand at it. So he became a guest lecturer for all grade levels—from elementary school up to college—teaching the younger generation how to become active in protecting the planet.

As Brian stared down at some of the notes the students had written to Zac, he inwardly smiled. *Of all the things I've tried to pass on to him, it makes me happiest to think I exposed him to the joys of teaching, not just learning.* Then he shook himself out of his reverie, recalling the task at hand. Five minutes later, Brian located the boxes of parts he was looking for, returned all the others to the shelves, and locked the shed behind him before racing off to the marina. It was time for their next adventure.

❋   ❋   ❋

That night, the house was still, with everyone fast asleep. At 2:00 a.m., the light on the speaker of Brian's voice-controlled intelligent personal assistant flashed and announced an incoming call from Oscar. Brian, groggy and disoriented from being awakened so abruptly, unburied his head from his pillow and responded, "Answer call from Oscar."

"Connecting," the device responded.

Brian sat up on the edge of his bed and yawned. "Hey, buddy… changed your mind and want to come with us?"

Brian could hear Oscar's heavy breathing on the other end, and he spoke rapidly with intense emotion. "Brian, listen carefully. This is an urgent call. It's truly a matter of life and death. Literally, I could get jailed for making this call and have to be fast. How long would it take you to provision *Quark II* for another long voyage?"

Brian shook his head to wake himself up. "Oscar, what the hell? Have you had a few drinks? Are you okay? We're pretty much done preparing the boat for our trip. Did you forget we're heading out in a few days? Just need to add some fresh food. What are you talking about?"

"No, I haven't been drinking, and this isn't a joke. I forgot you were going, but it couldn't be better timing for what we're up against. This is deadly serious. Just listen, please listen," Oscar pleaded. "You have just a few hours to act. All the borders will close shortly, and you'll be restricted from travel after that. Everyone will. So get out and get out now. Lea just boarded a plane for the Marquesas. The best I could do was to give her masks and antibiotics. I'm not sure she'll make it out before things close down. You need to head there right now. It may be one of the last safe places in the world for the next year or more.

"Remember when we talked about the possibility of North Korea having a biological weapons program? Well, now it's confirmed, because we've been attacked. North Korean sleeper agents disguised as janitors wore backpack sprayers to disperse a biological agent in airports, train stations, and subways around the world. They had it narrowed down to anthrax, smallpox, or the plague, and now the agent has been definitively identified as *Yersinia pestis*—pneumatic plague, with a two- to six-day incubation period. This is one of the world's most virulent human pathogens, classified by the CDC as a category A select agent.

"Look, all hell is about to break loose, Brian. I'm trying to save your lives, so listen carefully. Get to *Quark II* and get as far offshore as you can. Do it quickly. Leave everything behind and go. Well, take masks and antibiotics. I'm staying behind to lend my expertise to manage this and to help work on a vaccine. That's all I can do for you and your family. Please watch over Lea when you get there. Please. I have to go. Love you, buddy. Be safe. See you on the other side of this. Take care."

The call disconnected. Stupefied, Brian sat on the side of his bed for a few moments staring into space. He had to digest what Oscar had just said. Was this for real? Was he having a nightmare he needed to wake up from? How could he still be breathing when he felt like this? *What the hell? This is not a drill! I need to act quickly. I have lives to save. Thank God they're here in the house with me. Except for Hannah. She's doing research on the reservation. How can I help my precious Hannah? There's no time!*

A sensation of bitter cold traveled down Brian's spine and gripped him tightly in his gut. *So this is it. I need to stay calm. Our lives depend on my cool thinking.* He quickly roused Zac, Avram, and Olivia and briefed them on the dire circumstances. He urged them to get ready to leave immediately. "Now!" he yelled. "Grab you bug-out bags and let's bolt!"

Olivia's eyes watered and her voice shook. A vein throbbed in her forehead. "Brian, *please*. I beg you to let me warn Gus and my dad. And Hannah!"

"Of course, of course, I'm trying to reach Hannah right now, but she isn't picking up. Damn it! Why isn't she picking up? Try Gus, but do it quickly. There's nothing we can do for them now except to call and prepare them. Being on the reservation will provide them with some protection from contaminated outsiders. But you need to do it with care or Oscar could go to jail." He briefed her on what to tell Gus. "Make sure they know not to implicate Oscar in this."

"I'll speak to Gus in my dialect, okay? He'll understand it."

"Yes, that's good. Call. Hurry. We need to leave now."

As the men bustled around the house grabbing whatever essential items they could, Brian could hear Olivia talking to Gus. Although he didn't understand what she was saying, the panic in her voice made her emotions easy to read. He hoped she'd remembered everything he'd told her to communicate to Gus: to bring all the families that had not interacted with outsiders to the reservation. Those who had contact would have to wait out the incubation period at the perimeter. Everyone was to bring all of the seeds, honey, canned goods, masks, antibiotics, water, and fuel they could load in their cars. Frequent hand washing was a vital preventative practice, he'd warned. He'd told her to tell them to park the cars strategically, so their batteries and fuel could be used if it turned out to be a long ordeal.

Olivia wore a grim twist on her mouth when she ended her call. She told Brian that Gus would take charge and notify Hannah, her father, and the ranch hands. Through her tears, Brian assured her that was all she could do. "But we won't know if any of them make it until we return," she sobbed. "*If* we return."

Brian had everyone up and out of the house within fifteen minutes. Luckily, they still had possession of the truck Avram had rented at the airport upon his arrival, as well as Olivia's van. Zac and Olivia headed to the twenty-four-hour supermarket for more dried fruit and anything fresh while Avram drove to the gas station with all the jerry cans they'd already brought back from the marina earlier to fill for their trip. Before departing, Brian sprinted to his hidden vault for his stash of gold, critical documents, firearms and ammo. If he understood the implications of what was happening, he wouldn't be able to use cash or credit cards. He also grabbed a bag of antibiotics and masks. Zac's case full of Nikolai's tapes and journals was sitting on the coffee table. On impulse, he grabbed the case with the recorder and batteries.

As he headed toward the door, a rueful snicker escaped from his lips—he'd never been more grateful of his hoarding habit, knowing the spare boat parts were already loaded on board, and he was also thankful that the boat had extra tanks for long-distance travel. *Along with the jerry cans of diesel Avram's getting, we should have enough… we should have enough.* There was a watermaker on board, so drinking water wouldn't be an issue, and they had plenty of MREs stored for emergency meals.

After loading up his car, Brian returned to lock the door of the house. His fingers trembled as he turned the key. *Will we ever be returning to this house, our lives? Will Hannah be okay? How can I leave her behind?* Feeling the chill of the forty-five-degree night air, he reopened the door and grabbed a jacket. He stood and looked around the room one last time, turned out the light, and left. *Life will never be the same now…*

Brian met up with the others at the marina. In spite of the cool night air, sweat dripped down his face. They abandoned their vehicles, loaded up *Quark II,* and were thirty minutes off the coast when the first reports came in; people were dying, lots of people were dying. Brian hoped Lea would make it to the Marquesas without becoming infected.

At the helm, Brian's face was passive, and he breathed deeply. "Okay, here we go, gang. You know the old adage, head south until the butter melts." Brian's attempt at lightening the mood fell flat.

They were all speechless. Numb. Olivia sat near Brian and stared out into the sea holding her head in her hands. She turned to him, tears in her eyes. "Brian, tell me what's happening. I need to understand. I told Gus to pass out masks and goggles and to immediately use antibiotics as soon as anyone showed symptoms."

"I wish I knew more," Brian said. "Oscar often told me this threat has been building for years. People assumed North Korea was isolated and not capable of what we now know they are. It was reported that they got strains of the biological pathogens that cause diseases like the plague, smallpox, and anthrax from some source in Japan back in the late sixties. It was only a matter of time."

Avram sat next to Olivia and put his hand on her shoulder, trying to soothe her shaking. "I know how upsetting this is, and as Brian said, it was just a matter of time. In spite of the Biological Weapons Convention of 1972, countries continued to make biological weapons. Russia has stockpiles, and North Korea and Iraq were thought to also have these weapons. People were worried about nuclear weapons and focused on that, but they were warned that some countries also possessed chemical weapons and had ongoing biological weapons programs. Bill Gates even warned world leaders about this in 2017 and talked about how small terrorist groups could turn biological viruses into weapons and that governments were way too complacent about the level of risk. Unfortunately, he was right."

"I just can't believe this is happening. It's all so surreal." Olivia wrung her hands. "My brain just can't conceive of this!"

Avram's nostrils flared, and he wrinkled his brow. "We knew North Korea established a biological weapons program back in the sixties and produced weapons by the eighties. Of course, they've always denied it. Because they were vaccinating their own soldiers against smallpox and anthrax, we figured those would be their biological weapons of choice. There's been lots of reports that they're in possession of at least thirteen different biological agents, including those I said, as well as the plague."

Zac sat on the other side of Olivia and held her hand in his. In a soothing voice, he said, "I'm so sorry this is happening. I know how worried you are about your dad, Gus, Hannah, and all of the ranch and reservation people. Oscar previously told us that the United States has been aware of these possibilities for a long time. They anticipated it would be delivered via aerosols. Aerosols are pretty easy to disperse, as they're cheap and invisible. And unfortunately, international travel is a huge factor in how disease spreads.

"Apparently, if I understand correctly what Oscar told Uncle Brian, the North Koreans were working on a bioengineered drug-resistant strain of *Yersinia pestis*, the bacterium that causes the plague, using recombination technology. Released in aerosolized form—in places like airports and train stations, where the terrorists sprayed them—the bacilli can remain viable in the area for about an hour."

Olivia was speechless and just shook her head.

"It's been targeted as a biological weapon for quite some time because of the ability to mass-produce it with aerosol dissemination," Brian said. "There's a high fatality rate, even with the administration of antibiotics."

"It's been one of our greatest concerns," Avram said. "Even in the eighties, they were working on creating superbugs, resistant to treatment, by splicing together bits of DNA so they would kill faster. We even heard North Korea had been experimenting on their political prisoners. Heaven help mankind."

"Is there any chance our loved ones will live?" Olivia clutched at her throat and stared at Avram with beseeching eyes. "We have Gentamicin, Cipro, masks, coveralls, and gloves at the hospital on the reservation. I hope they take the necessary action with Gus having the info I gave him. Will that help?" Olivia asked.

Avram sighed and rubbed his temples. "Well, maybe, I certainly hope so. I'm so sorry to say this, but I do want to be honest. Pneumatic plague has a high fatality rate even with fast treatment. Treatment needs to be given within twenty-four hours. Who even knows with a possibly genetically altered version? At least life is pretty much self-contained on the reservation, and that's a good thing. So let's keep our hopes up."

"I feel so guilty leaving our loved ones behind. I'm going to call upon the Great Spirit to watch over them now." Olivia closed her eyes and began to chant.

No one said another word. They headed directly offshore into international waters toward the Azores, some eight hundred miles off the coast of Portugal. Olivia had felt seasick before the last line was untied at the dock. Zac held her head for several minutes, inoculating her with his healing energy until she fell asleep. When she awoke, the seasickness was gone.

They used a single sideband radio for long-distance communications. Brian monitored the airways, and they were all horrified by the news. Even accounting for the sensationalism of the American press, the world appeared to be in devastating chaos. It was hard for Brian to keep his mind on task. *I can't stop thinking about Hannah… I feel like I deserted her.*

For the time being, the southerly breeze was steady and strong. They knew that getting to the Panama Canal would be dangerous if they made the route between Cuba and Florida, so they agreed to take a safer, longer route. With a boat designed for racing, Brian estimated it would take them about ten days, depending on weather conditions. They sailed east of Puerto Rico and then swung due west to the canal, not knowing what to expect. Avram kept diligent watch for marauders, pirates, and other threats.

As they got close to the marina near the Panama Canal, Zac prepared the flags while Avram was at the helm. Once they arrived, they found themselves in a sea of yellow flags.

"What are they all for?" Olivia asked.

"Lots of bug-out boats here... The flags are flown by vessels that are declaring they're free from any contagious disease and requesting boarding and inspection by port state control," Zac said.

Brian spoke to the group after radio communication with the port authority. "This is pretty serious business going on here. Canal officials have always had strict guidelines for traversing the canal, but nothing like this. All tolls for the Panama Canal previously needed to be paid in cash; now payment to pass has to be paid in gold. I have it stored well out of sight. It had to be placed in a special container, and now it has to be washed with disinfectant before being pulled to the shoreline. Unfortunately, even gold doesn't guarantee safe passage during times like these."

Brian was right about it being strict. Every day for a week, they had to stand for fifteen minutes at the bow of the boat in order to be inspected through binoculars by the Panama Canal authorities that were looking for telltale signs of the plague. It was a nerve-racking experience because they witnessed people on boats who showed signs of illness, and those people were immediately shot and their boat destroyed. They weren't allowed onshore during the quarantine period. They still had some boat repairs to attend to, arranging for a robotic captain to guide their transit, and then waiting to be approved to proceed. It was a stressful time. They waited for two nightmarish weeks.

"How do we get through this canal if we're ever approved?" Olivia asked as she stood at the bow of the boat.

"The Panama Canal operates using a system of three locks," Zac explained. "In order to cross from the Atlantic to the Pacific, or vice versa, ships must travel through Gatun Lake, which is eighty-five feet above sea level. The locks raise and lower the ships from sea level in order to travel the lake."

Finally, they were approved to proceed. They were aware that ships normally stopped for several hours in Gatun Lake at the middle of the canal. But due to the circumstances, changes had been made and they traversed quickly—the authorities made it clear that travelers would be shot if there was any dumping as they passed from lock to lock and onward to the ocean.

Brian released a sigh of relief when they finally passed through the last lock and into the Pacific. He knew things could go wrong very quickly if he wasn't on the ball. At least none of them felt they were in danger of becoming ill—and even if they did, they felt reassured by Zac's healing presence.

After the sun set, the men took turns at the helm in four-hour shifts. With Zac at the helm, Brian sat next to Olivia on the foredeck with a cup of coffee. "How much longer until we're there?" Olivia asked.

Brian laughed. "You sound like a little kid on a road trip. It depends on the weather and the winds. With the speed this boat can go, I estimate about another three weeks, give or take a few days. Hang in there. You're doing great."

At times the seas were pretty rough, and Brian could see Olivia was stressed from the motion of the boat. Zac tried to distract her with fishing and dolphin watching, but most of the time, she did her best to stifle her feelings of pure terror.

They'd finally crossed the equator, and just being in the Southern Hemisphere gave Brian the terrifying sensation of being so far from Hannah. Hopefully, he'd be able to make contact with Oscar soon to get an update on how things were going back home.

At last, the mountainous ridges and volcanic peaks of the Marquesas rose from the sea. Brian was at the helm preparing to be battered by the powerful currents known to the area. The French Navy was on patrol but really didn't need to turn anyone away. The length of the cruise had eliminated all those who were infected.

They made landfall at Hiva Oa, and the check-in process took longer than they'd anticipated. They were required to post bond with the gendarmes for each person on the boat. Once completed, they headed to what was to be their new home for the foreseeable future—Tahuata, a small island with a population of fewer than one thousand. Lea and her family—descendants of the original inhabitants—were anxiously awaiting their arrival.

Brian took a deep breath and exhaled. They'd made it. But thoughts of home and the loved ones they'd left behind were always present. The concerns were overwhelming to Brian, and he choked back his emotions. He knew this was a time for being strong and calm. But he couldn't help but dwell on the what-ifs. What would the world look like when they returned? Would they even be *able* to return?

The questions, the doubts, and the anguish weighed heavily on his mind. For now, they were safe.

But was anyone else?

Chapter Twenty-One
Zac
2025

Z AC, LIKE HIS father, enjoyed the habit of daily meditative walks. Due to their location near the equator, the seawater was always warm. Shuffling his bare feet through the turquoise water of picture-perfect Hanamoenoa Bay—with the grainy sand gently massaging his feet and the morning sun warming his back—gave him a sense of peace.

The geographical isolation of the island provided them with a sense of security from the chaos going on in the world around them. The lush vegetation, the rugged landscape, the sparkling waterfalls—it was all the universe's poetry. Zac felt fortunate that they'd escaped the initial impact of the pandemic and that he was safely with his loved ones in a stunning, bountiful environment. Yet, he couldn't stop worrying about all those who were suffering.

Brian and Avram spent time fishing off of *Quark II*, and their plan was to use the resources of their boat to help the locals who were now partially cut off by the pandemic. Supply ships stopped coming, and they'd begun to ferry supplies between local islands until normal trade could be reestablished. Since cruise ships were no longer in service, the village sculptors, who relied on selling their intricate and unique bone and rosewood carvings and jewelry to tourists, were negatively impacted.

One morning, Zac met Olivia on their favorite part of the beach to enjoy a breakfast of freshly baked baguettes, papaya, pamplemousse, and coconut water. While they ate and chatted, Avram and Brian approached and plopped down on the sand next to them.

Avram grinned and pointed to the food spread out on the blanket before them. *"Profiter du petit-dejeuner?"* he asked.

"Oui," Olivia responded with a laugh. She handed them each a baguette.

"I have news," Brian said, his voice rising a few notches. "Thanks to satellite communication, I finally spoke to Oscar. I'm beyond happy to report that he's okay. And the news is… are you ready for this?" He paused. "Gus, John, and Hannah all made it through this. They're okay too!" He blew a puff of air out between his pursed lips.

Great sighs of relief and tears of joy followed his hopeful message. "He said most of the ranch hands and people on the reservation made it, although, sadly, there have been some losses. Oscar is doing his best to take care of the management of our house while we're gone, but in all areas, things are really in chaos and his advice for us is not to return yet." Brian hesitated and shook his head. "Schools and businesses are closed. There's a great deal of disinfecting going on as well as management of the dead. Hospitals are way overcrowded with insufficient staff and medications. Food supplies and essentials aren't getting in. The large number of deaths has impacted so many services. Plus, people are isolating themselves and afraid to leave their houses. There's difficulty getting any kind of supplies and basic life necessities.

"Oscar recommended we stay put until he gives the all clear. I feel like I can breathe again with the news that they're alive, but now I'm worried about their well-being. My fears have weighed so heavy on me. Not only do they have to deal with the pandemic, but due to the drought and another dreadfully dry year, fires are raging again in the Pacific Northwest and down the West Coast. There aren't enough emergency personnel to manage this. That's the last thing needed right now."

Zac pressed his lips together in a thin line. It actually hadn't crossed his mind that they wouldn't be returning home right away. He hadn't thought about the aftermath of this disaster. There were so many other things he'd been obsessing about that he hadn't really thought about the future until Brian said they should stay in place. At least they finally now had some communication, and, thank heaven, those closest to them were okay. But he couldn't stop fretting, and that underlying current of worry became a part of the landscape of their lives.

*   *   *

Several months quickly passed on the island, and Zac felt gratitude for the life they'd temporarily been given. Living on a boat and enjoying the splendor of nature with its bountiful tropical vegetation was a gift. The island people were kind and welcoming and always willing to share their limited resources. Learning the village ways of dancing and making music brought joy to their lives and served as a distraction when thoughts became heavy. Zac, Olivia, and Brian joined in with the villagers, to their great delight, playing drums and unique instruments. They spent their days snorkeling, riding bikes and horses, hiking, and fishing. With all that they were given, it made Zac feel a bit guilty for missing his previous life—he had so much he wanted to accomplish.

Brian and Avram were very adaptable and never complained, but Zac knew they harbored the sadness of the friends they'd lost. Avram hadn't been able to contact Yaffa or any of his family. Zac sensed he was quietly grieving. Considering the circumstances, Olivia was doing remarkably well and easily fit in with the islanders. Surprisingly, since shamanism had always been a "men only" tradition here, the natives embraced Olivia as one of their own and invited her to help with ceremonies and to assist with healings. She was in her element, except for the nagging "no-see-ums" that loved to bite her and cause her misery. The annoying insects left huge welts on her skin that itched like crazy. With his healing powers, Zac was able to ward them off so that they were no longer attracted to her.

Without all of his typical scientific and academic pursuits occupying his time, Zac found himself ruminating about the impact of the pandemic all around the world. *Should I have used my gift of healing in some way to help other people? Could I have done anything to prevent this disaster from happening? Should I be back home now, helping?* He'd originally thought it was best to use his gift for something larger in scope than healing ailing individuals. Still, it kept him up at night. Was he doing the right thing?

Zac's stomach ached whenever he thought about how humankind had brought so much pain and suffering upon themselves, intentionally attacking one another in the name of power and control, and the ongoing pursuit of stealing land and resources from others. What he'd learned from the Polynesians was the beauty of their beliefs. They demonstrated their inherent understanding that they were all interconnected and that what happened to one impacted all of them. They never hoarded their resources—they shared what they had, even with outsiders.

Zac experienced sensations of withdrawal being away from the lab. *I'm so lucky that Brian grabbed that case of tapes and journals. I need to think of other things than the devastation going on. My work helps keep me distracted from negative thoughts.* Between fishing and snorkeling, he spent a lot of time on the beach replaying tapes he'd previously listened to but hadn't had the knowledge to understand at that time. The challenge Zac faced was how to apply the information he was learning from his father's work. The combination of his own education, his father's information, and input from the best scientists Avram had introduced him to placed him in a unique position. His father's work with cells and energy states fascinated him, and he realized that the possibilities for applying these energy states went beyond cells. Tesla had theorized he could use the gravitational rotation of Earth to provide all of the power mankind would need. Zac wanted to explore these concepts further.

✳   ✳   ✳

On a Sunday, while most of the islanders were at church, Zac dragged his case of journals and tapes to the beach where he had hung a hammock for leisurely reading. He listened to them all now, some several times, except for the one marked Pimsleur: Learn To Speak English For Russian Speakers, Level II. He recognized the name Pimsleur as a language learning system that preceded Rosetta Stone and Babbel. He had no interest in listening to the tape his dad had apparently used to improve his English speaking skills. In fact, he wasn't even sure why he hadn't previously tossed it.

Picking it up, he noticed the label was peeling off at the corner. *This is interesting. What's it covering?* He tore it all the way off. Underneath was another label written in faded black ink: Sparkman Energy Experiment #BB 54-1992. *What? An energy experiment conducted by my dad back in 1992? Could this be the tape I've been looking for all these years? Right here under my nose the whole time? Was this mislabeled tape yet another one of* his father's decoys? Something to throw people off track?

Zac's hand shook as he hurriedly inserted the tape into his recorder, then reclined in the hammock to listen. He instantly broke out in goose bumps as soon as the introduction played and his father started dictating the date and topic. Finally! This was what he'd been looking for—the tape was the recording from his dad's final experiment. His last tape. More and more, as Zac listened, he began to understand the full implications of his father's work. In his beginning experiments, plant cells responded to energy shifts by increasing the energy states around them. But his last experiments were conducted to determine how a mammalian cell would react. *This is beyond fascinating*, he thought. Zac could tell from his father's voice that he was clearly excited about the next phase of his research.

After listening to all of the tape, and then again, Zac turned off the recorder and sat up on the hammock, staring out at the sea. *I'm dumbfounded.* The effects described in the experiment matched many of the traits that Zac possessed—the ones he referred to as his "gift." *Did I somehow end up being a part of my dad's experiment? If so, how?* He played out the sequence of events in his mind. Just how did he come to possess the heightened energy state his father had developed? *Let's see…,* he thought. He wrote it all out in bullet fashion on a piece of paper:

- *Dad died before I was born.*

- *He hadn't known Mom was pregnant.*

- *Olivia said that the day Dad died, Mom went into the lab to hide his journal and other important work before the agents came. She was in there a long time.*

- *Uncle Brian found her pearls in the area of the secret cave.*

- *Mom reported to Olivia that she'd had a pain in her abdomen that had caused her to pass out.*

• *Mom was in the cave in early September, and I was born in June.*

He felt he was on the cusp of finding his answer when a distant memory jogged his brain, providing him with a lightbulb moment. Thinking back many years ago, he remembered when Olivia brought home the two journals she'd found at the ranch. At the time, he'd been most intrigued by what he might discover about the father he'd never met and spent hours studying each page of the notebook. The sketches and experiments had intrigued him with ideas he'd wanted to re-create. When he decided to look through his mom's journal, though, he'd discovered it was locked. It had felt too painful to read her personal thoughts, and knowing what a private person she was, he felt like he'd be an intruder if he did. *I remember Sarah telling me that women's diaries contain secrets... Oh my God! Maybe the answer I've been seeking all along is actually in Mom's writings?*

Fortunately, both journals were still in the case next to him, so he reached down and pulled out his mother's cloth-covered diary. Using his jackknife, he cut through the strap to bypass the lock and flipped through the pages, glancing at the dates of the entries. The last time she'd written in it was dated September 3, 1992. It made sense. It was the end of that particular story of her life.

He flipped to the beginning of the entry and started reading about what she planned to plant in the garden that season and how sad she was that just last month her period had come, indicating that, once again, she wasn't pregnant. At that, he closed the diary abruptly and rubbed his temples. *This isn't right. I'm invading her most personal thoughts—thoughts she obviously never intended anyone to read.*

Later that afternoon, Zac took a walk with Olivia through the lush, wild island landscape and explained his dilemma and his reasons for not wanting to continue on with his mother's diary.

Olivia turned to Zac and placed both of her hands on each of his cheeks and stared directly in his eyes. "Zac, hear me out. I never asked, but I always just assumed that you had read it and that if there was anything you'd wanted to discuss, you would have come to me. Let me encourage you to go ahead and read it now. I knew your mother very well. She was a mother to me too. I *know* she would gladly and happily share her innermost thoughts with you, her beloved child."

"Are you sure?"

"I am completely sure, my Child of Light. Trust me on this."

He did always trust Olivia, so an hour later, he was back on the beach, diary in hand, looking for the best spot to plop down. Leaning his back against a coconut palm tree, he felt his hands trembling as vivid memories tumbled through his consciousness. The last day he saw his mother crossed his mind. She was talking on TV, the ground rattled, and she disappeared out of his life forever. The anguish of his loss was always present. *With the powers I have, why couldn't I have saved her? Why?*

With great pain and tears, he read her last entry. *I hope this is okay with you, Mom...*

> September 3, 1992
>
> Here I am recording the most horrible day of my life. Thank heaven Olivia is with me or I think I would completely fall apart. My heart is shattered, and I'm a broken woman. My love, my life, left me today. I've never imagined such a grievous pain. It's ripped a part of me away—the part of me I loved the most. The part of me that was Nikolai's heart. It's a loss so deep, an abyss of darkness. I'm hollow, empty. My love, where did you go and why didn't you take me too?
>
> Our last night together was intoxicating, and forever I will only want more of you. To taste you. To hold you. To love you. How is it possible

I will never feel your arms around me again and never feel your breath intermingled with mine?

I wish I understood why this had to happen. The only comfort I have that soothes my soul is that you died happy. At least you were able to realize your passion with a wonderful discovery that you hoped would change the world. Your joy and enthusiasm about this achievement was such an aphrodisiac to me. The delight on your face when you showed me what you had achieved will be forever magical to me. Your beautiful dancing cells☐ If you could have only seen that magnificent gleam in your eyes when the energized cell healed the one next to it. You did it! If only you could have completed your next experiment on your mammalian cell and changed the world. Perhaps☐ the world was not yet ready for that.

You will be happy to know (you probably already know) that I quickly went to hide your work. No one can have access to your discoveries. No one. The world we live in just isn't ready, as it is a world that seeks power and control and hoarding of knowledge and resources to monetize and weaponize.

I raced to your lab to hide all evidence of your discoveries. But, my darling, I don't know what I did. I was leaning over the table where your experiment sat ready to begin, and I must have hit the timer you'd set and turned it on! In your plant experiment, the activated cell caused the damaged cell to increase its vibrational state until they vibrated at the same higher frequency. It was glowing. Well, I tried to get a better look at the HeLa cell, and I wedged myself tightly between your accelerator, the table, and the microscope. The timers you'd set suddenly went off, and I saw a glow around the apparatus that grew into an unusual colored light. At that moment, the room burst into bright light followed by complete darkness. There was a clicking sound and then a sharp pain pierced my abdomen, and I must have fainted on the table. When I woke, the projection scope had been pushed to one side and the accelerator to the other. My love, I don't know what I did!

I had no idea how long I'd been passed out, so when I came to, I rushed to hide everything. I hid it in *the fake storage area and removed the tape from the recorder along with the evidence of the experiment—I hid that too. No sooner had I come through the outer lab doors than the agents were there to confiscate your materials!*

I hope I protected everything as you would have. I can't write any more. My tears are drenching this paper I write on. I don't know how I'll live without you, my Nikolai. All my love through all eternity. Until we meet again. Forever yours.

Zac was thunderstruck. Rendered speechless. He finally knew the truth—he'd been zapped when he was a developing zygote in his mother's womb! Olivia always called him a Child of Light, but he was actually *the* Child of Light. He couldn't believe what he'd read! Something told him not to share his discovery of the source of his gift with Olivia, but he couldn't wait to tell Brian and Avram. With that mystery solved, he could now move on to concentrate on other things. There was so much to accomplish. But there wasn't much he could do in terms of making the equipment he needed for his experiments on Tahuata, and he also had no idea what it would be like when he returned home.

Zac now felt fully ready to set his objectives and goals. He knew precisely what he wanted to do. Continuing his father's work with cellular energy states and developing safe sources of energy was important to him, so first, he'd modify his father's plans for the particle accelerator he'd found in the lab with this new information he'd just discovered. There were hungry people in the world to feed, now more than ever, and he knew that the experiment he couldn't wait to carry out could help.

After that, he wanted to explore the intriguing possibilities of how his father's energy discoveries would apply to outer space. Zac calculated that it would take ten more years to achieve the more grandiose plan for space travel.

Like his father before him, he'd begin with plant life.

❋   ❋   ❋

Another month passed, and Zac was thrilled to see how well Olivia continued to adjust to this new way of life. Perhaps something about it reminded her of her life on the reservation, and she seemed to be in her element on the island using her shamanic skills for healing. The more the native islanders sought her out as a shaman, the more interested Zac became.

As they sat in their favorite spot on the beach, soaking up the morning sun and talking over a cup of tea, Zac asked Olivia to explain her work with the islanders to him.

She squinted as she looked up to the sky, scrunching up her nose, thinking before she spoke. "I don't talk about the process much," she said, "as my father requested long ago that I not share his teachings. But to you, I'm comfortable sharing my ways. In fact, it was your father who told me that the word 'shamanism' comes from a Russian word, and it refers to a person 'who sees in the dark.' When I travel on a shamanic journey, I shift from this realm to a different realm." She brushed away a long strand of hair that had blown across her face from the breeze. "What I'm referring to are altered states of consciousness that normally people don't use. I step into these other realms, receive my wisdom and advice from the spirit world, and then I come back to this level of consciousness and heal the person or community in this physical world. My father referred to it as a 'shamanic state of consciousness.' It's not a conventional reality recognized by your average person."

Zac gave her a crooked smile. "I'm fascinated by this side of you that I really know nothing about. Tell me more."

She mindlessly picked up a handful of sand and let it softly sift through her fingers. "So, to understand what I do, you must understand the concept that we are not separate physical beings. We're a part of the wholeness of the universe—of all that is. I create gaps of consciousness, which I can then step into. Intense rhythmic stimulation can alter states of consciousness, and I do this through my chanting and drumming. Something you're very familiar with."

Zac grabbed her hand and squeezed it, nodded his head, and smiled. "Indeed, I am."

"Sometimes I work with energy healing similar to the way you heal. A shamanic healer knows how to move and manipulate the energy of someone's body and can pass on wisdom coming through from the spirit realm, but true healing must take place inside the spirit of the individual. When I talk to the people here, they recognize this. They understand it."

"Interesting. Go on…"

"In my shamanic journeys, I'll sometimes use plant medicine healing. Entheogenic plants are not looked upon as drugs, but as sacred medicines."

He cocked his head to the side. "Like ayahuasca or peyote cactus?"

"Exactly. And these lovely people use *Piper methysticum,* also known as 'kava kava,' which Hannah actually introduced me to, as it is used on the Hawaiian Islands. They call it 'awa' and use a special varietal called 'Hiwa.' Here, on this island, it's interesting, as the kava isn't limited to only shamans as some other plant medicines are. It's not considered hallucinogenic but has psychoactive effects. They have some special strains they've shared with me. Kava can facilitate contact with our ancestors and spirits of the departed. And they use it here in their rituals and ceremonies to help them maintain a connection to the spirit world. You'll see them using it socially too."

Zac leaned forward and directly connected with Olivia's eyes. "Wow, that's so intriguing. I'd like to try it."

She didn't hesitate. "Of course. I'll make some, and we can have it this evening. You can try it with me. I've been using the kava in ceremonies here. They make the drink, called 'grog,' by pounding dried kava root into a powder. Then they mix it with water and strain it. It's drunk from a bilo, the half shell of a coconut.

"Lea told me that kava has been used by Polynesian shamans to get them into a trance and commune with their gods and ancestors." Olivia laughed. "Warning. It tastes a bit like bitter mud or dirty water."

Zac laughed too. "I can deal with that. Can I experience the kava and chanting without you going on the shamanic journey for me? I'd just like to experience the effects. Maybe Uncle Brian and Avram would like to as well."

"I'm sure they would. We can do that tonight. Let them know not to eat dinner tonight, please. You either. I'll mix up some of my version of the grog with a little addition I add to make it stronger, and I'll bring us some kava bilos—the bowls we'll drink from. Would you mind stopping to see Lea and picking up a couple of drums and a didgeridoo for you?"

Zac let out a whoop and slapped his thigh. "Warning right back at you. I haven't played the didgeridoo for a long time. But no problem. I'll pick up those things and catch up with you later."

※　　　※　　　※

Evening fell after a glorious sunset, and everyone returned to the boat for the night. Of course Avram and Brian were up for the kava experience and didn't even mind skipping dinner. They gathered together on the trampoline on the boat, and Zac handed each person a drum.

"No one is on any kind of medication, are they? If so, I don't want you trying this," Olivia said.

Zac and Brian shook their heads, then Avram said, "I was on blood pressure medicine years ago, but then I started a new health regime"—here he gave Zac a conspiratorial wink—"and I haven't been on anything else since."

Olivia instructed everyone to begin with shamanic breathing. Then she rang a bell three times, and Olivia, Zac, and Brian began to drum in the way they always had. Olivia poured the grog into the kava bilos and handed one to each person to drink, and then she began to chant. They drank the kava, and Zac switched to play the didgeridoo while Brian drummed and Avram followed Brian's lead. It felt like old times jamming in their basement.

As he played, Zac noticed his lips became numb, and he could no longer form a seal on the didgeridoo. Soon, his tongue felt numb as well. A warm and tingly sensation coursed through his body, and his perception of time seemed distorted. The tension he held in his neck and shoulders melted away. Bright colors zoomed in and out in front of him as he mind-traveled into an altered state of consciousness.

It was at that moment that a mystical vision began to materialize before him. Something like a mist emerged as his vision continued to fully formulate, surrounding him in a surreal fog. A presence appeared as vibrating energy—a feminine energy—and she manifested above his head, the image developing like a Polaroid picture. She hovered before him, palms outstretched with Earth, Gaia, floating and rotating just inches above. It was his mother, Virginia. His eyes were fixed—he was mesmerized, in awe of her presence. The vision was nothing less than hypnotic and took his breath away as a sensation of sadness rushed over him. He missed her deeply. Pushing his sorrow aside, he gave in to the moment in order to experience the gift of seeing her face once again and basking in the presence of her loving energy.

The materializing vision was faint at first, but her image sharpened, as did his joy at seeing her. It was definitely her.

Satisfied it was indeed his mother, Zac lifted his eyes to gaze into hers and waited to see if she spoke. Was the sorrow in her eyes for him? He reached out with his hand to touch her. "Mother, I…"

In a soft voice that sounded like an echo, she spoke. "My son, I'm here with a message. I love you very much. I'm always with you. I come now to help you release your guilt. For some reason, you are thinking that because of your powers and your ability to heal that you were responsible for saving the people who've perished. Know this. The situation that's now impacting the world is not on you. Preventing this situation or fixing it is not what's expected of you. You're assuming a responsibility that goes way beyond what even you are capable of.

"The planet is in the midst of a major shift. It seems to be happening suddenly and quickly, but it's been mounting for ages. This shift is like nothing humans have ever seen. What's happening now, the disasters you see going on around you are ultimately the responsibility of mankind.

"Mother Earth is a living entity, and all living organisms seek balance—they strive to maintain homeostasis. Life is a dance of adaptations and modifications. All things exist in a relationship. Mother Earth has now reached her tipping point. As mankind overpopulates, overextends, overuses, and overexploits, she's making corrections to achieve her balance. The warnings continue to fall on deaf ears. You have the opportunity to be the messenger, the harbinger of things to come. Instead of looking at these occurrences as disasters, look at them as blessings. They're motivators to bring about the changes that are needed. When enough people are persuaded, then the solutions will come. As a rule, people tend not to take action until something negatively impacts them. With human beings, sometimes things of a monumental nature are needed to accomplish this. And sometimes disasters become the ignition spark to create astonishing technological breakthroughs leading to enhanced levels of global cooperation.

"Without these monumental changes, Earth is on a trajectory to more major catastrophes, and sometimes it takes disasters to wake people up—to motivate them to make changes. The message is to stop being complacent, to take action now. Everyone must do their part.

"For years, Earth has been sending out messages in the form of whispers. Always, always listen to messages when they are in the form of whispers. Because if you don't listen, and you don't hear them, they become shouts. And if you don't listen when they are shouts, they become screams. If you continue to ignore them, they become larger and much louder until you can't do anything but hear the message. Remember… first come the whispers. I love you, my son."

Her image disappeared into a fog, and Zac slept.

✻ ✻ ✻

As the sun rose over the horizon, Zac woke to the sensation of feeling slightly disoriented—something seemed different to him. He rubbed the matter out of his eyes and glanced around. Everyone was asleep where he'd last seen them sitting the night before—stretched out on cushions on the boat trampoline—leaving the empty kava bilos scattered about as the only indication of what had transpired the previous evening.

Although his pulse was sluggish, likely due to the kava, Zac couldn't contain his excitement. He'd seen his mother! *What an unbelievable experience.* It was her, and she'd left him with a message.

"Wake up, everybody," Zac said, his voice heavy with emotion. "You won't believe what I have to tell you!"

CHAPTER TWENTY-TWO
OLIVIA
2027

THE WATER TWINKLED in the sunlight like stars that had dropped from the night sky. Olivia reclined in Zac's hammock on the beach, contemplating life. What they'd hoped and prayed for was finally coming to pass—they were going home. Home! Oscar had finally given the all clear, and they began to prepare *Quark II* for departure from the place that had provided them with safety and love for the past two years. Thinking of the long boat voyage back almost made Olivia decide to stay on the island, but Zac had taught her how to sail over the past couple of years, so she felt more secure to handle whatever came to pass on the sea.

Over the past week, she'd spent a great deal of time pondering. *How has life at home changed?* Oscar was conscientious about giving them updates, but actually seeing things in person would be different. Was home still home?

In some ways, she was horrified by the information Oscar had shared, but in other ways, she was greatly relieved. From his reports, it sounded like life would never be entirely the same, but maybe that wasn't a completely terrible thing.

Oscar had told Brian that international plans for such disasters had been in place long before the pandemic took place, but actual preparation was lacking. It was next to impossible to determine where to focus limited funds, as there was no way to predict what type of threat and where the threat would occur. Prior to the pandemic, most reports indicated that the next major outbreak would be influenza, but if bioterrorism was involved, they suspected it would be anthrax. Even with all the international disease reporting and surveillance networks in place to ensure that a disaster on that scale would be thwarted, it was always a guessing game. The CDC had been on hyperalert since 9/11, and their Epidemic Intelligence Service had a detective team constantly investigating suspicions of bioterror.

Some of the cities in the United States that had been targeted were a surprise to Olivia: Washington, DC, and New York were obvious choices, but random spots down the East Coast had been hit, and the West Coast had been relatively spared. She didn't understand why Boise, Idaho, and Las Vegas were targets, but then nothing about the attack made sense to her. Fortunately, Montana and Maine weren't hit by the initial attack, but every state, every country, was affected by the repercussions.

Thankfully, since the Crow Reservation was relatively self-quarantined, most everyone survived. The ranch was also fairly protected with few casualties. But when the main cities were hit, hordes of people fled to more rural environments, so no place was totally spared.

The disease had spread rapidly in densely populated urban environments where people relied on public transportation. Oscar's initial description of events sounded like hell, and the cost of recovery numbered in the trillions.

Olivia played out in her mind the pure pandemonium she'd envisioned. Oscar had informed them how difficult it was, nearly impossible, to escape the cities. Borders immediately closed, and all mass transit shut down. People in cars, desperate to escape, sat on roads and freeways in complete gridlock. Many succumbed to the illness and died while waiting to escape, leaving cars stranded in the roads, blocking traffic, making it impossible to navigate. Looters stormed the cars, disregarded the dead, and stole whatever they had brought with them.

It didn't take long for people everywhere to turn on one another for the sake of self-preservation—the inner savage was quickly released. Stores ran out of supplies within a few days, and gangs were immediately established to obtain the necessities of food, water, guns, and ammunition. People who attempted to hunker in place were invaded by the hostile groups and thrown out of their homes and cars.

With people dying and fleeing, there just weren't enough living bodies to operate power plants, water utilities, and waste management facilities. Electricity went down. Gas pumps were empty. There was no running water, no working toilets, and no one to collect the trash and waste debris, causing rats and flies and other vermin to come out in droves, creating additional illnesses.

Communications shut down—no Internet, Wi-Fi, or TV. There was no refrigeration, no freezers, no fresh food, no working traffic lights. Planes were grounded, trains sat idle on their tracks, and buses stopped rolling the minute their tanks were empty.

Hospitals quickly reached overflowing status and doors were barricaded. Dead bodies piled up with no system to dispose of them, creating a stench and even more disease. There were no police, fire, or first responder services. International trade shut down. Production stopped. Banks closed down with no money in the ATMs. Money and credit cards were no good anyway. Postal service ceased. There were no alarm systems protecting homes, stores, and businesses, and no law enforcement to respond even if there were.

Infrastructure crumbled, affecting shipping and distribution centers, server clusters, and basically all of the interconnected modern technology.

Vacation resorts were the first areas survivors fled to, as well as agricultural areas where people thought they could grow food. Survivors had to develop, with limited resources and technology, a plan to deal with the debris of bodies scattered everywhere—close to two billion people worldwide had died.

Olivia felt simultaneously guilty and grateful that they had been living a life of ease while others suffered. But they all knew another catastrophe could hit at any time. Such incidents cause life-altering changes in attitudes.

At least Oscar was able to hold on to their home in Maine, which in itself seemed a miracle. Brian had paid for the purchase of the house in cash, and Oscar had asked some friends, who'd fortunately gotten out of New York early, to live there and watch over it. They were lucky this time. It was incredible that the disaster struck as they were prepping for a sailing trip. Things might have been very different if that hadn't been the case. Would this be a warning sign that people would heed? Would there be another global attack of this scale?

Zac had explained that in spite of the horrors of pandemics in the past, a few positive things came from them. Fewer people meant less demand on resources. He'd even read how biodiversity has a way of recovering over time with fewer humans using resources and causing pollution.

It would pain Olivia to say good-bye to the people she'd come to care about on this island, but her desire to be with Gus and her father was overwhelming. She'd long ago packed up her feelings so she could move on with the new life that was forced upon her, but now, at the thought of going home again, the sensations of anticipation flooded her. She missed her loved ones so much and thought about them and their well-being every day. She understood that good-byes were simply a part of life and never easy.

As Olivia helped ready the boat for the journey home, she saw Zac standing alone on the beach staring off into the distance. She approached him and placed her hand on his shoulder.

"My Child of Light... what has you so pensive?" As he turned to look at her, she saw grief written across his face.

Choked up, he couldn't respond.

She placed her open palms on his cheeks—her familiar gesture of comfort. "Tell me what it is," she said, her voice full of concern.

He stroked his beard and released a deep sigh. "I understand this, I truly do, but for my own selfish reasons, I'm not okay with it."

She gave him a puzzled look. "With what? I don't know what you're talking about."

"Sorry, I thought he'd already told you. Avram... Avram's not returning home with us." As he released the words, he released his tears.

Zac continued. "He said he's eighty-six years old and returning to Israel, with all the loss and changes, was more than he could cope with. Things are really bad there. And as you know, his darling Yaffa and all his family died in the pandemic, so he has no home to return to. He said he feels comfortable here and wants to live out his remaining years in a place of peace without the chaos he'd be returning to. His whole life has been one of chaos. Now, he just wants peace."

Olivia's eyes welled. "Oh, I didn't know he'd made this final decision. We'll miss him very much."

They walked together, shuffling their feet in the sand. "He's made good friendships, and people here care deeply for him," Zac said. "But the thing is, so do I. I want him to come home with us. He always has a home with us."

"Of course he does."

"Brian talked to him and invited him to live in our house with us. I mean, we're fortunate. Oscar said we have a home to come back to, as amazing as that seems. So we're lucky. And there's room for Avram there. I don't understand why he wouldn't come back and just be with us."

Olivia reached for his hand and squeezed it. "One of the hardest things we have to deal with is other people's choices. I'm sure he's searched his soul and decided what's best for him. We'll surely miss him very much. But in some ways, it'll be like starting over for many of us. Things back home have changed, and sometimes when you're very old, change is something that doesn't come easy.

"He's a proud man and doesn't want to end up being a burden as he continues to age. He's mentioned that," Olivia went on. "The villagers here will care for him. I know this is painful for you—for all of us, but especially you. Letting go is difficult, and you'll need to move into a state of love and grace for his sake so that accepting his decision will bring you to a place of greater peace. It's the hardest part of moving forward in life. Your love for each other will never die."

Olivia hoped she was giving Zac some comfort, but his face was still full of sorrow as he told her, "I thought he was going to come with us, but then he expressed that his reluctance to stay here, where he truly wanted to be, was because he didn't want to cause *us* pain. I know he loves us all, and he was also worried about there being one less body to crew on the way back, but he said he's old and tired and the peaceful lifestyle suits him. I don't want him to do something he doesn't want to do because I'm standing in the way of his decision."

"Well, I certainly can help crew now," Olivia reassured him, "since I've learned so much about sailing over the past two years. It'll never be anything I look forward to, but I can do my part." She looked off into the distance for a moment before continuing. "I hope everything goes smoothly having Lea on board. I relate to her fears—she's a land-lover like me."

"Brian's aware of her concerns and has already re-rigged the jacklines from bow to stern on both sides. We'll all use our sailing harnesses with tethers like we did coming here. I already tested the bails on the clips of the tethers. She'll be fine, and with everything I owe Oscar, keeping his wife safe will be my top priority."

"Agreed. You know, I admire you that you're not trying to hold Avram back—that you want him to make the best decision for himself. We'll do a collective drumming this evening with the villagers to help us with this monumental transition."

❊   ❊   ❊

That evening, their last on Tahuata, Olivia led the ceremony with the villagers. She dressed in a brightly colored shaman gown with a beaded headdress made for the occasion by Lea. She premeditated about the ceremony to put the intention forward to ask the spirits for a safe voyage for the travelers, for a gracious thank-you to the islanders for taking them in and treating them as family, and to ease the pain of leaving them, especially dear Avram.

Everyone gathered in a circle with Olivia in the center, holding a rattle and her drum. Zac and Brian skipped the kava since they were on duty on the sailboat the next morning, but the villagers passed around the bilos to share. While they were drinking, Olivia cleared the circle with the sound of her rattle. She began the ceremony by addressing the group.

"Rhythm is our universal language. It's one we all speak without the need for words, and it resonates as vibration deep in our souls. We all understand this language. Tonight we celebrate the wonder of life—of our connection as human beings. Tonight we beat our drums to express the joy we've had in our coming together as one. As we physically separate tomorrow, we know that our hearts are never apart. We are always interconnected just as the sun is to the moon and the moon to the sea. Every one of us is a part of the great cosmic system. We are a little bit of the stars and a little bit of the sand on the beach. We are the universe. We will drum to remember our one unified heartbeat."

The collective beat of the drums, gentle and in harmony, throbbed into the night air, hypnotic and mesmerizing.

❋   ❋   ❋

They all rose early the next day; it was time to leave—and time to say farewell to Avram. Olivia stood close to Zac to lend her moral support as he said good-bye. She'd been through his pains of separation before with his mother and his friend Sarah. She could feel the struggle he was going through to release Avram.

She stood stoic and watched as Avram and Zac embraced in one last, enduring hug. The corners of her lips turned upward as she saw the familiar unusual-colored light flowing from Zac's hands into Avram's body. She realized he had turned on his power, his light, to imbue Avram with healing energy one more time.

Avram stepped back from the embrace placing both hands on Zac's shoulders as he gazed deeply into his eyes. "I love you. You've been one of the greatest gifts I've been given. I'll always think of you as a son." Avram pressed the pad of his index finger to the pad of his thumb and reached over to touch Zac's chest. He drew his fingers in a line from Zac's heart to his own. "I just drew an invisible thread linking your heart to mine. We are forever connected."

Zac, choking back his emotion, wore a strained expression on his face. He closed his eyes as he rolled his head back and sucked in a deep breath. "I love you so much. Thank you, thank you for all you've given me. I hope I make you proud. There are no good-byes, only see you laters."

They vigorously clasped hands.

"*Shalom aleichem,* Zac Sparkman."

"*Aleichem shalom,* Avram Epstein."

They released their grasp, and Zac pressed his lips tightly together, turned on his heel, and quickly walked away. Olivia felt the thud of his anguish flowing through her body.

It was her turn to say her good-bye to Avram. She stood before him, touched her hand to his wrinkled cheek, then wrapped her arms around him in an embrace.

"Many blessings to you, my good friend," she whispered in his ear.

"And to you as well, dearest Olivia. Peace be with you, always."

Lea boarded *Quark II* first, along with Olivia. Standing at the stern of the boat, Olivia watched Brian through her binoculars as he motored the dinghy across the harbor to say his final good-byes and pick up Zac. To her delight, she spotted a rainbow—something she often witnessed on the island—which she took as a good sign. She could see Brian gesturing with his hands as he talked to Avram, then he leaned in for a lingering hug. She didn't have to hear what was said. She knew. Brian and Zac returned to *Quark II*, and they all began their long journey home. As she continued to stand at the stern of the boat, she watched Avram onshore waving until he was just a speck on the sand.

Brian radioed Oscar informing him when they'd be arriving in Maine. Oscar, Gus, and Hannah had all traveled to Portland to get the house ready and to greet them when they arrived. One last time, they let down the fenders, docked *Quark II,* and secured the lines.

Olivia looked up after disembarking. As she walked up the ramp of the marina, she could see the faces of people she loved looking through the window of the on-premises restaurant. There never was such joy. Olivia cried out and laughed at the same time. No amount of gratitude could have been greater than what she experienced at that very moment. They were all alive, well, and together again. They had a home to return to. She kneeled down on the ground and chanted to the Great Spirit in gratitude. She looked on as Oscar cried as he hugged his wife. Their grown children and grandchildren were there to greet her. Brian picked up Hannah and twirled her around, laughing and joyously singing. Zac fiercely grabbed on to Gus, giving him a huge bear hug.

Olivia was exhausted. She thought she could sleep for a million years. She stood from her kneeling position and gazed into the handsome face of Gus as he stood at the end of the ramp, smiling at her. She ran straight into his arms, burying her face in his chest. She lifted her head and raised her eyes to lovingly gaze up at him. "I'm home," she said. "I'm home."

PART SIX
2037–2039

Treat the Earth well: it was not given to you by your
parents, it was loaned to you by your children.
—Ancient Indian Proverb

CHAPTER TWENTY-THREE
ZAC
2037

IT WAS THE final days of autumn in the Pryor Mountains when the fleeting weeks of intense red and gold colors yielded to the cold gray and white of winter. The Sparkman ranch hands were busy preparing for the change in seasons.

Zac, relaxing in his new leather recliner, waited in the study of the ranch house while his digital assistant quickly organized and analyzed the data he'd entered to calculate the cost projections for the next quarter for his Sparkman Global Healthy Food Project. While he waited, he scanned the room and decided the house was sorely in need of some updates and fresh paint. They hadn't done many renovations over the years, and it was time to modernize.

He heard Brian singing in the kitchen as he prepared vegetables to stir-fry for their evening meal. The doorbell rang, and Brian yelled out, "I'll get it."

Zac heard Brian's cowboy boots clomping across the wooden floor, and after he opened the door, Zac picked up the sounds of muffled voices. Out of curiosity, he sauntered to the front door to see who was there.

Brian turned toward Zac when he heard him approach and rolled his eyes. "Hey, Zac, these two gentlemen are here to see you."

Zac stepped forward to get a look at them. "To see me?"

A man, probably in his thirties, medium height, in a suit and tie, stood at the door and said, "Sorry we didn't call first. We only had this address to contact you—didn't seem to have a current phone number I could find."

Sure you didn't, thought Zac. *Of course you have access to my phone number.* After all the years of being surveilled, he always immediately recognized a government agent. *The whole men-in-black thing is a bit dramatic and out of step with modern times,* he thought. Every agent he'd ever met looked like they'd been born in a suit, broad-shouldered, and wearing an expressionless look on their face. They appeared to be on high alert, looking back and forth to the right and left as though someone were going to jump out and attack them.

"So you're Dr. Sparkman? I'm Special Agent Crawford, and this is Special Agent Brockton." They each handed him their identification.

The second agent looked like the spitting image of the first. Zac studied their IDs and handed them back to the men. The old ones kept retiring and new ones kept replacing them.

"Yes, I'm Zac Sparkman. What can I do for you gentlemen?" He noticed Brian standing to the side, rubbing his jaw and wearing a scowl on his face.

"Wondered if we could have a few minutes of your time," Agent Brockton responded.

Should I cooperate or not? Zac thought. "Well, this isn't the best time. We're in the middle of making dinner. What's this about?"

Agent Crawford, maintaining his emotionless expression, rocked back and forth on his heels, shifting his weight. "Sorry for the inconvenience, but we were in the area and just had a couple of quick questions about your food project."

"I have lots of literature I can give you. Come on in and sit over there." Zac pointed in the direction of the couch. *Better to play nice and stay up-front with these guys.* Both men sat where Zac directed them.

"I'll go get you some information about the project." He glanced at Brian out of the corner of his eye, messaging him not to leave. "Join us, Uncle Brian."

Zac turned to the agents. "Gentlemen, this is my uncle. Dr. Brian Sutter."

Brian shook hands but remained standing with his arms across his chest while the men sat. They didn't speak.

Zac returned with two folders and handed one to each man.

Agent Crawford accepted his and said, "You've quickly become quite the VIP, Dr. Sparkman. Your project is very impressive. Your work has now become legendary, interestingly, and it seems that quite a few articles have been popping up online connecting you with your father, Dr. Nikolai Sparkman, in a series of what used to be conspiracy theories."

Zac sat on the edge of one of the easy chairs and laughed. "So what's new? What's that got to do with my food project?"

"Just small talk. Wondered what you thought of those theories."

"Which ones are you referring to? The one where my dad got his ideas and information from aliens? Or the one that says the extraterrestrials gave him materials and highly sensitive plans for advanced technology? I'll just say, people have always had a hard time accepting his level of genius and found all sorts of theories to discredit his work."

"Yeah," Agent Brockton responded. "Those and then some. You know, things that were once tinfoil-hat ideas back in your father's day no longer are just conspiracy theories. More than sixty-six percent of the population now believes there's life outside our planet."

Zac chuckled. "So you think my food project has something to do with that?"

"I'll be direct," Agent Brockton continued. "Word has it that your father developed a unique type of energy. As a matter of national security, we follow up on all tips. We're interested in your energy system in relation to your food project, so we thought we'd come straight to you."

Zac's mind drifted back to stories he'd heard about his father, some of them from Avram. He'd always known what the government surveillance was about—weaponry, plain and simple.

It actually all started with Nikola Tesla, not his father. Tesla had experimented with and created inventions using scalar energy. According to the historical accounts Zac had read, the U.S. government wasn't interested in Tesla's work, but the Germans and Russians were. One of Avram's scientist contacts told Zac that after Tesla's death, the Russians had gotten hold of his research and inventions—one in particular identified as a particle beam weapon.

Starting in the 1960s and continuing for decades, there was a space race going on—a race for world domination. What nation *didn't* want to gain military supremacy in space? Somewhere around 1960, President Khrushchev announced that "the Soviets had some superweapons." In fact, Zac had even been told that there had been a cover-up in 1977 in which the Russians shot down American shuttles and satellites with particle beam weapons, and that the United States also had secret weapons that used Tesla's technology.

It was said that the Soviet scalar weapons were capable of destroying the United States, and upon Nikolai's death, the U.S. government had evidently become suspicious that he hadn't actually broken allegiance with the Russian government and had been secretly working with them on weapons. After scrutinizing the journals and notes they'd confiscated from Nikolai without finding what they were looking for, the government assumed his information had been secretly squirreled away—and thus agents had kept their eyes and ears on, first, Virginia and, then, Zac all these years.

From everything Zac understood, and with confirmation from Avram, his father had serious worries that his cellular energy discovery would be weaponized. He wanted only to offer solutions to the world that would provide mankind with what it needed to sustain itself and advance, not further its obsession with weapons. And that's all Zac wanted too.

Zac felt Agent Crawford staring at him. Caught up in his thoughts, he had missed what he'd said. "Sorry, would you repeat that?" Zac asked.

"Your setup for the food project… Can we have one of our guys take a look at your design plans and equipment?"

"Hey, guys, I can assure you my project has nothing to do with weapons. All I'm trying to do is help feed the world," Zac said.

Agent Crawford scanned Zac up and down, apparently trying to read his body language. "We've been told by several reliable sources that you might be utilizing some unusual source of energy similar to your father's suspected area of focus. So I'll ask again: would you be willing to let our guys take a closer look?"

Zac let an uncomfortable silence fill the room for a few moments before he responded. "Well, this *is* my personal proprietary information"—he sighed deeply—"but I'm happy to go over the basics. And I've got to tell you, I've addressed this topic with a string of agents like you, ad nauseam, for years now. So again, for the benefit of the new guys: the day my father died, agents—your peers—came to retrieve all of his work and equipment. They swooped in, while my mother was still in shock, and took everything they could find. I was left with nothing of his—no journals, no lab equipment, no notes—and he died before I was born. Honestly, I'd love access to his work. As I've offered countless times before, I might even be able to assist the government's efforts if I were allowed to see what was confiscated."

"What about you, Dr. Sutter?" Agent Brockton asked, turning his gaze to Brian.

Brian finally spoke, still standing with arms crossed. "Sadly, I only met my brother-in-law once before he died, and I had no idea what he was working on. Nor would I understand it. My expertise lies in mathematics."

Zac walked toward the front door, suggesting the meeting was over. "I have your contact info, gentlemen, and I'll check up on who you are. If everything you've claimed is legit, I can get some additional information to you. But that's all I really have to offer. And my offer stands: if you're willing to turn over my father's work for my inspection and study, I may be able to help you in the ways you're seeking. Until then, that's all I have for you."

Both agents simultaneously stood. "Thanks for your time, Dr. Sparkman, Dr. Sutter. We appreciate you seeing us without prior notice. We'll be in touch."

After the men left, Brian closed the door, shook his head, and frowned at Zac. "I guess you'll have to pull the same Trojan horse trick your dad did—give them information that leads nowhere. This is getting really old."

"It is. I'm tired of being watched. My dad was right. Even after all these years, and maybe even more so now, the world is not ready for his discovery. All mankind seems to think about is how to dominate."

"I thought things would have changed after the pandemic, but it doesn't seem that way. I'm going to finish making dinner. Call you in a bit."

✳   ✳   ✳

Zac returned to his recliner to think. Brian's comment caused him to remember how he'd felt after his return home from Tahuata. After two years away, his attitude on life had changed. Initially, he was so grateful that his country still had an infrastructure to return to. He woke up every morning, glad to be in his own bed, happy that the lights went on and the toilet flushed. He appreciated what they'd all previously taken for granted: a mattress and a pillow, a coffeemaker, food in the refrigerator and cupboards, and clean drinking water from the faucet. And, of course, electricity.

He knew from experience that a disaster has a way of making a person feel grateful. But it didn't seem to last for long. As life continued on, most people seemed to acclimate to what they had, and then the desire for more and more emerged again.

Once they'd returned home, it was apparent to Zac that there were fewer people, yes, but even with that, resources were growing more scarce again as the population increased, causing an exceptionally high demand. At the same time, climate change caused more droughts and severe weather conditions, so crops couldn't sufficiently grow.

The simple fact was that all commodities had quickly been depleted. People had tapped what was easily accessible, so the search moved to the far reaches of Earth, like the Arctic and in the oceans. The planet had been exploited—its natural resources drained.

Once back home, Zac was anxious to dive into the work he'd constantly contemplated on the island. He'd had two years to think about the details of the projects he was eager to implement. He'd been obsessed with the information he'd found in his mother's diary, where he'd discovered the source of his special powers, and he couldn't wait to get back to the lab to carry out experiments on his own remarkable DNA.

As nostalgic and comforting as it was to be back in Maine, Montana offered more of an opportunity for all of Zac's loved ones to be together. After having gone through the bioterrorism experience, everyone just wanted to be near one another, so Brian rented out the house in Portland, and they headed to the ranch, with Olivia deciding to move in with Gus.

Zac thought about how there was now a net gain in the world population of one person every fifteen seconds. With the ever-increasing population, nations were clamoring for clean water and food. It was no surprise that farmland had become the number one global commodity—those people who possessed the most fertile land for crops had become the ones with control and power. Zac wasn't concerned about obtaining power; his mission was to provide a safe and plentiful source of food.

Once he'd gotten settled in at the ranch and established his home office there, multiple organizations were chomping at the bit for Zac to work for them. The world had lost many great scientists, and before his departure, Zac was respected as a young, promising, contemporary genius in mathematics and physics.

He'd immediately set to task researching and consulting with Avram's microbiologist friend on using extractions from his own unique DNA and coding the genes into plasmids with electrical current. His experiments combined with Nikolai's findings led to meeting his goal of producing the desired modifications in traits he sought for the survival of plant life in such conditions as drought and extreme temperatures. He used his connections at the Santa Fe Institute to create a think tank to begin a company to produce his modified seeds, activating them by using his father's process for cellular energy and waveforms.

The community at the Santa Fe Institute had, with some prodding, come to realize that scientific thinking had become too rigid and controlled by committees that were often narrow-minded and tended to approve projects that furthered their own agendas. They had no idea how advanced Zac's and Nikolai's work was in the fields of cell biology and physics. They were more than delighted to become involved in his food project, as few had guessed the extent of the devastating effects the altered climate would have on the ability to grow crops.

Now Zac had to deal with the government again and needed to come up with a strategy to throw them off track as to what he was doing—or, more specifically, how he was doing it. He had modified his father's discovery by amplifying energy without harming the host, using his cells to emit waveforms that transformed the cells around them to create vast amounts of energy. Using his modified accelerator, Zac was able to harness and focus the power needed to create the particles and waveforms.

Always conscientious about protecting the technology from abuse, seeds were shipped to a facility Zac had created near the ranch. It was a thrilling and satisfying moment when he'd demonstrated to his partners that his SES—Sparkman Energized Seeds—grew successfully with a fraction of the water and no pesticides. Best of all, most were perennial and would continue to produce food for years.

The scaled-down model of the accelerator from his father's designs was housed in a high-security building, along with the treated seeds that were then distributed around the world. Once the potential for his discovery went public, a deluge of requests for the seeds flooded the ranch.

By creating new food sources that withstood harsh elements without causing a reaction in the body's immune system, Zac had developed new tools for man to survive the perfect storm of plague, climate change, and diminished food production. He felt satisfied knowing that soon, a world ravaged by years of illness and poor nutrition would begin to heal.

But it was only one step. There was much more that needed to be accomplished for the planet to survive, let alone thrive. There were still many mountains to climb, and Zac's seeds were only the beginning.

❈　　❈　　❈

The smell of Brian's stir-fry wafted through Zac's nostrils, jolting him from his reverie.

"Soup's on," Brian called.

"This looks great. Thanks for cooking," Zac said as they sat down to eat. "What time will Hannah be back?"

"Probably not for a couple more hours. She was helping Olivia with a ceremony on the reservation. So right now it's just us guys."

Because he was so hungry, Zac shoveled down his food. Once he became aware of that, he slowed down his pace. "I'm feeling stressed after the beady-eyed agents' unannounced visit. Want to do a bilo of kava tonight? I'm in the mood for some relaxation, and Olivia left a pitcher of her special concoction in the refrigerator."

"Sounds good to me. You have some ideas on how to mislead these guys?"

"Yeah, I have a few ideas. Last thing my dad would have wanted was to have his world-altering discovery misused. Like you, though, I know that some of these so-called conspiracy theories about space and weaponry are really more truth than fiction. Ultimately, I'm sure the underlying objective the government had for funding my dad's work was to further secret military motives."

"Absolutely. And I have to say… there are times I have many more questions than answers as to where some of Nikolai's drawings and sketches—the very otherworldly ones—originated from," Brian said.

"I think about that too," Zac said as he pushed himself back from the table. "Dinner was great, thanks again. So let's get into relaxation mode. A bit of drumming, a bit of chanting, and some kava sounds good right now. If you want to set that up, I'll clean up and take care of the dishes."

As Zac loaded the dishwasher, he thought again about the kava-induced communication he had with his mother while still on Tahuata. He'd tried unsuccessfully to reproduce the experience but so far had been unable to do so.

Brian set out the drums in the living room along with two bilos filled with kava. They sat on the floor, tailor-fashion, while they drummed and chanted as Olivia had taught them. Soon, Zac felt the familiar numbness on his lips that spread like slow-moving lava throughout his body. The relaxation seeped through his muscles, leaving behind a sensation of heaviness and warmth while all his cares about the government agents melted away.

He didn't quite understand what had happened in the dream when his mother first appeared, only that he was an integral part of some kind of message and he needed to listen.

To his delight, the mystical vision he'd hoped to see materialized before him. Once again, the feminine vibrating energy manifested above his head—his mother had returned. Like before, she hovered before him, palms outstretched with Gaia floating and rotating just inches above. A sensation of comfort drifted through him. He listened carefully as he heard her speak in her soft, gentle voice.

"I'm here, my son, listen to me carefully. My time is brief. This message is given to help sustain humanity. Last time I was with you, I told you that mankind needed to heed the warning signs Mother Earth was sending because *first come the whispers.* Unfortunately, the whispers were not heeded in a large enough magnitude, and now the world is experiencing the messages as shouts that have materialized in severe earthly reactions as seen in disasters and shortages of resources.

"Each human being needs to do more to heal and balance the planet, and it needs to be done quickly. You've accomplished so much with your seed project, my son. I'm so proud of your hard work and endeavors. But as you know, this is only a step toward the work that needs to be accomplished. Mother Earth will continue to speak, as she is seeking balance and these messages are now becoming screams. They will increase and become amplified until every last person hears and understands.

"During your future nightly dreams, you'll receive information of what is coming to pass. Continue to share these messages with your fellow scientists, as well as with all of humankind.

"People must not wait for someone else to bring about the necessary changes without attempting to change themselves. Each individual is responsible for the script that is being written at each and every moment.

"They have a choice of what legacy they wish to leave—a world plundered and raped due to greed and corruption versus the personal gratification of a life lived in harmony with nature with a healthy population that flourishes and prospers.

"Mankind needs to realize that the entire biosphere is alive, in the sense that it has a consciousness. The universe is made up of vibrating energy that is interconnected and affected by each and every thing that takes place in the universe. The spirit of the living Earth is Gaia.

"For those who think there is nothing they can do, remember this change requires an internal shift that everyone can accomplish. Humans must live in their hearts and release their egos.

"It's time to make a choice. Will people choose to save themselves from their own self-destruction? Will there be a coming together of all, working in harmony and cooperation, or will things continue as they are, heading down a path that will end in the annihilation of this civilization?

People must understand that it isn't up to someone else to save them. Their power is within and always has been.

"My dearest son, please leave them with this message.

"Open your eyes. Heed the warnings. Do not blame anyone or anything else for this situation, for it is mankind that's the author of this story. What will you write on the next blank pages?

"I love you, my son… I love you."

CHAPTER TWENTY-FOUR
ZAC
2037

ZAC STOOD IN the center of their recently renovated ranch house kitchen, admiring the completed project, albeit still a bit confounded by the technology. It was a far cry from the kitchen he first stood in with his mother years ago while she made his favorite vegetable soup. He could almost smell it cooking. Forty years later and the kitchen would look unrecognizable to her. Everything was synchronized and controlled by an electronic device. Along the length of the southern window, there was an indoor area—dirtless—for growing food. The best part, at least as far as he was concerned, was that each appliance was self-cleaning. Olivia mentioned she hadn't yet learned how to use the hologram chef, 3-D food printer, or the gadget that measured the nutritional values of all ingredients. Of course Zac loved the refuse bin that instantly biodegraded anything plastic. Sensors controlled each and every function. The refrigerator actually kept track of available ingredients and placed a reorder when needed, with a drone delivery.

Olivia told Zac she'd had to learn an entirely new way to cook— gone were the old favorite meals of yesteryear. Global fisheries were now depleted, and the price of meat had skyrocketed, leaving most people eating plant-based diets.

It always felt like old times to Zac when he, Olivia, and Brian met, just the three of them, at the ranch. This time, they only had a few days to spend together before going their separate ways, so Olivia decided to break in the newly remodeled kitchen and prepare a home-cooked meal. Zac's plans were to return to the East Coast for the next stage of his space mission, Brian would be heading back to Maine for an adventure on *Quark II* with Hannah, and Olivia was, of course, staying in Montana with Gus.

As Zac stood in the kitchen, his mind continued to flood with more memories. He remembered sitting at the kitchen table putting together his favorite Barney and Baby Bop puzzle while his mother sang songs to him and baked chocolate chip cookies. It was always a time conducive to intimate sharing about their day.

Zac glanced up as Olivia entered the kitchen through the back door, emerging from the garden with a basket of peppers. She watched as Zac examined the various new high-tech gadgets. "This kitchen is a bit intimidating, isn't it?" she said with a chuckle. "A part of me misses the good old days."

"I hear you on that! What can I help you with? What are we making for dinner?" Zac asked.

"I'd love some help. Sit at the table, and I'll bring you some bell peppers to cut up the old-fashioned way." After he positioned himself at the table, she brought him a cutting board, knife, and the basket of vegetables.

"We're making eggplant and chickpea curry. You can seed and dice those peppers for me, please, while I roast the eggplant. First I have to figure out how to turn the oven on." The sound of her joyous laughter made Zac feel happy.

Zac chatted while Olivia prepared the eggplant and boiled the chickpeas, updating her on his latest vision of his mother in which she'd foretold what he'd be shown in his future dreams.

"So tell me your thoughts about this. What my mother predicted in my last vision has now happened. It's like the universe is downloading the future directly into my head while I sleep. I have to say, it's all very disturbing. I've delivered the warnings to the Santa Fe Institute team, created video podcasts, published an audiobook, written multiple web articles, and met with politicians to address these issues through policy, but I know there's always more to do—more people to reach, more to change."

"Personally, to me," Olivia said, "your greatest feat was your leadership and organization of the most impressive nonviolent march on Washington in history. Almost every big city in this country, as well as in other countries, participated. That's an incredible accomplishment, Zac. Because of you, your World Climate March brought your message in front of billions! When I was walking in the midst of hordes of people carrying globes on sticks, wearing Earth hats, and raising their giant cardboard cutouts of the planet as they paraded down the streets, it made me so proud of you. It's so evident that there are people who do care and people who are trying to get the message out there." Olivia emphasized her point by waving her wooden spoon in the air.

"Thanks. It was an impressive turnout. Still, so many people resist the facts that seem so obvious to me. The visions of the future that are downloaded into my dreams actually haunt me. I've seen the upcoming destruction of wildfires sweeping across southern Europe, an earthquake of a magnitude over 8.1 near the equator, unprecedented superstorms in the American Southeast, a huge Mississippi River flood… it goes on and on and on."

Olivia shook her head. "Those are not things I would care to have dreams, or rather nightmares, about, and I only hope these are things that *could* be and not things that *will* be. After the horrors that have happened over the past ten years, how much more can we take?"

"It's disconcerting. I've run out of ideas of how to be more effective. I'm done chopping these. What else can I do?"

"You can set the table if you want."

Zac continued the conversation as he stretched his arms to the upper shelf in the cupboard to grab the plates. "However, it's fascinating to see my mother again. I'm infatuated with these visions. I know they're nothing new to you, but I find them awesome. She's intent on getting her message out, and she repeats the words 'I am, I am.' I'm not exactly sure what she means, but I have a pretty good idea. What do you think?"

After adding cumin and garam marsala to the sauce, Olivia turned on the timer to let the pot simmer and sat at the table with Zac. "That's a topic near and dear to my heart. Mother Earth is more than a metaphor to my people. Indigenous wisdom says she's a living, breathing entity we must respect and honor—not in the human sense of the word, but she's still very much alive. Do you remember the verse I taught you? 'All is interrelated…' "

Zac grinned and interrupted. "I do. 'All is interrelated. Heaven and Earth, air and water. Where they are not together, there is only an incomplete piece. Who else is the enemy of Nature but he who mistakes himself for more intelligent than Nature, though it is the highest school for all of us.' " Zac recited.

Olivia smiled broadly. "That's it. It's from Mother Earth that we live. It's said that to lose consciousness with her is to lose touch with life.

"The 'I am' statement refers to the healing power of the universe. In a way, it's a calling out for healing energy. I remember telling you a story about this years ago when we were walking on a beach in Cape Cod, about how we must honor Gaia, the spirit of the living Earth. Mother Nature has a consciousness, because we're all connected to all aspects of the cosmos; 'I am' part of all that is. On any given day, so many people go from their home to their means of transport to their office and home again, and they miss out on any kind of connection with nature. And many people have difficulty recognizing their own connection with people outside their own family, much less their connectedness with Earth, a living, conscious entity, and the web of connection that extends far beyond our three dimensional world. That's what I love about being here on the ranch, working in the garden, and being on the reservation."

Zac got up to fill the water pitcher for dinner. "You know, that's so true. I'm so happy when I feel that closeness with nature, for me, especially out on the sea. That's when I feel at one with Mother Earth… Or when my feet are bare, and I walk in the grass, I feel a visceral connection. It was also the best part about being on Tahuata where I learned so much about living in a close relationship with nature and how to respect it."

Olivia nodded. "The individual who heals the self, heals all."

Zac lifted his eyebrows in thought. "What's interesting is how it all fits so snugly into science. Einstein recognized that everything in our universe, including us, is connected to each other at all times. When you affect one thing in the universe, everything is impacted in some way. My own father discovered something that connects the energy of the universe to all things—a unified theory. This energy allows cells to function at a state that has never been explained before. The space probe I developed uses the same kind of energy." He stroked his trimmed beard. "My ideas on space, my probe, are all things I want to further develop to help sustain and improve life."

Zac had a hard time containing his enthusiasm about his probe. He thought about it constantly. He found it both fascinating and intriguing that there was a space renaissance going on at an even more accelerated pace than what had occurred in the sixties—only this time, it was with private companies taking the lead. Space was being explored and exploited by many countries due to Earth's natural resources having been depleted and contaminated. Space travel, space mining, and the development of colonies on other planets had caught on not only as possibilities, but as necessities. Minerals and ores were now so scarce and expensive that it paid to mine on large asteroids.

With his reputation as a pioneering, well-established scientist, Zac made the probe project happen by delegating most of the seed project income to it, along with the financial commitment of a foundation controlled by deep-pocketed private investors who were extremely interested in planetary development.

This funding allowed Zac to build his Arthur C. Clarke (ACC) Antigravity Propulsion System and the Sparkman Multifunctional Galactic Probe, known as the SMGP, to safely and quickly penetrate deep space. He brought together the leading scientists from a variety of specialties to plan what was needed for his interstellar enterprise. Now the units had been assembled into the spacecraft that he'd christened the Sailfish, in honor of his and Brian's love of sailing and because the sailfish was the fastest fish in the ocean. He was ready to commence the first round of tests and was eager to initiate the next steps.

Zac stood and gazed out the window for a few minutes and then turned and stared deeply into Olivia's eyes. "You have such a depth of wisdom, Olivia. There's so much to explore in this cosmos of ours. With open minds and hearts, think of all we can accomplish to help humankind. When I look at my dad's sketches and notes, I get this sense of wonder at his creativity. And I keep having these thoughts of where this planet would be right now had he lived. So many inventions and other things had been shut down in history for various—"

He was interrupted mid-sentence when Brian burst into the kitchen, plunked a brown bag down on the counter, and grabbed Zac, then Olivia, giving them each a huge hug. Wearing the cowboy boots he always wore on the ranch, he bounced on his toes and rubbed his hands together, wearing the expression of a child at his birthday party. "I brought champagne. We're going to celebrate that *Sailfish* craft of yours. God, Zac, it's good to see you! How are things going with the project? Tell me everything! Did you just get in?"

"It's always great to see you too, Uncle Brian. I got in about two hours ago. I'll update you on the probe—in fact, you won't be able to shut me up. But right now I was just talking to Olivia about Dad's work. I was telling her about that drawing we discovered in his journal years ago. The one that was jaw-dropping. Remember it?"

"Remember it? Of course I do. Very distinctly." Brian turned one of the kitchen chairs around and straddled it. "Quite a few of his drawings looked otherworldly."

"Well, now I recognize years later, after training and study, how some of his renditions have actualized. For example, one drawing clearly was a solar sail space vessel. I plan to create one myself and send it on my probe into space," Zac said.

"What's a solar sail?" Olivia asked.

"They're so cool. Think of something that looks like a giant kite in space. In a way, it acts like a mirror, and when a photon from the sun hits it, it bounces off the sail and transfers its momentum. But I plan on exploring ways to accelerate the speed of the sail using solar wind. Hopefully, the *Sailfish* will unfurl a fast-moving sail in the near future. I knew you'd like the idea, Brian, 'cause I'll use solar wind to propel a giant sail—it'll be like sailing through the sky instead of the sea."

Brian laughed. "Great concept. I hope I live to see it. If I keep getting Zac's famous healing sessions, I may live to be one hundred and fifty."

Zac responded with a serious tone of voice. "There's no doubt about the energy treatments, Uncle Brian. Both of you are physically about twenty years younger than your actual age. My electromagnetic current is zapping and altering your DNA."

"Just don't revert me back to infancy," Brian said with a snicker. "I much prefer being an adult."

"Same goes for me," Olivia chimed in.

Olivia returned to the counter to stir the sauce. "I didn't realize that your father was into space exploration along with the million other ideas and concepts in that brilliant, unusual mind of his."

"Olivia, you wouldn't believe the stuff he drew sketches of. Brian and I were mesmerized. He had a plan for orbiting solar arrays that absorb direct sunlight and beam the energy back down to stations on the ground via radio waves. That's now been accomplished, actually. But he also had a unique inexpensive method for transporting those materials into orbit. That was the downside of the original plan—the cost."

Olivia placed bowls of cilantro rice and the steaming curry dish on the table, along with a basket of warm, crusty bread. "Dig in, you guys. I hope this tastes good. You know, I've always been curious how Nikolai came up with such ideas. Do they just pop into someone's head? Do they dream it?"

Brian and Zac briefly gazed at each other, then Zac watched Olivia's eyes darting back and forth between them. "What? Don't hold back… tell me!" she said.

"It's an interesting concept that Avram, who specialized in archeology, spoke of. He referenced an expert, by the name of…" Zac rolled his eyes up to the left as though searching for the information in his head. "Brian, what was his name?"

"I don't remember exactly… maybe Dr. Sharma?"

"Oh, I think that's right. Avram said Dr. Sharma was convinced that much of the ancient architecture in India came from information received from extraterrestrials. He said it's all documented in India's Sanskrit texts. It's been said, by one camp of individuals, that those ancient texts were given as a gift from a superior intelligence as a guide to benefit mankind."

Brian couldn't contain his enthusiasm. "Right… right… he said that the ancient Vedic texts have information, diagrams, and instructions for very advanced space devices, as well as advanced medicine. Some of them were the same diagrams Nikolai had in his journal." Brian jumped from his chair. "Let me sketch one for you." He grabbed a piece of paper and a pencil. "He had drawings of vimanas, ancient flying machines. Avram said the Chinese found some documents, written in Sanskrit, that they'd interpreted about twenty years ago, and what they discovered were instructions for interstellar spacecraft. Some researchers recently printed 3-D models based on those instructions, tested them, and found they could actually fly." Brian sketched out a drawing and handed it to Olivia. "One of them kind of looked like this. Looks like a flying beehive, doesn't it?"

Olivia looked at the paper. "It does," she said. "Sometimes I believe there's no such thing as discovery—only rediscovery. Everything to be known is already out there. We just need to find it. That's really fascinating. There's so much we could learn if we only were open to it."

"By the way," Zac said, "this curry dish you made is outstanding. Please pass the bowl so I can have some more. So... according to my father's notes, only when mankind is ready will the secrets of the universe be revealed, and where they'll be discovered is in space and deep in the seas. The information is currently being given to those who are open-minded and ready to receive it—meanwhile, preparing the rest of mankind for what will be revealed."

Brian leaned over and lightly squeezed Olivia's shoulder. "And, Olivia, those are wise words you just spoke. If you think outside the norm, you're often considered crazy—like what happened to Tesla, who some ended up labeling a madman."

"Space technology is so important now, with companies searching for planets to colonize," Zac said, "and methods and means to extract resources from asteroids and all. But for me, what I'd like to accomplish is to actually make contact and communicate with advanced extraterrestrials. Imagine what an opportunity that could be. I believe interstellar communication is right there on the horizon. Avram said I shouldn't bother looking into outer space as extraterrestrials have already been here and still are. Even if that's so, I want to explore the great beyond."

Olivia stood and went to the counter where three ramekins sat. "I made us crème brûlée for dessert." She brought the dishes to the table.

Brian beamed and rubbed his hands together. "You're so sweet. My favorite dessert!" He waited for Olivia to sit, holding his spoon poised above the hard caramelized top. "What's disappointing are all the years our country lost out on the achievements we could have made because the government turned away from our space program. Other countries have certainly benefited from exploration. Think of all the jobs it has created in other countries. I doubt the West can ever catch up because after the space race between India and China heightened and China took the lead, they've made tremendous leaps and bounds. What they've discovered has been astounding."

"Well, China went to space for the purpose of industrial development," Zac added, "and they certainly are succeeding. After building their newest space station, they quickly followed with successful manned missions to the moon and Mars."

Brian continued to dangle his spoon above his ramekin, swinging it as he talked. "Don't forget their search for intelligent life in the universe. For that, they built the largest spherical radio telescope in the world."

Zac nodded. "Thank goodness so many private companies fund various space projects. Space is now controlled by private international corporations, and I'm very grateful for the support and backing we've received through their grants and interest in our work."

Olivia reached over and clasped Zac's hand. "You were always obsessed with space, ever since you were a little boy. It's amazing and wonderful that now you're making your dreams come true. When we moved to Bennington, you insisted that Brian put stars on your bedroom ceiling in the pattern of the Hercules constellation."

Zac slapped his hand on the table and let out a hoot. "Oh yeah! I almost killed Uncle Brian when he fell off the ladder because I kept insisting he climb up and make the star Epsilon Herculis brighter."

Brian reached over and tousled Zac's hair affectionately. "Thank heaven, no pun intended, I got it right without breaking my neck. It was a labor of love."

Zac laughed, and his eyes shifted to Olivia. He hesitated briefly. "I don't know if my mom knew or mentioned this to you, but in his journal, my dad describes how, back in the 1960s, he and a team of fellow scientists in the Soviet Union had made extraterrestrial contact."

Olivia's eyes shot open wide. "What? I never heard him mention that."

"Yeah, it's true," Zac said. "I have to tell you this. Back in the sixties, the Soviet Union was really a contender for leadership in the space race. In 1961, they sent the first human into space. As a young scientist, and a genius in math and physics, they had my dad working on various space projects. It's been said, but we don't know the facts, that in 1943, when Tesla died, his papers were stolen from his safe. No one knows for sure who got them, but it wasn't long after that Russia appeared to be replicating his designs: his lightning machine, radio equipment, his wireless transmitter—"

Olivia interrupted. "Oh, like the one I helped you make a model of years ago."

Zac grinned and nodded. "Yes. Apparently, Tesla transmitted radio waves said to reach the far ends of the solar system and beyond. I also read that he received a signal from outer space that came via serial numerical codes. Other people have too, like Guglielmo Marconi. Marconi said he received an interplanetary signal, and a guy named David Todd, an astronomer, said he recorded extraterrestrial signals as well."

Brian, in his excitement, interjected. "And other strange things have happened—like voices heard, in an unknown language, reported by an astronaut named Gordon Cooper, who was talking to mission control from his Project Mercury capsule when he heard them. There are lots of reports like that."

Olivia glanced at Brian and laughed. "You're so funny. You're so caught up in this, you're holding your spoon over your dessert and haven't even cracked the top yet."

Brian laughed and jabbed his spoon into the hard golden sugar crust. He took a spoonful. "Ahh… creamy goodness. You've got the magic touch. Thank you."

"So back to my dad," Zac said. "According to Avram, my dad and fellow Russian scientists were told to build a tower like Tesla's—a two-hundred-eighty-foot tower. He said they received signals they had no doubt were from outer space."

"Avram had some fascinating stories to tell," Brian said. "He said the Soviet Union was extremely cooperative, but with the dissolution of the KGB, tons of secret documents were smuggled out or sold, revealing confidential information on all sorts of topics, one of them being UFO reports. They had thousands of reported cases and proof that extraterrestrials had visited because they have remnants of crashed spacecraft that utilized technology not yet invented on our planet."

Olivia brought coffee to the table and poured everyone a cup. "I can't say I'm really surprised to hear that. There are so many mysteries in life. I remember when I was a young girl and looked up at the Milky Way with my father, it was always so magical and mysterious. It seemed clear to me, in all its enormity, that life must abound in the great cosmos. So much space—beyond what we can humanly conceive. I don't believe that human beings are the center of anything. Some of my people believe that the great visionaries throughout time have been given advanced information from a superior intelligence to help forward mankind on Earth. Your father may have been given the gift of such information. Who knows?"

Zac pressed his lips together and nodded. "Yeah, I've heard that too about various visionaries. Not just people from the past either, but also people like Steve Jobs and Elon Musk. Were they given information to rapidly advance our technology? Maybe. My dad's journals are full of space illustrations and information that we hadn't conceived of yet. He even documented the places where we should look for intelligent extraterrestrial life. His information also includes warnings for mankind."

Olivia hit her palm to the side of her temple. "Ahh… do I really even want to know? Tell me…"

"Basically, it boils down to man must stay clear of nuclear power and be very wary of letting artificial intelligence get out of control."

Brian scraped the final remnants of custard from his dish and licked the spoon. Then he cleared the dessert plates and returned to his seat. "Now, how 'bout I crack open that bottle of champagne I brought to toast your *Sailfish*?" He grabbed the bottle to pop the cork while Olivia retrieved the flutes.

Once opened, Brian poured the bubbly elixir and handed Olivia and Zac each a glass. "Zac, how long can you stay before heading back to work on the probe? I'm going to stay here as long as you're here, then I'm heading back to Portland. Hannah and I are taking *Quark II* out. She may be old, but she's still well maintained. I'm talking about the boat, not Hannah," he chuckled.

"I need to leave on Sunday."

"And I'll take care of things here," Olivia said. "I'm so glad we had this opportunity for just the three of us to be together, like old times. Now let me offer a toast before we drink.

"Cheers to your success, my Child of Light, and to your future success with the Sparkman Multifunctional Galactic Probe, and to some future exciting and beneficial conversations with the extraterrestrials." She giggled. "Zac, your uncle and I could not be more impressed with your achievements—we're so proud of you, and we love you with all our hearts."

"Hear, hear," Brian said. "My exact sentiments."

They drank their champagne, and Zac said, "You know what I'd love to do after we're done? A jam session. Anyone game?"

"Of course!" they responded in unison.

As they stood to clear the remaining dishes, Zac turned to Brian, lifted an eyebrow, and spoke in a hushed tone of voice. "Uncle Brian, we need to go to the lab tomorrow. I have something very important to go over with you."

Brian stood still as he examined Zac's stern facial expression. "Well, that sounds a bit serious. First thing in the morning, okay?"

"Perfect," Zac said as he nodded his approval.

Zac gazed at the two people who had raised him with such love and devotion. He knew their family was one of the more unusual ones, but he couldn't have asked for anything better. He recalled his mother repeating his dad's favorite quote: "Love is where the wise man builds his home."

Spending time with his family was great, but he was also anxious to get back to analyze the test results from his probe and start the next phase. He had a strong gut feeling that a discovery was looming on the horizon. He just hoped it was going to be a good one.

CHAPTER TWENTY-FIVE
ZAC
2039

Z AC GLANCED AT the calendar on his watch to remind himself of the date: June 20, 2039. Today was the day he'd been looking forward to for years—sending his spacecraft into interstellar space.

His team was prepped and ready at the command center, and the excitement was electric. These were the moments the crew lived for—the real action. Typically, only a small percentage of their time was spent on controlling missions; the bulk of their work, by far, was consumed by developing the action plan, with the remainder dedicated to training. But today was a day where all things culminated.

Zac remembered back two years ago, when he'd sat in this same chair, his eyes darting around the room, taking in the hive of buzzing activity. In the burgeoning age of commercial spaceflight, he'd been thrilled that space exploration was progressing at a fast and furious pace. He remembered dreaming, as many scientists had, about discovering a functional means of speeding up the process of getting to the far reaches of outer space, once considered impossible. Zac had believed his dream had come true when his *Sailfish* spacecraft with its embedded Sparkman Multifunctional Galactic Probe and ACC Antigravity Propulsion System was launched.

Over the years, both wealth and fame had been showered upon Zac for his agricultural innovations, but he'd made it clear that his dream was to take man's quest for the stars as deep into space as possible.

After life had settled down from the turbulent times following the pandemic and launching the Sparkman Global Healthy Food Project that was now feeding and nourishing the world, Zac had finally been free to work on the most intriguing challenge yet: increasing the speed of space travel. Einstein had predicted—in 1916—the existence of gravitational waves: invisible cosmic ripples that occur when massive objects move through space-time and travel at the speed of light. The discovery that they actually exist was considered a pivotal scientific moment. The waves were shown to distort space-time, causing a "warp." With that finding, along with further understanding of the electromagnetic and field forces of deep space, Zac had envisioned spacecraft that could be constructed in space and sent not just to planets—but now the stars themselves were within reach.

His goal was to travel beyond the solar system into interstellar space, but one of the things Zac needed to devise first was a high-speed space-craft. To Zac, there was no point in spending vast amounts of money on a spacecraft that had a transit time of hundreds of years or more. He knew he had to overcome the restriction of the speed of light. Although warp speed was once thought to be only a science fiction construct, it was now a possibility. And though it was said that an object with mass couldn't move faster than the speed of light, Zac understood that, with warp speed, it wasn't the craft that would be moving, it would be space itself. The distortion of space would move the craft in a space bubble by creating a wave where the space in front contracts and the space behind expands. In order to expand the space, negative energy would be required. Creating negative vacuum energy was the key to making it functional, since a spacecraft would need negative energy at large densi-ties. With his father's energy discoveries, Zac was able to produce the negative vacuum generators—a technology that the *Sailfish* utilized with its doughnut-shaped oscillating ring around the craft.

As space warp expands and contracts space, the resultant benefit is speed. With Zac's plan, his spacecraft would travel at a highly acceler-ated rate. He believed the waveforms, which operated differently than the speed of light, had uses that far surpassed man's current comprehen-sion. The key was within Nikolai Sparkman's journal, where Zac had uncovered the answers that led to amazing breakthroughs in multiple fields from agriculture to medicine and now space travel.

The next challenge Zac had to solve was a guidance system. Any spacecraft traveling at greater than .75 light speed needed an antigravitational guidance system to avoid crashing into asteroids, stars, planets, and debris.

After many a failed experiment, Zac's spacecraft was designed with such a system. Deep inside of it was a small box developed on the basis of his father's findings—a device only Zac completely understood. The guidance system had the ability to work well at any of the speeds the ACC Antigravity Propulsion System could produce.

From the preliminary design review, to the assembly facility, to ground development and test preparation, Zac had overseen each step of the project. Once the probe was attached, it was sent on test missions taking it beyond the moon and back in order to test the cutting-edge drive system technology. Whereas, theoretically, the *Sailfish* could complete the trip in several minutes, Zac decided not to take any chances. The lunar test missions were plotted to take two hours. Due to Zac's inherited skepticism of governments, he didn't want to let on as to the speed capacity of the *Sailfish* yet. Not even Zac knew the actual top velocity the drive was ultimately capable of achieving.

✳   ✳   ✳

One of the flight engineers, hurrying through the control room, bumped into Zac's chair, jolting him back to the present moment and the current task at hand. The *Sailfish* was in geosynchronous orbit and completing another round of tests. Tracking stations around the world had been feeding in the latest positioning data, all of which was collated and assessed before sending the initiating signal that would begin fine-tuning the craft.

Zac now stood on the threshold of his second greatest accomplishment. He sat on the edge of his chair, rapidly tapping his feet on the floor, busy reviewing the initial data stream from the probe. He read and reread the data. *This has to work. I know it will*, he thought.

He glanced around the room to see that everything was in order. Over the past couple of years, the command center had gone through an overhaul to modernize some of the outdated equipment. A multitude of large screens surrounded the room, with a series of curved, built-in consoles with monitors facing them. Each station handled a specific function. Behind the consoles was a glass partition for visitors to observe the inner workings of the missions.

Zac returned to the business of watching each screen with great intensity. He could never assess all the input coming in; he was looking for patterns, flows, or anything that felt off. He was familiar with each planned study and had overseen the loading of programs and equipment for each.

Herman Broderick, his chief programming engineer, stood behind Zac, looking at the monitors. He was a burly man, almost menacing in appearance, but really as gentle as a lamb. He unwrapped a submarine sandwich and handed half to Zac. "Here. Just a reminder that you *are* a human being and you do need to eat once in a while. The body actually requires some nourishment." He held the enormous sandwich in his two hands—calloused, with nails bitten to the quick—and took a huge bite as a creamy white sauce dribbled down his lips into his scruffy beard. He licked each of his fingers one by one, making a slurping sound, then wiped his beard with the back of his hand.

Without turning to look at him, keeping his eyes steadfast on the screen, Zac accepted the sandwich, setting it on a piece of scrap paper sitting on the desk. "Thanks."

Herm continued munching on his sandwich with his mouth open, garbling his words. "I'm going to grab a cup of coffee to wash this down. Want me to get you one too?"

Again, without breaking eye contact from the screen, Zac replied. "Uh… what? Oh, coffee. Yeah, sure. Black, please."

"Be right back. Hold down the fort."

When Herm returned with two cups of steaming coffee, he once again stood behind Zac, looking over his shoulder while he continued to watch Zac's monitors. He set one coffee cup down next to Zac's untouched sandwich and proceeded to gulp his own while it was still practically boiling hot, burning his tongue in the process. "Crap," he yelled out.

Zac muttered something incomprehensible in response. In deep concentration, he didn't have much time for inconsequential talk.

Herm scanned the screens with his eagle eyes. "Wait a minute, what was that?" He pointed to the screen with the hand that held his coffee, spilling some on the floor in the process. He knew the programs by heart, and he was certain something unusual had appeared on the monitor: it was briefly there and then gone in an instant.

"What the heck?" Herm sat down next to Zac. "I need to rerun this test. I saw something." He repeated the test. "Hmm… nothing is showing up."

Zac chewed his lower lip and scowled. "What do you think it was?"

"Um… I'm not sure. It was only there briefly, and I probably would have missed it if I'd looked away for a second. I'm going to run everything once more."

He set to task as Zac observed. *I can relax. If Herm can't detect anything, it's all good.*

Once again, Herm reran the test. "All clear," he said. "My mind was probably just playing tricks on me."

Zac blew air out between his lips and sighed. "Whew."

An exuberant television reporter, a science nerd in appearance, flitted from work station to work station. Her enthusiasm from bearing witness to the awe-inspiring events unfolding right before her very eyes was more than evident.

She approached and stood to the side of Zac, recording device in hand, as he studied his monitor. "Dr. Sparkman, I met you before. I'm Barbara McClusky from BR-TV news. Do you have a moment?" She extended her free hand to shake.

Zac patiently and happily made time for anyone interested in his projects, thoughtfully answering their onslaught of questions. He swiveled in his chair, turning to respond to the woman vigorously tapping on her electronic device.

"Sure," he responded as he shook her hand.

"I have a question. Is it correct to say that the *Sailfish* made it to the moon in two hours?"

"Yes, that's correct," Zac said. "One of the things that the *Sailfish* provides is the speed that we need. The old Apollo rocket ships took three days to reach the moon."

Herm interjected. "That's right. Early probes to Mars and Pluto could pass by the moon in under nine hours, and that's without decreasing speed to enter lunar orbit."

Barbara pulled an empty chair next to Zac's and sat. "I have so many questions to ask after reading some of your work. Could you explain more to me about how antimatter has the ability to shut off quantum entanglement and its impact on antigravity? And, of course, that leads to my additional questions about your antigravity propulsion system."

Zac glanced at the back of the room and beamed. "I'm so sorry, Barbara, but my aunt and uncle just got here, and I need to greet them. Herman will be glad to answer any additional questions you have." He smiled and shook her hand again and bounded to Olivia and Brian, wrapping them in hugs. "You made it! I didn't think you'd get here on time."

"Horrid traffic. We didn't miss anything, did we?" Brian was grinning from ear to ear.

"This place has changed a lot since the last time we were here," Olivia said as she looked around. "I'm going to have to take a self-tour. I'm so impressed. This is such an exciting day." She gave Zac another hug.

"You haven't missed anything yet. You guys can come sit by me and watch the action. You need anything? Coffee? Bottled water?"

"Zac, I'm going to sit over there in the visitor section," Olivia said. "I don't want to get in the way. This moment's for you and Brian." She squeezed his shoulder. "I'm good." She took off to scope out the updated environment while Zac pulled up a chair next to him for Brian and pointed to the various monitors. "This one's used as a PC, this one's for access to telemetry analysis, and this one's for the audio communication system. We all have a headset and a set of loops. The flight controllers sitting at their consoles will be using telemetry to monitor the mission in real time."

Brian's whole face lit up as his eyes darted from monitor to monitor. "I can't wait to see what this craft of yours can do in terms of speed."

"I'm excited about that too, but right now my major concern is to safely guide her as she soars through space. It's my special box, tucked away aboard the ship, that's my survival insurance at these tremendous speeds."

"So much to think about," Brian said, shaking his head. "After it leaves orbit, then what happens?"

"It'll take the *Sailfish* about a week before we slow the engines as she approaches the outer limits. Once in place, each system has to be individually triggered for tracking: activation of each programmed task, calibration of the measuring instruments, and general review of the craft's integrity. Hours of prep will be needed before turning the probe's multiple antennae and satellite dishes toward Earth to begin calibrating several hundred computerized instruments."

Brian shook his head. "I'm so impressed, Zac. Just so impressed."

❈   ❈   ❈

Finally, it was time. The entire room was as hushed as a library. Zac's fingers trembled with eagerness and anticipation. "Okay, team, this is it," he announced. "The moment has come! Stand by… five, four, three, two, one. Engage drive at one one-thousandth light speed."

With minimal gravitational forces holding back the *Sailfish*, it quickly moved out of Earth's orbit. Multiple satellite and ground-based tracking stations followed the craft, as most of mankind held its collective breath waiting to see just how quickly the *Sailfish* could travel through space. There was no telling what future discoveries could be made.

Initially, the control room remained quiet as everyone concentrated on their jobs. Later, the excitement became palpable. People clapped, slapped backs, and cheered. Everything had gone by the book. Someone popped the corks on several bottles of champagne as an explosion of laughter and chatter filled the room. With the craft at the outer fringes of the solar system, its signal would take some time to reach Earth. First, radio waves would confirm the general position of the spacecraft, then, after an hour, laser signals would begin connecting the probe to a cleverly designed network of laser stations that would fix its exact position and create an optical laser link to Earth.

Feeling buoyant and riding on the high of success, Zac stood to address his colleagues. "Everyone, everyone, gather round. I just want to commend all of you on a great job. Thank you all for the unusual hours you've been keeping. I know you're all exhausted. Now go home. I'll keep an eye on things tonight. Go get some sleep. As you all well know, there's so much to do over the next several days that we'll all need to be rested and alert."

No one argued. The probe had been programmed to turn its attention toward Earth and wait silently in space until everything was ready. Nothing more needed to be done for now.

Since Zac planned to spend the night in the control room, Brian and Olivia ordered take-out food to share with him before they headed to his apartment for the night.

Zac was tired. But it was a good tired, earned from all his hard work and effort.

He briefly fell asleep at the console. Once again, his mother visited him, echoing the words "I am, I am."

CHAPTER TWENTY-SIX
ZAC
2039

H E DIDN'T HAVE much time to spend with Brian and Olivia during the week after launching the *Sailfish* into deep space, but at least Zac was able to have dinner with them each night. They understood he had to work, as there was still a great deal of preparation he needed to attend to. He felt comforted to have their support, and he enjoyed their lively discussions with an appreciation of how their viewpoints, one from the world of science and one based on ancient wisdom, often seemed to coincide.

This morning they were leaving to return home, and after he said good-bye to them, Zac drove to work and entered the control room with a steaming cup of coffee in hand. Some of the staff had already assembled in the control center and had begun analyzing the incoming data. The probe was in place at the edge of the heliosphere—as detected by the plasma wave instrument—functioning and awaiting its next command. Zac conferred with staff and several scientists who'd contributed to the *Sailfish* project about a series of experiments he wanted to proceed with.

A few years prior, Zac had been involved with a privately funded unmanned Martian project that was studying the Earth and yielding copious amounts of data. Zac suggested tuning the probe toward Earth from its position in the far corners of the solar system in order to compare the Martian data to what the SMGP would produce. There was a consensus to run the experiment, and for the better part of a day, calculations were made, instructions set up, and, finally, the first signal was sent to the probe to focus its systems on a tiny planet millions of miles away—Earth.

The laser navigational stations around the world lit up and sent the positioning signals. Next, the probe was informed that all of its instruments would be coming online in a specific sequence. As the data was collected, some of the input was analyzed at the control center while other data was sent to the scientific teams that had developed that particular experiment. Once everything was collected, the probe would be placed in limbo until the information and the probe's responses could be assessed and the next target selected.

While monitoring an incoming data stream, Herm's attention was provoked. He called Zac over. "Did you see it, Zac? It happened again. That momentary change in the program pattern." Zac nodded. Herm was the only person besides Zac who'd detected it. He called it to the attention of others, but no one else had noticed. "I must be sleep-deprived or something. I guess it's just a ghost pattern. Nothing serious. They all acted surprised when I asked if they'd seen it."

"You sure?" Zac asked. He knew sophisticated programmers could readily identify ghost program variables, but this flutter wasn't like any of those and others would have noticed. Herm was sure he'd seen something, but what? *I wonder why we're seeing it again...*

Zac knew more about the probe's functions than anyone on the planet, and for this phase, he was needed to ensure that the interconnectivity of all the programs was properly functioning. They couldn't afford for even one individual component to fail. The extensive network within the guidance systems was all Zac's responsibility. The source of power for the probe remained a secret, and everyone who was connected with the project was required to sign a confidentiality agreement.

"Alpha Team up," Zac said to the group, after checking his watch. The Beta and Gamma Teams, exhausted by the sheer volume of data they were collecting, put their programs on standby and left until their next shift.

Zac's experiment wasn't on the manifest, and even the Alpha Team was unaware of the small signal box that had been placed in the craft. Zac had pushed his father's work a step further by taking the super-energy states he'd discovered and developing them to the most macroscopic level yet.

Nikolai's research had unlocked key energy states at the cellular level, and in the same way nonlinear mathematics and physics had grown out of Newton's and Einstein's understanding of the universe, Zac sought to discover if these energies existed at the planetary level. For now, he still needed to keep his father's work a secret, and if his suppositions proved true, most of his findings would be given to the world free of charge.

After a full day of analyzing data, Zac's eyeballs literally ached and his eyelids were on the verge of closing. Before he left to go home to get some sleep, he sent a command signal for a data dump into the computer in his office. *This information is for my eyes only. I want one more look to ensure everything is ready.*

Zac dashed home, grabbed a sandwich, took a shower, and was eager to crawl under his sheets for some deep sleep. Meanwhile, the control center personnel worked in teams around the clock until all of the systems had come online and were functioning.

As soon as Zac's head hit the softness and comfort of his pillow, he felt his body start to disassociate from his mind as he drifted into a hypnogogic state—somewhere between asleep and awake—where reality begins to warp and distort. It was in that space where the mystic, surreal vision of his mother once again emerged. He was now familiar with her soft, haunting voice and with her hands holding the rotating Earth.

"You are tired, my son, so just listen. It's now the moment to give the world its final warnings. Time is short. People must know what's coming and why. There are those who will not survive what's about to happen, but for those who do, they must make the choice as to how they're going to continue living their lives. This is not said to produce panic. It's to let Earth's people know that they can and must make changes. It's up to them to do so. Now, instead of words, I'll show you."

As she'd said, the messages didn't come in words. Instead, Zac received them as though they were movies of actual events—clear pictures, in high definition, materialized before him, and none of them were like the Earth he'd ever seen before. He was aware that the pictures were generated from somewhere very far away, where time was of no consequence.

He could see it all. The great monuments around the world had been built on energy lines that, when connected, created the formation of a web—an electromagnetic field of energy, an energy web referred to as an "Earth Grid." Everyone and everything was a part of the matrix on this grid—connected in a synchronous manner, operating in a cosmic dance of infinite energy. The intricate web covered the planet in a connection of consciousness, moving in a fluid constant state of adjustment as it continually balanced itself to find a state of harmony and equilibrium within the Earth, mankind, and the entire cosmos.

Zac was mesmerized by how every particle on the planet was in constant vibration, and the human body was constantly responding. Human beings both received and transmitted the vibrations, and every cell in every body responded accordingly as they continually adjusted to the ongoing fluctuations of the energy in the universe.

Zac finally understood his role and place. His father had discovered what connects the energies of the universe. All cells have it and it exists across the universe itself. Zac had been able to unlock this phenomenon in food sources, allowing cells to function at a state that had never been seen before, with the ability to remain stable in almost every environment. The probe Zac had developed used the same kind of energy. He understood that he was an integral part of the message.

As his mother vocalized the now-familiar phrase "I am, I am," he understood that Mother Earth is a living entity, a part of the great cosmic web, seeking balance and equilibrium. In the visualizations that played before his eyes, he saw that the life force, the pure energy, contained measurable and immeasurable frequencies that wind and weave their way through everything—constantly moving, constantly flowing. Everything has a rhythm, everything vibrates to its own frequency. Zac realized that space was not empty; the invisible web of the universe was everywhere. It's the "I am" simply because it exists.

For Zac, his experience was straight out of the book *The Christmas Carol*, where Scrooge was visited by three ghosts who changed his viewpoint about the meaning of life in one night. The information flowed sequentially into Zac's mind: how Earth functioned and how the web of energy was connected throughout the universe. He knew there were precedents for such phenomena in science. Physicists had discovered that electrons separated by great distances could be synchronized with no time delay, operating beyond the speed of light.

The intensity of the visions jolted Zac out of his bed. His head was spinning with what he'd seen, and he had to talk to someone, but it was the middle of the night. He knew who'd be up that he could talk to. Uncle Brian. Zac placed his call.

Brian's head of tousled hair showed up first on the screen, then his smiling face appeared. "I was just relaxing in bed thinking about you, and all of a sudden your call came in."

"Well that connection, that synchronicity we have, is just what I need to talk about with you, Uncle Brian." Zac gave his lowdown, in a nutshell, describing what he saw in his vision from his mother.

With wide eyes, Brian shook his head in amazement. "This is fascinating. Go on, you know how I love this stuff. Tell me everything."

"At first I saw visions of networks: systems of interconnected threads. In the beginning, they seemed to be disconnected random flashes, but then... they constructed themselves and organized in front of me like I was sitting in the front row at a music concert. I saw each section tuning their instruments, and then with the conductor's raised arms, each section became part of a symphony."

"Like the music of the universe... ," Brian said.

"Yes, yeah, and it was a sound unlike anything I'd ever heard before. But slowly the sounds changed, and everything broke down. I felt crestfallen as the pictures defragmented, until it all turned to one picture of total desolation. Then the vision stopped."

Brian winced, then stroked his forehead. "What? That's it? Like the end of the universe?"

"No, wait... Earth was still a planet, but not one of solid matter. You and I have talked about this—how matter isn't really solid; it's made up of constantly vibrating energy. Then—get this—time crystals started to appear with their atoms arranged in a pattern that not only repeated in space, but also repeated in time. They were oscillating at their lowest energy state—something we thought was impossible. Then, after I was shown Earth in a deconstructed state, in a time-lapse movie, it reassembled as pure energy states, each component working with the other. The parts flowed together exchanging their energies. First, it was the seas driving the waves, then it was wind generated from heat, followed by forests releasing gases that recirculated as vibrant waveforms to the plant and animal energies roaming the surface. Everywhere mankind wasn't present, things were in balance.

"It was an amazing visualization. I was actually seeing the electromagnetic fields of the Earth! In my mother's professional writings, she referred to what I just saw in this vision as ley lines, which she defined as a straight fault line in the Earth's tectonic plates. But it's interesting that Olivia has referred to these same energy lines as spirit lines, and as a shaman, she said she uses the energy in these lines to help her contact the spirit world. The ley lines all lead to the energy grid covering the Earth.

"Everything became crystal clear to me. This is the energy my father worked with. This is what Tesla spent many years of his life working on, and he said it's the primal force in the universe. He was able to take the natural scalar waves of the Earth's surface and the atmosphere and harness it to produce power—static scalar negative energy. Harnessing electromagnetic energy! Then in the vision, I saw the physical manifestation of quantum entanglement, antimatter, and antigravity. All of this information is like completing a giant jigsaw puzzle that had missing pieces. I can see the gestalt of it all.

"Then I understood Dad's drawings—someone or something saw this before from a great distance away."

Brian closed his eyes, inhaled a deep breath, and slowly released it. "Like the information you'll be receiving back from your probe from far off in distant space?"

"Yes."

"Wow. This is mind-boggling," Brian said.

"I understand it's my job to represent Earth. My mother said I'm going to be receiving messages of dreams foretelling future events, and I need to alert mankind to prepare and unite in our healing powers as we are intrinsically intertwined. This is so much responsibility, Uncle Brian. I'm not sure what more I can do. How can I help us to globally evolve to a place where we honor life here on Earth and beyond?"

"Zac, your heart is solid gold. But in spite of your gifts, you are still a human being. There's only so much you can do. You can't change others; only they can do the changing. The most you can do is to enlighten them. I feel like I'm channeling Olivia here, but for Earth—and for the universe, for that matter—to create harmony on this planet, human beings must learn to create that harmony within themselves. It's going to be up to the people to decide if they're going to continue to cast aside the inherent laws of the universe while they keep causing the chaos that ignites the cataclysmic changes. Man must live in harmony with all and uphold the order of the universe. It sounds like a day of reckoning is here. Zac, you are only the messenger."

❈　　❈　　❈

The next morning, feeling dragged down with the responsibility on his shoulders, Zac entered the control room wearing a solemn look on his face. Everyone was already busy at work. He met with the Project Designation committee and persuaded them to wait to move the probe to a new location. *I'm glad they agreed with me.* He was feeling a pounding headache coming on and went to his office to treat the pain with his healing energies. As he bent his head into his hands, covering his eyes, he drifted deeply into a meditative state when the first of the specific precognitive dreams began. It wasn't one he wanted to see.

It was an earthquake that hadn't happened yet. Centered off the coast of Jakarta, the quake would register at 9.5 and set off a huge tidal wave in Southeast Asia in which more than 500,000 people would die.

He had to warn them. He had exactly eighteen hours.

CHAPTER TWENTY-SEVEN
ZAC
2039

ZAC ACTED AS quickly as possible, using the Global World Emergency Contact Council to alert the world of the pending disaster, but the warning fell on deaf ears. He felt frustrated that, even with his reputation, he still wasn't taken seriously by those in power, and the Indonesians weren't about to evacuate a couple of million people based upon Zac's hunch. None of the global seismic alert systems indicated warning signs associated with earthquake activity.

When the quake actually hit, the effects were devastating. The death toll was the highest from a natural disaster in recent years, with more than half a million dead or missing. In spite of being the person who was trying to save others, Zac felt guilty. *What more could I have done? If only we'd all listened to the whispers…*

Zac was well aware that questions arose from within and outside his core group, wondering how he could have had information that even the global early warning system hadn't indicated—suddenly, he realized he was under suspicion. He'd been so intent on trying to save people that he hadn't thought through how he'd explain his ability to foretell the future. *They're starting to mistrust me. I'm losing my credibility. I can't say this information came from the probe because that's not its purpose.* Besides, other scientists had access to the same information, and none of them had any knowledge of the events to come. The reality struck Zac: he wasn't a hero, he was a suspect.

At a hastily contrived news conference, Zac persisted with his attempts to warn people about what was to come. He felt it was his obligation to save those he could, and he'd already received a vision with new information about another pending crisis. He saw a rather innocuous tropical depression in the southwestern Caribbean appearing, and he knew where it was headed—the depression would rapidly move into a storm. This time, in response to Zac's warning, there was a negative reaction from the U.S. Weather Bureau. The bureau said that Zac's forecast was irresponsible, that there wasn't a single computer model that showed his prediction was possible.

Twenty-four hours later, wind speeds increased to a staggering 156 miles per hour, turning it into a Category 5 hurricane. What was the point of jeopardizing his future when no one believed him anyway? A handful of people listened and drove northward and inland; however, by the time the U.S. Weather Bureau acknowledged that a major storm had developed, for most of the people in its wake, it was too late. The panicky exodus from the coast produced massive traffic jams, and the gridlock caused many to die in their vehicles as the storm ripped and roared through the area. In what seemed like only moments, the storm devastated southern Florida.

Zac wasn't surprised when government agents showed up at the control center looking for him—in fact, one of them was the same guy who'd shown up at the ranch to question him about the food project's energy source a few years ago. When Special Agent Brockton appeared in the control room with his team, Zac showed them to his private office. He tried to prepare himself for the accusations that surely would come. Since his interstellar project was privately funded, they probably wouldn't threaten to shut it down, but they demanded answers, and Zac had none that satisfied them.

"Dr. Sparkman, you're held in very high esteem around the world," Agent Brockton said. "If not for that, you'd be in an undisclosed facility talking to us right now. Many years ago, your father's work seemed like science fiction. However, with what's happening right now, we suspect that you and your father's work are behind the recent disasters. We know this has always been about your secret weapons program. Now in the privacy of your office, come clean and tell us how you have weaponized the probe and what it is you want. We can do this the hard way or the easy way."

Speechless, Zac pondered how to reply. *There's no way I can tell them the truth. They'll think I'm either lying or deranged.*

Zac answered as best he could. "As I've mentioned before in interviews with the government, with the media, I'm clairvoyant. That ability has nothing to do with weapons."

"So, what... you're the Second Coming? The Messiah? Anointed by God? Sounds pretty fantastical to me. You have forty-eight hours to reveal how this works."

Zac shook his head and sighed. "Do you understand what clairvoyance even is? Have you heard of Edgar Cayce or Baba Vanga? It's the ability to foresee events. There's nothing sinister about it."

After another twenty minutes or so of irrelevant questions and fruitless answers, the agents left. Once they'd gone, Zac tried to conjure up some support, or at least sympathy, from his own team, but when he looked around the control room, all he saw was blank stares of disbelief, turned heads, and shrugged shoulders. Zac felt very alone.

In spite of the fact that he was being looked upon as a possible terrorist, Zac felt compelled to continue sharing what he was learning from the visions that kept appearing as downloaded imagery in his brain. Governments continued to balk at his messages in spite of the accuracy of his earlier predictions; but in time, regular citizens worldwide began to listen because lives were being saved due to his warnings about wildfires, pestilence, storms, earthquakes.

Feeling under pressure and scrutiny, several of the scientists on the probe project resigned, and two of them completely shut down the experiments they'd devised. Zac knew the U.S. government questioned his coworkers time and again, yet no one knew of any connection to the probe that was millions of miles away and the catastrophic events that were unfolding. All eyes were on Zac.

Eventually, Zac was brought before a Senate Select Committee. He wasn't surprised that he'd been summoned, but he didn't know why the proceedings were so secretive in nature—no reporters, no cameras, no transcriptions were allowed. As had happened with the government agents, the committee members posed questions that Zac couldn't answer to their satisfaction. How had he gone about weaponizing a peaceful mission? What was his purpose? Who was he targeting? How did he control the effects? What were the codes that gave him control?

He sat in front of his microphone, in suit and tie, trying to sort out how his good intentions had come to this.

"Dr. Sparkman," the senator from Illinois began, "if you refuse to give us the answers we need right now, consider yourself and your project finished. We will not allow you to cause any more disasters to occur."

Zac knew this was all futile. "I don't know how many times I have to tell you that I am not the cause of these disasters. I've weaponized nothing. I'm merely alerting people as to what is to come."

"And we ask you one more time: how are you predicting what's to come?"

"And I'll answer you one more time. I told you I'm clairvoyant. Why would I give out warnings of what was going to happen if I had nefarious intentions? That doesn't make any sense."

"Sorry, that psychic bit doesn't fly. No psychic can make predictions with the specificity and accuracy that you do. This is getting old now, and it's time for us to take alternative measures."

The only thing Zac had going for him was that by the time he appeared before the committee, he'd become a folk hero. His warnings had saved many people, and they didn't care how he'd obtained the information—only that they were alive because of it. He tried his best to convey not just the warnings, but also his understanding of Earth's consciousness and its interconnection with humanity. Pressure was mounting on the government to make Zac's information public and to release him. But Zac was aware this wasn't going to happen until the various government entities got answers, and when they didn't get what they wanted, that's when it happened. Suddenly and unexpectedly, while he was working in the control room by himself, Zac was whisked away during the night.

❊　　　❊　　　❊

Zac knew he was in a large fortress-like building—most likely the U.S. government's highest-security facility, sitting threateningly, like an ancient gargoyle, on a hillside just outside New York City. Just moments ago, he'd been brought there by a V-45 vertical takeoff and landing aircraft. From the air, through the mesh covering his eyes, he caught a glimpse of the gray concrete facility—cold, silent, and foreboding—its rooftop capped with isotropic antennae radiating power in all directions.

The VTOL aircraft had hovered briefly before landing. No time had been wasted as they dragged him to a room where they uncovered his eyes just before shutting a thick steel door with a loud clanging noise that startled him. Zac was now in a prison pod so dark, he couldn't see his own hands in front of his eyes.

He knew what would happen in the following days—the enhanced interrogation techniques. He'd read about it before—the twenty-four-hour interrogations with sleep deprivation, followed by loud, blaring music played through headphones they would force him to wear while placing him in stress positions. He couldn't believe that in this day and age, people would still use physical means on another human being. To Zac, any physical harm to another living thing was unspeakable. *What have I done? Why do this to me? How can they think I'm a terrorist?* He wasn't so much scared as confused.

If he didn't come forth with the information they wanted to hear, Zac knew what their next steps would be. Deep brain stimulation—where they'd use increasingly stronger electrical impulses to probe his brain cells to extract information; and, to deal with the public, only one strategy was left open to the government on such short notice. They had to discredit him.

They'd injected him with ketamine, a powerful tranquilizer that also produces psychotic behavior. He used his healing powers to shake off the effects with minimal success. As soon as they informed him he'd be seeing a specialist, he understood they'd use a psychiatrist to declare him insane and a danger to himself and others.

So now... he waited to see the specialist. Meanwhile, without his warnings, more and more people would die.

CHAPTER TWENTY-EIGHT
DR. WELLINGTON
2039

ZAC WOKE UP on a blood-and urine-stained mattress on the floor in the dark prison pod, waiting for the specialist to see him. He could smell the stink emanating from the stainless steel toilet in the corner. He shook his head, trying to eliminate the confusion in his brain from the injection they'd given him. All he could do was try to subdue the effects with his powers. Thankfully, none of his captors understood what Zac's capabilities were. He couldn't use his gift to harm others, but he could use it to try to battle the powerful drugs. His main concern was how many people would die while he was in custody.

He heard the sound of the code being entered into the keypad and the automatic opening of the heavy door. Two burly guards grabbed Zac from the mattress and shoved his limp, groggy body onto a motorized chair they propelled with a remote control down a tunnel. They stopped outside an office.

A woman stood in the doorway, waiting for him. Her name tag read *Dr. Wellington*. The guards guided Zac into the exam room at the back of her office, his wrists magnetically restrained to the armrests. A highly regarded psychiatrist who'd graduated at the top of her class at Harvard, Dr. Wellington had been the government's first call for this unusual assignment. The NSA's background check had given her the highest clearance a consulting physician could have, and she'd been thoroughly briefed on who Zac was, his various accomplishments, and what he was being accused of. She was known as an expert in the criminal mind, with terrorism as her specialty.

Dr. Wellington stood before Zac. She was forty-six years old, with chestnut brown hair twisted into a bun on the back of her head, wearing the traditional white lab coat and black "smart" glasses that were currently relaying to her all of Zac's medical data. She peered over the glasses at the guards. "Release him from his restraints, then that will be all, gentlemen. Given his condition, I think it's safe for you to wait outside the door while I complete his exam."

The hesitant guards peered at Zac menacingly. One of them pressed a button on his device to release the magnetized arm restraints, then they closed the door behind them as they exited.

Dr. Wellington stood to the side of Zac's chair, looking down at him as his head hung against his chest. "Hello, Dr. Sparkman, you're safe now." She placed her hand on top of his to reassure him.

This was the only communication-secure office at the heavily guarded facility, which Dr. Wellington had made a condition of her employment. She wanted complete privacy during her examinations. Zac appeared to be rousing in this new setting, and she encouraged him. "I need you to fight through the fog now—to overcome the effects of the drugs they've given you." She was already aware of his special abilities.

She took a seat across from him as she observed his labored breathing. "Dr. Sparkman, can you hear and understand me? My name is Dr. Wellington, I'm a psychiatrist, and I'm here to evaluate you. How are you feeling?"

He nodded. "Yes, I understand you. And I feel like crap. I have a horrendous headache, and I think I'm hallucinating."

"I'm going to examine you now." She clipped a scanning device to his index finger, and it immediately provided her with ongoing digital readouts of his blood pressure, pulse rate, heart rate, blood glucose levels, and body oxygen consumption rate.

"Dr. Sparkman, Zac, I want you to listen to something and see if you recognize it."

She walked over to a metal cabinet, slid her hand into a drawer, pulled out two objects, and returned to sit in the chair in front of Zac. She performed a specific beat on a handheld drum—a rhythm she'd played often over the years. At first, he continued to allow his head to rest on his chest, but as he kept listening to the familiar beat, he slowly raised his head to gaze into the eyes of the woman sitting before him. A tear rolled down his cheek.

"Remember this, Zac? Forever you and me?"

She placed the drum in one of his hands and the beater in the other. With her hand on top of his, she lifted his hand with the beater to re-create the rhythm they'd played together so many years ago. Soon, he was making the beat on his own. He traced his finger over the child's painting on the face of the drum. "Dorje?" he said. He looked up into her face again, this time studying it intently. "Sarah? Is it possibly you? Sarah?" He shook his head. "Now I know I'm hallucinating."

"No, Zac, it's really me. It's Sarah. I'm here to help you." She stood behind him to give him a hug around his neck, then she went to the door, opened it, and said authoritatively to the guards, "This is going to take a while. I need to wait for some of the effects of the drug to wear off before I can evaluate him. He needs to sleep." She closed the door and returned to Zac.

As he slowly regained clarity, they talked as though they'd never been apart. Although there was so much ground to cover, they only had limited time today, so they made the most of it, with Sarah assuring Zac that she was aware of the full extent of his grim situation and that she was prepared to do whatever she had to do to get him out of it. Then she did her best to fill him in on all the lost years between them.

Sarah had never forgotten him, she told Zac. To her way of thinking, the soul doesn't forget a connection like they had, but for some reason she knew they weren't meant to be together until now. The invisible thread connecting them had never been broken, just stretched. She'd followed Zac's celebrity over the years but hadn't contacted him as she didn't want to stir up her emotions while she'd been married. Once divorced, however, she'd always planned to get in touch… but she never thought it would happen like this.

Sarah knew what the government had planned for him, and she vowed to help him escape. Any plan would have to involve Olivia and Brian, they both agreed, so Sarah needed a way to buy time for Zac so they could set things in motion. But the situation was dire, because Zac's probe was considered to be the most advanced weapon ever developed. As such, the authorities involved in Zac's case now included the top military brass, and nothing would deter them from obtaining the secrets of the assumed weapon.

✳   ✳   ✳

While the inner world of government officials wanted to lock Zac up forever or make him vanish, the outside world was at odds. Still reeling from the devastations that had plagued the Earth, the masses positioned Zac as a symbol of hope and as their protector. Once the news leaked out that Zac was being held, people from all over the world began protesting his incarceration, especially when the natural disasters didn't stop—and now without his warnings. Foreign governments began to complain as, one by one, their countries fell victim to floods, earthquakes, and volcanic eruptions. When a group of Nobel laureates and government bodies jointly appealed to the president of the United States for Zac's release and appearance before the UN General Assembly, the White House knew it had to do something to head off the pressure. So the NSA and the military devised a scheme to neutralize Zac's impact and label him a terrorist.

Sarah Wellington's skills and experience were well known to the government. She'd been working with government agencies for years, and after proving herself highly valuable in case after case, her judgment was trusted completely. Once she'd been informed of the details of the plan to discredit Zac, the authorities had numerous questions for her. Could she keep Zac sufficiently subdued for a meeting with the press and with the General Assembly? Would she be able to convince him it was in his best interest to give the speech they'd written for him? They needed a way to control what he said, and Sarah convinced them she was the right person for the job. She was given the clearances she needed to be in charge of the operation, but if she dropped the ball on this, she knew, she'd quickly be replaced by someone else, which would terminate her access to Zac.

Meanwhile, Sarah's own plan for Zac required both Olivia and Brian. Shortly after he'd been taken into custody, Olivia had become frightened for Zac and had moved somewhere in the area to be closer to him. Zac suspected she'd be at an Indian reservation, but he couldn't give Sarah any further location information. Sarah knew of a Native American who worked as a janitor at the NSA facility and managed to pass a handwritten message to him when he was cleaning her office. It was her only chance. She had to believe that his heritage was stronger than his loyalty to his job, or it would be the end of the line for both Zac and her. Thankfully, her hunch was right.

Harold Handman was known as Big Hands to his tribe. He didn't live on the nearest reservation, but he visited every weekend to work with the local kids to keep them out of trouble. Swiftly and cleverly—forgoing use of cell phones and all technology and instead relying on verbal communications among his people, often spoken in native tongues—he set about finding Olivia. When he accomplished his mission, a meeting between Sarah and Olivia was quickly set.

Even though there was no known prior connection between the women, and even though it was a weekend, when no one would watch Sarah leave work or have cause to doubt her actions, she wasn't taking any chances. She rented a car and drove to the reservation at night. Initially, her headlights cutting through the blackness aroused suspicion among the tribesmen milling about, but once Olivia rushed out to greet her, the men relaxed.

"Oh, Sarah," Olivia cried, instantly embracing her, "I'd recognize that face anywhere." Olivia cupped Sarah's face and kissed her on the cheek. "Are you here to help my Child of Light? Do you know where he is? I've been so worried."

Sarah nodded. "Yes, and I need your help."

"Whatever I can do."

Sarah felt a wash of relief at Olivia's warm greeting. The pressure on her was overwhelming, and she was grateful for this moment's release. She knew her plan meant the end of her career. It would not only revoke all clearances she'd ever held and erase any trust ever placed in her, but it would sever her ties to the government forever.

In a quiet, safe spot within the reservation, Sarah explained her plan to Olivia. "There's a meeting planned with the UN General Assembly. The purpose is to discredit Zac and force him to admit to the world that his probe is a weapon. I'll be there with him, and I've been granted allowance to have one psych tech with me—we'll remain in control of Zac as long as he acts and speaks as directed. My superiors have agreed to use heavily armed security only if necessary. I was given a code that I can use if I need them to intercede." She stopped to take a deep breath. "What you can do to help is to take on a temporary nursing job. Are you game to play the role of my psych tech?"

Olivia squeezed Sarah's arm. "Of course I am. Whatever it takes to help my Child of Light. But won't they discover that I'm the one who raised Zac when they do a background check on me?"

"I have a plan for that too."

"Just tell me what to do."

They sat for the next hour with Sarah outlining her plan to Olivia, who agreed to bring together a meeting of tribe members she thought would be key to a favorable outcome. Upon convening the meeting, Sarah discovered an unexpected bonus: three of the men worked at the UN building in New York. They were mostly providing janitorial services and, like many minorities, went largely ignored in their daily routine. Sarah immediately recognized what an advantage this could be and was thankful that the tribal meeting had been closed to any members not directly involved with the plan.

Next, back in Olivia's room, Sarah handed her the phone she'd brought along for this purpose—an untraceable phone—so they could call Brian together and talk to him securely on speakerphone. Sarah had such fond memories of Brian and felt saddened to hear the anxiety and fear in his voice over Zac's fate. They filled him in on the plan, and his addition to it was the icing on the cake that Sarah needed to make it complete. Brian excitedly told them that *Quark II,* totally refit and ready for another circumnavigation, was available to utilize for the escape plan. Out of habit, ever since the bioterrorism event in 2025, Brian told Sarah, he'd kept the boat fully provisioned in the event that they'd ever have to make another last-minute departure. Yes, he could set off for New York right away, and once he was there, with an hour's notice, he knew where he could secure a temporary slip in the East River.

Sarah's shoulders relaxed for the first time in weeks. It was all falling into place.

*   *   *

When she returned to work on Monday, Sarah immediately placed a requisition for an experienced psych tech from a psychiatric center at the local Indian reservation. The request was initially questioned, but she'd been expecting that and had already prepared a plausible justification. She explained that she wanted a woman who was skilled at working with men who needed to be controlled with medications, someone with a low profile, unknown to the medical community at large. She convinced her superiors that any of the government techs would stand out like military bodyguards, whereas a smaller, older woman standing by her side would seem less threatening to all, especially to all the citizens clamoring for Zac's release. A skilled professional ready and able with a syringe would be all they needed, she argued. It would take up too much valuable time to find, secure, and screen a staffer from a major New York hospital, but she personally knew a nurse who had a history of asking few questions and following orders in difficult situations.

True, Olivia had an obvious connection to Zac that could easily be discovered during the vetting process, but Beatrice Hightower did not. She was close to Olivia in age, worked at the reservation's mental health facility, and had nothing in her background that would set off any red flags. So a qualifying résumé was hastily drawn up, the reservation doctor drafted a reference letter, and in one sitting, the tribal leaders made the necessary changes to documents that turned Olivia into Beatrice. An advantage of having a nation within a nation was their self-governance.

As hoped, Beatrice passed her government screening and was allowed to join Sarah's team. Now it was time to turn her attention to Zac himself and prepare him for what to expect at the UN. She'd already briefed him on what was happening in the outside world since his captivity—the cult following he had, the dissolving lines between religious and scientific beliefs, the government's unyielding conviction that the only way to maintain order was to get him to admit that his weaponized probe was causing all the devastating planetary events. Sarah explained to him that should he deviate from the speech written for him, he was to be removed from the podium at once, and she'd been instructed to have "Beatrice" immediately sedate him.

Sarah and Zac were ready to deploy their own part of the plan. In the days leading up to the UN meeting, Sarah and Sarah alone administered Zac's medications, which she'd replaced with saline. In front of his handlers, he played the part of sedated patient protesting the injections, and she kept up the appearance of nothing other than an objective psychiatrist monitoring her patient.

They both were buoyed by the news that Brian had safely reached the city and that *Quark II* was docked at a little-used commercial pier just a few blocks away from UN headquarters. And Zac felt comforted knowing that Sarah and Olivia would be by his side as he gave his presentation.

There was only one problem Sarah didn't know how to address. She didn't have the heart to tell Zac that the military had taken over his probe project and that they and many of Zac's former colleagues were scouring the data for some clue as to how it was powered. *I'll tell him later. It'll devastate him.* Zac had already told her they'd never find the information they sought. Even if they found the source Zac had created, it would take them decades to understand it.

Sarah knew the cost of any failure to her plan. *If I mess up, I'll ruin all of our lives. Everything has to work. It just has to.*

CHAPTER TWENTY-NINE
ZAC
2039

FOR ZAC, WITHOUT the powerful drugs in his system, his normal dream state was returning. On the night before his trip to the UN, while sleeping on a moldy mattress on a cement floor with one threadbare blanket for a cover, his mother appeared again.

This time in his vision, Zac and his mother were together on a boat. Virginia stroked Zac's hair and looked deeply into his eyes.

"Zac, my dear child. You did nothing wrong. I'm so sorry that you've been through so much pain. Understand that you're free to choose how to respond to what is about to unfold." She reached over the side of the boat and ran her hand through the shimmering blue water. "Look, my son." Peering down, Zac saw the crystal clear ocean teeming with life. "The Earth is not trying to destroy humankind—humans can only do that to themselves. She has no malice; her only desire is to heal herself and find her balance and harmony. To do that, she must respond to the injuries the human race is inflicting upon her. She's a living thing with consciousness. She is, she exists, and people must listen.

"If necessary, Mother Earth will eradicate what is no longer working. Tidal waves can wash away coastal villages, volcanoes melt away cities, and forests reclaim land over time. To Earth, the span of millions of years is only a heartbeat. She has time on her side to erase and rebuild. This isn't the first civilization to teeter on the brink of extinction. There's little time left, and she'll shortly reveal herself to the world. There will be choices to be made and little time to make them."

"I have been through so much, Mom. They've betrayed me, hurt me, and ridiculed my work. Friends and colleagues turned on me when I needed them. Why should I help a humanity that ignores all that it has been shown?"

"That, my dear son, is a choice only you can make. You will try and they may not listen. You will try and nothing may change. That's what choice is all about. I can only show you what is true." As his mother faded, Zac was shown a vision of what was to come the next day.

In the morning, he woke before opening his eyes in the darkened room of the psychiatric ward in the facility. In that space between dreaming and wakefulness came the familiar words "I am."

It was the day the government planned to force Zac to give the presentation written for him to disparage all that he stood for. Suits and ties were way out of character for Zac, and he felt foreign in the garb they made him wear. He feigned lingering sedation from the sugar pills he'd been given the night before while two guards lifted him into a motorized chair and then into an armored van, where Sarah, Olivia, and a guard were waiting. He and Olivia almost broke down when their eyes first locked on each other, but they quickly regained their composure. As she had done so many times before in his life, she gave him her imperceptible, all-knowing nod.

It had been prearranged that Sarah would give Zac a final injection to temporarily render him sufficiently awake to read his—rather, the government's—speech. While the driver of the armored van waited, Sarah helped Zac remove his jacket, and she administered the saline injection. He dutifully followed the directions she'd given him on how to appear to come out of his sedated state. The aggressive guard shoved his face in front of Zac. "You act up and the doc here gets shoved aside and I take over. Got it?"

Zac nodded yes.

✳   ✳   ✳

The gallery of the General Assembly was filled to capacity. The room was a cacophony of different languages, all being shouted at once. The stage was set, and Olivia propelled Zac in his motorized chair onto the platform and assisted him to the podium.

The entire audience rose with applause when Zac appeared with Olivia and Sarah by his side. The speech he was about to give was far from what the officials had written for him. *How much time will I have before they pull the plug? Will they really do it in front of the world's leaders and all these cameras?* His hands shook, and he worried he wouldn't find his words. He was more concerned for Olivia and Sarah than for himself. He knew the members of the tribe were in place to assist and provide distraction when needed. While the military might strong-arm him, he doubted they'd use weapons in the UN building. They were all counting on that, along with the element of surprise and a well-executed plan.

Zac tapped on the microphone, and the room went quiet. His voice was surprisingly strong and clear as he addressed a room that fell completely silent to hear his every word.

"Ladies and gentlemen, dignitaries and representatives of the world, I'm here to deliver a simple message. Our planet, Earth, Mother Earth, is a living entity and one to be reckoned with."

Immediately, several of the agents moved toward the podium. This was not in the script.

"I may have only moments here, and you may have only moments left to make the right choices. This is my message. Mother Earth is not at war with us; she's merely defending herself from our abuse. She's causing these disruptions, not my probe, as she adjusts her energies to seek harmony and balance. The probe is not a weapon, and your well-being is my main concern.

"We've been misguided in our relationship with our planet, fighting over land which is not really ours and referring to Earth as a thing. Earth is not ours to own. You and I are passing through something that's far more eternal than we are, yet we live on a part of Earth and claim it for ourselves without the slightest understanding of what it really is."

By now, the security team had received their orders through their earpieces and started moving in on Zac. But the moment they did, the entire audience erupted in a collective demand of "*No!*" The guards froze in place, taken aback by the deafening scream, and they too stared at Zac, seemingly mesmerized by his words along with the rest of the audience.

Zac hurriedly continued. "There's nothing I can tell you that you don't already know except for this. Earth has the power to remove us and has previously done so to civilizations that were here long before ours. Millions of years before our most recent recorded history, others have not heeded the warnings and have been rendered extinct."

At that moment, the projection screen behind Zac—a screen that wasn't even on a second before—unexpectedly lit up with images that arrived from an unknown source. Scenes from Zac's visions were conveyed onto the screen, with videos of Earth and its energy grids, in time-lapse photography across the universe, connecting its energy lines to every human being, rock, tree, animal, insect, plant, and molecule of water. The audience sat spellbound watching what was happening.

Zac had no idea what or who was allowing him to still stand there, but he wasn't going to waste the opportunity to keep talking. "I am here to tell you Earth has erased prior civilizations and started anew. We're not the first inhabitants of this world, and the way we've treated it, we may not be the last."

The audience broke out in gasps and whispers, sounds of awe mixed with confusion, reverence, and fear.

Then it happened. It was so sudden that Zac was caught off guard, as was everyone else. The lights flickered, and everything plunged into darkness. A loud electrical humming noise overwhelmed the room. Zac's ears began to ring, and people covered their ears and shook their heads. Every speaker in the room began to crackle, then hiss, and a moment later, the familiar voice from Zac's dreams, his mother's voice, spoke the words: "I am." At first, her cadence was slow and steady as she repeated the words over and over. The Native Americans in the assembly kneeled down and began a quiet chant. Behind him, Zac felt the gentle tug of Olivia's hand. While his mother distracted the audience, it was time for their escape.

Zac saw it play out in his mind's eye exactly as it had unfolded in his vision from the night before. The guards were the first to regain movement, advancing on what they thought was Zac, but their flashlights, like everything else in the room, didn't work. Their earpieces crackled with the same words. Every cell phone in the building, every sound system in New York, every radio and TV station in the world played two words over and over. Zac realized Earth's consciousness had broken through, and it felt like life itself was suspended. He was aware that the words were being communicated out loud in every land and every language, perhaps even reverberating throughout the universe. There was no mistaking the message. Finally, everyone was listening.

With everything at a standstill, Zac's exit strategy suddenly became much easier than any of them had anticipated. He even knew what would happen next. In his vision, he'd been warned that there'd be the possibility of strong electromagnetic waves of a type never seen before. They would interfere with anything electrical, rendering everyone transfixed, and yet no one would be hurt—planes, for example, would safely land before their systems would die. And amid all this pandemonium, it would be at least forty-five minutes before the guards realized that their prisoner was nowhere to be found.

✳   ✳   ✳

The trip by pedicab took about ten minutes. Zac was so anxious to get to safety that he couldn't even take the time to admire the majestic sky, to relish the outdoor air, the first he'd breathed in months. The moment they got to the pier, he dashed out of the vehicle, ready to board *Quark II*. Brian was on deck readying the boat for departure. None of the electronic systems were working, but the boat was stocked with maps and, of course, the sextant so Zac could navigate.

Olivia and Sarah started boarding right behind him when he suddenly turned to them. "No, I'm sorry. I can't let you come with me. My mother will continue to reveal herself just long enough for me to get out of reach. But soon everything will recover, everyone will recover, and they'll come looking for me. I must go through this part alone. You, too, Uncle Brian.

It'll be the hardest thing I've ever done to leave you guys here, but you've taught me well. You've taught me what to do, and I'll be fine."

Sarah broke down in tears. "Zac, no! This wasn't the plan—we've talked about this; you know I've been planning to go with you all along. My professional reputation will be shot after this—there's no point in me staying. And I don't want to lose you again, Zac, please. I won't lose you again. I have to come with you. I *have* to!"

Tears formed in Zac's eyes as he stood there staring at Sarah—not wanting to lose her again either but not wanting to put her life in danger. He didn't know what to do.

Olivia, choking back her own tears, gently took Zac's arm. "My Child of Light, she's right. Sarah must go with you while the world collectively decides what course to take. There's no safe place here for her now." Olivia looked pleadingly at Zac. "You played your part and delivered the message. If you both stay, you'll be deified or damned, and that will take the focus away from the critical issue. This Earth binds us all, and now that we all know that, there can be no more excuses.

"Zac, you cannot and must not be a part of what comes next. You've been alone long enough. You and Sarah are together now, bound the way your parents were. Sarah, I'll contact your family and let them know what happened. You'll both know if and when you can return again. There are no words to express the love I hold in my heart for both of you. Until our paths meet again, my beloved ones, know that I'll always be with you. Now, both of you, go. Go!"

Zac held Olivia by the shoulders and gazed deep into her eyes. He knew those eyes so well, the eyes of his surrogate mother, and he knew he may never see them again. *If I tell you and Brian just how much I love you and how it kills me to leave you, I know I won't go. I need to be strong so I can leave.* He kissed her on each cheek and pulled her tight to his chest. Then he held her at arm's length and said, "Go back to the reservation in Montana, with your people. If and when we can return, I'll come find you. Uncle Brian and Hannah will go with you. You'll all need the protection the tribe can give you. Olivia"—and here his voice did begin to break—"you've been a mother, a protector, a mentor to me. You've *always* been there for me, and I love you to the moon and back."

Olivia, nearly collapsing from the pain of releasing Zac, attempted to smile through her tears. "To the moon and back."

Brian walked back and forth releasing the lines that held *Quark II* to the dock as Sarah boarded. Zac knew how hard this moment was for him, this man who'd turned over his whole life to raising a boy he never planned to have. As Zac watched him ready the boat, he saw him remove a wad of tissue from his pocket and dab at his cheeks and nose.

When Brian finally looked up, with red-rimmed eyes, Zac walked forward and faced the man who'd breathed life into his soul. He was an old man now, the father Zac might be parting from forever. *How can I do this? How can I leave him at this point in his life?* Zac refused to believe this would be their final farewell.

"This isn't good-bye, Uncle Brian," Zac said, trying to sound cheerful. "We'll be together again. We haven't finished all of our adventures yet!" Then his voice turned serious. "Did you put the extra signal box I gave you on the boat? And don't forget to check the one in the lab from time to time." But then he couldn't hold his emotions in any longer. He rubbed his eyes with his thumbs. "There's not another person like you in this entire universe. I'm profoundly grateful to you, and I love you with every ounce of my being."

Brian pressed the palms of his hands together, touching his fingertips to his nose and blinking rapidly, trying to contain his own flood of emotion that desperately needed release.

"It's there, Zac. In our secret compartment, along with some gold and important papers. Everything is provisioned for you. I wish I could go with you, but I understand. To let go of you now... well, it's just inconceivable to me. From the moment you became mine, I've never wanted to let you go. You're my son, my pride, my greatest joy. And I love you beyond measure." He tried to crack a smile. "Now, do your best to bring *Quark II* back to me safe and sound, you hear? We still have places to explore."

After one final agonizing embrace, Zac jumped aboard and shouted, "There are no good-byes, only see you laters."

Then Brian turned to release the final connection *Quark II* had to land.

❄   ❄   ❄

The breeze that came up from behind the boat was perfectly placed to drive it down the East River and toward the ocean. Zac watched as his surrogate parents stood side by side on the pier, clinging to one another, waving until they were just small specks in the distance, just two shadows blending in with the background.

Zac would navigate by sextant until Mother Earth released her hold on humanity. It was very, very quiet, except for his radio repeating the only message the world would hear for the next several minutes, then it was up to them to decide:

"I AM, I AM, I AM."

❄   ❄   ❄

Somewhere out in space, with all connections to Earth suspended, the lack of contact was itself a signal to the small box tucked inside the probe. The box glowed as it signaled the SMGP probe's antennae to rotate 147 degrees away from Earth. The positioning program began its search of the stars, looking for a specific pattern, then locked on a group of stars many light-years from Earth. The ghost glitch, undetectable until now, had replicated itself in several key programs. No longer a program ghost, it took command of the probe. While the whole of Earth was focused on the two words "I am," another means of communication was formulating and being sent through deep space back to Earth. It was a reply to a brilliant male scientist who'd sent his own message via his probe to a specific location that had been documented in his father's old leather journal decades ago. Within a few days, the reply would be received using technology only one living person on Earth understood.

EPILOGUE

Why should the Earth be the only planet supporting human life? It is not singular in any other respect.
—Albert Einstein

IT HAD BEEN a few weeks since Zac and Sarah sailed away on *Quark II*. Not an hour went by that Brian and Olivia hadn't wondered about where they were. They hadn't received any word from him, but they didn't expect to, as they knew Zac had to stay completely off the grid. The worldwide devastations continued to occur without the benefit of Zac's warnings, but after the "I am" messages, world leaders had immediately commenced talking about changes that needed to be made. Brian was pleased the global dialogue had begun, but he doubted it would have much impact on the disasters.

Meanwhile, Hannah, Brian, and Olivia lived under the protection of the reservation at John Medicine Crow's house. Brian wanted nothing more than to relieve his anxiety by slipping into the lab to check the computer with the attached signal box as he'd promised Zac, but he had to tread carefully. Like the reservation, the ranch was also under constant surveillance for trespassers—Gus had security patrolling the perimeter of the reservation and the ranch twenty-four seven.

The last time Brian, Olivia, and Zac had dinner together at the ranch, Zac had shown Brian the setup he'd concocted in the secret lab. He'd connected a signal box on his computer, similar to the one on the probe, and he'd asked Brian to stow one on *Quark II*.

With Herman's help, Zac had worked on an advanced version of a multiplex binary coding program that Zac showed Brian how to use. Zac had told him of his plan to send a message to possible extraterrestrial intelligence when his probe went into interstellar space. He'd endeavored to be very cautious about putting Earth in a compromised position—the last thing he wanted was to be viewed as a threat within the universe.

Before the launch of the probe, Zac had decided to send a message in binary code, as others had done in the past. Deciding what to send was the question. Based on the Arceibo message sent by Carl Sagan in 1974, Zac included a graphic of the solar system, highlighting Earth's position. He wanted to send something unique as well, so he decided to send a selfie, some content known only to Zac, and a message in code with the question, *Where should we look to find you?*

※   ※   ※

Finding himself obsessed with his thoughts, Brian could no longer wait. He alerted Gus that he was going to sneak onto the ranch premises, and Gus and his men covered for him that night.

Brian slipped into the depths of the cave to the inner sanctum of the secret lab. Once behind the waterfall and wall, he heard a sound—the steady eight beats of Beethoven's Fifth playing repeatedly over and over. He stopped dead in his tracks as his heart raced and beads of sweat broke out over his forehead. His breath was shallow and rapid. There it was—the sign that something had been received. But what? He didn't want to get his hopes up, but the excitement surged through him like an electrical storm. He powered on the computer while the machine ocularly scanned his iris, allowing him access.

He logged in to the program Zac had created and read the message that popped up. *Is this from Zac or something or someone else?* A series of binary numbers appeared. Brian quickly ran them through the converter and came up with:

45.3833° N, 107.8340° W

He scratched his head. GPS coordinates. *What are they for? Does Zac want me to meet him somewhere?* Brian entered the coordinates, and within seconds, the computer map pointed dead center to the Crow

Reservation. *What?* He didn't understand what it meant. *Why am I being led to the reservation?* Feeling stymied, he closed up the lab and returned to the reservation to talk to Olivia and Hannah.

✳　　✳　　✳

The next morning, the three of them sat at the kitchen table. Brian explained what had happened and shrugged his shoulders. "I don't know what it means," he said.

Olivia nodded. "Okay, this popped into my head. Some of the men were talking about a discovery they made yesterday on the southwest field. I believe this is what you're meant to see. It appeared overnight—a crop circle surfaced. Some of my people are fearful of them and prefer not to talk about them or go anywhere near the area."

Hannah sipped her coffee. "I'm familiar with them. Strange patterns that appear in crop fields in a short period of time, usually overnight. The phenomenon was well known in England; however, they were determined—sometime in the early 1990s—to be hoaxes after two men came forward claiming they'd been making them for years."

"Yes, I've read about them too," Brian said as he paced the floor. "In the past, they were thought by some people to be either human hoaxes or signs from ETs or time travelers, but after that, there were reputable scientists who stepped forward and declared that some crop circles were definitely not man-made. In fact, it was proven that the crop circle debunkers were debunked themselves. Apparently, they'd been paid off by the government to make people *believe* the circles were a sham. There's always been a marked military interest in crop circles and secret government knowledge about ETs that they didn't want introduced to the public at large, so declaring the whole concept a hoax was probably just another cover-up. It's hard to know what's real. There was a well-respected scientist who'd studied crop circles for over twenty years and found, in some, that there was a technology involved that still can't be explained today. He and his team studied the circles in great detail using stringent methods of assessment. The scientist explained that telling a genuine crop circle from a fabricated one was like telling a fake painting from an original. He said you can tell a fake from the real ones by various signs, like where the crop is bent and the level of details in the fallen crop."

"Well," Olivia replied, "I can tell you that no one in this tribe made this crop circle, and with all the security patrolling the perimeter, no outsider got access to the reservation either. Someone once said the worst thing to fear is having a settled point of view. I've seen so many things throughout my life that challenge my preconceived beliefs. I try to always keep an open mind."

Brian clapped his hands and rubbed them together. "I absolutely agree. This may be what we're looking for. Lead me to it. I'll get the truck."

Walking through the field, the trio could see there was a pattern—some of the crops had been bent halfway up their stems; they curved but didn't break. From their perspective on the ground, they couldn't tell what the design was.

"Hannah, would you mind getting our drone from the truck? Let's get some aerial shots for perspective."

"Sure thing," she said.

While Hannah headed back to the truck, Brian handed Olivia some crop samples to bring back to the lab. He picked out some cuttings from crops that appeared to have been blasted out on one side. The entire field was punctuated with crystal particles and pieces of black stone—the same kind of stones Brian had found back in Nikolai's desk in Montana. At the time, he'd identified them as shungite-fullerenes—carbon and silicate minerals found only, to Brian's knowledge, in Karelia, Russia, in an ancient deposit.

Nothing entered the field while they were present—not a bird, not an animal. The air was unusually still.

Hannah undertook the task of setting up the drone and taking aerial photos of the crop circle while Olivia gathered samples of soil in containers she had in her medical bag.

"Hey, Olivia," Hannah shouted, "I brought the Geiger counter from the truck if you want to take some readings."

"Okay, I'll mark the spots if the numbers are elevated." Olivia took readings and then announced, "Guys, right here it's showing an elevated reading of 123 CPM." She continued to mark spots and Hannah photographed them. With their samples, photos, and readings, they drove back to Johns house.

✳   ✳   ✳

Once again in the dark of night, Brian slipped onto the ranch to sneak the samples into the lab. He removed the card from the drone and inserted it into the computer. Watching the drone footage was fascinating as well as shocking. It appeared as if what he observed was similar to a crop circle he'd seen online before. Part of the circle appeared, in binary code, to produce a replica of an alien being: a large bald head with two black eyes and a small nose and mouth. *Their own version of a selfie?* Then Brian had a lightbulb moment. Was this possibly a response back from the message Zac had sent into space with his probe? He'd sent his own selfie, Brian knew… were they reciprocating? The second figure within the crop circle was a rectangle of binary code that he needed to translate.

He opened Zac's decoder program on the computer and, one by one, painstakingly entered each series of numbers from the rectangle. *What else did Zac send as a message? Oh yeah, he asked the question: Where should we look to find you?*

Fantastical ideas pummeled Brian thoughts while he waited for the program to finish decoding. *I wonder if Zac got this same message on his signal box?* Within minutes, the translated message appeared.

Brian sat without moving a muscle for over fifteen minutes staring at the screen, stupefied, until the meaning of the message finally registered. He knew beyond a shadow of a doubt that it was the answer to Zac's question:

We Are Already Here

Thank you for reading *The Exigent Earth*. If you enjoyed this story, please:

- Help other people find this book by writing a review on Amazon
- Make this book a selection for your book club
- Ask your library to carry it
- Tell your friends to buy it and read it
- Spread the word on social media
- Please enjoy the other novels by Beverly Knauer, *The Line Between* and *The Soul's Hope*

THANK YOU!

ABOUT THE STORY

The storyline for this book came to me in a dream—a dream I readily shared with my then nine-year-old son, Jonathan, who struggled to understand the ending. During our conversation that followed, we imagined some of the twists and turns that are now peppered throughout this book.

I made a promise to my son that one day he would hold a book in his hands that captured the essence of the parts of the story that we wove together.

That nine-year-old boy is now thirty and continues to be a creative spark in my life. It's taken quite a few years, but he now has a special book to add to his library.

— Murray Rosenthal

About the Authors

Multi-award-winning author **Beverly Knauer** is devoted to giving her readers fiction novels that stimulate out-of-the-box, thought-provoking content that expands the mind and imagination.

Through writing and teaching, she enjoys sharing her knowledge of esoteric wisdom as demonstrated in her two visionary novels, *The Line Between* and *The Soul's Hope*.

During her career as chief of rehabilitation services for the county of San Diego, she administrated and managed a program that provides physical and occupational therapy services for children with physical disabilities. After retiring from that position, her time was freed up to fulfill her passion for writing. She believes that fiction is a safe way to explore new ideas, as it allows readers to gently trespass into the experiences of others in order to test out the waters before adopting new concepts for themselves.

Since the first Earth Day, which began as a national teach-in years ago, Beverly has been an advocate for environmental protection awareness. She makes her home in San Diego, California.

You can contact her at:

Facebook page: https://www.facebook.com/beverlyknauerauthor
Author page: https://www.authorbeverlyknauer.com/
Twitter: https://twitter.com/authorbevknauer
Instagram: https://www.instagram.com/beverlyknauerauthor/

❋   ❋   ❋

Murray Rosenthal is a world-renowned, board-certified psychiatrist, researcher, and lecturer. Even after a thirty-year career, he's not one to retire. Currently, he's managing a farm in Fiji and mentoring young entrepreneurs in the medical arena.

Murray thrives on adventure and travels extensively, including trekking throughout Southeast Asia and, more recently, sailing around the world. Through his travels, he has seen firsthand the profound changes our planet is experiencing, and he feels an urgency to rectify the situation.

He has been a lifelong science nerd, especially in regard to up-and-coming technologies.

He and his equally adventurous wife share their home in Lake Tahoe with their canine pal and delight in the successes of their adult children, Jonathan and Samantha.

Murray can be contacted at Murray@hyperion-research.com.

Acknowledgments

Contributor
Janet Rosenthal

Copyeditor
Cindy B. Nixon, Bookmarker Editorial Services

Book Cover Design
Christian Bentulan, Covers by Christian

Beta Readers
Carol
Jana
Georgia
Shaun